The Cicada

The Cicada

INGE MELDGAARD

A Novel

Published by Aquinine Books
51 Roy Street, Donvale
Victoria, Australia 3111

Australian distributor:

Digital Print Australia
135 Gilles Street, Adelaide
South Australia, Australia 5000
www.digitalprintaustralia.com
books@digitalprintaustralia.com

Revised Edition: July 2013

National Library of Australia Cataloguing-in-Publication entry:

Author: Inge Meldgaard
Title: The Cicada
ISBN: 978-0-9807097-0-4
Dewey Number: A823.4

Cover design and artwork by Inge Meldgaard
Website: ingemeldgaard.artworkfolio.com

To my sister Tove, with love.

'Heaven's gold is kindness of heart.'

Warwick Collins
The Rationalist
1993

This edition of *The Cicada* is the result of several revisions since it was first published in 2009. I sincerely hope the reader will enjoy this substantially improved version and go on to read its sequels, *A Death In The Making* and *The Seed Gatherers*.

MAIN CHARACTERS

The Willsmere Scientists – Melbourne, Australia

Karla	Geneticist
Mik Theophanous	Botanist
Tamara Solanum	Agricultural Scientist
Søren Thorup	Zoologist, on temporary assignment from Greenland

The Other Scientists

Martha	Environmental Scientist, Lamington, Queensland, Australia
Meng Jarrah	Australian Palaeontologist employed by the Papuan and Myanmarian Governments as a Research Coordinator
Zago	Federation Research Coordinator, based in Oslo, Norway
Sirinya	Federation Researcher, Serro do Cachimbo, Brazil
Eduardo Arreza	Federation Researcher, Serro do Cachimbo, Brazil
Owain	Brother to Gwenllian, Melbourne-based government Research Coordinator

The Peacekeepers

Chiu Liow Jones	Melbourne, Australia
Welcome	Criminologist and Psychologist, Melbourne, Australia
Freddi	Jamaican, on assignment in Myanmar, half-sister to Chiu Liow

The Federation Special Investigation Unit, based in Luzern, Switzerland

Rohan Maerz	FSIU Coordinator
Morag MacIain	FSIU Investigator

The Australian Information Technologists, Melbourne Central Computer Site

Lance Melrose Naylor	Senior Systems Technologist
Gwenllian	
Marika	
Thanh Fong Lau	

The Cats

Fliedermus	Companion to Mik Theophanous
Possum	ditto
Red Matilda	ditto
Shela	Companion to Freddi
Aurora	Companion to Rohan Maerz

Others

Kenjiro Kakura	Director of Wyvern Meridian
Mervyn Bradshaw	Sponsor of Bendigo Theatre Company
Erminio	Senior Research Assistant, Epsilon Pty Ltd Brazil

PROLOGUE

Despite the grim laws of nature and the effect of human arrogance taking its toll in famine, disease, war and environmental degradation, in the year 2050, the world's population reached ten billion, and by 2090, had risen to twelve billion. By 2135, with a population of fifteen billion, Earth was now in a state of crisis. Species extinctions increased exponentially and the planet's ecosystems were at breaking point.

The sick, the frail, the prematurely born and the disabled could no longer gain access to dwindling medical supplies and overextended facilities, so died in their hundreds of millions. Life expectancy dropped to a meagre fifty-six years in even the least affected countries – while women continued to give birth in agony and sorrow.

As the world's climate became increasingly unstable, and the wealthier nations began to feel the direst impacts, an awareness of the need for global government developed. The United Nations Assembly was transformed into the World Federation of Nations.

Economic and technological aid, together with political incentives, were offered to those countries unable, or unwilling, to introduce population control or effective resource conservation measures. Some resisted what they perceived as interference and closed their borders, nationalising foreign-owned industries in a vain attempt to exclude the outside world. Others saw themselves as powerful enough to defy both the Federation and the inevitable consequences of their actions, so declared war – and solved their population problems by losing.

By the middle of the twenty-third century, the world was finally at peace, but had lost most of its natural forests and other wild places. Humans now numbered a mere three billion.

Two hundred years later, a massive global effort is in place to restore Earth's devastated ecosystems, but the Federation is about to face an enemy who even they may be unable to defeat.

PART I

CHAPTER ONE

As Karla walked along the riverbank, enjoying the sharp, clean scent of eucalypts and the unusual summer coolness of the early morning, a faint, blurred image began to form in her mind. When the image grew clearer, she broke into a run, her heart pounding. Two minutes later, she paused outside Willsmere's vast research complex, catching her breath and glancing at the security system's retina scanner. The gates silently opened and the young woman walked swiftly along the smooth, gravelled walkway. There was another agonising wait while a second retina scan was performed, allowing the massive wooden doors of the main building to finally swing open.

By the time Karla reached her laboratory, sunlight was pouring through the windows, all too clearly showing the ruins of what had been her life's work. The once beautifully presented plant specimens, painstakingly catalogued over the past ten years, were now a brown pulpy mass, mixed with shards of plastiglass from the nearby culture cabinets. An acrid smell of burning permeated the whole room. The cat, Fliedermus, was there, crouched inside an empty storage cupboard, tail lashing from side to side, eyes huge and ears flattened in rage.

Controlling herself, Karla spoke softly: 'I'm here; you're safe now. Where's Mik?' She crouched down to hold out a hand. 'Is he in the other lab?'

Fliedermus leapt to the floor, snarling, hackles raised. She hurled herself frantically against the closed door to the second laboratory, scratching the surface with her long, needle-sharp claws. Karla suddenly knew what she would find. When they entered the room, the cat's vivid imagery ceased and an icy calm replaced the fear in her mind. Even so, Karla's hand trembled as she cautiously lifted a curl of Mik's hair away from his forehead, revealing an ugly gash. A trickle of blood stained the sleeve of his loose white shirt. Fliedermus licked his cold hand and mewed piteously. Slumped over his keyboard, he didn't respond.

'Mik,' whispered Karla, her voice strained. 'Mik,' she called, more loudly this time, 'can you hear me?' He still didn't respond, so she pressed her fingers to his neck, feeling for a pulse, which, to her vast relief, was strong and steady. Placing her hand onto his computer's identity pad, Karla asked for an ambulance, then spoke to the medtech who answered, giving brief details of the situation.

Shortly afterwards, the computer informed her that Willsmere's security system had authorised the approach of an ambulance, which was soon hovering on the grassy verge outside. However, by the time two cheerfully competent ambutechs strode in, Karla was beginning to feel dizzy, and even slightly faint from shock. Taking a few uncertain steps towards them, she hesitated, took a deep breath, and put a hand to her forehead. One of the women immediately took hold of her arm and helped her sit down. Meanwhile, the second ambutech examined Mik, and then together, the two women lifted him onto the hoverbed they had brought with them.

When they turned to speak to Karla, she pointed to the longhaired brown tabby crouching nearby, who was watching them all closely. 'That's Fliedermus, Mik's cat,' she said. 'While I was still outside the gates, I could sense her calling me...warning me of what had happened. She was in *my* lab when I arrived and this door was shut. She must have stayed in there all night.' Tears gathered in her eyes. 'I thought Mik had been killed!'

'Yes, we understand how you feel, Karla, but overall, your colleague seems fine,' said one of the ambutechs, with a reassuring smile. 'The cat may even have helped him. It'd be an idea for her to come along with our patient, if that's okay with you?'

Fliedermus answered for Karla by leaping lightly onto the hoverbed and curling the tip of her tail protectively around one of Mik's feet.

As the group moved slowly towards the main entrance, Karla's friend, Tamara, came running in, alarm drawn on her round, dimpled face.

'What the blazes is going on here? Why is there an ambulance? Is that Mik? What's happened to him? Karla, are you all right?'

Karla put an arm around Tamara's shoulders, saying, as calmly as she could manage, 'Someone's broken in and they've attacked him; Fliedermus warned me just before I arrived. Apparently he isn't seriously hurt, but the ambutechs are taking him to the nearest medcentre and want her to go as well. I think it's best if we leave them to it and take a look around. My lab's completely wrecked... Aside from that, I don't know if there's any other damage, or if anything's been taken.'

Angrily blinking away the sudden tears, Tamara made an effort to stop her hands from trembling, then gave Karla a quick hug and turned away to catch up with the ambutechs. She could see Mik's colour was improving and hesitantly touched his face, then stroked Fliedermus, who gently rubbed her head into Tamara's hand. Drawing back, she linked arms with Karla, who had followed her, and together they walked silently alongside the hoverbed until it reached the waiting ambulance. Once everyone was on board, it hummed softly and lifted off, rapidly disappearing from sight.

When Tamara placed her hand onto the identity pad of Karla's computer, it failed to respond to her voice, so she checked the power source to make sure it was still on. It was, although the screen was completely blank.

'Damned idiots!' she exclaimed. 'They must've completely wiped it, or there'd be *some* response! Why bother? There's nothing here that isn't on the network as well.' Tamara swore again, needing to release the anger that for the moment had replaced her earlier fear.

She and Karla had already discovered that all the hand readers from both laboratories were gone. It could only mean that someone had stupidly, senselessly – and possibly dangerously – tried to interfere with Willsmere's research. No one had done that for over a century. Not since 2337, when an obscure group made their final attempt to steal the frozen gene pool of their 'martyred' cult-creature, the Queensland cane toad.

'We'll have to notify the peacekeepers,' she concluded.

'Yes, and Zago,' agreed Karla, running a hand through her already tousled hair, 'she'll need to know what's happened, though before we do, we'd better check the other computers.' She stretched her arms and flexed her broad, strong shoulders, trying to ease the tension in them. 'Sorry, but I need to clear my head. I want to take a quick walk outside. Could you call the peacekeepers? I expect they'll only want the basics to begin with... I won't be long.'

Tamara noticed that Karla's normally healthy countenance was pale and drawn. 'Sure,' she replied, smiling bravely, but with a catch in her voice. 'Hopefully I'll have some coffee ready by the time you're back.'

Making an effort to remain calm, she identified herself to the other computer in the laboratory, then instructed it to run a full operational diagnostic. After following the same procedure for Mik's and then her own, all three computers reported their systems to be normal. Her own asked if she wanted anything else done.

'Yes,' she replied, 'please contact the nearest peacekeepers.'

The screen soon displayed a cheerful dark-complexioned face, topped by an unruly mop of straight black hair. The peacekeeper identified himself as Chiu Liow Jones, while the routine message "Identity Confirmed" appeared at the bottom of the screen, together with the date: the fourteenth of November 2450.

'Thank the Sun we've got building scanners linked to this machine,' thought Tamara. 'At least I can show them what's happened.' She stuttered a few times, and then in an artificially cool voice, said, 'My name is Tamara Solanum. I'm a research scientist and someone has assaulted my colleague, Researcher Mik Theophanous, and vandalised our laboratory here at Willsmere. If you wish to verify this report, you can request a scan of Room WL1201.'

The cheerfulness on the peacekeeper's face became a touch less so, and Chiu Liow Jones allowed a hint of surprise to enter his otherwise steady voice. 'That's unusual, and yes, I will scan. Thank you.'

As she waited, Tamara reverted to a childhood habit of twisting a curl around a forefinger, then mentally rapped herself over the knuckles, knowing how distracting it could be to others.

Finally, the peacekeeper said, 'I'll be with you in about ten minutes. Please make sure any witnesses are available.'

Karla returned at that moment, looking a little more like her usual confident self. Tamara stood up, saying, 'You weren't long. I haven't even made the coffee yet.'

'What did they say? I don't imagine they'd get many reports like this.'

'No, I don't suppose they would. A peacekeeper by the name of Chiu Liow Jones should be here any minute.' Tamara busied herself at the room's small servery, glad of the distraction, and handed Karla one of the filled cups. 'We might as well go out front and wait.'

They had barely seated themselves on the steps leading to the building when a Melbourne Peacekeeping Force patrol car arrived. It skimmed over the tops of the massive river redgums surrounding Willsmere before settling on the blue-green lawn. A tall figure wearing a dark blue uniform extricated itself from the driver's seat and strode towards them.

Producing an ID card, and without any further preliminaries, yet with a friendly smile, the peacekeeper said, 'Please, tell me what happened from the time you arrived until now.'

Slightly intimidated, despite his amiable manner, Karla introduced herself and held out a hand, which he briefly shook. Given the circumstances, she managed to relate her experiences in a remarkably concise fashion. Tamara listened carefully, while at the same time closely observing the peacekeeper's face. His expression remained blandly cheerful, although a small telltale quirk of the mouth showed his keen interest. Once Karla's account of the morning's events was finished and recorded, Peacekeeper Chiu Liow Jones asked to be shown the centre. They began with Karla's laboratory, which she shared with Søren Thorup, a zoologist.

'What was in the hand readers?' asked Chiu Liow, after Karla told him what the empty storage cupboard previously contained.

'A couple had copies of certain aspects of our recent efforts to produce new food crops using our own unique genetic engineering techniques. I work together with Søren Thorup, who's here on temporary assignment from Greenland. We're trying to create new environmentally sustainable and resource-efficient food sources, in the form of plants that have the same type of complete protein normally found only in animals. This type of work's been around for centuries, but for various reasons, until fairly recently, very little succeeded.' Karla kept her voice as steady as she could, although the idea of someone else now having access to some of their more critical work, particularly before it had been thoroughly tested, was unsettling, to say the least.

'How remarkably interesting,' said Chiu Liow, raising an eyebrow. 'Your work is obviously important to both Australia and the Federation. Did the hand readers contain anything else?'

'Yes, one held an earlier version of a knowledge base I've worked on for almost ten years. I'm mapping the DNA of around five hundred newly discovered plant and fungus species. The current knowledge base is linked to an enhanced intelligent decision-making system which models new genetic combinations...and all this has been erased from my computer. There was also a great deal of test data and software we'd developed. Søren's other work, with previously unidentified insects and arachnids, is kept in here too, but *his* computer seems fine.'

'What would happen if something was completely lost?' asked Chiu Liow, frowning.

'It depends what it was, but we have back-ups of everything in our own secure area, as well as on the Luzern network... Surely they couldn't have gotten in there as well!' Karla's voice rose and she put a hand to her mouth, then immediately made an effort to control herself.

'Perhaps they only wanted the actual information and ignorance caused them to accidentally delete your computer's contents,' replied Chiu Liow, noticing how tense both women were.

'No, the computer itself would've prevented accidental erasure,' said Tamara, her tone harsher than normal. 'The only way it could've been done would be by somehow introducing a very large power surge to just this workstation.'

'I see,' said Chiu Liow. 'Have you lost anything that can't readily be replaced?'

Karla pointed to what was left of her reference collection. '*That's* what I won't be able to replace in a hurry. My plant specimens... It's taken me so long to find them all!' She sat down on the nearest chair and gazed up at him, completely at a loss as to why anyone would want to break in and destroy their work.

'Why are these particular plants so important?' The peacekeeper had never before had any reason to look into the details of Willsmere's work.

Shaking her head in frustration, Karla shrugged, then explained that apart from their environmental value and potential medical significance, it was important to their food sciences to have full records of as many potentially edible species as possible.

'All the sites I obtained them from are recorded, of course,' she continued, 'but a few of the places are murder to get to, and some of the species are extremely rare. Fortunately, we have a full set of duplicates of all my original specimens in the Federation Herbarium in Oslo, together with their frozen gene pools. We also have the DNA and tissue samples from the specimens I've finished with in our secure cryogenics store – which doesn't seem to have been opened – and most of their genomes are now in the knowledge base, but there were still thirty-two to define and enter. The problem is, there's no way I can quickly obtain return samples from Oslo for the ones I still need to work on. They always seem to take forever to do anything...' For a moment, Karla covered her face with her hands, then looked up at him, tears in her eyes.

'You have my sincere sympathy, Karla,' said Chiu Liow, briefly placing a hand on her shoulder. He turned to Tamara, who was now sitting down as well, her arm linked with Karla's – they both needed the simple reassurance of touch.

'What are you and Researcher Theophanous working on?' he asked.

'We do the core research that determines which species and other interventions are required to rehabilitate the forests, grasslands and other natural areas the Federation has decided aren't damaged beyond repair. Part of my role is to work out which regions can survive as true wilderness and which can only be used for plantations, or other types of agriculture. We also mass-produce embryos of the more fragile plants and animals, then use them to re-establish wild populations.'

'Thank you. Now, I need you to answer some questions regarding how entry into the building – and afterwards, the laboratories – could have occurred. I assume you have standard security procedures?'

'Of course we do, Peacekeeper,' said Tamara, rather tersely, 'but you'll have to check with the infotechs at central security to find out if they've authorised anyone for entry without telling us...which I doubt; I'm responsible for liaising with them. Either way, our security system here is still doing the retina scans at the gates and at the main door...which means the identity of whoever got into the building might be in its database.'

'Well,' said Karla, with a slight pressure on Tamara's arm, 'the chances are that there won't be any record. My guess is that everything's been erased by now. Mind you, to do that without leaving any trace would be incredibly difficult. All the security system's transactions are logged, of course.'

Chiu Liow hesitated before replying, but quickly realised that without too much trouble – he hoped – it should be possible to obtain help from the Federation's Special Investigation Unit to look into the issue. Still, security matters aside, there was enough for him to follow up that didn't require their specialist personnel.

'Yes, I imagine the records *would* be gone by now,' he said, frowning slightly. 'So, presumably Researcher Mik Theophanous isn't implicated. I see no logical reason for him to sabotage your work and then arrange for someone to assault him... Have either of you determined whether his computer, or anything else in the laboratory, or for that matter, anything in the remainder of the building, has been interfered with?'

'I've run a check on both Søren and Mik's computers, as well as my own, and they've verified themselves to be fully functional and intact, but we haven't had time to check either lab thoroughly...and certainly not the rest of the building,' replied Tamara, brushing a curl away from her face. 'It'd take ages because it's so big, but our building maintenance computer will know whether anyone's entered other parts of the complex since Karla and I left yesterday, at around 22:30 – if the records haven't been changed, of course.'

Chiu Liow nodded. 'Very well. Thank you.'

'Do you want to see the other labs first, or the scanner records? We can show you where the console's located.'

'I think it would be best if you check your own laboratories after we have seen what the security system has to tell us,' he replied, in his oddly formal manner and with another gentle smile. 'I am quite certain you can be trusted to let me know of any disturbances you might find, but at this stage, please do not clean or tidy anything away. I will call in our forensics team to examine your laboratories, the grounds, and the remainder of the building.'

During their walk to the security console, Chiu Liow had the opportunity to observe his companions. Tamara appeared to him to be of Anglo-Celtic descent, with short brown curls, grey eyes, fair skin, slightly stubby nose and a wide, friendly mouth. She seemed like someone who lived firmly in the present. Karla showed her northern European background in her greater height, broad shoulders, high forehead, fair hair and bright blue eyes. Despite being understandably upset, her mouth had a determined look, and he could imagine that once the trauma of these events had been dealt with, the work destroyed last night would be painstakingly reproduced, no matter how long it took. Casting a surreptitious glance at their left hands, he noted that neither of them wore a fertility ring, which didn't surprise him as he estimated their ages to be only in their early thirties.

They turned a final corner then waited outside a large, plastiglass-enclosed room containing, Tamara told him, the computer and the robotics controlling Willsmere's security, internal climate and general facilities. The door opened for them after routine retina scans confirmed their identities. Karla requested a report of everyone who had entered the building and its rooms since midnight the previous day and the present time. The screen neatly tabulated times, rooms and names. All the names

– other than those identified as the two ambutechs and the peacekeeper – were those of staff members. Mik's name was shown as not having left until this morning, but otherwise, Karla and Tamara were the last to leave yesterday and the first to arrive today.

Karla, out of habit, thanked the computer, which replied that she was welcome, its tone soft and somehow reassuring. Nevertheless, she could feel herself becoming faintly nauseous and briefly laid her hand against the hard, cool surface of the console. The information confirmed that either a staff member was involved and had somehow managed to bypass the security system, or their database had indeed been altered during the night.

'We will need to interview them all, as well as the information technologists at the central computer site,' stated Chiu Liow, echoing Karla's thoughts. 'Would you be so kind as to ask for a full set of identification records?'

To his surprise, the request was answered by the computer without Karla having to repeat it. 'Ah, I see,' he said, peering at the screen. 'I have right of entry to this building and to this room, so I suppose I also have rights to certain information held in this system. Presumably it can all be transferred to my comlink?'

'Yes, it can,' said Tamara, 'but because you don't normally work here, you'll have to enter your ID number for confirmation, together with your handprint.'

Chiu Liow did as she asked and the computer announced that the records had been successfully transferred. 'History has a depressing tendency to repeat itself,' he murmured, checking his comlink to make sure he had the information.

'What do you mean?' asked Karla.

'Oh, I have a strong interest in ancient architecture, which inevitably leads to a study of history and social trends. I find it helps me understand my role as a peacekeeper, so even though these types of crimes might be uncommon now, they weren't in the past.'

'Look, I don't want to appear unconcerned,' interrupted Tamara, frowning, 'but could we postpone the chitchat until we at least see how Mik's doing?' She had become red in the face as she spoke. 'Sorry, I don't mean to be rude, Peacekeeper Jones, it's just that I'm finding it hard to deal with the idea that a member of staff, either here or at central security, is involved. In fact, I'm finding it almost impossible to believe any of this has happened!'

She turned away, embarrassed by her brief outburst, and asked the computer for an update on the condition of Researcher Mik Theophanous. After a brief delay, the screen cleared to show the face, identity number and name of a medcentre practitioner, who was able to give her the information she asked for.

'Researcher Mik Theophanous is now conscious and has no serious injury, Researcher Solanum. He'll be well enough to leave here by tomorrow morning and has requested that you take him home at 11:00. The injuries to his head appear to have been caused when he was struck from behind with a heavy object and then fell onto something with a sharp edge. The cut on his forehead may even have happened afterwards if, for example, he wasn't rendered unconscious and turned to face his attackers. Either way, his injuries should heal within two weeks. Also, he may have been sedated, since neither blow would have caused him to remain unconscious for long. However, we found no trace of anything in his bloodstream.'

The practitioner paused for a moment to see if Tamara had any questions, but as she didn't, continued: 'After tomorrow, he won't need any medication or other treatment, so unless there are unforeseen complications, I won't be allocating any home aftercare. Unfortunately, he suffered concussion and at this stage is unable to speak with us about what happened. To help him recover emotionally, I suggest you attempt to talk it through with him at the earliest opportunity. Although,' he added, with eyebrows raised, 'I gather he actually has three cats. He must be an extremely well-adjusted person!'

'Thank you, Practitioner Sanderson,' said Tamara, managing a small smile. 'I'll be there tomorrow at 11:00.' Turning to Karla, who had brightened a little at the news, she exclaimed, 'Well, that's a relief! Though I must say, it all sounds really weird. Anyway, I'll tell him what's happened here today...so maybe he'll be able to talk to you soon, Peacekeeper Jones.'

Tamara led the way to the building's main entrance, a rather vague expression on her face. Noticing, Karla smiled for the first time that morning. She had seen that look before, but never, until now, associated with Mik Theophanous.

While the two women examined their laboratories, Chiu Liow made arrangements for the forensics team to attend, then indulged himself in a short but leisurely stroll around the grounds of Willsmere – even though, outside, the full heat of the day felt almost as if he had stepped into a furnace.

Bellbirds echoed loudly throughout the grey-green forest nearby, contrasting strangely with the harsh cries of aggressive wattlebirds. An intricate cobweb, spun during the morning by an ever-industrious spider, caught his eye as he passed. In its centre, the owner waited patiently inside a curled-up leaf for its first meal to arrive. Smiling, Chiu Liow wished it luck.

Earlier, as his patrol car approached the research station, the peacekeeper had reverently admired Willsmere's impressive nineteenth-century towers, and he now silently gave thanks to the people of the twentieth century for having the foresight to preserve so much of the building, as well as its ancient trees. He slowly passed his hand over the ornate brickwork of the original boundary wall, then gazed up through the dense canopy of a gnarled oak. Chiu Liow realised that Willsmere must once have been a landmark – before the older, low-lying, coastal regions of Melbourne were partially submerged during the late twenty-first century, due to the effects of global warming. The immense complex now sat at the top of a gentle rise leading down to the mouth of the Yarra River, several kilometres away. It overlooked a city which had become the 'Venice' of the south, replacing the ancient and entrancing original. 'Such a pity,' he thought, with a sigh. 'So many beautiful places lost forever.'

Even Willsmere's history was a sorrowful one, and despite the heat, he shivered, imagining the tragic lives of the inmates of this former 'Kew Lunatic Asylum'. Were the patients of the nineteenth and twentieth centuries able to appreciate the beauty of their surroundings? Or had the beauty been created to allow the community to congratulate itself on its willingness to give only the 'best care' to those unfortunates? What were the words he had once read about Willsmere in the National Australian Library? "It has been too big a problem for people to consider and they have shuddered and walked away."

Shaking his head, Chiu Liow walked on a little further, thinking about all the old cities that were once situated conveniently by coastal harbours or large rivers. The ancient centres of inner London, Stockholm, Copenhagen and Amsterdam were now ghostly ruins, surrounded by water and inhabited by shadows, while the newer, and yet still relatively old, cities of Vancouver, Miami and New Orleans had been destroyed by the unleashed violence of tidal waves. The tidal waves followed a worldwide series of massive earthquakes, during which Japan and the American state of California were destroyed, together with countless other vulnerable regions and low-lying island states.

Many historic inland sites had succumbed as well – to the wreckers' ever-hungry machines in the drive to find more living space for both the world's refugees and its burgeoning population. There was neither the time nor the will to preserve the ancient monuments, artworks and buildings as the multitude of wars and other catastrophes of the twenty-first and the twenty-second centuries finally drove Earth's people into a desperate fight for survival.

Melbourne was more fortunate than many other coastal cities, being sheltered from the worst storms by Port Phillip Bay. Some of the older buildings in the central area were lost, but those which had been well built, or were strategically placed on the summits of low hills, survived as islands in a shallow and gentle sea. The noise, smell and dirt of the city's streets were, in time, replaced by the grace and silence of solar-electric powered watercraft. The walls of the buildings, once covered in grime from exhaust fumes, returned to their original colours, and after almost two hundred years, the sunlight now sparkled on clean waters.

Narrowing his eyes, Chiu Liow looked into the distance, bringing himself back to the present. 'We survived,' he thought soberly, 'even though our ancestors didn't leave us much!'

'Your report is not the first to reach me, Karla,' said Federation Research Coordinator Zago, her face creased with a thousand wrinkles and her voice holding the slight quaver common to those of extreme old age. 'Here in Luzern, we have received news of two similar incidents: one from Brazil, three months ago, and the other from your sister laboratory in Queensland, just twenty minutes before you called. Unlike you, they were fortunate at the Lamington station not to have anyone working late, which meant no injuries were sustained.'

'I see by your face I have upset you with this news,' Zago continued, using the more formal language of her generation and background, 'and I am sure the violence will have disturbed you all gravely, so please replay this transmission for Mik. I want him to understand how deeply I sympathise with him.'

'Yes, I will. Thank you... But what happened at Lamington?' Karla found herself tensing as she waited for the reply.

'We are greatly puzzled by the damage there. Like you, some of their results were erased from one of their computers. This is only a minor inconvenience, of course, and although the plant stocks still under indoor culture were harmed, I am thankful to report that they were not entirely destroyed. However, this, together with the loss of a large number of their test plants, will delay the outcome of their outdoor growth trials by some one and a half years. Naturally, we will coordinate extra personnel to assist you in developing a fresh set of embryonic plants for them, once they have established what was lost. How long do you estimate it will take you and your colleagues to determine exactly which losses *your* laboratory has sustained?'

'I can tell you now. We were incredibly lucky in one way, because our frozen gene pools are completely intact. I don't know if whoever did this ran out of time, or was scared off for some reason, but I'm thankful to say that they didn't get around to vandalising any other labs – only mine. The embryo cultures in Mik and Tamara's lab are untouched, so the only real loss is my original species collection. Fortunately, Søren's set of little creatures hadn't yet been transferred from Lamington... Oh!' Karla's eyes widened. 'Zago, are you sure *they* weren't damaged?'

'Ah, yes, Karla... Do not excite yourself unnecessarily,' murmured Zago. 'I will arrange for a transfer of samples from Oslo once you give me a complete list of what you require. If *I* do it, they may move faster than they would for you. Also, if they realise there has been no culpability on your part, they will be more ready to part with their treasures.' She chuckled at the thought of overcoming their bureaucratic resistance, then added, 'In the meantime, in case it is needed, I will arrange a permit for you to return to the sites from which you obtained the specimens.'

'Thank you, Zago.' Karla felt both relieved as well as a touch foolish. She should have realised Zago would deal with the situation promptly. Their Research Coordinator was a precise and meticulous woman, with almost eighty years experience in the ways of the scientific community and its necessary – although at times excessively irritating – flock of seat-warming functionaries. 'What happened in Brazil?' she asked. 'We haven't heard anything about them.'

'The event was not reported to either the public or to anyone outside the immediate circle of people who needed to know. We felt the news would only cause widespread alarm and that no benefit would be gained by notifying other centres. The local peacekeepers could find no trace of the perpetrators, nor any sane rationale behind the attack. However, the fact that there now appears to be a pattern of incidents changes the situation. A comprehensive report will be sent to everyone in our network, as well as to the Federation's Special Investigation Unit.'

'What about the staff? Was anyone hurt?' Karla kept her thoughts to herself. For once, Zago was wrong. They should have been told.

'I am sorry to say that two of our researchers, Eduardo Arreza and Sirinya, were injured, but thank goodness, not seriously. Unfortunately, they were unable to identify their assailants in any way.' Zago briefly shook her head and frowned. 'None of their computers appear to have been tampered with, but some of the frozen plant and animal embryos were, regrettably, stolen. No fungi were lost, however, because we think the perpetrators were disturbed at this point by the no doubt unexpected return of Eduardo and Sirinya.'

'I see!' exclaimed Karla, shocked. 'I'm so glad they're all right... What do you think the FSIU will do?'

'I expect they will liaise with the local peacekeepers and provide enough resources to ensure the investigation proceeds without delay. Presumably they will also ensure security measures in all our centres are thoroughly examined and improved where necessary. Now, Karla, is there anything else I can do for you before I go?'

'No, thank you. The forensics team is here at the moment. Once they've finished going through everything, I'll concentrate on cleaning up. I think we'll all feel a lot better once we've sorted out the chaos. I'll let you know if anything new turns up.' Karla tried to smile, but failed.

Understanding, Zago nodded and bade her a fond farewell. Karla returned the greeting then closed the connection, preoccupied and deeply disturbed by the news the Federation Research Coordinator had given her.

When Tamara went to the medcentre the next morning, she found Mik sitting up and watching Fliedermus perform graceful gymnastics on the curtain bars surrounding the bed. Quite clearly, there was very little wrong with either of them.

'Hi there, Mikko. Want to go home?' said Tamara, with a grin of relief. The dark smudges under her eyes showed how difficult it had been to sleep after a long day cleaning up the mess at Willsmere, as well as dealing with the news of the attacks on the other two research stations.

At this point, Fliedermus scampered to a spot above Mik's shoulder, hanging by her tail and dangling a furry face directly in front of Tamara's. The creature burbled happily, batting at her hair with one paw, then suddenly, with an extraordinary display of aerodynamic agility, up-ended and leapt into Tamara's arms. When she nearly fell backwards with the weight, Mik burst out laughing and Tamara simply had to join in. She gave Fliedermus a kiss on the nose, then handed her to Mik, saying, 'Here, take your cat and let's get you out of here.'

Mik climbed out of bed with some difficulty, as his beloved feline was by this time sitting on his chest. 'Come on, move!' he implored her.

Pretending to be insulted, Fliedermus leapt to the floor, built up speed, and skittered sideways towards the door, arching her back and tail as she went.

'If she's like this now, you'll have to help me when I get home to the others,' said Mik, smiling as he watched Fliedermus. 'They'll probably be hysterical. I don't suppose anyone thought of telling them where I was?'

'As a matter of fact, yes, we did. I went to your house, let myself in, and got pounced on by Red Matilda. She glared at me for ages before getting my message that you were okay and that I had no intention of invading your privacy! Meanwhile, Possum was hiding under the bedcovers. She poked her nose out just as I was going, so I hope she came out later to eat what I left for her, assuming Red didn't grab the lot. That cat's a monster!'

'Well, I didn't name her Red Matilda for nothing. Haven't you read any twentieth-century history?' said Mik, with a teasing grin. 'Anyway, Fliedermus is creating havoc. We'd better move, and I'm sorry, but you can't watch while I get dressed!'

Tamara poked her tongue out at him, but obediently turned around while he put on the clothes she'd remembered to bring. He really did look wonderful, she thought, studying him for a moment after he tapped her on the shoulder to let her know they were ready to go. Even being attacked and spending a night in a medcentre had done nothing to change either his sense of humour or his general appearance. If it weren't for the mark on his forehead, it was almost as if nothing had happened.

They presented themselves at the main reception area, where Mik pressed a thumb against the keypad of the computer with "Patient Arrivals and Departures" displayed on its screen. After the usual exchange of information, and once he'd been issued with a record of stay and aftercare instructions, Mik and Tamara left the building, led by an overjoyed Fliedermus. Outside, the small blue flowers of the trafficway's living surface spread before them in a dense carpet. Its beauty and delicate scent seemed to invite them to enjoy the warm, sunlit day.

'According to my aftercare schedule,' said Mik, briefly putting an arm around Tamara's shoulders, 'I'm supposed to go home and rest. Furthermore, I'm to have 'a close friend' with me until morning. Do you think you'd qualify?'

When Tamara mumbled something indecipherable, Mik laughed, his voice rich and deep.

'I do believe you're blushing, Researcher Tamara Solanum. Would you rather I contacted Søren? He should've returned from Lamington by now. I'm sure he'd be enthralled at the idea of spending a day and a night by my bedside, instead of advancing the cause of science by another twenty-four hours.'

Fliedermus gave his game away by rubbing herself against Tamara's legs, purring loudly. Tamara giggled and looked him straight in the eye. 'If you want to tease people, my friend, you'd better leave your cat at home.' Mik pretended to be chastened, but utterly failed to convince her.

The two friends walked on towards the medcentre's public callstation, Mik in his usual lively way and Tamara matching his stride. When she entered Mik's address code into its small, robust terminal, the screen glowed yellow and showed the message "Transport in 5 minutes". As they waited, Tamara told him what had happened at Willsmere while he was unconscious. It appeared the practitioner in charge of his treatment had already given him the basics, yet although Mik was recovering well, he still had no memory whatsoever of the night's events. He could only remember working peacefully, listening to his music – then waking up in the medcentre bed with Fliedermus asleep by his feet. He now found it hard to control a sense of complete outrage at the wanton destruction of Karla's work. Nevertheless, he also had to admit to feeling relieved that so little damage had been done to his or anyone else's.

Once their transport arrived, they both sat quietly during the short trip, not wishing to discuss such sensitive matters in public. When they were alone again, as they walked, Tamara continued her description of the events and gave him the news from Research Coordinator Zago. Mik said very little. It was all too much to take in.

By the time they arrived at Mik's home, the sun glinted on its greenhouse entrance, where, inside, a riot of greenery and brilliantly coloured flowering plants displayed the botanist's vibrant taste. When he pressed the security keypad with his thumb, the door slid aside to admit them. Following the circular staircase down into the house proper – which as a private dwelling in this particular part of the city was built below ground level – they entered the main living room, which was lit by a plastiglass sun dome in its ceiling. The temperature of the house was kept within reasonable limits by the insulation of the earth surrounds, so the room felt delightfully cool and the air fresh and pleasant. As was customary, the building had self-sufficient energy, water, and waste disposal systems that supplied fertiliser for the small outdoor garden of food plants, which Mik tended with loving care.

As soon as they walked in, an enormous golden-red cat leapt from an armchair and bounded over to greet them. Mik crouched down to rub his face against hers, laughing as Fliedermus attempted to swat Red Matilda's waving, bushy tail. Red Matilda turned and cuffed her playmate over the ear, and then the two capered around the room, rolling over each other in their excitement. A little grey head appeared from beneath a ruffled floor rug and the smallest of the household's trio of cats appeared: Possum. As Mik stood up, she sidled delicately up to him to wind herself around his legs, purring noisily. Tamara bent down and, with some effort, managed to pick her up. Possum immediately nestled into her cradled arms.

Leaving the other two cats to their antics, Mik, Tamara, and her furry bundle, went through to the kitchen, where Tamara collapsed thankfully onto the nearest chair. The worry of the past twenty-seven hours eased as the cat's effect on her began to take hold.

'Mik, I think you'd better take Possum away from me. She's nearly sending me to sleep.' Possum immediately stopped purring and snuffled into Tamara's ear.

Rubbing the side of his slightly crooked nose, Mik quirked his eyebrows and said, 'Apparently I'm not allowed to remove her. We wouldn't want to risk sending her back under the rug, now would we? I'll keep you awake by creating a midsun masterpiece. What would you like with your food, Tamara? A good pinot grigio or a nice soft merlot?'

'Well, neither. You're supposed to be taking it easy and definitely not drinking alcohol. How about you sit here with Possum and I get something for us both instead?'

Mik paused in mid-stride towards the pantry and turned back, then picked up Possum and obediently sat down on the chair opposite, an expression of mock remorse on his face, which soon disappeared as he replied, 'Just don't wreck anything, Tamara. I know you're not interested in cooking.'

She picked up a lemon from the fruit bowl on the table and threw it at him, missing completely when he ducked. Possum leapt off his lap and scrabbled around after the fruit where it had rolled underneath a small side table. Sniffing carefully, she decided it wasn't edible and patted it one last time with her paw, just enough to make it roll a little further, then gazed up at Tamara, eyes wide.

'No, it's not a toy,' answered Tamara. 'Sorry.' When she got up from her chair to retrieve the lemon and wipe it clean, Possum pressed herself against Tamara's legs, tail in the air, and was rewarded with a piece of soft cheese. The cat carried it over to her own special place by the kitchen sink, where she contentedly ate her treat.

Tamara watched for a few moments, and when she turned to ask Mik what he wanted to drink with his meal, found he was no longer in his chair. Instead, he was fast asleep on the living room couch, with Red Matilda and Fliedermus snuggled up beside him, also sleeping soundly. For once, Mik's hands were still, one of them resting on Fliedermus, the other tucked beneath his cheek, where long, thick eyelashes lay on his warm, sun-browned skin. Feeling guilty, Tamara took the chance to study him, gently stroking the smile lines deeply etched around the corners of his wide, mobile mouth. Then, unable to resist the temptation, she followed the outline of his eyebrows with her forefinger. They were spaced widely apart and towards their outer ends, the black hair grew a little longer and stood straight up, as if in perpetual surprise, giving him the appearance of an habitual comic. He muttered something in his sleep and turned over. Tamara quickly drew away.

CHAPTER TWO

Rohan Maerz looked out over the city of Luzern from his suite in the office tower devoted to the employees of the Federation's Special Investigation Unit. As its Coordinator, he was faced with an unusually perplexing situation and it seemed that, regrettably, action was unavoidable. Earlier during the day, the disruption to his morning routine in the form of an insistent call from Research Coordinator Zago had thoroughly annoyed him. Not only had her call been worrisome, it had been long. So long, in fact, that his coffee was stone cold by the time he returned to it.

Sighing, Rohan reflected that he'd not even had the chance to eat an extra round of pastry before another call interrupted his breakfast. This time, it was some obscure peacekeeper from Australia, of all places, and only after the conversation ended did it occur to him to wonder how this person had managed to contact him directly. Chiu Liow Jones must possess a high degree of initiative and an unusual amount of ingenuity to have been able to short-circuit the pleasantly complex bureaucracy with which he surrounded himself!

Turning from his contemplation of the intricate facade of the old hotel opposite, he was about to treat himself to his usual mid-morning meal of glacé fruits and more coffee when the door was flung open and Morag MacIain marched in. Her expression told him to abandon the idea of food.

'Ah, hum...I gather the reports were interesting, Morag?'

'We have a problem, Rohan. There's absolutely no doubt in my mind that these attacks form a pattern. The *pattern* is that they don't make sense. The most junior of my investigators knows enough about computers to realise that wiping them clean is a waste of time! Of course, I can well understand why someone would want the stored information. What I find hard to comprehend is the degree of corruption of security personnel that gaining access to the sites and then to these databases would have required. All our information and communication systems are totally secure – or at least I thought so – which means it's virtually certain we're dealing with on-site sabotage, coordinated by someone with worldwide access to infotechs. Otherwise, whoever did all this must have a frighteningly high level of expertise to have been able to bypass our security, or worse still, has extremely high-level access.'

She paused at this point and her features relaxed. There was no misunderstanding the longing looks Rohan was casting at the small office servery. 'Perhaps you'd be so kind as to offer me a cup of your excellent coffee? I've had no time to stop all morning.' Morag could rarely resist teasing her colleague, so, brushing away a lock of bright auburn hair from her forehead, she added, 'You seem a bit parched yourself. Have you been pushing yourself too hard?'

Rohan grimaced, then fussed over the coffee preparations for several minutes. Finally, and feeling only slightly embarrassed, he arranged a selection of his favourite sweet fruits on a priceless Spode plate, together with the iced cakes he'd hoped to keep for the afternoon. Still, the sacrifice would be worthwhile if it kept Morag in a good mood.

They enjoyed their delicacies in companionable silence for a while, before he said, 'Priority investigation, I'd say, wouldn't you? When do you want to begin? Could I suggest you draw up a plan listing the resources you need, site priorities, and a proposed timeframe? Oh, and may I also ask you to outline a report schedule? It does so help me to refrain from worrying unduly.'

Morag's slender fingers handled the porcelain coffee cup with loving care. Its beautiful green pattern matched her eyes. 'I'll do that for you. I'll even make sure you have it all before you leave this evening. Despite there now being five sites involved that we're currently aware of, with a little luck, it shouldn't be too long before I obtain the full details.'

She stood up and moved over to the window, taking a few moments to enjoy the panorama – this peaceful city that represented order and beauty to most citizens of the Federation. At the same time, however, Morag experienced a vague sense of disquiet. The crimes to be investigated were uncommonly vicious and outside her previous experience. Turning to Rohan, she added, 'I suspect the Australian laboratories will yield more answers than the others. That peacekeeper, Jones, is a rarity. I can't remember anyone else from the Federation forces managing to get through to you without having to speak with your minions first. He must have caught you unawares. Your conversation with him was...frank.'

Rohan had the grace to blush. 'I was having breakfast. You know I get easily flustered at that time of day. In any case, my computer indicated he had security clearance of a very high order. I did at least notice that much before I answered the call, so do get on with the job, Morag, and don't stand there smirking at me!'

Morag laughed, then before leaving the room, helped herself to the last of the iced cakes. Rohan returned to his earlier study of the view, his mind speeding through the possibilities. He was certain she would get to the bottom of the matter; Morag had never failed in the past. He did regret her eating the last cake though, but preferred not to order any more. His great size and well-known craving for sweets already caused him a considerable degree of social embarrassment. Colleagues had been known to turn down invitations to dine with him. They were, in his opinion, only those who held extreme views on over-consumption, and who prided themselves on wearing their clothes until they were almost in tatters. He chuckled. Really, there were limits to how far social etiquette should be taken!

Studying the evidence before her, Morag could see that the research sites which were attacked fell into two groups. The first, supervised by Federation Research Coordinator Zago, dealt with new food crops, timber plantations, and restoration of tropical rainforests and other priority environments. Three centres in this group had been sabotaged: two in Australia – situated at Willsmere in Victoria and at Lamington in Queensland – and one in the Brazilian Amazon basin. The second group was supervised by Research Coordinator Meng Jarrah, an Australian currently living in Oslo and employed by the national governments of the countries where her laboratories were situated. Two had been attacked and were located in Papua and Myanmar.

Morag was curious about this woman and did a quick search, to find she not only supervised other researchers, but also carried a high voluntary workload consisting of her own studies in palaeontology. Meng Jarrah was, it seemed, one of the few scientists capable of quite literally bringing the past back to life. To date, her laboratories in Myanmar and in Niu Bougainville, Papua, had managed to use the preserved remains of two extinct life forms to extract their genetic tissue and recreate the living organisms. Unfortunately, the animals died soon after they reached the embryo stage. Nevertheless, worldwide excitement had been generated and she became the unwilling focus of intense lobbying from every nation wanting to share in the glory.

Much to her disgust, apparently, Meng Jarrah also gained the attention of nutters like the Cane Toad Preservation Society of Australia. This group tried to bribe her personnel into turning their attention to the living and monstrous descendant of this pestilential creature, which they saw as being unfairly persecuted. They argued that the researchers would achieve far better results using live tissue rather than preserved remains, and they could therefore perfect their technique in a shorter period of time – even though this had already been done centuries before with other species and with significant success. Fortunately, Meng Jarrah, being an Australian, had direct experience of the frightening destruction the modern-day cane toad, like its much smaller ancestor, was capable of. The society had been thrown out on its collective ear. Meng Jarrah's only reported comment was, "I hope a cane toad spits on them."

Morag laughed, then went back to her collection of evidence. She noticed that all the attacks occurred late at night. In those instances where laboratory staff returned to or were still on the premises, they had been violently assaulted and rendered unconscious before having a chance to see their assailants. That in itself was peculiar. Villains were usually able to obtain immobilisers quite readily – why not these people? One of the Myanmarian researchers was still in a coma a whole week after being assaulted. She wondered if there was even a small chance he might have seen enough to warrant the particularly brutal treatment at their hands? Morag made contacting Meng Jarrah a priority.

In contrast, however, in no instance was the damage to the laboratories as extensive as she would have expected, while the erasure of databases had been inconsistent, haphazard and relatively minor. Even the thefts were inconsistent, although this may have been due to the intruders being interrupted. The specimens stolen were, nevertheless, of great value. In all, the thieves gained a large number of frozen plant and animal embryos from Brazil; a range of new species of plants from Australia; various experimental tropical timbers, also from Australia; the preserved remains of a small set of extinct rainforest species from Myanmar; and a single, recently obtained, twentieth-century soil sample stored in the Niu Bougainville laboratory. The booty also included a vast amount of genetic and ecological knowledge. So, if the attackers had sufficient power and connections to suborn people at central security sites, or were capable of using highly sophisticated means to bypass security systems, it seemed safe to assume they were not common vandals and had a highly specific purpose in mind.

After giving the situation more thought, Morag spoke to her computer, describing the information she wanted and asking for the names of all suitable investigators free to follow up on what could be provided. It told her there were only seven organisations of the particular type in which she was interested.

Apparently, a number of private companies and collectives funded their own research into food crops, forestry products or both – although she imagined that none of these organisations would usually be in a position to realistically compete with Federation or other government-sponsored efforts, relying instead on the published material routinely made available. Still, perhaps one of them was attempting to enhance their research capacity in this nefarious manner in order to improve their ability to compete?

No, it just didn't seem likely. Although three of the organisations were large enough to have more than a single research site, and one had a diverse set of interests and operated globally, none of them appeared to have the resources to organise a coup of these dimensions, or even any known motive. It also appeared that none had previously earned the attention of the Federation's Special Investigation Unit.

'Well, they'll certainly get it now,' she thought, and rapidly entered instructions to be sent to the chosen investigators. Wanting quick results, Morag allocated one to each organisation. As an afterthought, and when she was suddenly struck with an overwhelming desire to speak to anyone who had managed to out-fox Rohan Maerz's network of bureaucrats, she asked her computer to contact Peacekeeper Chiu Liow Jones. The computer beeped and said, 'Please confirm your call. It is 05:00 in Melbourne, Australia.'

'It's confirmed, if the number is on alert,' she replied.

The call was put through and Morag was impressed to see a wide awake, calm face smiling cheerfully at her from the screen. She had expected the peacekeeper to appear somewhat frayed at this hour.

'Good morning, Peacekeeper Jones. My name is Morag MacIain. I am an investigator with the FSIU and I understand you've spoken with our good friend, Rohan Maerz. Congratulations!'

Chiu Liow allowed himself a smug grin. 'I am honoured by your praise, Investigator MacIain. Uncooperative people annoy me intensely, so it has been a pastime of mine for many years to annoy them in return. I also felt the situation at Willsmere warranted prompt attention. Although FSIU Coordinator Maerz would almost certainly have acted in due course on the information received from Research Coordinator Zago, I wished to ensure that my own peacekeeping force was kept informed as the inquiry proceeded. It is possible we could even assist the Special Investigation Unit.'

Morag was impressed by the man's quiet assurance, yet amused by his formal manner. 'Thank you, Peacekeeper Jones. Tell me, how well do you know the members of the Brisbane Peacekeeping Force?'

'I have had many dealings with them and have obtained a high level of cooperation when needed, Investigator MacIain.'

'In that case, perhaps you could liaise between them and our people? Your Willsmere situation isn't unique. An attack on a sister site in Lamington, Queensland, occurred on the same night. Have you heard about it?'

'Yes, I scanned our crime statistics for any similar incidents. My Brisbane colleagues are now working in coordination with us. I would welcome your involvement too, as we do not have sufficient access authority to the relevant network segments – or possibly even the computing expertise – to fully examine the security aspects of the case.'

Morag tried hard to keep her growing excitement from showing. One of the Unit's many difficulties was the not infrequent obstruction from local peacekeeping forces. Perhaps these were different. 'You don't happen to have contacts with any peacekeepers in Myanmar, Papua or Brazil, do you?' she asked hopefully, raising one slim hand towards the screen.

'Indeed. I have a personal friend working in Papua, a family member working in Myanmar, and a former colleague working in Brazil. Why do you ask?'

'Over the past three months, there have been five similar incidents all told. The other three occurred in Niu Bougainville, Papua; Mandalay in Myanmar; and Serra do Cachimbo in the Amazonian State of Para, Brazil. Given you're already involved with the investigation into the two attacks in Australia, perhaps you could provide liaison with local peacekeeping forces in these other countries? I'm sure the FSIU would benefit from more cooperation than we're usually given. You also have the necessary security clearance to deal directly with me. Would you be willing to assist?'

Chiu Liow's face betrayed a flicker of gratification at the unusual request. 'I would be pleased to, Investigator MacIain, and I am sure my contacts in the other countries could obtain a transfer to the local Forces of the regions you have mentioned. Can I assume you will send copies of the relevant material without delay?'

'Yes,' replied Morag, smiling broadly. 'You should receive it all very soon!'

Once his screen cleared, impressed by Investigator Morag MacIain, Chiu Liow Jones allowed himself a broad, satisfied smile. No obstructive inclinations there! He also had to admit she was beautiful. Wavy auburn hair, green eyes and a sprinkling of freckles across her straight, finely moulded nose. He liked the laughter lines around her mouth and eyes, too. She wasn't young, but then, neither was he. Still, such fantasies would need to be set firmly aside, although he hoped to meet her in person some day. The chances of that, the peacekeeper concluded wistfully, were probably remote. He returned to the reports he had been reading before the call interrupted him. There was now the added, and alarming, dimension to consider of a further three attacks on research sites; but for the time being, his immediate priority needed to be the case at hand.

Forensics had so far found no trace of whoever broke into Willsmere, suggesting this was no common criminal – which they already suspected. Furthermore, none of the other secure areas of the building were recorded as having been entered in an unauthorised manner by any of the staff members present before Karla and Tamara left for the night. Neither had there been any damage done to these other areas, or losses from any other computers.

So far, it seemed highly likely that the attacks on Lamington and Willsmere occurred before midnight, when the regular security updates were performed. This meant the timing of the security breach depended upon how the systems were managed, because at midnight, temporary, or guest, entries would be erased and could only be restored at official request on a daily basis. At the same time, identities registered as having 'permanent' right of access were matched with those registered as being either current employees or authorities with appropriate entry privileges, such as himself, all of whom would need to be examined. Perhaps he could suggest to Morag MacIain that her investigators share this particularly prickly part of the burden?

The most plausible scenario seemed to be that the breach had been organised from within the government division responsible for, amongst other things, communications, transport, and buildings security. As a result, each infotech employed by Melbourne's Central Computer Site needed to be interviewed at length and their movements crosschecked. Fortunately, there were only thirty-seven of them: five for each twelve-and-a-half-hour shift and two for emergency relief. The names of every friend, family member and close acquaintance to whom they would admit were already being checked against the Force knowledge base, on the off-chance that a link or pattern might exist. Chiu Liow expected the final results to be available by the end of the day.

Meanwhile, he began by going through the list of employees present at Willsmere during the day of the attack and making an interview schedule. Permission would be required to access the information held in the Government databanks on each of them, as well as all the other potential suspects. The interviewers would use the background information to help them target their questions. Usually they made do without, as most crimes were not serious enough to warrant the breach of privacy. Taking one last look at the bright sunshine outside, and with a sense of longing, Chiu Liow commenced the tedious job of entering the formal request for access to all the necessary records. He hoped the conversation with Morag MacIain would go a long way towards convincing the Speaker of the House of Representatives that permission should be granted, once she had viewed the recording.

Karla yawned and rolled over. Her videoscreen showed a day of brilliant sunshine. The view gave her enough incentive to get out of bed and eventually wander into the dining room, where Tamara and another woman were already having breakfast, and by all appearances, talking earnestly. Karla found this the only trying part of living in one of the communal houses, preferring at least a good hour to herself first thing in the morning. Still, this was a small price to pay for not having to do any domestic work. She took her time choosing from the food and drink available at the buffet. The fresh coffee sent out an appealing aroma and the tossed tow salad looked just right. Karla loved towes, not just because they looked and tasted good, but because they held a sentimental attraction for someone in her profession: they were one of the very few plant-animal survivors of twenty-first century genetic engineering.

Taking her tray over to Tamara's table, she smiled and sat down, then lifted the soymilk jug and poured some of the rich, creamy liquid into her coffee.

'Well, Tamara, how's Mik?'

Tamara's other friend laughed and got up from the table. 'I'll leave you two to talk in peace. I've just been given a highly coloured account and don't think I could cope with a repeat version. See you both later.'

Tamara looked embarrassed. 'See you, Anne. Have a good day.'

'How come you didn't have breakfast with Mik? I thought you were still supposed to be nursing him... Or is he better already?' Karla couldn't prevent herself from grinning. A good night's sleep had helped restore her sense of humour.

'Oh yes, he's fine now,' replied Tamara, her voice tinged with sarcasm. 'It's that blasted cat of his, Possum. Every time I sit down, the animal jumps onto my lap and goes to sleep and then I start nodding off as well. I was lucky to have woken up at all this morning! I don't think I would have, except that Fliedermus obviously thought it was time I did. She started chasing her tail on my bed at 07:30 and nearly squashed Possum in the process. Anyway, I got up and was just starting breakfast when Possum curled herself up on my feet. Before I knew it, Mik woke me half an hour later. Would you believe, Possum and I were snuggled up together underneath the table. It was totally embarrassing! When I walked out, he was laughing himself silly...so I know he's perfectly alright!'

Karla tried to appear sympathetic and failed. 'You should know better than to be embarrassed. Mik's cats are his darlings and he was most likely laughing at Possum. My guess would be that he left the cat with you on purpose so you'd sleep well. You should have given him a chance to explain. It's not like you to get into a huff like this. You've worked with him for five years now. Don't tell me it's the first time Possum's sent you to sleep.'

'You're right of course, Karla. It's just that when he got hurt, I realised how much I cared for him. I've been talking it over with Anne, but I don't know what to do because if he doesn't feel the same way about me, it's going to be very hard to work together. I guess I'll have to rake up enough courage to ask him straight out.'

'Why don't you wait a bit, Tamara? What you're experiencing may simply be the natural concern anyone would have for a close friend. We're all confused and vulnerable at the moment, so I'm sure Mik won't mind if you take more notice of him than usual. After all, I suspect it won't be long before he'll be feeling quite fragile himself. It's mainly the cats who are helping him appear normal.'

'You're right. Thanks... Anne was talking about fertility applications and all that sort of stuff. I must admit, she almost had me convinced, though I can't really imagine myself doing that right now... Work's too interesting. Anyway, just because I'm fond of Mik doesn't mean I have to get all clucky.' Tamara stood up. 'Have you finished eating yet? I'd like to get back to Willsmere.'

Karla shook her head. 'No, I've hardly started, so why don't you go on ahead? I won't be far behind.'

Tamara sighed, but realised she was being impatient and left Karla to eat in peace.

Mik sat completely still, holding his head in his hands. He was perfectly sure that if he didn't, it would fall off. The semi-euphoria of his treatment by the medcentre, mitigated by Fliedermus' soothing effect, had worn off and his head ached abominably. What really did happen at Willsmere? The memory, which had totally disappeared at first, was now beginning to return. He could visualise himself sitting at his workstation, deep in thought, his furry friend asleep by his side. Fliedermus had suddenly growled and when he turned to see what was wrong, an incredible pain at the back of his head was the last thing he could remember. He hadn't caught even a glimpse of his assailant.

Possum put a paw on his knee and meowed softly. When Mik picked her up, he immediately felt calmer. Even his headache eased. Crooning, she butted her forehead against his chin.

'Don't do that, cat. It hurts.'

As his 'little' grey cat settled down on his lap and gazed lovingly into his eyes, a startling idea came to him: Fliedermus would recognise the intruder! He was almost sure of it, then felt himself go red in the face. Suggest to the peacekeepers they use a cat as a witness? Was it even legal? Mik doubted it, despite their amazing powers.

CHAPTER THREE

When his computer signalled an incoming call, Mik rose to acknowledge it and Søren appeared on the screen, immediately saying, 'Mik, I hear you are hurt! This is terrible, my friend! Even worse, I understand you are also alone, and Tamara tells me you have insulted her, otherwise she would not have left. You must apologise, and meanwhile, will have my company instead. I admit this may not be as intriguing a prospect, but it isn't every day one is hit on the head.'

For once, Mik had no witty reply to Søren's banter. 'How soon can you get here?' he asked instead. 'I've just had a really weird thought that I'd like to talk to you about. Do me a favour too, would you? Bring something for us to eat at midsun? I don't have the energy to prepare anything.'

Søren smiled. 'Forty-five minutes, and I will be there. We will eat in your delightful greenhouse and I will try not to interrupt you for at least five minutes.'

After precisely the time stated, the household security system chimed, announcing Søren's arrival as he stood outside the front door, burdened with a great deal of food. Mik pressed the keypad to allow him to enter, then slowly climbed the stairs to the greenhouse, his knees feeling weak with the effort. He stared at the food Søren had brought, which he was already arranging on the table with an eye to effect – he had even thought to bring a tablecloth. There was enough to keep them both going for at least three days!

With a final artistic flourish, Søren bowed to Mik, saying, 'Please, sit, and tell me all.' A touch embarrassed, Mik began. Every now and then Søren shook his head in sympathy. The expression on the delicate, classic features, together with the directness of his dark grey eyes, contributed to an overall effect of deep concentration on every word his friend spoke. The concentration wasn't feigned. As a zoologist with, amongst other things, a particular interest in cats, Søren was in a good position to give Mik a judgement on the soundness of his theory: that Fliedermus might be able to identify his assailant.

'It is reasonably well known,' said Søren, once Mik had finished speaking, 'that cats are able to receive and broadcast emotions clearly and strongly. What you put forward is that they could also remember scenes and experiences long enough to recognise someone with whom they had previously come into contact only the once. Furthermore, you are suggesting they are capable of broadcasting their emotional memory should they meet the person again. Very well, I accept your hypothesis. A cat such as Fliedermus, who has bonded strongly with you, would quite likely be an adept. Even before cats were genetically engineered to become what they are today, they were renowned for their long memories. I cannot imagine she would fail to recall such a traumatic event as a physical injury to her companion. So, we will contact this peacekeeper of yours and put the proposition to him – at once!' Søren leapt to his feet and energetically began to remove the remains of their meal from the table.

'I thought you said "at once",' Mik remarked, raising an eyebrow.

'Some things take precedence. I will not have it said that I left your greenhouse in a state fit only for the toads your nation despises so deeply. Orderly habits go with an orderly mind.' He carried the tablecloth outside, shook it carefully, folded it neatly and put it away. 'We must rinse these dishes and then wash them after we have spoken to Peacekeeper Jones.'

Søren fussed about for a short while longer before asking the computer to contact the said peacekeeper. The computer disappointed them both by stating that the number contacted was not answering because its owner was asleep.

'Why is this person sleeping during the daytime, just when we need him!' fumed Søren. 'Tell me, computer, how long will he be asleep?'

The machine answered that Peacekeeper Chiu Liow Jones would awake at 18:30, but would not be available until 20:00. Could it take a message?

'Tell Peacekeeper Jones that Researcher Søren Thorup of the Willsmere centre has contacted him regarding a possible means of identifying whoever it was that attacked Researcher Mik Theophanous. He will please return my call on this number as soon as possible.' Søren waggled a finger at the screen for emphasis.

They occupied the next half hour tidying the kitchen and speculating upon the reasons for the raids on Willsmere and the other research centres, then watched the recording of the conversation that had taken place between Karla and Research Coordinator Zago two days earlier.

'I can't understand why they didn't take more from Willsmere than they did,' said Mik, when it was finished. 'There was all the time in the world.'

'You forget, Mik, that at 24:00 each night the security system is restored to retain only permanent access entries. If, for example, our unknown villain isn't someone with permanent access and they arrived at the perimeter wall shortly after 22:30, when Karla and Tamara left, they had at most only one and a half hours to gain entry, obtain what they wanted, then leave the building and grounds and be well away from the area before an alarm was created. Perhaps that isn't much time in a strange complex and with strange computers. Besides, Fliedermus would have been a complicating factor.'

'True, and thank the Sun she wasn't hurt!'

'Has she told you what happened?' Søren found it difficult to imagine how, precisely, the attack had been managed, given the cat *was* actually present.

'Yes, but it was a while before she did. I think Fliedermus was waiting for me to feel better before showing me what she saw and heard. Apparently there were two intruders and her first image is of my being hit on the head, then immediately having a blanket thrown over her and being put into a cage. They then proceeded to wreck the place, and after they'd finished taking what they wanted, carried her into your lab, let her out and quickly closed the door behind them. I suppose the cage and blanket were removed in case they could be used as evidence.' Mik shrugged and ran a hand through his hair, his expression grim, imagining how Fliedermus must have struggled and cried.

At this point, the subject of the conversation made her presence felt by licking Mik's bare toes. Despite his gloomy mood, he responded by rolling the cat onto her back and scratching her stomach. Absorbed in each other, neither noticed Søren's expression of wistful longing. He had been constrained to leave his own beloved feline companion in Greenland, due to her refusal to travel in the cargo hold for the duration of the long flight. He sighed softly. Already he loved Fliedermus dearly, but she was no substitute.

Breaking in on the increasingly boisterous play, he said, 'Mik, I am sorry to interrupt, but you must contact our little Spud and apologise for your behaviour this morning. She is most disgruntled, so you should do it now.'

"Little Spud" was a private joke, since Søren was a diminutive one hundred and sixty-five centimetres tall, fully fifteen centimetres shorter than Karla, who was merely average height. In return, Tamara sometimes referred to him as 'Alf', the Danish word for 'pixie'.

Mik had the sense to agree without comment. He wasn't up to the teasing he would otherwise have received if he'd given any indication that an emotional attachment appeared to be developing between Tamara and himself. Even he would have doubted it if Fliedermus hadn't reacted to the atmosphere between them at the medcentre the previous morning – although Mik sincerely hoped Tamara's usual down-to-earth nature and solid common sense would prevail. Her outburst this morning was completely uncharacteristic. Somewhat wary of what she would say now, he asked his computer for Tamara's comlink code. After a few moments, she appeared on the screen, wearing a strangely noncommittal expression. Søren discreetly left the room.

'Hi, Tamara. I'm still alive, as you can see, despite being deserted this morning. Luckily, Søren arrived to keep me from death's door, so I've been wined and dined, so to speak, in grand Scandinavian style. Say you forgive me, and promise to come over tomorrow morning. *I* promise to keep Possum away from you!' Mik raised a pleading hand towards the screen.

Despite her best efforts, Tamara couldn't keep a straight face. 'Sure, Mik, I guess I can stand your company a bit longer, but how do you expect Possum's going to take it if she's locked out of the room?'

'Well, we *could* take them all for a walk. Red and Possum haven't been outside for three days. Let's do that after breakfast. You *are* coming over for breakfast, aren't you? Søren's brought enough food to last the week.'

'That'd be great. I can only stay until midsun, though. There's still a lot of work here that needs doing; we're liaising with Lamington now to restore the plant stocks they lost.' Tamara paused. 'Have you listened to the recording Søren brought for you?'

'Oh yes. And I think I might have a way of helping the peacekeepers. I've talked it over with Søren and he agrees it's feasible. My proposal is that Fliedermus and I should be present when they interview their suspects. I'm sure she'd react if any of them were actually at Willsmere the other night. I don't think a cat's ever been used as a witness before, but I can't see why they shouldn't be. I'm hoping Søren's expertise will help convince the peacekeepers it's worth a try.'

'What a fantastic idea!' cried Tamara. 'I love it! Can't you see a suspect just about wetting themselves if Fliedermus went berserk!' She calmed down, and with a giggle, added, 'Still, come to think of it, you'd better put a collar and lead on her if they do agree. We wouldn't want her charged with manslaughter, would we. Or would they charge you? Never mind... I shouldn't be laughing at such grisly ideas. Obviously, I've still got an instinct for revenge... And I thought I was such a gentle person.'

'It takes a situation like this to find out how easy it is for people to become violent. It also shows how lucky we are to have survived our ancestors, who weren't as finicky,' replied Mik, not finding what she said at all funny. 'Anyway, I'm getting far too serious and I don't think my poor head can take it. I actually went into shock again after you left, if that helps.' He pulled a wry face and shook his head.

'Well, it doesn't, you know. It makes me feel guilty. I also feel like a total idiot. Normally I'd have laughed right along with you, so I think I must've been in shock too. The other thing, dare I say it, is that you're important to me.' Tamara blushed and felt her heart rate increase. 'Now I've done it,' she thought, biting her lip.

'Thanks, Tamara. You're important to me too. If *you* weren't around, who'd take care of my cats when I'm away on field trips...and water my plants, come to think of it?' Mik grinned, while Tamara glared at him. 'Just joking,' he added. 'I noticed how Fliedermus behaved yesterday morning at the medcentre. Don't tell me you didn't... And by the way, you're looking a lot better today than you did yesterday.'

'Mik, if I didn't have your precious cat's projections to rely on, I think I'd come over right now and stomp all over your biggest and juiciest pumpkin patch! As it is, I'm going to inform Karla what a ratfink we've got for a botanist! See you tomorrow,' she finished by saying, before abruptly ending the call.

Mik smiled to himself. Despite the situation, life was definitely improving – not that it wasn't pretty marvellous anyway, when it came down to it. Whistling a passage from *Carmen*, an ancient opera he'd once seen, he wandered off to find Søren, who, as it turned out, was engaged in exchanging growls with Red Matilda. It was a ridiculous pastime, for Red knew perfectly well he wasn't being genuinely aggressive. However, Søren adored making use of opportunities to study what he termed 'cat psychology' and Red Matilda was more than willing to cooperate. She was able to mimic almost every sound Søren produced, but seemed intent on always having the last 'word'. As a result, the cacophony was fast reaching unbearable levels. Meanwhile, as Possum hid beneath a rug, Fliedermus stared at the two in disgust, shoulders hunched and tail swishing vigorously from side to side.

'Shut up, the pair of you!' shouted Mik. 'My head's starting to hurt again!'

Silence reigned for a moment, and when Søren calmly pronounced that Red Matilda was a highly intelligent cat, she leapt at his chest and knocked him to the floor.

'Yeah, I totally agree,' said Mik, turning his back on them and leaving the room.

Peacekeeper Chiu Liow Jones rolled onto his back, savouring the last memories of his dream. Morag MacIain had featured in it, and for some strange reason, was here in Australia. 'Must be wishful thinking,' he murmured. Stretching, he lay in bed for a few more minutes, gazing up at the ceiling. Not needing to return to duty until the next morning, he had the entire evening and night to himself. This was a novelty, as his large number of voluntary hours far exceeded the twenty-five-hour working week everyone was required to perform. Investigative work was addictive, that was the problem. Even his sleep was interrupted occasionally with a solution to some dilemma neatly presented to him by a subconscious that kept dutifully ticking away.

He eventually got out of bed and walked over to glance at his computer. Its message icon winked steadily. Resisting the urge to listen to the message immediately, Chiu Liow wandered into the bathroom, and before allowing the small spa to fill, performed the *Shil Lim Tao*. Most people allowed their practice of Wing Chun kung fu to lapse once their first years of formal education were over, but the peacekeeper found this daily training routine indispensable to his physical and mental wellbeing.

The exercise finished, and with an appropriate sense of serenity, Chiu Liow relaxed in the hot, bubbly water, enjoying the sunlight filtering in through the room's skylight. When the need for food began to impinge on his thoughts, he dried himself and decided not to bother dressing, but kept a robe handy in case the computer chimed an incoming call. After a 'breakfast' of apple and strawberry fruit juice, fresh coffee, and a small bowl of oatflakes with soymilk and honey, a relaxing half hour disappeared all too quickly in browsing the Federation's central library for general news. Sighing, Chiu Liow put on the robe and asked for his messages. He was soon jerked out of his pleasantly tranquil state of mind into one of concentrated attention: Morag MacIain was arriving the next morning. She would be here, in Melbourne! If he wasn't careful, he would start believing in fate!

His mind buzzing, he watched the next message, then asked for Researcher Mik Theophanous' comlink code. The response to the call was almost immediate. Although Chiu Liow hadn't met the researcher, he had seen file images of him and quickly adopted the serene expression reserved for his official duties, as well as the cheerful tone of voice.

'Good evening, Researcher Theophanous. I gather Søren Thorup has used your comlink code as a contact point for me. I believe he has information regarding a possible means of identifying your assailant?'

'Pleased to meet you, Peacekeeper Jones. Yes, he's here with me now. We've been waiting for your call.'

Mik smiled politely and moved away to allow Søren to speak with him. Chiu Liow was momentarily taken aback by the unusual beauty of the man before him, enhanced by his mass of golden curls: angelic was the archaic term used to describe such features. However, the angelic impression was soon discarded when Søren began by saying, 'Peacekeeper Jones, I gather? We were becoming impatient. It is now 20:20. We were told you would be available at 20:00. My sense of humour suffers from being kept waiting.'

Chiu Liow brushed his hair away from his eyes and managed to prevent himself from being startled into an apology. He couldn't remember being reprimanded for lateness by a member of the public before, but supposed it was the man's democratic right to do so and chose to ignore the complaint. Instead, he raised an eyebrow and said, 'I would appreciate your thoughts on the matter you contacted me about. Please, be as concise as you can.'

In contrast to his earlier manner, Søren smiled sweetly and said, 'Mik and I have decided that Fliedermus would almost certainly be able to recognise the persons who attacked them, and believe this means she and Mik should be present when you interview your suspects. Naturally, Mik accepts he would be bound by law to complete silence on the contents and outcomes of the interviews, other than any matters directly affecting our work or wellbeing here at Willsmere or Lamington.'

Leaning back in his chair, Chiu Liow considered him carefully before replying: 'How would the cat tell us she recognised someone?'

'That we cannot be sure of, but she would...somehow. Possibly by snarling, possibly by flattening her ears, perhaps by lashing her tail. She may even raise her hackles and attack, so Mik suggests we have her on a leash. However, Fliedermus may do nothing at all, other than give us a psychic impression.'

'The concept is novel, yet has a great deal of merit, Researcher Thorup. If we can bring someone to trial, we could ensure the panel of experts relevant to the case includes one with a sound understanding of cats. However, the Judge may not have a knowledge base relating to cat behaviour. Perhaps you could help us by developing one?'

'Certainly,' replied Søren. 'I don't suppose it would do my reputation any harm.'

'Good. I notice you said "persons". Does the cat know how many there were?'

'Yes. It seems there were two. One attacked Mik, while unfortunately the other managed to put Fliedermus into a cage before she could react. Clearly, they knew Mik had her with him and came prepared.'

'I see. Thank you. This is highly valuable information. Now, would you please be kind enough to return Researcher Theophanous to me?' Chiu Liow smiled briefly, impressed by the zoologist, in spite of his rather strange mannerisms.

'Indeed. Farewell, Peacekeeper. Keep well,' replied Søren, with a parting smile. He left them to discuss the interview schedule, and in the meantime, wondered what Fliedermus would have done if she hadn't been caught by surprise and then confined in a cage.

Aside from the case having such sinister overtones, this assignment already appeared as if it would be highly enjoyable, thought Morag, chuckling to herself as the airjet landed at Melbourne's Tullamarine airport. Without doubt, Peacekeeper Chiu Liow Jones would have been greatly surprised when he received her message the previous evening.

After collecting her luggage, Morag quickly found the customs area and managed to expedite her passage through by placing her forearm, with its embedded FSIU identity chip, beneath the electronic scanner. Outside the main airport building, she revelled in the fresh scent of eucalypt trees and the sense of open space. Boarding the nearest waiting transport, she entered her destination into its terminal as the Rialto building, Collins Street, Melbourne. When the other passengers from the latest flight had filled the railcar, it moved smoothly off and Morag sank back into her seat, prepared to simply enjoy the sights. Upon arriving at the Parkville exchange, content with life, she waited by the water's edge for her next transport to arrive and passed the time in admiring the view of the city's skyscrapers, a short distance away.

The last leg of the trip to the central part of the old city took only five minutes. Having never before seen an image of the Rialto tower, Morag marvelled at its bright blue, gleaming surface. The multistorey building was entirely covered in glass, which today reflected the cerulean sky. Glass in such quantities was a rare sight, seen only in the surviving architecture of the twentieth and twenty-first centuries. Quality sand was too scarce a commodity these days to squander on such ostentation. Where plain glass remained, the panes were usually converted into solar-electric cells.

Once inside the building, Morag took an elevator to the twentieth floor, one of several reserved for use by the Melbourne Peacekeeping Force. She was met in the foyer by Chiu Liow Jones. He was much taller than she imagined, and judging by his grip when they shook hands, immensely strong. A moment of mutual admiration passed between them.

'Your city is very beautiful, Peacekeeper Jones,' said Morag, with a friendly smile. 'I must try to mix pleasure with work while I'm here. I trust you're pleased the case is receiving the high priority you asked for?'

Making a quick assessment of her personality, Chiu Liow decided there was no need to assume his usual expression of cheerful serenity; this woman would not be so easily fooled. Instead, he found himself welcoming the opportunity to relax into a more natural manner, so grasped her firmly by the elbow and steered her towards his office, saying, 'Thank you, I'm delighted, believe me.'

Morag was not accustomed to being physically taken charge of in this manner, but her sense of humour told her she was being paid the compliment of immediate acceptance. When they were alone, away from potential eavesdroppers, he gave her a succinct account of the theory put forward regarding the possibility of using a cat as a witness to the assault on Mik Theophanous at Willsmere.

'I agree the concept is a fascinating one and deserves consideration,' said Morag, 'but I do hope you're not pinning your hopes on this feline version of an identification parade? For example, whoever engineered the security breach may not have been physically present during the assault. In fact, it's highly likely they weren't, and even if you do find any of your culprits this way, I'll still need to analyse the goings-on at your central computer site, as well as at Willsmere, to see if they've left some trace that'll incriminate them. A cat's evidence alone won't be sufficient to charge them. Also, it may be difficult to find a link between suspects, because we can be sure there's someone else, or some group, behind all this. Speaking of which, have you obtained background information on the employees at Melbourne Central yet?'

Chiu Liow silently handed her a storage module containing the analysis of all the information held in the Force knowledge base relating to the staff members employed at the site – which included the thirty-seven infotechs, their families, friends, and close acquaintances. His list of possible Willsmere suspects was there too, extended to include everyone who worked at the research centre, as well as officials with permanent right of entry to either site.

'I've made a request for access to government data on all these people,' he said. 'There may be something we can use. Unfortunately, as far as we can tell, no one else was present in the building during the attack on Mik Theophanous...and there were no members of staff present during the attack on the Lamington research station either, although that may have been their good fortune.'

'I could give the request a nudge by talking to your Speaker, if you like?' suggested Morag, moving over to Chiu Liow's computer. It accepted her voice pattern and put through a call to the House of Representatives. A woman with a rather hard-bitten appearance answered the call: 'The Speaker is asleep at present. She chaired an all-night session of Parliament. Could you call back in around eight hours?'

'Well, yes, I could, but prefer not to,' answered Morag, with a polite smile. 'Would it be asking too much for you to look into a request put through to your office by Chiu Liow Jones, of the Melbourne Peacekeeping Force, with regards to an urgent need for government-held information on a list of potential suspects in a serious criminal case?'

The woman hesitated. 'Our office *has* received the request, but the Speaker hasn't had time to consider it... Would you be willing to add your endorsement?'

'Yes, I would, and look forward to having it answered. Perhaps the Speaker could keep in mind that the case is being given high priority by the Federation's Special Investigation Unit, and that until it's solved, even Parliament's own communications network might not be secure.'

The woman in Canberra blanched as Morag ended the call.

Turning to Chiu Liow, Morag smiled sweetly and said, 'Stop laughing, Peacekeeper Jones! Have you ever tried doing this before? Most politicians and bureaucrats think their own small worlds are all that matter. With luck, I can revise their opinion.'

Chiu Liow was still regarding her with amused admiration, but replied soberly enough. 'Yes, I've tried twice...six years and twenty-one years ago. The first was denied and the second accepted. We usually manage reasonably well without the information, but for this case, since we're not dealing with an ordinary crime, I believe we need it. I'm particularly interested in additional financial information and business dealings, as well as commercial and professional connections. Any material that could throw light on their career aspirations and backgrounds would be useful too, including personal vulnerabilities – such as difficulties retaining a position, for example.' He paused, then added, 'Let's hope our Speaker will dislike the sense of insecurity you've managed to give her secretary. Meanwhile, would you like some coffee or tea – or anything else?'

Charmed by him, Morag accepted, and they enjoyed a short break in companionable silence before she turned her attention to the information on the storage module. All the Melbourne Central Computer Site and Willsmere staff members, as well as the relevant officials, had MPF records, having undergone comprehensive security checks before being given approval to work in their area and to have access to relevant sections of the worldwide communications network referred to as the 'lattice'. Routine monitoring of certain key aspects of their lives was also something they were required to accept.

Morag noticed that only a few of their family members, friends and associates had MPF records related to their being employed in occupations with similar security requirements. However, reading on, she was intrigued to see that the nephew of an ambutech with right of entry to both the Site and to Willsmere had been convicted of illegal hunting, which was a relatively rare offence that said something about his willingness to take unusual risks. Apparently a friend of an emergency services employee also had a criminal record: in this case, assault of a fellow employee. In terms of any other traits that were even slightly out of the ordinary, the analysis of the available information showed that one of the infotechs had a father who was a Member of Parliament; a second had a brother, who was employed as a research coordinator with the Department of Agriculture; while one of the infotechs was the daughter of a peacekeeper.

'Hmm...not much promise here,' thought Morag, 'unless, of course, we get a few insights from the information the government gives us.' For a moment, she toyed with the idea that the son of the Member of Parliament might be the worm in the apple, as children of prominent people were sometimes more precocious than others, but then dismissed the possibility as being no more or less likely than any other.

Aloud, Morag said, 'Chiu Liow, it seems we have only a handful of people who have some trait separating them out from the rest, which is precious little to go on.'

'That's to be expected,' he replied, with a slight smile. 'After all, if the staff members and officials *were* suspicious characters, they wouldn't have obtained positions with high security ratings. Also, if there's an organisation behind these crimes, they'd be just as careful in terms of who they approached. Still, someone's the culprit, and there has to be a reason for their behaviour. In my opinion, it's almost certain an infotech has been subverted, and it has to be someone who'd be fairly sure of not being found out. So, perhaps we should have a psychologist on the case?'

'Yes, excellent idea. Once we have more to go on, we'll have something for them to work with during the interviews. How good *are* your MPF psychologists?'

'There's one who I think would be perfect. He's written a research paper on the history of computer crime and would be more than happy to work with us. His name is Welcome. As you might guess, he has a sense of humour.' Chiu Liow grinned, then stood up and stretched. Turning to Morag, he said, 'Do you want to go out for our midsun meal? It's a beautiful day.'

Morag returned the grin and they spent the next hour walking along the foreshore, thoroughly enjoying each other's company and pausing only to sit at an old wooden table to eat the food they had bought at a small shop on the ground floor of the Rialto.

In front of Karla lay a range of carefully preserved plant specimens, neatly arranged in rows and in alphabetic order. She touched them all in turn, taking deep pleasure in the hope of new life that each contained. Research Coordinator Zago had been better than her word, the specimens having arrived from Oslo in what must surely be a red-tape-slashing world record.

One and a half weeks had passed since the wreckage of the laboratories and all physical traces were now gone from Willsmere. The psychological traces, of course, remained; they were merely less sharp. So although Mik was healing well enough to be back at work tomorrow, he would not have the chance to settle down and enjoy his research: there were still the interviews to be dealt with.

Karla was relieved to see that the relationship between Mik and Tamara appeared to have returned to normal, although Fliedermus purred more than usual when the two were together. Also, Karla had noticed that their intended work schedules coincided more than in the past. Still, if they wanted, and as long as they were sensible, they could easily enjoy a warm working relationship as well as a loving one in their own time. Taking this last thought one step further, Karla wondered if they would eventually become bondmates and perhaps even apply for fertility rights... She mentally shuddered at the thought of having to give up a career for ten years just to rear a child. Ugh! Karla had to admit her maternal instincts confined themselves to baby plants!

Reluctantly turning away from her new set of specimens, she turned her attention to the list of lost embryos and test plants sent from Lamington and began to compile a replacement schedule. With the assistance of the entire research team, additional stock could be grown and sent to

Queensland in around three weeks, at which point the staff at Lamington would take over their development to ensure they were acclimatised to local conditions.

Just as Karla was finishing this task, Tamara arrived. 'Hi Karla. Where's the Alf today? I thought he would've been helping too.'

'Um...just a minute... I need to save this.' Karla turned around. 'If you mean Søren – though I must say "Alf" suits him – he was in earlier this morning, but left a message saying he was intending to spend the day putting together a knowledge base on cat behaviour for use by the Judge. It seems the Judge doesn't have anything on cats... Anyway, he also told me that a woman by the name of Morag MacIain, a Federation Special Investigator sent from Luzern, contacted him about the break-in and the idea of using Fliedermus as a witness.'

Karla ran a hand through her hair, stood up and moved closer to Tamara, speaking in a low voice: 'This is all sounding pretty grim, don't you think? She's an expert in IT, so perhaps the Federation agrees that there's a connection between the attacks on Willsmere, Lamington and Serra do Cachimbo. And...there have been two others! Do you remember reading about that Australian palaeontologist, Meng Jarrah? Her laboratories in Myanmar and Papua were hit as well! A Myanmarian researcher was so badly hurt he's still in a coma. They think he may have seen too much. It's incredible he even survived, after what they did to him.'

Karla paused. She felt sick at the memory of Mik's injury. How much worse must it have been for those who discovered the Myanmarian? It was likely the injury to his mind would be even more serious than the injuries to his body. Karla stared at Tamara for a moment, lost in thought.

Her face pale, Tamara exclaimed, 'Oh, how awful! Poor man! I hope he recovers and they catch the mongrels who did this! What did they get away with from the labs?'

'It seems they stole the remains of a small number of extinct rainforest species from Myanmar, while the Niu Bougainville lab lost a twentieth-century soil sample which was to be used to model the physical and biological structure of rainforest soils from that period. Both of them also lost a great deal of data, though they had back-ups of course. The soil sample might have been irreplaceable, but Meng Jarrah sent portions of it to both Oslo and Coordinator Zago. They're old friends apparently and Meng Jarrah thought Zago might be in a position to help tie her team's studies in with the work being done by Lamington.'

'It's always been obvious there's a connection between the crimes,' said Tamara, frowning, 'so it would hardly be surprising if the Federation agrees. What I can't understand, though, is why anyone would want to steal our work or Meng Jarrah's. Amongst other things, all the labs are working on projects associated with re-establishing rainforests, either for ecological purposes or for timber production. Also, Meng Jarrah's team may be at a point where they can recreate some of the extinct species needed to complete and stabilise certain ecosystems. So, what I mean is, it's all going towards the public good, and anyway, the research results will be published as soon as they become available. There haven't even been any really prestigious prizes for more than a century for being first in scientific discovery...not that anyone could get away with cheating, I wouldn't think.'

'Yes, you're right, but there *are* private companies, and who knows, perhaps *they* might benefit from stealing our research,' replied Karla, with a grimace. 'Anyway, let's leave it up to the investigators. We've got our own work to do. I contacted Lamington this morning and spoke with Martha to give her the good news that my samples have arrived from Oslo, and also to let her know how we're progressing with their replacement needs. She estimates that their trials have been set back one and a half years and told me that morale was pretty low, which is awful. Still, she said they were pleased when Morag MacIain contacted them. I'm looking forward to meeting her, aren't you?'

Tamara agreed, and they worked steadily throughout the rest of the day, stopping briefly only for meals. By 20:00, both felt they had earned their credits. Before going home, they tidied the laboratories and left a message for Mik and Søren to say they were choosing to work the following day. This meant the whole team would be together for the first time since the attack. Chatting quietly to each other, they left by the front entrance. Being the last to leave, the lights dimmed and went out once the gates swung shut behind them. The evening was warm and still and the scent of honey myrtle sweetened the night air. The cicadas had started their evening chorus, while the first stars were just beginning to show. In a mood of quiet reflection, Tamara linked arms with Karla and they turned to walk towards the nearby river. The gentle ripples along the shallow banks and the murmur of the water exercised an almost hypnotic effect, allowing them to forget for a while that they were in the midst of one of the world's largest cities.

CHAPTER FOUR

Gwenllian, Marika and Thanh shared two shifts at Melbourne's Central Computer Site. For twelve and a half hours, twice a week, they relied on each other in a relationship of unquestioning trust. After having met at one of the social events organised for staff members, and finding they had a great deal in common, the three asked to work together. As highly trained specialists, they were part of the small team keeping the communications, transport and security systems within the State of Victoria in perfect working order. Despite the tradition of social equality in Australia, the three felt ever so slightly superior to their other colleagues, mainly due to their having such influential family members: Marika was the daughter of a peacekeeper, Thanh the son of a Member of Parliament, and Gwenllian had the rare joy of having a brother, who worked as a research coordinator with the Department of Agriculture.

The libraries, medcentres, training centres, transportation systems, financial systems, private homes, commercial and government buildings, as well as comlinks, were all linked to segments of the intricate global network that formed the lattice. Overall responsibility for maintaining the lattice lay with the Federation, but each country had its own section to manage and where there were semi-autonomous states, or where the country was particularly large, as in Australia's case, some tasks were delegated to regional centres.

All those who worked at Melbourne's Central Computer Site held a highly responsible position and were extremely well trained. In return for their time, the staff were provided with all essential services, received a quota of scarce resources, and in addition, a number of credits with which to buy the goods and services provided by private enterprises. In this respect, they were not unduly privileged as all workers received similar rewards, but they were held in high social esteem.

During this particular shift, the topic of conversation was the same as that which had occupied Gwenllian, Marika and Thanh for the past two weeks: the investigation by the Melbourne Peacekeeping Force into the security breach connected with the assaults on the Willsmere and Lamington Research Centres. They had each been interviewed immediately after the incident at Willsmere and Gwenllian was to have her second interview tomorrow, while the others were to have theirs the following day.

'How can I prove I had nothing to do with it? How can any of us prove it?' Gwenllian's voice rose in anger. 'I mean, as far as they're concerned, if I can design applications to detect hoax transport calls, I'm probably capable of breaking the sites' security systems...not that I've ever looked into their design – I just provide the MPF with data if attempts at unauthorised entry are detected anywhere in Victoria...although there aren't usually many to report, thank the Sun!'

'Yes, but Gwen,' said Marika, in a reassuring voice and after drinking the last of her tea, 'we're all involved with security work of one type or another. As far as I'm concerned, the only thing they mightn't like about *my* personal history is the multitude of career changes. They'll probably think I'm a suspicious character on that information alone! Anyway, it's all going to seem like magic to the peacekeepers; I doubt if any of them have an IT background.' With eyebrows raised and a tight smile, she added, 'All the same, I hope they get the best specialist investigators available so that we *do* have someone who knows the difference between one infotech's expertise and another's.'

Thanh had said little until now. His father had taken great pains to distance himself from the investigation, being unwilling to even discuss the case with his son. Thanh was understandably dismayed, because for once, he had counted on his father's moral support during the ordeal.

'I don't think their investigators will find out who did it,' he said slowly. 'Anyone with that level of expertise would be highly intelligent and careful enough not to leave any trace. What horrifies me is that this criminal could do something else. Can you imagine what a person like that might be capable of?'

Gwenllian finished her tea and absentmindedly poured some more for Marika. 'You know, you're right, Thanh. If someone is wicked enough to deliberately allow unauthorised access to a high-security research centre, I hate to think what else they might do. They could even attempt to get into private files. If someone had been convicted of an offence, for example, and it was discovered, their life could be made a misery!'

'What if they could break into the Federation's distribution system, or the financial system, or even Parliament's records? Or what if they could alter the Judge's knowledge base! It's all too dreadful to think about.' Marika shuddered.

'We're not the only ones they'll suspect,' said Thanh, his voice as optimistic as his words. 'What about all the other staff members here and the officials with right of entry? One of them might have a background in IT. A lot of people are fascinated enough to play around with computers, but don't want to work at it regularly. Still, we'll know more once we've had our second interview. Meanwhile, I've got a nice little security problem of my own to solve before midsun. You'd hardly believe it, but someone working in the Ferntree Gully medcentre has actually tried to increase their salary by tampering with the database. What a twit!'

They went back to their work, each with their own private thoughts. At midsun, Gwenllian ate her meal outside while she read the day's news reports. Sometimes she found the atmosphere of her workplace oppressive and today was one of those days. Last autumn, she had used all her saved credits to take a trip to Norway, just to savour the sense of freedom and the grandeur of high, cool mountains. A sense of utter frustration made her long for another such escape from routine. Perhaps in three years she could go to the steppes of Siberia. Three years! It was a long, long time. Still, with luck, it might be sooner. Before returning inside, a brief walk around the neat parklands surrounding the site helped, but only a little.

When Marika finished work that evening, she decided against going straight home. The night was cool and the stars bright, while a gentle breeze brought her the scent of the sea, even this far inland. A sudden impulse made her stop at the nearest callstation, where she entered the address of the Willsmere research centre. Ten minutes later, Marika boarded the transport and in another half hour was standing on the riverbank, staring up at the white towers. No lights were on, or at least none she could see from here. Stepping softly, she walked across the smooth lawns and stood outside the gates. They were closed to her, as well as to any other unauthorised person. It was hard to conceive of having the courage to walk through those gates, gaze calmly at the next security scanner, then walk unerringly to the laboratories with... What *had* been in the person's mind? She would quite likely know soon enough.

Thanh lay in his bed staring at the skylight. He loved to study the stars. They reminded him that life wasn't all petty and trivial. The whole universe lay out there waiting – waiting for someone like him. He knew there was so much more in life. Look at his father: one of the most brilliant Members of Parliament in Victoria! As the youngest infotech in the security section, Thanh had already achieved more than most of the others who had been there far longer. It wouldn't take many years before he'd be ready for an even better position.

He rolled out of bed and threw his pillow at the wall. Somehow his father never seemed to know his son even lived in the same city! The only time Thanh could remember him actually paying attention for any length of time was when he told him about his application for fertility rights. Even then, his only response had been to say he would oppose it until his son was legally an adult. It didn't seem to matter to his father that he loved Rebecca and that they desperately wanted a child.

What did it matter that they were only seventeen? Their seventeen compared with twenty-seven if intelligence and ability were anything to go by! Why, at five, he could play the flute, so sweetly it brought tears to his mother's eyes, and Rebecca held her first exhibition of sculpture at nine, with every piece sold by the end of the day. But their chance was gone forever. Rebecca died at only nineteen from a rare viral infection. After ten years, the grief had not left him, nor had Thanh's hate for his father.

Morag pored over the personal information released by the Speaker of the House of Representatives. She saw that a number of those on Chiu Liow's list had travelled overseas for business or recreational purposes, one of whom was an infotech and who was also registered as having an interest in undertaking private research that might possibly be of some relevance to their case. Moreover, this same infotech was the one who had a brother, and he in turn was a shareholder in Teak Australia, a private company she was already investigating.

One of the other people on their list turned out to be a director of Teak Australia, as well as a business partner of one of the Central Computer Site's administrators. This administrator appeared to have no training in information technology, had a blameless career and personal life, and in his spare time ran a small furniture import company. No doubt he also had an interest in any commercial advantage that might result from research done by his business associate's company.

They had thrown their net very wide indeed, so although these connections with Teak Australia seemed too good to be true, it could be mere coincidence. 'But really, it *is* stretching it a bit!' muttered Morag to herself.

Reading on, she found that four infotechs, two administrators, and three building technicians had suffered financial embarrassment at some time, all despite their steady careers and adequate income. Additionally, seven of the permanent research staff from Willsmere and five of the infotechs had failed to enjoy stable careers with steady advancement. Of these, one turned out to be the infotech whose father was a peacekeeper.

There were others who shone in their chosen professions and so perhaps were more often confronted by temptation than those whose lives were relatively placid and confined. Within this particular group, she noted with interest the remarkably early application for fertility rights by the son of the Member of Parliament, the infotech Thanh Fong Lau, and its subsequent abandonment after the tragic death of the young woman involved. However, despite this setback, Thanh Fong Lau appeared to have enjoyed an outstandingly successful career and had received a number of awards for original contributions to information technology. It occurred to Morag to wonder if his ego might be large enough to be tempted to break security systems which to all appearances had remained unbroken for over sixty years. 'Perhaps his job isn't challenging enough and he needs something to break the boredom? Definitely a possibility after all,' she concluded.

Finally, a few of the remainder had migrated to Australia, but other than these sparse facts, the suspects were to all appearances normal, law-abiding citizens with few outstanding features.

Feeling optimistic she could use the information, little as it was, Morag glanced at the time and hastily finished her coffee. Before the next round of interviews began tomorrow, she wanted to discuss everything with Welcome and Chiu Liow. Walking swiftly down the corridor of the Rialto, she went over in her mind the arrangements made for inspecting the Central Computer Site in person. Morag had spent her first available morning examining the methods used for logging the security database transactions. As expected, they were standard and, in theory, tamper-proof. The design of the database was also standard, as were the application access controls, device handling procedures, maintenance routines, and regulations covering the production of the occasional hardcopy report. Nevertheless, despite all these time-proven procedures, the human factor remained. *No one* was incapable of occasional negligence or oversight, so this could very well be the key factor.

Entering Chiu Liow's office was becoming a pleasure, and today the pleasure was heightened by the presence of Welcome. Of medium height, with mousy brown hair, a button nose and double chin, he was totally unremarkable until he spoke.

'Good morning!' said the psychologist, beaming at her. 'Now, let's find out what dark secrets we've discovered. No sociopaths amongst them? Not even a single practitioner of one of the old creationist religions with a fanatical hatred of genetic engineering?' When Morag laughed, shaking her head, he waggled his eyebrows and added, 'Pity... We'll simply have to do some hard work instead.'

Morag laughed again, enjoying the sound of his warm, deep, melodious voice, then gave him a quick kiss on the cheek.

Mik Theophanous was due to arrive ten minutes before each of the interviews on his schedule and was to be thoroughly briefed well beforehand on the suspect's background. On cue, Morag and the two peacekeepers heard a scuffling outside the door. When Chiu Liow opened it, a furry shape ambled complacently in, restrained by a short leash attached to Mik's wrist. As Welcome knelt down to formally introduce himself to the cat, Fliedermus put a paw on his knee and for a moment gazed into his eyes. Satisfied, she tucked herself up by her companion's feet.

'She's on her best behaviour,' Mik explained, smiling broadly and putting his hand out to Morag. 'It's a great honour to meet you, Investigator MacIain, and I'm sure my colleagues would enjoy meeting you too. I hope Fliedermus won't be any trouble. She's used to being on a leash when I take her for walks, but I'm sorry to say that even with the research into cat behaviour that Søren Thorup has done these past few days, we still can't predict what her reaction would be if she meets the person who had a go at me.'

By this time, Mik had released Morag's hand, but she found herself more than usually aware of how attractive he was in every way, particularly his good-humoured expression. 'Far too young for me,' she thought, but returned his smile as he met her eyes. Noticing, Chiu Liow abruptly suggested it was time they went to the interview room. Morag raised an elegant eyebrow and turned to look at him, then touched him lightly on the arm and followed Welcome, who had already taken a few steps towards the door.

Once everyone was seated – with Welcome, Mik and Fliedermus remaining slightly in the background – the first suspect was ushered in. With every appearance of cool appraisal, Gwenllian looked at each of them in turn. A twitch of the eyebrows betrayed her surprise at seeing a cat in the room. Fliedermus returned her gaze, flicking her tail and uttering a low growl. When the cat's ears flattened, Mik stroked her head, but she ignored him, and although Chiu Liow heard the growl, he appeared to take no notice and instead began the interview.

'Your name is Gwenllian,' he said softly, 'and you work as a systems technologist at the Melbourne Central Computer Site, having worked there for the past twelve years. These details, and the others which follow, are in our files due to the routine security check performed when you first applied for the position. However, before going further, I must inform you that this interview is being recorded and your answers will be used, if necessary, as evidence. You were free to request that a Witness be present, but I understand you chose not to do so. This displays commendable confidence.'

Gwenllian inclined her head in acknowledgement of the compliment, but didn't reply, so Chiu Liow continued: 'You graduated from Monash University with a Doctorate in Information Technology in 2436, then spent two years travelling in South America and Papua before commencing your current official employment. In your spare time, you work with your brother – who is a research coordinator with the Department of Agriculture – on a joint project investigating the commercial potential of an expert system designed to analyse depleted soils and recommend remedial treatment.'

Morag noticed Gwenllian's nostrils twitch in contempt at the term 'expert' system. She scribbled a note and passed the hand reader to Welcome.

'Gwenllian, you appear to be a highly talented and ambitious person,' said Chiu Liow, leaning forward to emphasise his words, 'so why have you chosen to jeopardise your future?'

Startled out of a growing sense of complacency, Gwenllian answered without thinking. 'But I haven't! I only collect and report data on attempted break-ins. You should know that!'

Morag quickly took advantage of her loss of control. 'What do you mean by "only"? I'd have thought someone with your qualifications would be given far greater responsibility.'

Gwenllian flushed at the jibe, but soon regained her poise. 'Surely your files show I also have prime responsibility for the integrity of the transport request validation system? My method of detecting hoax calls has been adopted worldwide, and my professional reputation is good and solid, I assure you. I certainly couldn't be bothered jeopardising it for the sake of helping someone break into a building!'

Chiu Liow pretended to consult his notes, then looked up and said, 'Can you tell us specifically what type of expert system you and your brother are developing and what, if any, profit you expect to gain from it if it's successful?'

Again Gwenllian's nostrils flared. 'I prefer not to use the term "expert" system. The correct name for these types of applications is a knowledge-based system. To refer to them as "expert" is misleading and dangerous. They can never replace human judgement and should never be relied upon in any absolute sense. Even with our highly advanced self-learning systems and natural language capabilities, a computer is only a machine. I admit that our intelligent decision-making systems perform as well as most human experts, but they *can* malfunction on occasion and we're still unable to code the intuitive leaps humans can make.'

She paused, then said, 'Together with a new and different approach to analysing soils and making recommendations for improvements, one of the advances my brother and I are working on is a type of early warning, malfunction self-diagnosis ability. It's quite a simple concept, yet strangely enough, until now, hasn't been done overly well with such highly complex applications as ours.' She forgot herself and grinned. 'Still, I expect you're more interested in finding out if what we do has any commercial potential.'

Chiu Liow nodded, managing to convey an appropriate level of humility.

With a brief smile, Gwenllian continued, now perfectly at ease: 'We'll begin field testing the application in three months time and if the trials are successful, we should be ready to publish the results and market it within a year or so. Of course, the Federation and the Australian Government will be given first option, and we expect they'll take it up. On the other hand, given the time it takes for them to make up their minds, draw up a contract and arrange for payment, we may offer it to any interested private companies.'

Morag felt it was time to jolt the woman again. 'Have you received any expressions of interest yet?'

Gwenllian's eyes narrowed and her expression changed to one of polite withdrawal. 'I'm sorry, but that's not a question I'm prepared to answer, even in a general way. If this interview eventually becomes a matter of public record, I'm not willing to have it said that I was tempted to betray confidential information.' She folded her long, slender hands and straightened her shoulders.

'Perhaps you'd prefer a change of subject. Do you intend to pursue your interest in travelling overseas in the near future? We gather you visited Norway last year. I myself frequently travel to Oslo.'

'Then you're more fortunate than me. It'd take three years to save enough credits for another holiday. I'll just have to make do with the occasional field trip around Australia with my brother.' Gwenllian looked away for a moment to hide her expression.

Chiu Liow put the next question, again changing the subject. 'You and your brother live in a private dwelling in Mount Eliza, which has been extended at your own expense in a manner that can only be termed luxury accommodation. Please tell us how you managed to afford the extensions.'

'Quite frankly, Peacekeeper, I would have expected you to have consulted our taxation records. They contain all our sources of income, and as I haven't falsified my statements, I have nothing to say.' Gwenllian frowned in annoyance, the resentment in her face clear to see.

'We *have* studied your taxation records. They tell us that your only additional source of income is the occasional payment for articles published in journals, so the question remains... How have you paid for the extensions to your home?'

'I haven't paid for them. My brother has, so I suggest you study *his* taxation records, if you haven't already. You'd see that he's a major shareholder in Teak Australia. Even though it's a small organisation, they have the highest commercial reputation of all the private companies importing teak into Australia from Myanmarian plantations. The company has operated for more than one hundred and twenty years and has always maintained complete integrity. Their profits are high because of the demand for wood. We would *never* associate ourselves with anyone involved in raiding tropical rainforests for timber. I hope this answers your question. My brother will confirm what I've said when you interview him, as I'm sure you will.' Her tone had become increasingly hostile.

Chiu Liow turned to Welcome. 'Do you have any questions for Systems Technologist Gwenllian?'

Welcome gave a small start, seeming to bring himself out of an introspective reverie. Gwenllian also appeared startled, abruptly turning her head to look at the inconspicuous person whose presence she had almost forgotten. As she did, her attention was caught by the presence of the cat. It was staring at her intently and Gwenllian felt a distinct projection of concentrated anger. When she gasped in surprise, Welcome stood up and walked over to her.

'My name is Welcome,' he said, smiling. 'The cat's name is Fliedermus, and with her is the researcher who suffered an injury during the trouble at the Willsmere laboratory. His name is Mik Theophanous. It's a great pity the building's security system isn't as infallible as your transport request validation system appears to be. If it were, we wouldn't be here today. Now I'm sure this is all very stressful for you, but you must understand that the crimes which have been committed are extremely serious.'

He brought his chair closer and sat down. 'We want your help in solving this puzzle. It's unavoidable that you're a suspect, as are dozens of others, and they'll all need to be interviewed. However, not many of them would be able to give us the help you can. It's also vital you clear your name, and I can't really see you having sympathy for an infotech – or anyone else for that matter – who allowed the centre's security systems to be tampered with, which I gather is regarded as being virtually impossible.'

Welcome noticed that as she met his eyes, Gwenllian seemed to be struggling to regain her balance. With a tremor in her voice, she managed to say she was sorry, she'd lost her perspective, and of course the crimes were horrifying. 'It's an enormous strain on all of us. We've spoken of little else these past two weeks. So far, no one's been able to work out how it was done. My colleague Thanh, whose father is a Member of Parliament, says that questions are being asked and the Opposition is having a field day! Thank goodness neither they nor the media are allowed to release any of this until the case is resolved. There'd be widespread panic.'

Welcome patted her shoulder as she gazed at him. The room was quiet, except for a low growl emanating from Fliedermus.

Gwenllian turned to look at her again. 'Why is the cat growling? I've never heard anything like it! In fact, I've never been close to one of those creatures before.'

In a low, pleasant tone, Mik said, 'Would you like to take a closer look?' He stroked Fliedermus and the growling stopped.

She shrank into her seat and shook her head. 'No thanks, this is close enough for me. I'd prefer to just get on with the rest of the interview, if you don't mind. If there's anything I can tell you that would be of help, I will.'

'There is nothing else for the present,' said Chiu Liow, 'although we would appreciate your noting down anything at all suspicious that might occur to you and reporting to me once a week by comlink.'

He rose and ushered Gwenllian out of the room, then walked with her to the elevator and wished her a pleasant remainder of the day.

'Now what do we make of all that?' he asked, upon his return to the interview room. 'Our feline detective reacted to her, but I'm fairly sure she didn't break into Willsmere.'

'Well, it would've been surprising if whoever was responsible for fiddling with the security system also assaulted Researcher Theophanous,' said Welcome, idly playing with a loose button on his cardigan. 'If the scale of this operation is as great as we think it is, it wouldn't be particularly wise for such a valuable person to take the physical risk, and for that matter, I can't see someone like her being party to the vandalism that was such a distinct aspect of the evening's entertainment.'

'Mik, what do you think your cat was reacting to?' asked Morag.

'As far as I can make out, her reaction was to Gwenllian's hostility towards all of us,' he replied, still stroking Fliedermus, who seemed to have fallen asleep. 'I don't think it was strong enough to fit in with a feeling of guilt, or anything directed purely at me.'

'Unless she *has* done something wrong but is egotistical enough not to feel guilty,' remarked Welcome. 'She's without doubt highly intelligent, somewhat arrogant, devoted to her brother and their joint research project, has a strong sense of privacy that she's willing to defend, and has enormous pride in her work, but suffers from a sense of being stifled and restricted. From this point of view, Mount Eliza is a highly indicative area for her to live in. It's by the sea, has a large area of intact bushland, and attracts those who can afford to build personalised housing. So, as far as I'm concerned, Gwenllian has the qualifications to be our culprit...on the systems side of things only, of course.'

'She certainly wishes to be materially wealthy and has a strong urge to travel, which at the moment is frustrated by a lack of credits,' said Chiu Liow thoughtfully. 'This makes her vulnerable to temptation, and I agree that Gwenllian would be capable of creating the security breach, but I feel that as a matter of pride, she would make sure the method used could not be repeated by anyone else. Also, seeing you fit and well, Researcher Theophanous, would, if she *is* guilty, reassure her that little real damage has been done. In other words, Gwenllian would be able to rationalise her actions. Unfortunately, this would also increase her confidence in her abilities, so unless you can find out how it was done, Morag, she's the type who might yield to further temptation. The potential for blackmail, for example, would be vast if other security systems could be broken.'

Morag brushed a stray curl from her forehead and contemplated the ceiling for a few moments. 'I don't like it,' she said. 'Her indirect association with one of the private companies on our investigation list is a matter of public record, and she would almost definitely know that one of the Central Site's administrators has a direct association with Teak Australia. They probably discuss business over morning coffee when they're on the same shift! Arrogant, Gwenllian might be, but not blind.'

'Yes, Morag, what you say is probably true,' replied Chiu Liow, in a gentle tone, 'but she may have adopted the tried and true method of getting away with crime: think innocent, therefore behave consistently innocent, well aware that without concrete proof there can be no conviction. Gwenllian could be so sure proof is unobtainable that she might well be laughing at our expense.'

'I suppose so, and I do agree with you both that she has the expertise to get away with this – that is, if I weren't here. The very fact that not one single transport hoax call has gone undetected since her new system was installed three years ago proves it, but I just don't like it, even though in so many cases the obvious suspect *is* usually the guilty party.' She sighed, then said, 'I certainly think we should interview the remaining infotechs before we let on about my own background in security systems. Whoever did this is most likely feeling very smug. Meanwhile, I intend to continue looking into the procedures used at the Central Computer Site, and my instinct tells me psychology is the answer, not technology.' Morag smiled at Welcome, who warmly returned the smile.

'Let me guess, learned friend,' he said. 'My studies of the history of computer crime show that most were made possible due to the lack of appropriate human vigilance. We've learned to minimise the need for it by maximising the use of such things as software robots, firewalls of various types, centralised software distribution, and intelligent decision-making systems, all of which make it easy to become complacent. Therefore, the question we must ask ourselves is, "For which routine security checks are humans still necessary?"'

'That is indeed my line of thought, equally learned friend,' replied Morag, giving him a mock salute.

After the day's interviews, despite feeling utterly fatigued, Mik returned to Willsmere. Fliedermus rested her head on his knee during the trip and he could feel her sympathy soothing his mind, but to help him prepare for the next session the following day, he wanted to share the experience with his human friends. Despite her initial attitude, Gwenllian in particular had impressed him. 'She should've gone in for one of the agricultural sciences, like Tamara,' he decided. 'Gwenllian's the type to prefer being out in the open, not cooped up in a high-security building.'

By the time they arrived, Karla, Søren and Tamara were busy preparing a meal. When all four shared the same shift, they tended to treat it as a special event, exchanging gossip and professional information. Søren, as usual, was taking the trouble to make the table look attractive, while Tamara kept them entertained with the latest anecdote, picked up from friends in their communal household.

'Did you know that someone's been caught trying to steal a chook from one of the farms?' she was saying. 'He was reported as being convinced he could overcome his sexual difficulties by eating more meat, and had watched the farm every day for two weeks to work out how to get around the security alarms. It turned out that the system was turned off for fifteen minutes once a fortnight for routine maintenance. He snuck into one of the enclosures, grabbed a chook, stuffed it into a bag, and was almost out of the grounds when he was confronted by the manager's pet emu. The bird had seen the bag and probably thought it contained food. When nothing was offered, it turned nasty... They've got really beady little eyes, you know, and they race towards someone they're after with their beaks snapping! Anyway, by this time, one of the farmers had heard all the noise and was out in time to rescue his precious hen. The silly bloke who took it has been fined two weeks pay and has to see a sex counsellor...*and* the poor bird got such a fright, it didn't lay for a whole week...' She broke off as Mik entered the kitchen. 'Mikko...you look awful!' she cried. 'What's happened?'

He collapsed onto the nearest chair and gave a weary account of his day, insofar as he was able, given that the legal and more personal aspects of the interviews, together with the subsequent discussions, were confidential. 'It's a gruelling timetable, but it *is* fascinating. However, I don't think any of the Central Computer Site people physically broke into Willsmere, and I seriously doubt if it was someone from here, which means I'm not sure now how much use Fliedermus and I will be.'

'My dear Mik, even if she doesn't get the chance to fly at the face of your assailant,' said Søren, waving a hand to emphasise his point, 'I am *quite* sure your dual presence would prompt *some* reaction from whoever is responsible for organising the break-in; at the very least, they would almost certainly be taken by surprise.'

'Well, this Gwenllian I've already told you about was definitely put out by Fliedermus growling the whole time...*and* she wasn't too happy at the idea of getting any closer to a cat. On the other hand, her reaction is probably normal for a lot of people. Just being involved in a case like this would be enough to rattle anyone.'

He looked up gratefully as Karla put a steaming hot cup of coffee into his hand. 'The most amazing thing, though,' he continued, 'was the relationship between the research she and her brother are doing and the work Meng Jarrah's group in Niu Bougainville are involved with. Once this is all sorted out, I'd be interested in finding out if Zago would be willing to approach them with an offer of a contract that allowed both Gwenllian and her brother to work jointly with us, as well as with Niu Bougainville.' He paused to sip his coffee, then said, 'Assuming the twentieth-century soil sample Meng Jarrah's group has is in good enough condition, they may be in a position to provide useful input with a view to using it as a basis for the reconstruction of current day tropical rainforest soils.'

'Truly?' said Karla, sitting down next to him, keenly interested.

'Yes,' said Mik, with more energy in his voice now. 'It's likely, for one thing, that the soil micro-organisms present now are either different from, or at least present in different proportions to, those that were there when the forests were healthy. If there are some that can't readily be reintroduced from elsewhere, for example, and the sample doesn't contain live specimens, Meng Jarrah's workers might even be able to recreate them! Can you imagine the impact that would have on our Lamington project?' Mik waved his hands around to illustrate his point as he suddenly jumped up from his chair and began pacing the floor, his fatigue forgotten.

'Personally,' said Tamara dryly, 'I think it's all too much of a coincidence. What if Gwenllian and her brother have decided they can make a fortune with this new application by selling it off to private enterprise before our projects are well off the ground? Sabotaging *our* work would be a neat way of making sure they got the leading edge in the market. It wouldn't matter how suspicious it all seemed if there was no proof...and if she's such an expert in security systems, then presumably there'll never be any.'

'That's true, Tamara, but why sabotage our work and not yours?' asked Karla. 'I mean, you and Mik are dealing with agricultural projects just as much as Søren and I are, and the big money for private enterprise is in agriculture and forestry, not in identification of rare species...unless they're being used for research, of course, which I must admit Søren's and mine are.'

'Yes, and it depends upon how we look at it. Mik, from what you've already told us, Gwenllian wants to improve soils directly and immediately, which can be expensive to maintain. Karla, you and Alf are trying to find a way of using *depleted* soils to produce high-quality protein, through either genetic engineering or the use of suitable new plant species. If your research succeeds, that means there might be less demand for Gwenllian's. Mik and I, on the other hand, with Søren's help, are approaching the problem from rather a different angle: improving soils in the long term by providing the organic matter, plants, fungi, micro-organisms, insects, *etcetera*, needed to restore natural ecosystems. Still, if the Lamington growth trials remain as promising as they've been up until now, maybe they thought attacking them and delaying the project was more effective than worrying about what Mik and I are doing at the moment?'

Tamara screwed up her face in thought, then added, 'Either way, I honestly find it hard to believe Gwenllian and her brother are the ones doing all the scheming. How could she have tampered with the security systems in Myanmar, Papua and Brazil? Unless, of course, she's found a way to break through network barriers...but personally, I think there has to be someone else involved and it has to be someone who's extremely wealthy or powerful.'

At this point, Søren interrupted Tamara by saying, 'It's time to eat! This good food must not be allowed to get cold. We can continue the discussion afterwards.'

Despite their consuming interest in the investigation, the culinary creations demanded another form of consumption, so silence reigned for quite some time. Eventually Mik broke it by saying that he wanted a good, uninterrupted stretch of work to take his mind off the events of the past two weeks.

'Sounds good to me,' said Tamara, with a grin. 'Let's all get together and have dinner at your apartment, Søren. Say, at around 19:00? We can continue our theorising then.'

Thanh walked slowly home from work, choosing the quieter avenues. He wanted the time and quiet to think through Gwenllian's indignant account of her interview that morning. He and Marika had listened intently to everything she said. They were intrigued by the presence of the Willsmere researcher and his cat, arriving at the obvious conclusion that the investigators were hoping to disconcert their suspects as much as possible. Marika had laughed at the idea. She had never been able to form a close relationship with a cat, although her mother made three attempts to introduce one into the household. Nevertheless, she certainly liked them well enough. As for the researcher, she looked forward to meeting him and was glad to hear that he appeared to have completely recovered from his injuries.

Gwenllian's description of the investigators and their questions gave little information about their probable areas of individual expertise. In fact, it seemed likely that none of them had an in-depth knowledge of security systems. Thanh smiled. He loved the sense of power his knowledge and ability gave him. The whole State of Victoria depended on such a small number of people. Occupied by this satisfying thought, he didn't hear the whispering of footsteps behind him and hardly had time to gasp before his neck was quickly, cleanly broken. His body slid gently to the ground. Fingers were placed on his neck to ensure no pulse was present. Nine hours later, a severely traumatised gardener reported the death to the Melbourne Peacekeeping Force.

CHAPTER FIVE

Morag, Chiu Liow and Welcome were in a sombre mood when they met to discuss the morning's grisly development. Chiu Liow shifted uncomfortably in his chair. Never in his long career had he been directly involved with murder. He had studied the records of the few Australian cases brought to trial over the past one hundred years, finding that only one person convicted of homicide was still alive in this country, held under house arrest for the past thirty-five years. She had made only one attempt to escape, but the microchip embedded in her shoulder made recapture inevitable.

'Morag, the method used to kill Thanh could have been employed by any physically fit adult,' he insisted. 'All our citizens begin kung fu training by the age of eight, at the latest. Also, there's no physical evidence at the scene of the murder, or on the body of the victim, to help us identify the killer, so I suggest we follow the plan we already have. We *cannot* allow ourselves to be diverted from the main issue. Our inquiries need to deal with another dimension, that's all. The implications of the murder are clear: our theory that we're dealing with a series of linked attacks on certain types of research centres seems to be confirmed and the intent behind these crimes appears to be as serious as we earlier supposed.'

Chiu Liow ran a hand through his already untidy hair, then absentmindedly, and without success, tried to pat it into some semblance of order. Folding his arms, and with a stern expression on his face, he said, 'I've notified the House of Representatives as required, but have requested that news of the murder not be made public until we've finished this investigation. Fortunately, the Government agrees. The less our adversaries know about us and what we're doing, the better.'

'We'll have to amend our interview schedule,' replied Morag calmly, pouring herself another cup of coffee and taking a sip. 'To find out more about Thanh will mean re-interviewing Gwenllian. We need to put her off balance, so I think we should ask her to be the second person to identify the body and then conduct the interview immediately afterwards. We could do it once we've spoken with Marika.'

Listening carefully, Welcome had been studying the tips of his fingers as he held them, tent-like, against his stomach, but looked up from his meditations long enough to say, 'Hmm, very true, Morag... A worthwhile strategy. Have you discovered anything else about our good citizens since we last met?'

'Yes, I spent all yesterday afternoon reconciling the programs used by the Federation's population database with the security systems used by Willsmere and Lamington, and took a close look at their transaction logs as well. I basically found what I expected. It turns out that a maintenance routine was used to insert the code needed to create the building access authorisations. It was all very cleverly done in terms of timing and covering of tracks, but it was unavoidable that the ID of the person who did it would be recorded somewhere.'

'And whose was it?' interrupted Chiu Liow, leaning forwards.

'The Senior Systems Technologist, Lance Melrose Naylor's, whose life is about to be severely disrupted for the next few weeks...at least! However,' and Morag also leaned forward, tapping Chiu Liow on the knee, 'I'm sure it wasn't him. Far too obvious... No, someone stole his identity. Now, I think you know that a nightly housekeeping run deletes each day's temporary authorisations at midnight and then creates a report. Therefore, before the report could be checked, this program also had to be tampered with ...which would require the use of yet another infotech's access authority, because, for simple security reasons, the same person wouldn't be allowed to make amendments to both programs, for use on the same day.'

'Let me guess, Morag,' sighed Welcome, rocking backwards in his chair. 'On the night in question, some poor person's ID is recorded as having edited the program producing these reports. Yes?'

'Yes indeed, Welcome, and there's no possible way he can prove it wasn't him because he was on shift that night. On this occasion,' and she consulted her notes, 'it was Systems Technologist Yilmaz Alavi. Nevertheless, I feel sure he had nothing to do with the security breach either. Again, too obvious. He'd also have to be a very strange person indeed to do it under the assumption that we'd never conceive of anyone being so brazen...if you follow me. So, it's still not out of the question that an administrator, for example, was the accomplice. Theoretically, if they didn't have the knowledge to do it themselves, the necessary code could have been written for them by an infotech – although there's a good reason for that approach being far too complex in an already tight situation.' Morag felt her shoulders tensing a little, so consciously relaxed and wriggled deeper into her chair to make herself more comfortable.

'And what's that?' asked Chiu Liow, standing up to fetch himself another coffee.

'There's an additional arrangement set up to prevent anyone working on an application *when* they shouldn't be, or *if* they shouldn't be at all. It's managed by a Senior Systems Technologist. This means that whoever made the illegal changes needed to know of a date when *both* these housekeeping programs would be authorised for amendment, as well as *who* would be authorised to do the work. They also needed to find an occasion that fitted in with a suitable opportunity for the physical break-in. These circumstances wouldn't have arisen very often, surely, and the information might only be available at short notice.' Morag waited to see if her colleagues had any questions, but as they didn't, continued her summary.

'Now that we know how the security breach was achieved in theory, I intend to find out more about the working environment at the computer site, as well as who had the greatest opportunity to steal handprints. I should be able to get both Alavi and Naylor to help us. I think they'll be so embarrassed their identities were used to break into their own systems, it'll be a hard job to prevent them from being too eager.'

'Good, let's hope that ends up being the case,' replied Chiu Liow, relaxing slightly and giving Morag a quick smile. 'For the moment, let's assume Thanh Fong Lau was our culprit and used the stolen identities. Why kill him?'

'We have the misfortune,' said Welcome, while this time contemplating the fingernails of his left hand, 'of not having had the chance to interview him a second time. He may have been killed to prevent just that, or given what we know of his personality and background, may have begun to entertain ambitions that were, if you'll excuse the pun, unwelcome to others. So, we should interview his illustrious father as already planned, but with great delicacy.' He looked up at them. 'After all, it's unlikely the father would be part of an organisation responsible for murdering his own son.' As Chiu Liow and Morag nodded, their expressions grim, Welcome added, 'It appears Thanh's mother is no longer alive, which means the only other sources of information we have at present are his workplace colleagues. I seem to recall that he nearly always worked the same shift as Gwenllian and Marika.'

While he was speaking, Morag had taken her coffee cup to the servery and was rinsing it out. She turned to them, cup in hand, saying, 'Yes, he did, so we can only do our best to make sure those two tell us what they know. Presumably Fliedermus and Mik should still be there when we interview Marika?'

'Yes, I believe so. Fliedermus' emotional reactions are definitely useful,' replied Welcome. 'We could almost employ her as a lie detector.'

Standing up, he slowly moved over to Chiu Liow's desk, climbed onto it, stretched up, and removed a smallish brown spider from a web clinging delicately to the ventilation panel. 'So, little fellow, how did you get in here?' he asked, taking it outside to the balcony and releasing it. His fellow investigators were regarding him with amazement and he apologised profusely. 'Do forgive me... I'm hopeless when it comes to leaving small creatures trapped indoors. I couldn't let it stay in here to starve to death, now could I?'

Morag and Chiu Liow giggled helplessly, while Welcome chuckled, glad he could distract them for a short while.

Marika calmly listened to the statement being made about her personal particulars by the peacekeeper, Chiu Liow Jones. Pre-warned by Gwenllian, she had asked for complete introductions before allowing the interview to proceed, then took the time to make herself familiar with everyone in the room, including the extraordinary cat and its memorable companion: Marika particularly noticed his long, black, curly hair – beautiful. Her eyes narrowed, however, as she studied Welcome's unremarkable appearance. 'Interesting that he's an MPF psychologist,' she thought. 'In which case, this interview is anything but routine. The woman, Investigator Morag MacIain, is a wildcard. I'd like to know what her speciality is!' With a small start, Marika realised Welcome was asking her a question. 'Sorry, what did you say? I'm a bit nervous. Please forgive me.'

'I asked how close you were to Thanh Fong Lau.'

'Oh... We just worked together. Mind you, that does mean we were reasonably close. Gwenllian, Thanh and I shared the same shifts for years, but he didn't confide in us about his personal life. We had plenty to talk about though. Our work is pretty well the centre of our lives.'

She winced then lowered her face to hide her tears. Fliedermus burbled an inquiry and jumped off her chair. Marika looked at the cat and at first felt its sympathy warming her mind, but after a few seconds, Fliedermus spat at her and leapt back onto the chair, tail lashing furiously. Turning to Mik, Marika apologetically said, 'Cats have never liked me, even though I like them. I don't know what it is.'

Mik didn't like her either, but smiled and nodded. He wasn't sure what it was about Marika that he didn't like, but Fliedermus clearly agreed with him.

Welcome settled back more comfortably into his chair and considered his next question. There was something disturbing about this woman. She grieved over Thanh's death, that was easy to see, and was almost certainly traumatised by the event, yet...what was it that eluded him? He decided to ask, 'What will you miss most about Thanh?'

'He was always enthusiastic and never ran out of energy,' replied Marika, with a small shake of her head. 'No matter how hard the problem was, he'd work until it was solved. He'd work twenty-four hours straight if necessary and never complain. If Gwenllian and I were getting tired, he'd give us a neck massage and a cup of coffee, then tell us to stop being useless.' She blew her nose, then rubbed a hand over her eyes like a child. 'He shouldn't be dead!' she cried.

'Why did the three of you usually work the same shift?' continued Welcome, without conveying any sympathy.

She sniffed and glanced at him. 'Because we had a lot in common and just sort of got on straight away. We're all rather good at our jobs...and ambitious, I suppose. I mean, Gwenllian wants to learn as much as possible so she can apply it to her private research. She loves travelling too and can't stand not being able to go on trips more often. Thanh wants to...wanted to...become the youngest Senior Applications Technologist in history. He would've been, too. Me, well, I'm just into being someone other people have some respect for. I've taken a long time to settle into a proper career and now I'd like to make the most of it – earn a really substantial reputation in my field.'

'And what *is* your field, Marika?' asked Morag softly.

'Um...how can I explain... You *could* call it three-dimensional graphics. It's an idea that's been around for hundreds of years, but there's never been much commercial demand for it. By the way, I don't mean 3D simulation on screens. I mean *actual* 3D. All the twentieth-century science fiction films assumed it would become a reality, but somehow it never did. I suppose the energy needed was too expensive, and there were easier ways for the entertainment industry to get the attention of the public.'

'I can't quite see how your position as an infotech specialising in systems security relates to your work in 3D graphics.' Morag tilted her head and managed to appear naive.

'Well, the connection isn't a direct one, though a high level of interest in quality graphics, as well as digital entertainment, have both traditionally been part of the IT world. By working in the field, I get to meet lots of people doing graphics who're also involved in the entertainment industry. We swap ideas and contacts. The people I deal with know I'm a professional, and that working in the security industry, I'd be reliable.' Marika allowed herself a slight smile. 'Reliability's worth a lot of credits, you know.'

Morag leaned forward. 'How far have you come with this work?'

'I'm well on track to finishing my first holographic prototype. The image is of a friend of mine playing the flute. It'll be projected, but will appear in three dimensions on a stage, just as if he were really giving a concert.'

Her listeners were impressed and momentarily silent, until Chiu Liow asked, 'Who is funding it?'

'I've got a contract with a theatre group in Bendigo. They have a few wealthy sponsors who're interested. If my prototype succeeds, I get my share of the profits. If it fails, I don't get paid and they lose their credits. Art and entertainment are always risky.'

'But you wouldn't like to fail, would you?' said Welcome, looking at her intently.

'I won't,' replied Marika, staring straight at him for the first time.

'Well, I think it's time we asked you a few more questions about your colleagues.' Chiu Liow smiled, as if to take the edge off his next words: 'I imagine you will have realised that one of you is most likely guilty of having assisted in arranging illegal entry to the Willsmere, and possibly even the Lamington, research centres. Can you give us any proof that *you* are not guilty of this?'

'No, sorry, I can't,' said Marika, straightening her shoulders. 'How on Earth could I?' Her voice had sharpened.

'In that case, can you offer us any evidence of someone else's guilt?'

'No, I can't do that either. We have enough to do without watching each other all the time. Our security clearance is of the highest order, so we don't go around being paranoid about our fellow workers. We devote our paranoia to the rest of the world!'

'Could you tell us about Thanh Fong Lau's work habits, then? For example, did he usually leave the site at a regular time, and did he leave at that time last night? And finally, do you know if he took any particular way home that he generally kept to?'

'Yes to the first question, and yes to the second... As to the third, I can't say,' replied Marika tartly.

'Do you know where he lived?'

'Yes, in Blackburn.'

'Which is only a fifteen minute leisurely walk from the Central Computer Site. Has he ever mentioned taking public transport instead of walking?'

'No, he always walked, even if the weather was terrible. He said it was the only real exercise he did, other than yoga.'

'So someone could easily have waited for him in a secluded parkland area like Blackburn in order to quietly murder him.'

Tears once again trickled down Marika's cheeks. This time she didn't bother to lower her face. Chiu Liow was immune to such displays of emotion, but he allowed her time to regain control. When she did, he asked her for the name of the theatre company sponsoring her holographics project. When Marika gave it to him, he ended the interview by standing up and leaving the room, without looking back.

'That had to be one of the best performances of 'a friend displaying grief' I've ever seen,' said Morag afterwards. 'Does she think we're all of subnormal intelligence? If I remember correctly, she spent eight years – and highly successful years at that – performing with 'Victoriana', usually playing the tragic heroine in nineteenth-century dramas.'

'And our furry detective didn't think she was genuine either. Poor Fliedermus. You're being exposed to some terribly negative emotions lately, aren't you?' crooned Welcome, gently stroking the cat's head while Mik disentangled her claws from the shoulder of his loose white shirt.

Apparently at some point the cat had left her chair to sit on Mik's lap. He hadn't wanted to disturb the interview by freeing himself, and consequently, some repair work would be necessary before this particular garment could be worn again! Sighing inwardly, Mik told the others what he thought of the interview.

'As far as I could make out, Fliedermus reacted in a highly typical cat fashion to someone who is totally unable to form a relationship with them. Welcome, you should be able to confirm what I'm saying, but I suspect people like her don't usually have much genuine sympathy for anyone else, human or otherwise. In fact, they're incredibly egocentric.'

'Oh yes, Mik, I agree with you completely,' replied Welcome, smiling slightly as he gave Fliedermus one last pat. She licked his hand.

'At least she didn't seem as arrogant as Gwenllian,' remarked Chiu Liow. 'I'm sure you'd agree too, Welcome, that Marika is a person who would drive herself to succeed. Otherwise, she'd hardly have undertaken such an enormously difficult and hazardous an enterprise as that of entertainment holographics. The financial returns of success could be vast, but on the other hand, failure would mean many years of work for nothing – although she appears to refuse to entertain the idea of failure.'

'Yes, Chiu Liow, I do agree, and believe Marika can take equal place with Gwenllian at the top of our list of live suspects.' Welcome paused, then turned to Morag for her thoughts.

'I think you're right,' she said. 'In my opinion, Marika is technically capable of the security breach and her awareness of the field of holographics brings an interesting point to mind. To gain temporary permission to enter a secure area, the applicant must present themselves either at the Central Computer Site or to a gatekeeper, if there is one. The workstations used to process these applications are kept behind a plastiglass screen and are never left unattended. A touchpad placed outside the barrier is used to record the applicant's handprint, which is matched with the Federation's population database. The database has the person's retina pattern, identification number and other personal details, which are all crosschecked with the applicant. The final verification is a formal check with someone in a position of authority, who can act as a referee, if you like. If all is well, a record is written to the relevant security database, together with the dates and times for which the access is required.

'In the case of the Central Computer Site, the service is available twenty-four hours a day, seven days a week, whereas, if they choose to provide it, the building sites with high security requirements generally only maintain the service from 08:00 to 20:00, excluding meal times. So, with her knowledge of computer graphics, Marika is in an ideal position to be aware of and understand the procedures used to store and transmit images of finger and hand prints, as well as retina scans, and then match them with a database. She could also be aware of the techniques available for forging them…'

Chiu Liow was becoming impatient with this monologue, given he was fully aware of the methods and requirements for registering security accesses. Interrupting, he said, 'Wouldn't Gwenllian know even more about how these systems work than Marika, especially which details are important?'

'You're absolutely right, but I expect all three of them discussed their work at great length.' Morag smiled, a sympathetic twinkle in her green eyes. 'Now, I think we should take a break, don't you?'

'We've only just enough time before I leave to meet Gwenllian,' said Chiu Liow, standing up and stretching. 'May I suggest we go to the roof garden? I need a change of scenery.'

Gwenllian fought back the tears, hugging her knees as she sat on the floor, rocking slowly back and forth. Even though the Central Computer Site had been notified of Thanh's death, with an official request that only those who most needed to know were informed, the peacekeeper, Chiu Liow Jones, had personally contacted her with the news. His face was disconcertingly devoid of expression as he told her the time, place and manner of her friend's murder, and then requested that she formally identify the body. The young woman had cut the comlink connection before the grief became too much. Groping for her brother's hand, Gwenllian now sought the only comfort available. In two hours, she would face the investigators for the third time.

In Mandalay, a light breeze fluttered the leaves of the brightly flowering blue hibiscus growing outside the window of the room where Meng Jarrah's researcher lay. His eyelids trembled and opened. Within seconds, a medtech was at his bedside, monitoring his re-awakening from the coma which had claimed three weeks of his life. The expression on the researcher's brown-skinned face horrified the medtech: confusion, abject fear, and anguish.

The assault that took place during the attack on their laboratories had clearly been carried out with professional precision, as the injuries were sufficient to ensure coma, but not to cause death. The ruptured kidney had now been replaced with one grown from the researcher's own tissue by the medcentre's organ replacement unit, and his head wounds had healed well, while surgery had successfully rebuilt the fingers of his left hand, crushed by his tormentors. The single finger that had been severed and removed from his other hand was still regrowing and now measured almost one centimetre in length. However, should he be tempted to disclose whatever information he may have unwittingly gained, it was possible the missing finger would be sent to him as a reminder to keep silent; an archaic tradition still sometimes used by kidnappers and others to intimidate their victims.

A sigh escaped from the small form lying still and frail between the soft sheets. He lifted one hand, groped shakily, and then withdrew. As memory returned, tears trickled from the corners of his dark eyes. At least there didn't seem to be any brain damage, thought the medtech, raising a tiny bowl of healing tea to the trembling lips and supporting his head while the researcher drank the single mouthful. When he had finished, the medtech gently stroked his patient's high, smooth forehead until he fell into a healthy, relaxed sleep.

Ten hours later, the researcher re-awoke to find the medtech once more at his side. This time, the air was lightly scented with orange blossom, which soothed his mind, as did the tinkling of sweet music in the background. Again he drank the offered liquid, and again fragments of memory returned, but he pushed them aside, preferring the comfort of the warm, safe present. Weakly, he raised his right hand and looked in wonder at its small, new finger. He gazed questioningly at the medtech, who reassured him that it would reach its full size in another three months.

'Sleep,' he said softly, 'and when you awake, you will have your first meal in the shade of the courtyard garden. We have watched over you for three weeks and feel sure you have fully recovered. Even so, you may stay here for as long as you wish and there are no duties left undone which need worry you.'

The researcher slept. When he opened his eyes again, it was not the medtech who sat by his bedside, but Meng Jarrah. He could feel the strong, fine muscles of her arms tense as she lifted him onto a hoverbed. They moved quietly into the courtyard, where sunlight sparkled on the water of a small stone fountain. It seemed to him that the water laughed with pleasure. Once more, Meng Jarrah lifted him in her arms, placing him gently onto soft cushions before a low table, where a small bowl of jasmine rice awaited him, together with a sweet, fresh peach and a pot of fragrant green tea. Accustomed in the past to rely on her sound judgement in many things, he accepted her silence and enjoyed the simple meal. Once he had finished eating, she asked him what he wished to know.

He hesitated, looking at his damaged hands. 'I see I have had an accident. Can you tell me what has happened? I can recall almost nothing beyond working in our laboratory, then waking briefly, twice, and waking a third time to find you here.'

The practitioner in charge had told Meng Jarrah of the medtech's impression that their patient had regained his memory upon first waking. However, it would be no surprise if the researcher could not yet bring himself to relive his ordeal by describing it. Nevertheless, knowing her friend would want the truth, Meng Jarrah related the story of how he was found, unconscious and weak from loss of blood...but his mind was still fragile and he soon began to doze in the warmth of the morning sun.

'Time and care will heal him,' thought Meng Jarrah, studying his face. 'Meanwhile, we must hope he finds the courage to give us his evidence.' She eventually called for a medtech and left him to sleep.

An arrangement had been made for Meng Jarrah to keep her researcher company as often as possible until he regained his strength and confidence. She was given a room in the medcentre's community dwelling, which meant she could continue much of her work, as well as communicate in privacy with Morag MacIain in Melbourne.

On the way to her room, she considered how long they could afford to wait before questioning him. Morag had informed her the previous evening that they now had a Myanmarian peacekeeper assigned to the case and that this person was a member of the same family as the Australian, Chiu Liow Jones. Meng Jarrah was to meet the woman in three hours time.

Thanh's body lay in state in the chilly morgue, located conveniently near the Rialto building in the waterproofed basement of the old nineteenth-century law courts in Lonsdale Street. The only other body in this tastefully decorated room was that of an elderly person awaiting an autopsy. Thanh's father, Yuen Fong Lau, sat beside his dead son and planned his next speech to Parliament. Propriety demanded he spend at least two hours in public mourning a family member. He reached into his pocket and withdrew his comlink. It showed that only one hour and forty minutes had passed. Yuen sighed, but at long last, the time passed and he raised himself, knees creaking, and kissed his son's forehead for only the second time since he was born. He then smoothed the jet-black hair, turned, and walked away from what had been only a brief episode in his long life.

Upon leaving the morgue, he was greeted by the peacekeeper, Chiu Liow Jones, escorting a young woman. Her thin oval face was drawn, and the red, almost black, lipstick she affected contrasted strongly with her unusual, pale skin. Of medium height, with blonde hair pulled into a severe plait and eyes made artificially dark green by purely cosmetic contact lenses, Gwenllian was not the type of woman Yuen found attractive.

'May I introduce you to one of your late son's colleagues,' said Chiu Liow. 'Gwenllian, this is Thanh's father, Yuen Fong Lau.'

Gwenllian held out her hand, which Yuen grasped firmly. 'You will excuse me if I do not stay longer,' he said. 'I have many pressing matters to attend to...and the chill of the morgue to erase from my body.' He turned away, and without looking back, walked quickly to the staircase leading upwards and then out of the building.

Chiu Liow ignored Gwenllian's stunned expression and, grasping her by the arm, led her inside. She pulled his hand away and warily approached Thanh's body. It seemed to her that her friend could merely have been sleeping, but no technology was yet available to bring about that miracle. She touched his cheek, which felt like cold clay, then touched her own, which to her strained senses felt almost as lifeless. Turning to the peacekeeper, Gwenllian held out her hand in mute appeal against an irreversible sentence. Needless to say, her appeal went unattended.

'Sign this, please,' said Chiu Liow, without ceremony. 'His father has already done so.' Gwenllian did as she was asked, staring at the document as if she barely understood what it was.

'We can leave now, unless you wish to stay longer.' Chiu Liow checked the signature and looked down at her, waiting.

She shook her head, and they silently climbed the staircase towards the warm glow of natural light. Despite the sweetness of the air and the gentle breeze that blew sparkling ripples onto the surface of the water, her sense of confusion did not lessen during the short journey to the Rialto. Her ordered world of reliable technological solutions no longer kept her safe.

Gwenllian's manner during the third interview was in total contrast to that of the earlier ones. She rested her head in her left hand and answered the questions without comment. Yes, she knew Thanh had lived in Blackburn and that he preferred to walk home. Unlike Marika, she knew he frequently changed his route, and sometimes accompanied him as far as the nearest callstation. Did she accompany him last night? Yes, but not very far, as he hadn't chosen to walk in the direction of a callstation. Did she see any of the other computer site workers walking in the same direction, either before she left Thanh, or afterwards?

'There's usually a small crowd leaving at the same time. Unless there's a special occasion, not many stay around after the shift has finished. There are four callstations nearby, so three or four of us usually walk together, though Thanh wasn't popular and sometimes walked only with me. Last night, Marika kept us company, which was unusual, but didn't continue on with me to the callstation. I just assumed she was visiting a friend in the area. She often talks about him. He's the father of their fourteen-year-old son.'

Gwenllian raised her head and added, 'She's devoted to the boy and to his father, but finds the family gets along much better if they don't live together all the time. Marika puts so much effort into her holographics that she prefers to live in a communal house. I know her son spends a lot of his time there, helping with the design work, as well as with the routine programming.'

None of this was news to any of her interviewers, as the bare facts of Marika and her bondmate's successful application for fertility rights and their subsequent parenthood were on record. That they had lived apart since the child turned ten was also on record and was relatively unusual. The vast majority of parents continued living together after having successfully spent the mandatory ten years caring for their child on a fulltime basis. In Marika's case, the Federation had even announced a rare second-child quota only two years after her son was born, yet she and her fellow parent chose not to apply for further fertility rights, despite being given an opportunity others were prepared to break the law to obtain.

Although Welcome was surprised her application to become a parent had succeeded, he was not surprised by her success in being one. Her desire to succeed in everything she attempted would have given the necessary impetus to provide the child with everything he needed. However, the psychologist sincerely hoped her son was unable to make the subtle distinction between the love his mother most likely gave him in his role as an extension of her ego, and the type of love given selflessly and unrestrainedly.

'What was Marika wearing when she left you?' asked Chiu Liow.

'Just her normal clothes,' replied Gwenllian, with a puzzled expression. 'A loose, red, sleeveless cotton gown and black sandals, and she carried a small work bag.'

'And what were you wearing?'

'I was wearing a long, dark blue, silk cheongsam and matching slippers...and was carrying a parasol and work bag.'

'Where exactly did you part with Thanh?'

'At the entrance to Springvale Orchards.'

'Where did you part with Marika?'

'About fifty metres before the orchard entrance.'

'How long was it between the time you left Thanh and the time you made a transport request at the nearest callstation?'

'Five minutes. I walked through the orchards to the callstation on the other side.'

'And did you make a request for a direct journey to Mount Eliza?'

'Yes, I did,' replied Gwenllian, with a brief nod.

'What time did the callstation give when you entered your request?'

'I think it was 20:41.'

'Good... We can check that particular request and if it is as you say, we can at least be reasonably sure that you are not personally guilty of murdering your friend.'

Chiu Liow stood up, walked over to Gwenllian and took her gently by the elbow. 'You are free to go now. I suggest you continue your work routine. It may help soften your grief.'

Not expecting the sudden show of sympathy, Gwenllian met his eyes, blinked, and then lowered her face. 'Thank you,' she said softly. 'I appreciate your kindness.'

After Gwenllian had gone, Chiu Liow turned to Morag and asked, 'How can we be sure the transport request Gwenllian entered will be genuine?'

Morag's head was bent over her comlink, which, like most people, she carried everywhere. She waved her hand at him and kept working. After a few more minutes, Morag looked up, saying, 'It's genuine. There's a record for 20:41 from Springvale Orchards to Mount Eliza with Gwenllian's ID attached... It's highly likely that the time and place of this murder wasn't pre-planned, even if the murder itself was, so there wouldn't have been any point in tampering with the request records beforehand because no one could predict the exact time when an opportunity to kill Thanh would arise. However, I'll check the edit log, but to tamper with the callstation requests database would be lunacy. Breaking into *that* would be far more difficult than breaking into a building's security system.'

'Why so?' asked Welcome.

'The programs used to validate and enter callstation requests would have to be altered, and they're under the control of a knowledge-based code maintenance application. That particular system only makes required changes if it can be 'convinced' by an authorised information technologist that the change is necessary and logical. To make the system behave foolishly would mean changing the knowledge base, and quite frankly, I think that would be going to extremes.'

'Also,' added Chiu Liow, 'I find it difficult to see how a woman wearing a long, close-fitting garment such as a cheongsam could move swiftly enough to break Thanh's neck and then leave again just as quickly. If she was carrying a parasol and bag as she stated, they would also impede her movements. I can't see her being willing to pause long enough to put the items down and then retrieve them before leaving, either. Still, I'll check whether she was telling the truth.'

Morag and Welcome waited while Chiu Liow asked for the comlink code of the Central Computer Site's gatekeeper. A gnarled brown face appeared on the screen, blue eyes sparkling and alert.

'Hi, what can I do for you?' asked the elderly man.

'My name is Peacekeeper Chiu Liow Jones. This call is confidential. Are you alone?'

'Yes, indeed I am,' replied the gatekeeper, nodding vigorously.

'I am currently investigating a series of crimes associated with the Central Computer Site. Were you on shift yesterday?'

'Yes, indeed I was.' The gatekeeper was apparently economical with words.

'Can you tell me how the information technologists Marika and Gwenllian were dressed when they left at the end of their shift yesterday, and if they were carrying anything?'

'Yes, Marika wore a red gown and black sandals, and carried only a work bag over her shoulder. Gwenllian was wearing a long, blue cheongsam, slippers, and carrying a black sunshade with a blue fringe. She had her work bag with her too, which is quite a large one. Will that do you?'

'You are a priceless witness, Gatekeeper. Did the women leave together, and was anyone else with them?'

'They left together with the information technologist Thanh Fong Lau, and if you wait just a tick, I'll check what time they left.' He looked up again. 'Yes, yes, just as I thought. They left at 20:32 and walked together for a while in the direction of Springvale Orchards. Past there, I couldn't see what they did.'

'Many thanks. Now, you may already know what I am about to tell you, but if not, please accept my sincere regrets. Thanh Fong Lau was murdered shortly after you last saw him. He died immediately and would not even have been aware death was approaching. If you wish to view his body, it is at present in the morgue.' Chiu Liow paused, then added, 'If I remember correctly, you are the longest serving worker at the Central Computer Site, and apart from his family and friends, will quite possibly be the one most distressed by his death. You have my deepest sympathy.'

The old man's face had crumpled like that of a child. Tears ran down his furrowed cheeks and were wiped away by a clenched fist. Among the most trusted and respected of workers, gatekeepers symbolised care and security. This ancient had been friend and confidant to his fellow workers for over eighty years, yet could still remember each individual and take an interest in all. 'Will you tell me when you find the monster that did this?' he said at last, his voice husky.

'I will, I promise you, Gatekeeper.'

'Well, I think we have confirmation that Thanh wasn't killed by Gwenllian,' said Morag, raising an eyebrow. 'I'm almost certain she didn't arrange his death either. She may well be guilty of the other crimes, though perhaps without realising murder would be part of the agreement. On the other hand, Marika could have killed Thanh, or could have given information about the route he was taking to someone else. We can't check on times in her case, as it would have taken very little to follow and kill him, then make her way to her friend's house. How much do you think we'd gain by interviewing the father of her child, Welcome?'

'Not much, I'd say. Still, we can confirm the visit and its time, as well as her approximate state of mind on arrival. I suggest I call on him now, so we'll have *that* piece of evidence before we interview Thanh's father.'

Welcome set about locating Marika's bondmate. He was soon found at his usual workplace and appeared understandably nervous at the idea of having an interview with a member of the Melbourne Peacekeeping Force. Welcome made an appointment with him, then left and came back some seventy minutes later, looking pleased with himself.

'He knew Thanh had been killed,' he said. 'Marika contacted him this morning, after the Computer Site was notified. From his account, she was a great deal more shaken then than when we interviewed her. When I nodded sympathetically and stared at him, without saying anything, he eventually volunteered that she visited last night, straight after work, and stayed till well after midnight. Apparently she'd stopped on the way to buy some pastries for supper. I checked with the local pastry shop and they confirmed that a woman answering her description and wearing a red gown left there some time between 20:30 and 21:00. Now, if we can't imagine Gwenllian casually putting down her parasol and bag to murder Thanh, and then remembering to pick them up again before she left, we can't put Marika in the situation either. I mean, can you see her leaving a large box of delicate pastries sitting on the ground while she calmly murders her colleague, then just as calmly picking everything up again and going on her way to a family visit as if nothing had happened? Well, I can't.'

Morag sighed, and agreed that it didn't seem likely. 'All the same, it doesn't mean she didn't have time to tell someone else the direction Thanh was taking. It would only take a moment. Either way, at this point, I think we should definitely consider the possibility that Thanh was actually the one guilty of the original crime. Perhaps we can follow that line with his father. I see it's time for us to meet him.'

The three investigators walked to the reception foyer, where Yuen Fong Lau was sitting at one of the tables, speaking into his comlink. He put it away when he saw them approaching, stood up, held out his hand to Chiu Liow, and then to the others.

'I can give you only forty minutes instead of the full hour promised,' he said, with a polite expression of regret. 'My Melbourne office has called and there is an urgent electorate matter needing my personal attention. Please accept my apologies.'

'I am sure we can obtain all the information we require in that time, Yuen Fong Lau,' said Chiu Liow, bowing slightly. 'Please, come this way. May we get some refreshments for you?'

After having obtained tea and sweet cakes for Thanh's father and for themselves, they went back to the interview room. It seemed more appropriate somehow to treat him as a guest rather than as a suspect, however they were taken aback when Yuen Fong Lau himself began the interview.

'I wish to state that my son and I saw little of each other, despite living in the same house. It was primarily my bondmate's desire to become a parent, not mine. I loved Thanh because I loved her, and when she died, I ceased to love him. You will of course realise, I hope, that I was not prepared to deny my responsibility as a parent, so have done all that is in my nature to do. Unfortunately, this cannot replace love and I believe my son felt the lack. It is possible he even hated me.' He sipped his tea and ate a small cake while they waited for him to continue.

'Are you aware that I opposed his desire to obtain fertility rights together with a young woman named Rebecca? Since that time, he has been polite, respectful, and cooperative towards me, but nothing more. I regret to say that the crime committed at the Central Computer Site...I have read the report you sent to the House of Representatives...*could* have been committed by my son. He was astoundingly gifted, but may have seen this as a way of revenging himself upon me.'

To make sure he had their full attention, Yuen Fong Lau regarded each of them in turn before saying, 'I cannot account for his actions, or give you any help with information that would indicate the direction his life was taking; I have not lived in Melbourne for the past five months. My time has been spent undertaking a Parliamentary inquiry into the feasibility of introducing a limited level of public enterprise alpaca farming, primarily for wool... I hope you understand this is not for public dissemination.' He helped himself to another cup of tea and a second cake.

At this startling change of subject, his listeners were unable to prevent their astonishment from showing on their faces. If the Member of Parliament purposely wished to distract them, he could hardly have chosen a better method. Some countries grazed sheep where the natural herbivores had become extinct and grasslands needed to be maintained, yet they had not been farmed extensively in Australia for nearly three hundred years. Instead, the highly prized alpaca wool was used for clothing and other items, but was regarded as a luxury, produced and sold only by a small number of private enterprises. A public enterprise, on the other hand, would allow wool to be distributed as a free item, on a quota basis. Nevertheless, despite this good news, his attitude towards his son seemed extraordinary.

Morag was the first to recover and asked, 'Do you have any information at all which you think could help prove your son's innocence?'

'No, much to my regret, I do not. Nor can I give you any evidence of his guilt. However, I *can* give you a small amount of potentially useful information, which I came across in my travels around the country inspecting potential alpaca-farming regions.' He ate some of his cake, then carefully wiped his mouth with a napkin and smiled. 'As you most likely know, I am a member of the Parliamentary committee responsible for primary industry. Twelve months ago, an application by a South American company was made to purchase an initial one-hundred-year lease on two hundred and fifty thousand hectares of land, which at present is severely degraded but which was once prime timber-bearing, tropical rainforest. Mind you, that would be going back some three hundred and fifty years. They already have similar, although much smaller, leases in five other countries and have applied for three more.

'Their application appears perfectly reasonable and there are no suspicious circumstances associated with any of their worldwide operations. My attention was drawn to them only due to the condition of the land. Clearly, few governments would be willing to grant a lease on an area capable of immediate timber production, or even production within a time span related to the most advanced silvicultural techniques. However, in this case, the land in question is exceptionally poor.

'We must therefore ask, has this company developed, or do they have access to, new land restoration techniques that are not yet used, or even known of, by any Federation member government? If so, I wish them luck. If not, they could hardly damage the land any further. Nevertheless, I could not help making a connection between this application and the attacks on laboratories doing research into, amongst other things, re-creation and restoration of tropical rainforests... Did you want to ask a question Investigator MacIain?'

Morag had only raised her hand a few centimetres from the armrest of her chair. Startled, she replied, 'Ah...yes...I have two. Firstly, are you at liberty to give us the name of this company, and secondly, has the lease been granted?'

'I think, under the circumstances, that I *will* give you the name of the company, on condition you do not divulge it to anyone else unless your investigation requires you to do so. I must have an official secrecy agreement on this point, the reason being that the application has not yet been granted, although I expect it eventually will be. When it was first made, the proposal for restoring the land appeared technically lacking, but recent additions to the proposal have resulted in significant improvements. It seems they do their own independent research and have put forward a plan that has impressed our own experts, one of whom is Federation

Research Coordinator Zago. You may know her name in connection with the Willsmere, Lamington and Serra do Cachimbo research centres. She said that the work done by this company appears to be on par with our own, although they haven't so far managed to extensively field trial their concepts. However, they are prepared to bear the financial cost of failure, as well as donate any positive results to the Australian Government if they fall short of their own requirements. Our committee felt the offer was highly reasonable.' Yuen Fong Lau consulted his comlink. 'We have only ten minutes left. Is there anything else?'

'Yes,' replied Morag, 'the name of the company and contact names.'

'Oh yes, excuse me.' He entered a query into his comlink and gave her the results. 'I'm sure Research Coordinator Zago will be pleased to discuss their application with you. I don't think that would breach any of the few laws protecting private enterprises from having their commercial secrets stolen. We are, in any case, dealing with crimes serious enough to warrant breaching *any* commercial rights they might have.'

With these last words, the Member of Parliament stood up, shook each of them by the hand, and left the room.

CHAPTER SIX

Morag enjoyed the exchange with Research Coordinator Zago, whose great age gave her a warm sense of continuity and perspective. She was quite prepared to discuss the commercial application for the lease of a large tract of Australian land by the South American company, Wyvern Meridian, one of the companies on Morag's initial list.

'I can give you an undertaking for a detailed study of the similarities between the land regeneration proposals outlined in their application and the work currently being done by the Federation. If you wish, I can also offer to liaise with Meng Jarrah, who is ideally situated to evaluate an earlier application by Wyvern Meridian for a leasehold on Myanmarian land. It was granted two years ago and is now a timber plantation.' Zago leaned a little more heavily on the ornate staff she carried, waiting politely for Morag to reply.

'Thank you, Research Coordinator Zago. You have my deepest gratitude, but please excuse my asking, are you quite well? I can't help noticing you seem tired.'

'Yes, Investigator MacIain, I am quite well, just old.' Zago smiled. 'Still, it is a great privilege to have lived so long, and I am glad we will have the opportunity to work together. Please give my regards to your colleagues.'

Meng Jarrah had contacted Morag the previous evening to outline the results of her meeting with Chiu Liow's half-sister, the Myanmarian peacekeeper assigned to the case – an extraordinary woman, originally from Jamaica, who had named herself 'Freddi', and who was an awesome two hundred and fifteen centimetres tall, fully twenty centimetres taller than Meng Jarrah, who was by no means short.

It appeared that after consultation with his medical practitioner, Freddi and Meng Jarrah had agreed not to press the Myanmarian researcher for memories of the events at the Mandalay research centre. There was the risk he would develop long-term selective amnesia if they did, whereas with gentle treatment and indirect references to the harm he and others had suffered, there was a chance he would find the strength to confront his nightmare.

Shortly before the conversation with Zago, Morag had then spoken with Freddi to find out whether she had made any progress in other respects. According to Freddi's calculations, based on the damage done to the laboratory and to the researcher, as well as the nature of the information stolen, the time taken by the perpetrator need only have been some fifteen to twenty minutes and required only one person's involvement.

The problem was, however, that the crimes occurred during the evening of the site's annual festivities. All employees of the research centre, their friends and family members with temporary entry permits, together with numerous officials with permanent building access rights, were there that day, and of these people, thirty-two were in the building during the time in question. The thirty-two revellers, all of whom stayed late into the night, claimed not to have been in a fit condition to supply evidence as to each other's whereabouts at any specific time. Similarly, none of them were able to say whether or not someone was present who would not normally be given access to the site on an occasion such as this.

The Mandalay Peacekeeping Force had already scanned their own information sources for likely suspects, conducted a series of preliminary interviews, and made the necessary formal requests for additional personal data. Their psychologist was also attempting to eliminate suspects via a study of their psychological profiles. This was a time-consuming and painstaking task, which was expected to take at least another two weeks.

So far, their investigations had found no direct personal links with Wyvern Meridian or any of the other six private companies doing similar research to that of the Federation. The only indirect connection was the presence at the site festivities of a research centre employee who was also the owner of a transport corporation that held a contract with Myanmar's privately owned, long established, and highly successful timber production company with which Teak Australia traded. Apparently she had owned the transport company for two years, during which time it flourished at the expense of a number of smaller competitors. Although the association with the case was tenuous, so far this lead appeared to be the most promising.

Another outcome of their work was to narrow the field to two infotechs and one administrator capable of creating a security breach at the Mandalay Research Centre – if indeed there had been one, which was yet to be determined.

Morag had sufficient authority to access the databases of Myanmar's single central computer site, but due to a shortage of time and the necessity of acting without further delay, she delegated the task to another FSIU security expert. Their aim would be to find out whether anyone other than those already legitimately accounted for had been given temporary access to the research site, and if so, by whom.

In Melbourne, other more promising leads surfaced later the same day. Morag's enquiries established that Marika had made a comlink call from Springvale to South Yarra at 20:38 on the night of Thanh's death. The South Yarra comlink code belonged to a person who, when interviewed by Chiu Liow, freely admitted to having received a call from Marika at that time, and explained that he was one of the sponsors of the Bendigo theatre group with which Marika had her holographics contract. When queried about the content of the call, he informed Chiu Liow that it was very brief and only to confirm an appointment with the theatre group to discuss further development of the 3D prototype.

From the appearance of his residence, the man commanded considerable private means. Chiu Liow questioned him as to what his means were and was cheerfully told that he was fortunate enough to be a major shareholder in Teak Australia. The peacekeeper managed to maintain his usual bland expression as he heard this, and went on to ascertain that the sponsor had met Gwenllian's brother, Owain, on a number of social and business occasions, finding him to be "a truly delightful fellow, and his sister is quite stunning in every sense. Marvellous research they're doing."

Towards the end of their working day, Chiu Liow, Welcome and Morag met to discuss their progress.

'I have some news about the attack on the Federation laboratories in Serra do Cachimbo,' said Morag. 'It turns out the initial inquiries were entirely local and found no trace of the method used to gain entry. As you know, we were only notified three months later, after the other events occurred. My investigations have so far failed to find any traces of tampering with the security systems at their central computer site, so for the time being, we can only conclude that either the culprit had sufficient time to erase whatever records of their actions existed, or that in terms of the actual attack, we're dealing with someone who had a legitimate reason for being there on the night, as we believe may have been the case in the Myanmarian incident.'

She paused, and took a deep breath before continuing. 'Given the extent of these crimes, it's also possible that a security breach was contrived by someone who is a member of the FSIU. *We* are the only people on this planet with potential access to every corner of the lattice, as well as every Federation-owned and public computer system – or at least, that's the theory.'

Morag looked at each of her colleagues in turn, her expression very different from that of her usual optimistic, confident self. At first no one said anything. Chiu Liow's stomach muscles tensed and he could almost hear his own breathing. Welcome finally broke the silence:

'Five hundred years ago, a philosopher, whose name I can't recall, coined a phrase, "the wisdom of insecurity". Perhaps we've become too complacent in our beautifully ordered world and are now paying the price. We're shocked to the very core of our being at the thought that a member of the FSIU could have become corrupted, and yet throughout history the lesson has been that absolute power does indeed corrupt absolutely...not only the one who wields it, but those who trust and rely on them. We might ask ourselves, "Who guards the guardian?"'

'Federation Special Investigation Unit Coordinator Rohan Maerz guards us, and his bureaucracy guards him,' replied Morag in a low voice.

'In which case, we must consider the possibility that Rohan Maerz has, understandably, failed to be omnipresent and omnipotent, and that someone has escaped his net,' said Welcome, rubbing the tip of his stubby nose and pausing in thought. 'Unless, of course, he's chosen to amuse himself by becoming an expert in network and computer security.'

'I wish I could say it was impossible,' said Morag, with a lift of her eyebrows, 'but as much as it grieves me to even entertain the idea, I can't. Rohan Maerz is, in my opinion, the most intelligent person in the entire Federation government. He's also vulnerable in an odd way. You've seen him, Chiu Liow. What strikes you most about him?'

Chiu Liow grimaced and appeared embarrassed. 'He's grossly overweight.'

'He's also ostracised by many of his colleagues because of his weight problem and because he overeats. He's particularly fond of sweet pastries.' Morag slowly shook her head, wondering.

'How old is he and how long has he had the weight problem?' asked Welcome.

'He's seventy-three and I gather has had the problem his entire life. Our genetic screening of potential parents isn't always successful and he's even had to bear his particular burden alone. Both his parents died when he was only five and no one wished to adopt him, most likely because of his appearance. It's likely his compulsive craving for sweet foods started then, and my impression is that instead of trying to conform and control his weight, he's chosen defiance as a means of coping. For example, when he has guests to dine at his home, he often breaks all the cultural norms by serving at least five courses, one of which is frequently freshly killed fish.'

Puzzled, Welcome and Chiu Liow both gazed at Morag in surprise.

'Oh yes,' she replied to their mute question. 'He's one of our more peculiar citizens who keep fish tanks and offer their guests a choice of which fish is to be killed and then cooked for them. I've actually seen dinner guests stalk out of his house in rage and afterwards refuse to have any further dealings with him whatsoever. One even went so far as to throw her glass of wine in his face before leaving. Personally, I think they're over-reacting. I myself wouldn't choose to eat fish under those circumstances, but as long as they're killed humanely, I don't have any moral objection.'

'And how exactly does one kill a fish humanely?' asked Chiu Liow, his eyes wide.

'Rohan takes them out of the water and chops their heads off.'

Chiu Liow winced.

'Really, aren't we over-exercising our imaginations a little?' suggested Welcome. 'Just because the man's obtaining a quite reasonable and moderate degree of revenge on certain people who can only be termed zealots, need we suspect him of having become insane? I'm assuming this is what you mean, Morag.'

'You're the psychologist, Welcome, you tell us,' said Morag, then stood up and went to the servery for another cup of coffee.

'I suppose it's possible he's someone who's been pushed over that fine line between sanity and madness,' said Welcome, his head tilted to one side, 'but without studying his personal history in detail and having the chance to talk with him at some length, I'd find it difficult to say. Still, speaking as a peacekeeper and not as a psychologist, I think any attempt to place him under supervision would jeopardise our investigation. He's much too powerful for us to take the risk of him escalating his activities in response to any indication of suspicion on our part – if indeed he is our guilty party. I suggest we eliminate our other possibilities first.' Welcome stared hard at his feet for a few moments before looking up and saying, 'Could you get me some of that coffee while you're up? Do you want some too, Chiu Liow?'

The peacekeeper nodded, then stood and walked over to the window. The peaceful scenes of daily life in the city below formed a stark contrast to their own dark thoughts.

Having arranged to meet at his house for dinner, Mik arrived home to find Tamara already there, curled up on a large cushion, reading. He flung himself into an armchair, exclaiming, 'Damnation, these past few days have been a nightmare! I'd rather investigate plants than people any time.'

Fliedermus immediately jumped onto his lap, patting his face with a paw, her pupils dilated and glinting greenly. The cat's whiskers were pushed forward, giving her muzzle a fluffy, inquisitive appearance. Stretching, Tamara stood up, gave him a sympathetic smile, and said, 'Yes, I wouldn't fancy doing it,' then crouched down to stroke the cat's head, murmuring, 'Poor darling, it's hard on you too, isn't it?'

As she spoke, Fliedermus wrapped the tip of her tail around her wrist, and instantly, the atmosphere between Mik and Tamara became charged with tension. While the cat purred, they slowly reached out to touch hands, creating an ecstasy almost beyond toleration. Still linked by Fliedermus, their hands slid up and under the sleeve of the other's tunic, reaching smooth, rounded shoulders. Tamara caressed Mik's thigh, and felt his leg tremble in response, his muscles tautening. She pressed her lips to his throat, where the blood pulsed strongly, and felt her own heart pounding in response. As she raised her face to his, Mik tenderly kissed her mouth, then gently stroked her bright, brown, curly hair, drawing her down to rest within the warmth of his close embrace. They stayed there, all three, held together in rapture, until the moon rose, full and white, in the night sky.

Red Matilda broke the spell. Hungry, the cat had patiently watched, waiting until their tension was replaced by languorous calm. To be sure of getting their attention, she pounced on the nearest plant, tearing it to shreds, all the while emitting growls and snarls that could only have fooled a complete stranger into believing she was genuinely angry. In response, Fliedermus leapt from Mik's chest and bit Red Matilda's tail. The two kicked and nipped each other in mock rage, then flew apart, only to prance around, tails in the air, in front of their companions. As Mik and Tamara laughed helplessly at the display, Possum crept silently into the room to see what all the noise was about.

Smiling, Mik rose to his feet, lifting Tamara in his arms. She gazed at him, grey eyes sparkling in pure joy, and he set her down, clasping her to him with sudden, fierce passion. When Possum wound herself around their legs, again they felt as if the blood in their veins was liquid fire. Fliedermus and Red Matilda stopped their antics to watch, and then all three cats began to purr, whiskers and ears twitching, eyes glowing in the dim light of the room, their paws kneading the soft carpet in ecstasy as Mik and Tamara sank to the floor.

The moon had reached the middle of its course before Tamara awoke, to find herself still held within Mik's arms. She moved until her face was level with his and kissed the tip of his nose. He smiled sleepily and held her even closer. Earlier, Possum had snuggled into the curve of his back, and when she knew he was awake, stood up, stretched luxuriously, and licked his shoulder. Red Matilda was not as polite. As Mik rolled over, she trod heavily on his stomach.

'You're an oaf, cat!' he groaned, pushing her off. Turning to Tamara, he stroked her face then kissed each small breast. 'We'll have to feed the cats or suffer the consequences, my dearest little person.'

Tamara took his hand in hers and held it to her cheek, kissing his wrist, then sat up. Silhouetted in the moonlight, she seemed less vulnerable, freer, and altogether gayer than he had ever seen her. He too felt a new energy, a new vitality, coursing through him.

'I'm starving too! How pragmatic of me!' exclaimed Tamara, with a mischievous smile. 'Mik, let's not bother getting dressed. The cats won't mind, and it would just be a waste of time, don't you think?'

Standing up, Mik grinned, swept her into his arms and carried her into the kitchen, saying, 'I have no objections whatsoever, Tamara!'

The next day, at the Central Computer Site in Clayton, Morag MacIain strolled casually over to Lance Melrose Naylor's workstation, sat down nearby and studied him. She'd had no trouble recognising his mop of unruly brown hair and the broad shoulders that made him so distinctive. He was clearly in a special world inhabited only by the computing problem with which he was engrossed and only saw her when he turned around to pick up a graphics pen. Startled, Melrose blinked and swore, then realised who she was and immediately stood up, grinning an apology and holding out his hand. Morag stood as well to return the handshake, but allowed the silence to continue until it became acutely uncomfortable. At last, she said, 'I think you've blamed yourself for long enough.' Melrose blushed, his wry expression indicating his opinion of the situation. 'Tell me,' continued Morag, 'who, other than your own information technologists, has right of entry to this section?'

Melrose sat down again, while Morag remained standing. 'No one, other than your own people,' he replied, leaning back in his chair and folding his arms, 'as well as the usual lot: peacekeepers, ambutechs, emergency services personnel, and of course, the cleaners.'

Earlier in the day, during their comlink conversation, they had reached an implicit understanding that he and Yilmaz Alavi were victims rather than culprits, yet understandably enough, the knowledge that a colleague had stolen their handprints completely dismayed them. Under the circumstances, Melrose felt disinclined to discuss anything other than the precise matter in hand. Morag could only sympathise. 'So it's almost certain that none of the administrators could have arranged the security breach?' she said.

'Yes, that's right.' Melrose ran a hand through his rumpled hair. 'There are only three people who usually share shifts with both Yilmaz and me: Marika, Gwenllian, and in the past, Thanh. The timing of the whole exercise is too tight for anyone else to have done it, and I hate to say this, but almost any one of them could easily have worked out which programs to alter, and when. Here, see for yourself.'

Melrose turned to his computer and brought up the release schedules, which also showed actual transaction times and dates, together with the records of which infotech had worked on any given application. Turning back to Morag, he explained what they meant, the dark shadows under his eyes showing the strain he was under.

'These reports can be viewed by any infotech at any time, but can only be changed by whoever has the main responsibility for a particular application. For example, Gwenllian can only amend schedules relating to the transport request validation system. The transaction times and related information are generated automatically and can't readily be altered by anyone.'

'Given that we know which programs were changed and when, we need to know who could have filched your handprint and Yilmaz Alavi's,' said Morag, gazing at him expectantly, eyebrows raised, waiting. The chances of eliminating any of the three main suspects appeared very slim indeed unless Melrose or Yilmaz could provide enough useful information for them to do so.

'I know our prints are our main security measure, but we can't work in gloves!' As if to illustrate his point, Melrose spread out the fingers of his broad hands and held them out to her, palms upward. 'And we certainly can't go around wiping our prints off everything we touch! Working in a high-security environment like this is enough to make anyone paranoid, without having to suspect our own colleagues as well. Quite frankly, how could one of us have done it? We all have third-level security clearance!' Standing up, his shoulders hunched with tension, Melrose added, 'Yilmaz should be free by now. I suggest we have coffee together in the solarium.'

They passed through two doorways guarded by retina scanners before reaching Yilmaz Alavi's workstation. He rose to greet them, gripping the hand Morag offered almost as if she was reaching out to save him from disaster – as indeed in some ways she was. He gratefully agreed to the suggestion that they make use of the solarium for their discussion.

The solarium was the focal point of the site's social life. It was large enough to accommodate the entire workforce, but had cunningly contrived nooks that allowed conversations to remain private. The plastiglass roof soared above them, forming an immense transparent dome. At intervals, sections had been created using intricately designed coloured patterns, giving the sunlight streaming through all the hues of a rainbow. The floor, made from polished timbers of varying tones, gave a welcome contrast to the more utilitarian floor coverings of the remainder of the building, while a central fountain provided both a focal point and a pleasant background of natural sound. A great diversity of furnishings and forms of simple entertainment were provided, ranging from soft divans for those wishing to rest for a while, to dining settings and areas where musical instruments could be played without disturbing others.

Yilmaz led the way to one of the alcoves, where he and Melrose helped themselves to tea, offering some to Morag, who accepted, saying, 'I'm sure you both know what I want to find out. We have three main suspects and our interviews with the other infotechs here have given us a small but useful amount of information. For example, no one could remember any occasion on which either of you interacted socially with Gwenllian, which, in a small workplace such as this, is remarkable. However, it seems that you, Melrose, have had a close friendship with Marika for some years. We've also been told that Thanh frequently consulted you, Yilmaz, when he needed technical advice, and that if you left your position here, he was the one most likely to be appointed to it. Now, there are a few things we need to discuss: which of the three had the opportunity to unobtrusively steal your prints, did they speak to you on the day of the attacks on Willsmere and Lamington, and if so, what did you speak about? Who wants to start?'

Melrose finished his tea and carefully placed the cup on the low wooden table around which they were seated. He looked utterly dejected as he spoke: 'Marika knew which module I was working on that day and asked me to contact her as soon as I finished; we had arranged to meet for our evening meal. We didn't always eat together. She usually preferred to spend the time with Gwenllian or Thanh if they were working the same shift, which they generally were.' Melrose studied his hands. They were shaking slightly. 'I suppose this makes her the favourite.'

'Not necessarily,' said Yilmaz, putting a slender brown hand on his friend's shoulder. 'As one of his duties, Thanh monitored the production release schedule. The knowledge bases take care of implementation procedures, but the whole process has to be double-checked. He built himself a simple utility that noted the time any part of an application was ready to be put back into production. It would then notify him and he would check the schedule and begin monitoring...which makes him the ideal suspect. Still, Gwenllian worked closely with Thanh, so would have known what his methods were. She could have noticed what Thanh was doing and then checked the release schedule. Oh, and I'm almost certain she didn't speak to *me* that day.'

'Gwenllian didn't speak to me either,' said Melrose. 'I would definitely have remembered, because we rarely *do* speak to each other.'

'And what about the prints?' Morag reminded them.

'Marika could have taken mine any time,' Melrose told her, shaking his head. 'She usually offered to get something for me when we had meals or breaks together and often cleared away the dishes. Gwenllian or Thanh, on the other hand, would've had to sneak around our work areas or the solarium trying to pick up a print by chance. I honestly can't see either of them taking a risk like that.'

'No one I can remember has ever cleared away my dishes at work,' said Yilmaz, with a comical downturn of his mouth. 'Anyway, during this past year, I think I've only eaten about three meals in Marika's company, whereas I've spent a considerable amount of time down here discussing work issues and drinking tea and coffee with Thanh. I know I'll miss him...

Sometimes he'd even bring out his flute and play for us.' Yilmaz compressed his lips and shook his head wistfully. 'He was the sweetest player I've ever heard.'

'Did you say "flute"?' asked Morag, sitting up from the semi-reclined position she had adopted.

'Yes, flute. Why?'

'Have you ever seen the holographic work Marika's producing?'

'Yes, I have. Many times. Thanh modelled for it.'

'In that case, I'd appreciate your both keeping a close eye on her for me. She said during her interview that she only worked with him, nothing more. It seems this was a distortion of the truth.'

'If Marika was a horse running in the Melbourne Cup, I'd place my bets on her!' Yilmaz couldn't resist the joke, but earned himself a black look from Melrose.

'Just because *she* had the greatest opportunity and Gwenllian the least, doesn't mean Marika is involved in all of this. She's the perfect scapegoat!' Melrose sat forward in his chair, his face flushed.

'Well, if she's a scapegoat, she wouldn't stand much chance in the Melbourne Cup, I must admit,' quipped Yilmaz, still attempting to lighten the mood. However, neither Melrose nor Morag laughed, or even smiled.

Instead, Morag said, 'Gwenllian has a number of solid connections with the case as well, all of which could be coincidence, *or* they could put *her* into the position of being the scapegoat. To use your punting analogy, Yilmaz, I tend to think it's even credits on all three. There has to be some other way of eliminating two of them from the list. Could one of them have stolen your handprints directly from the database that stores them?'

'I doubt it,' replied Melrose, frowning. 'None of them have...or had...the authority to access it, so unless there was outside help, or they were capable of a great deal more than I think possible, we're left with them having to create forgeries. That particular database is surrounded with more layers of security than any other.'

'Thank you,' said Morag. 'I thought as much.'

'Have you had their comlink call histories analysed yet?' asked Melrose.

'No, I haven't,' Morag admitted, 'not all their calls; only the more recent ones. I'll get onto it today.'

'I'll put in the request for you, if you like. I know some of the people who work on that particular system. They're a bit touchy and defend the information as if it were a Federation secret. They do have a point, I suppose. Comlink privacy is a big issue and some people don't realise that tracing calls isn't the same as recording the calls themselves.'

Morag accepted the offer gratefully. 'If you look at their histories up to and including the fifteenth of November, that should be enough for the time being. When do you expect something to be available?'

'Tomorrow should do it. I'll forward what I find to you as soon as I can.'

'Excellent... Now tell me, if Gwenllian and Marika were temporarily suspended from duty, would they face any workplace issues once they came back, assuming they were eventually proven innocent?'

Yilmaz and Melrose were both appalled by the suggestion. 'Surely you wouldn't!' protested Melrose.

'I think I must. Gwenllian is already feeling vulnerable, which is what we want, but Marika appears to be made of much sterner stuff. We need to shake her, but we can't suspend one without suspending the other, otherwise Marika, if she's innocent, would always wear the taint of suspicion. Also, if either of them *have* had a hand in this, they'll no longer be in such a good position to wreak further havoc. Thanh certainly isn't, so if any further security breaches occur of a similar type, we'll know better where to turn our attention. And by the way, their suspension must be kept secret for as long as possible. I'm depending on you both to work out how to do that.'

CHAPTER SEVEN

Melrose preferred a quiet, routine life, relying on a few good friends and his work for stimulation and reward. His room in the communal dwelling was the place in which he felt the greatest sense of inner peace, and consequently, preferred not to bring anyone but his closest friends there. Marika had sometimes shared his bed, but as a child in need of comfort, not as a lover. She was a strange mixture of hardness and vulnerability, enormous ambition and great generosity. Throughout the years of their friendship, Melrose had never managed to reach through that tough outer layer during their working hours, and now, sitting alone with the results of the comlink traces before him, he reluctantly came to the conclusion that Marika had little in the way of an inner core of gentleness and human sympathy, something he always suspected might be the case. Listed amongst her calls was one made while she was at work on the day of the Willsmere and Lamington incidents, only minutes after the timestamp on the program that had been altered using his handprint as authorisation. The call was to someone in South Yarra by the name of Mervyn Bradshaw.

All Thanh Fong Lau's comlink calls, on the other hand, were related to his professional life, day-to-day affairs, his personal life as a musician, and on rare occasions, to his father. He appeared to have made no calls of a purely social nature within the past twelve months. His life had been solitary indeed.

Gwenllian's included all the expected ones, as well as many to numbers owned by commercial and research contacts related to the venture she and her brother had undertaken. The comlink codes of several private individuals appeared frequently, so unless these people were already accounted for, they would no doubt receive a visit from the peacekeepers within the near future. However, Melrose was relieved to see that Gwenllian hadn't made any private calls during the morning, afternoon or evening of the critical day.

Cursing the whole situation, he rubbed his hands over his tired, unshaven face, entered Morag MacIain's comlink code on his keypad, and waited. When she appeared on the screen, he absentmindedly noticed her complete change of hairstyle, then, frowning, said, 'I've managed to get the full call histories we spoke of yesterday, for the past two years. I'll send them straight through. It looks like you'll have what you wanted.'

'By the expression on your face, Melrose, I can guess whose history contains one made on the thirteenth of November. Marika?'

'Yes...unfortunately. In many ways, I wish it had been Thanh. At least he wouldn't have suffered.'

'Marika hasn't been found guilty yet, Melrose, so it's best not to jump to conclusions. Even though the evidence is accumulating, we don't have enough to make any accusations. Of course, we'll confront her with the fact she made a call at the critical time...and thanks, the report has just finished coming up. Ah, yes, I see... Our friend in South Yarra has surfaced at the critical moment, yet again.'

'Who *is* Mervyn Bradshaw?' asked Melrose, shifting himself closer to the screen.

'Oh, just a major shareholder in a timber importing company named Teak Australia, as well as being one of the sponsors of the Bendigo theatre group.'

'Really! Mervyn Bradshaw?'

'The very man. I gather you know him?'

'No, but Marika talked about her sponsor quite often, without actually being prepared to say who he was. All she ever said was that he's disgustingly wealthy. Knowing now that she called him, I imagine a close scrutiny of his income sources would send ripples through quite a few murky pools!'

'Yes...well...quite possibly. We should at least be able to justify a request for access to his taxation files, so we'll see what turns up. Personally, I suspect his pecuniary situation resembles an advertisement for detergent.'

'A what?'

'Peacekeeper Jones tells me that twentieth and twenty-first-century buildings were frequently used for things called advertisements.' Morag shrugged her shoulders and paused, then explained: 'Private enterprises would pay to have their products praised in public in the hope that more people would buy them. They used any form of media they could get hold of and buildings were amongst their favourites. Detergent was a substance used for cleaning clothes, as well as other things, and the advertisements often claimed it would wash them "whiter than white".'

'What if they were coloured?'

'I think we're getting side-tracked here... What I meant was that if our entrepreneurial friend is actually a villain, he would have ensured his financial transactions were all transparently legal.'

'Oh...I see. So is there anything else Yilmaz or I can do for you?'

'Not at the moment, other than keeping alert for any useful gossip you might hear.'

Morag felt keenly sympathetic towards Melrose, but knew there was little that could be said to ease his mind. She certainly had no intention of telling him about Marika's other call to Mervyn Bradshaw. It would be too heavy a burden of knowledge for Melrose to carry. If Marika was found guilty of having engineered the security breach at either or both of the research centres, and it eventuated that Mervyn Bradshaw was connected in some way as well, the likelihood that they would also be convicted of complicity in Thanh's murder was extremely high, in which case, they faced a life sentence in a high-security prison.

Once Morag and the brief distraction she had provided were gone, Melrose was left alone with only his bitter thoughts for company. The loss of two more highly talented team members, under circumstances almost too extraordinary to comprehend, threatened to send him into a state of unbelieving withdrawal – even if their loss *was* only temporary. He experienced a powerful urge to contact Marika in the hope that, somehow, she could convince him she wasn't involved, yet his strong sense of responsibility prevented him from doing so. Instead, he placed his head in his hands and wept.

Chiu Liow sat in his kitchen staring at a wall and frowning. Since the suspension of Gwenllian and Marika from their duties at the Central Computer Site, their movements and calls were being monitored. To date, other than not attending their workplace, neither of the two had deviated from their normal living patterns. As was customary when people were suspected of such serious offences, an identity chip had been inserted into each woman's shoulder. Gwenllian submitted to the small operation with white-faced despair, while her brother, Owain, protested stridently against the treatment his sister was receiving. He had needed to be physically restrained from assaulting the peacekeepers. Marika, on the other hand, remained grimly defiant throughout.

A tapping at the skylight reminded him that most other creatures were oblivious to the tribulations facing evolution's most complex creation. A kookaburra had developed the habit of demanding to be fed once a day by the former occupant of the house and Chiu Liow didn't have the heart to disappoint it. The bird only ate meat, so much to his distaste he placed an order for regular deliveries of chicken necks, derived from the geriatrics of the egg farms once they died. The kookaburra compensated his friend by serenading him in the early hours of the morning and evening – if raucous cackling can be termed a serenade. Grateful for the excuse to leave his work behind for a brief while, he went out to feed it.

On this particular day, the peacekeeper was pleased to find 'his' bird had brought a mate. It sat waiting complacently on the lowest branch of the swamp gum growing crookedly a short distance from his greenhouse. The old hand at the game perched next to the new arrival and raised its head to chortle, while in the background the sky glowed a fiery red as the sun began to set. The tranquillity of dusk would soon send the birds back to the hollow tree in which they reared their young, whereas Chiu Liow would return to his house beneath the ground to hunt out the evidence that might send one of two women, and possibly others, to lifelong imprisonment.

As the colours of the sunset deepened, Mik and Tamara sat in his greenhouse eating their evening meal. Afterwards, Tamara had promised to play her mandolin for him, and the news that she played such an instrument came as a pleasant surprise, for he himself played the laouto. They were each hoping to find the time to experiment with different pieces of music that would allow them to accompany each other, and perhaps even perform for their friends.

Revelling in the novel experience of having a bondmate, as they now regarded each other, Mik and Tamara had decided to live together for part of each week. The cats were delighted with the new arrangement, especially Possum, who displayed a small degree of jealousy whenever one of the others received too much of Tamara's attention. Red Matilda had already begun to tease Possum by biting her tail whenever she found her sleeping next to Tamara. The smaller cat invariably rose to the bait and attempted to swat Red, at which point she would leap into the place Possum vacated – Tamara swore Red Matilda could smile in an annoyingly smug manner!

'You know, Mik, if it wasn't for the investigations, I'd be so happy,' she said, helping herself to another serving of avocado salad. 'And in fact I think we're probably over the worst. Whoever's responsible has got what they wanted, so with a bit of luck, we'll be able to get back to our normal routine. From what Zago has told us, it looks to me as if some private company might've indulged in a bit of industrial espionage that went wrong, probably because they hired total incompetents to do the work. I bet they're wishing they'd never tried!'

'It'd have to be an awfully well-resourced company to operate on a global scale,' replied Mik, as he handed her the last piece of leek soufflé. 'I wonder if they've considered the possibility that it could've been the government of some country wanting to pull out of the Federation? Not everyone's happy with the Federation. There've been a few clashes at international conferences, as well as grumblings about not receiving enough quota goods. I've even heard of an argument being put forward that if a country produces a particular item, it ought to receive more than an equal share.'

'They're mad,' said Tamara, looking up from her plate. 'What do they want? To go back to a completely free-market economy?'

'I don't think they really understand what they're asking for, and don't know enough history to realise how easy it is to lose what we've finally gained after thousands of years of warfare.' Mik stood up. 'Anyway, my love, that's the perfect topic to give me indigestion. I'd rather tidy up all this while you finish...and then do you want to take Possum for a walk? It's her turn to have you to herself for a while. Crazy little pud...'

He bent down to kiss Tamara, stroking her brown curls. Having 'heard' what Mik said, Possum bumped the back of his knees with her forehead, then stood up on her hind legs and stretched up far enough to place her front paws onto his back.

'Ouch, cat, pull those claws in!' Mik reached around to lightly swat her. Pretending innocence, Possum dropped back down, rubbing her head against Tamara's legs instead and purring loudly. Tamara finished her last mouthful of food, and then, with the cat following closely behind, took the walking leash from its hook on the wall. She attached it to Possum's collar, gave Mik a rib-crushing hug, and left the house.

As they started off in the direction of the nearest open space, the sunset had faded to a soft yellow glow, and by the time the two crossed the trafficway, Venus was bright in the sky. The warm air brought them the faintest scent of the sea and they could hear the last twittering in the trees as the birds settled for the night. Crickets had started their nightly orchestra, but as they reached the edge of the open space, even these little creatures had retired. The silence was profound, with only an occasional bat flying overhead, until rustlings in the trees heralded the awakening of the night-time inhabitants of the bushland.

Tamara could feel Possum's contentment. Their mutual understanding had grown these past few days, until she could almost picture herself inside the cat's mind. 'I'll start thinking I've got a tail next,' she thought, giggling, but then stopped as Possum's mood changed from playfulness to alarm. They both halted. Tamara could see nothing to account for the cat's fear, which grew until the link between them snapped. Unable to understand why, she crouched down, murmuring, 'It's okay, there's nothing to be frightened of... I'm here; it's alright, my darling.' Then, with an effort, she picked her up.

Possum struggled, scratching her in panic. Dropping the cat, Tamara used all her strength to keep hold of the leash – but then she saw him, and was unable to move. As the smiling face came closer, Possum's madness sent her thoughts into turmoil, until she felt an overwhelming rage smash into her mind as she fell.

Morag MacIain sat in her office in the Rialto tower enjoying a short break as she looked out over the panorama of night-time Melbourne. There were relatively few lights in the central business district other than those of the waterjets, but beyond the coastline, glowing streams showed the busy nightlife of this vital city. Light railcars, airjets, and the blur of the occasional landjet, gave form to the darkness.

Research Coordinator Zago had supplied her with the promised report on the application by Wyvern Meridian for the commercial lease of a large tract of highly degraded Australian land, and it was proving to be highly informative. It seemed the company's land reclamation plans included research findings similar in many respects to those being produced by the Federation but which were yet to be completed or published. Certainly, there were also significant differences. The Federation's aim was to re-establish the former species composition of wilderness areas as closely as current conditions allowed, taking into account climatic changes, and to develop plantations or other agricultural projects only where this aim was unable to be achieved.

In contrast, Wyvern Meridian put forward a proposal based on the argument that there was no inherent value in re-establishing fragile ecosystems easily disrupted by the impact of introduced pests, climate change, and other human activities. Instead, they had modelled forests based on a diverse number of compatible and highly robust species which were not necessarily native to the area as it existed six hundred years ago. They justified their model on the grounds that it would require less time and company resources to implement and maintain, would still meet Federation land regeneration objectives, and would provide a greater level of production of goods currently scarce and in demand.

Clearly, if their model proved to be sound, they stood to gain massive financial profits, a significant degree of public support, and great scientific credibility. Evaluation of the application would, however, be difficult, given its entirely different assumptions. Robust species frequently became pests outside their own habitat, which meant that areas rehabilitated by Wyvern Meridian could conflict, in an ecological sense, with areas rehabilitated based on Federation principles. Therefore, Zago's opinion was that a decision on whether their application should be granted would not be made for some time. She had proposed that Mik and Tamara be given the task of evaluating the company's strategy in terms of its compatibility with Federation goals. However, the assessment of the internal integrity of the Wyvern Meridian model would be made by independent Federation researchers, who would also examine the Willsmere analysis and its conclusions.

Morag had also received the details of Wyvern Meridian's Myanmarian timber production activities over the past two years. Reading the information – provided by Freddi, Chiu Liow's sister – it appeared that despite the ideal climatic conditions of Myanmar and the comparatively fertile soils of the leasehold, their fledgling plantation had failed to flourish.

The contract with Myanmar's government specified they were to fully stabilise the area within fifteen years using native species of hardwood, and were to employ only local labour and contractors. The company had complied with the latter condition, but it appeared unlikely their trees would reach the required stage of growth within the period specified, despite a substantial investment in research and plantation development. Meng Jarrah's evaluation of their initial leasehold application showed that the likely cause of their lack of success was their having paid insufficient attention to the ongoing maintenance requirements of the land's soil structure and composition.

Freddi had also unearthed one very peculiar fact: the Mandalay Research Centre's employee who owned the transport company holding the sole contract with Myanmar's only long-established timber producer, had that day signed a contract with Wyvern Meridian, giving them a fifty-one percent shareholding. A ten percent decrease in their timber transportation charges was immediately announced, for which apparently public-spirited action they were praised by Myanmar's Ministry for Agriculture. To all appearances, it seemed that Wyvern Meridian was genuinely committed to the Federation's worldwide reforestation and land reclamation strategy.

Morag wrinkled her nose. Intuitively, she was sure the whole situation stank. As the only global company with timber production and processing interests, they could afford altruistic gestures in one country if they thereby gained elsewhere. With the Australian leasehold still under consideration, it was obviously in the company's own interest to behave in a benign manner.

Having done enough for one day, she stood up and stretched, then took a small mirror from her work bag to critically assess the effect of her new hairstyle; not normally vain, she had changed it due to the heat. Luzern was usually cold enough to make long, loose hair an asset, whereas Melbourne's humid warmth was making it distinctly uncomfortable. Swept up at the back and held in place by a silver comb, she had to admit the effect of the cascading waves was quite lovely. With a chuckle, Morag made a face at herself, closed the mirror, and asked her computer to contact Peacekeeper Chiu Liow Jones. Within seconds, he appeared on the screen, his face drawn and weary.

'You look ghastly!' she exclaimed.

'I *feel* ghastly, Morag. I always thought I agreed with life sentences for contract killers and terrorists, but now that I'm face-to-face with having to find the evidence to convict someone, it's hard. Almost *too* hard!' Chiu Liow paused, then said, 'Still, leaving that aside for the time being, I'm almost sure from the way Gwenllian reacted when the tracking chip was inserted into her shoulder that she's innocent. I also think that if Gwenllian *is* involved, Owain, her brother, is too, but he's completely distraught. They're almost closer to each other than bondmates. If they aren't guilty of anything, the longer this investigation goes on, the greater the chance they'll both be permanently scarred by it.'

'I agree... It's a bad situation for them. Have you managed to take a good look at the people Gwenllian makes regular calls to?'

'Yes, and there doesn't seem to be anyone suspicious. On the other hand, when Welcome told Marika we knew about the calls made to Mervyn Bradshaw, she just laughed!'

'And what did Welcome make of Marika's reaction?'

'Absolutely nothing, because she went on to ask if we'd bothered to find out how often she calls him. Welcome admitted we had and so Marika then asked if he knew anything about the laws of probability. Of course he said he did, at which point she refused to say another word.'

'So tell me, how often does she call him?'

'At least three times a week. It *could* be just coincidence that she made some at the critical times, or else it's possible they've built up a pattern of frequent calls over a long period because they knew we'd do a trace. I've looked at the records you gave me and the call pattern began around nine months ago...but that doesn't *prove* anything, does it?'

'No, it only means that for the time being both women remain under suspicion.'

'Morag,' said Chiu Liow, with an uncertain tone to his voice that Morag hadn't heard before, 'I'm badly in need of good company. Why don't you come over and tell me what you've found out today in person? You haven't seen my house yet.'

'Thank you, Chiu Liow.' She gave him a warm smile. 'I'd like that. See you soon.'

Morag was both disturbed by his unusual depression and quietly elated that he had paid her the compliment of inviting her to his home. Packing her things, she reflected on how long it had been since she enjoyed anyone's company as much as his. Ten minutes later, as she was about to step onto the plaza outside the building, her comlink beeped. It was Chiu Liow again. His lips were compressed into a thin line and the small screen showed he was even more upset than before. Her heart began to pound.

'What's happened?' she asked, managing to keep her voice steady.

'Someone tried to kill Tamara while she was out walking Mik's cat...the one called Possum. The cat killed him.'

Morag leaned against the wall of the Rialto and fought for control. 'Is Tamara dead too?' she said at last.

'No... She's fine physically, but has gone into severe psychological shock. We don't know exactly what happened, although it appears the cat attacked before the killer could touch her. His throat was torn out. I've never heard of anything like it! The cat's been taken into custody.'

'When did it happen, Chiu, and how were they found?'

'About half an hour ago. Mik heard the cat screaming. At least, he didn't *hear* it. It was inside his head and he received an image of Tamara lying on the ground, with blood everywhere. He followed the screaming straight to them. Possum was crouched over the man she'd killed, lapping up the blood. Tamara was unconscious, even though she hadn't been injured. We think the cat's rage may have impacted on her mind like a physical blow... Mik could hardly speak when he contacted me. They're both at the medcentre now and I'm about to leave to go over there. In the meantime, I need you to send for Søren Thorup to go to the Melbourne Detention Centre and attempt to communicate with the cat. It may be able to give him something we can use, if and when it calms down. At the moment, she's nearly mad with fear. I also want you to find Welcome and send him over to the medcentre...and Morag, I'm afraid I must ask *you* to go to the mortuary and arrange for formal identification.'

Morag nodded, and the screen became blank as Chiu Liow abruptly ended the call. She entered her priority transport code into her comlink, and within minutes, a silver MPF patrol car landed. Once they were skimming over the surface of the waterway, she quickly made contact with Søren. At first his face lit up with pleasure when he realised to whom he was speaking, but after her terse account of the reason for her call, his expression changed to one of horror.

'A patrol car will be outside your apartment within five minutes,' said Morag. 'I don't need to tell you that a great deal depends upon your work tonight.'

Søren, for once, had little to say. Not only did Possum's life depend on his ability to convince the people who were holding her that she reacted in the only way possible for her species, it also depended upon his ability to prevent an explosion of paranoia against all cats. He fervently thanked the good luck that had allowed him to have already entered a considerable knowledge base on cats into the Judge...and that Fliedermus' role as a witness had set a precedent for them to be given a degree of status under the law.

Next, Morag contacted Welcome, and unlike Søren and Chiu Liow, his expression changed only to the extent that the warmth in his eyes died. Without asking for further explanation, he confirmed that he would go to the medcentre immediately, then closed the connection.

Moments later, the patrol car landed on the soft living surface of flowering plants making up the arrivals and departures area within the Court precinct in Lonsdale Street, where Morag made her way to the mortuary.

*

In Luzern, Rohan Maerz walked ponderously back and forth across the parquetry floor of his office. Morag's inquiries were proceeding along the path he had privately predicted and he felt sure the various threads of evidence were on the point of converging. Until now, the whole sequence of events had been most satisfactory, except for the death of the information technologist, Thanh Fong Lau. This was tragic, and to his mind, totally senseless. The boy could hardly have presented a threat to anyone, and his removal only gave rise to a small, but telling, piece of evidence against his former colleague, Marika – whereas, alive, Thanh had provided a far more plausible third suspect.

The latest incident was even further beyond his comprehension, which was very wide indeed. Morag had contacted him with a brief summary of the attempted murder of the researcher, Tamara Solanum, as well as its gory consequences, promising to provide full details immediately they became available. Rohan shook his massive head. His contempt for the great majority of the human species seemed increasingly justified.

Heaving a sigh, he felt an overwhelming sense of boredom, relieved only by this new factor presented by the cat, Possum. Ridiculous name! He was greatly tempted to go to Australia to meet the creature. His knowledge of them was scanty, but sufficient to cause amazement at the animal's reaction to the body of the would-be killer. Lapping its blood! His body quivered with silent laughter. They were supposed to be vegetarian! The genetic engineers and behaviourists would have their work cut out solving that one! He reached for another chocolate éclair and ate it, then licked the last traces of cream from his fingers.

Having now returned to work for a few hours each day, Meng Jarrah's researcher sat quietly watching his friend as she finished her tasks for the day. Her precise movements and the careful, patient handling of the specimen on which she was working filled him with contentment. If only he could put aside the memories that had fully returned only this morning. Since then, he had sensed Meng Jarrah's keen sympathy and felt sure she was aware of his situation. Finally, he made his decision.

'I do not need to tell you what my fears are: you *know*,' he said softly. 'I will only say that I value our work as much as I do my own life and could not continue in silence, knowing a great evil is underway. I have remembered everything and wish to tell you what happened.'

Meng Jarrah turned to him, her expression grave. She briefly laid her hand on his shoulder and waited.

'You are one of the few people who have never asked how my artificial sight compares to normal vision, so I imagined you were well acquainted with the technology. There are many who work here, and some who visit regularly, who have asked about it. A few have felt uneasy when I responded. Perhaps they were only curious, or perhaps they wished to express sympathy, yet when I make it known that my vision is superior to theirs and in what manner, those few regard me with something akin to fear. I can only assume the fear is related to what may appear to be my uncanny ability to literally 'see' behind me without turning my head. Frequently, I forget to turn around before I speak to someone who has approached from behind. If they are new to the Centre, they are usually startled.' He paused and looked away.

'You saw who your attacker was,' prompted Meng Jarrah gently.

'Yes, I did, and he knew that I would. He entered the laboratory on the pretence of asking me if I expected to join the festivities again. I replied that I had decided to work through the night, then noticed his expression was strangely tense and recalled I had not, at first, turned to face him. He was close to me by this time, staring directly into my eyes. His blow took me in the chest and I fell backwards, into an old glass exhibition cabinet, which smashed and cut my head. As I lay helpless on the floor, he tortured both my hands, and I knew he enjoyed what he did. I heard him laugh.' The researcher stopped and held out his hands to her, unable to continue. Meng Jarrah took them in her own and knelt down beside him, looking into his face.

'Tell me who did this to you.'

'The Chairperson of the Ministry for Agriculture.'

CHAPTER EIGHT

Søren crouched several metres away from Possum, who sat with shoulders hunched, hackles raised and ears laid well back. Her pupils were fully dilated and blood still clung to her chin. She snarled if anyone moved, so Søren had asked that they be left alone. At first, the peacekeepers were reluctant, standing with immobilisers in hand, ready to fire if the cat leapt. One of them, however, had been sufficiently caring to hold out his hand to her – he had a cat of his own – but Possum bared her teeth and lashed out. The wound was serious enough to warrant medical attention.

Since then, two hours had gone by, yet still Søren had achieved nothing. The pain in Possum's mind communicated itself in waves of agony. He fought the anguish that threatened to overwhelm him, forced himself to send images of comfort and reassurance to the fear-crazed creature before him. Slowly taking his comlink from his pocket, he entered the code of the medcentre where Mik and Tamara had been taken. Speaking softly, and without taking his eyes off Possum, he asked for the practitioner in charge of Tamara's care. It seemed to take forever before he was put through, even though only a few seconds passed. Perspiration trickled from his brow as he forced himself to speak coherently to the practitioner. As he ran a hand over his face, the practitioner stood aside and Mik appeared on the screen, his eyes glazed, speaking with what sounded to be an enormous effort.

'Søren, thank the Sun you're there with her! Tamara's okay. They've treated her and she's been given a mild sedative. Welcome and Chiu Liow were here as well and they've agreed that we need to be with Possum...for all our sakes. We'll be with you soon.' He faltered on the last words and then cut the connection.

Another fifteen long minutes passed and finally Possum's tail stopped lashing. The security door slid back and Mik and Tamara stepped into the room, tears on their cheeks, tightly clutching each other's hand. Søren immediately noticed the change in Possum's mind. The violent pain became a pitiful wailing, a plea for understanding and forgiveness. Tamara quickly moved over to her, putting an arm around her rigid body. Mik hesitated for only a moment, then joined them and began cleaning the blood from the cat's face with his kerchief. The wailing gradually lessened and Søren suddenly felt sick. He realised his legs had cramped and his back hurt abominably. With an effort, he stood up, then carefully eased his muscles, breathing deeply and waiting while his two friends silently focused on Possum, willing the cat to remember, reassuring her of their love.

Warm soft darkness, living ground, new scents, new grimalkin from the far home... Tamara, my Wight now too... Possum, dreaming, scratching tree, claws sharp, stretching delight, running, catching leaf... Tamara laughing, happy... Hold me... Rub faces... A breeze... Strange wight!

A darkness came over Possum's mind. Disbelief seared through her, together with a desperate need to flee from the alien emotion. The wight with the crushing blackness came closer until she could see him. Tamara had stopped. Did she feel nothing? She did! She could feel Possum's terror, but the wight was too far away for her to know what he wanted. Possum strained against the sickness that threatened to send her mad. Tamara was trying to understand, trying to pick her up. She struggled against the encircling arms, pulling at the leash, which held her fast. *No! Let me go! Look at the wight!*

Tamara stood, frozen in horror, her face reflecting Possum's frenzy. Possum could see the wight's face. Tamara was staring at him, unable to run, to think, to react. The face came closer. It was smiling, but the blackness was growing, overwhelming them both. Tamara dropped the leash, forgetting Possum. The cat, freed from restraint, gathered herself to leap. The wight screamed, clutching at his head, and Tamara fell, her mind empty.

Possum hurled herself at the killer, knocking him to the ground. Hate filled her entire being as she tore at his throat. The screaming became part of her too, until the blood spurted and the voice became a ghastly moan, then ceased. Her heart pounding, her teeth gripping torn flesh, Possum's mind filled with an immense gloating. She snarled and sank her teeth deeper. The tip of her tail twitched. The wight was dead. Tamara was safe. Possum released the thing she had killed and backed away. The taste in her mouth was strange, sweet. An urge she had never experienced before crept over her. She gazed at Tamara and then at the dead wight. *Her* dead wight. She put her paw on the man's throat, but withdrew in disgust. It was wet. Sniffing at the dark blood running from the wound, Possum crouched down and drank.

From out of the stillness of the night, Mik's mind collided with hers. Possum recoiled from the body, a new fear threatening to overwhelm her. She leapt back as Mik ran towards them. His images were of her, drinking the blood, of Tamara lying still on the soft earth, of the torn throat of the man at her feet, repulsion at what she had done.

Don't hate me! He wanted to kill her! Possum suddenly vomited.

Mik loomed overhead, his arm raised as if he were about to strike her. Instead, he knelt down to cradle Tamara's head in his hands. Possum shared his misery and crept over to his knee, begging for understanding. While the confusion in her mind grew, she heard him speak to the small dark thing he always carried. Soon afterwards, the sound of approaching airjets impacted unbearably on her sensitive ears.

While Tamara was given into the care of someone whose thoughts were of warmth and healing, Possum's leash was gripped by a stranger. Her world in turmoil, she struggled, screaming, *'Mik! Don't let them take me from you!'*

But Mik's mind was filled with sorrow as he looked at her bloodstained face, her sweat-drenched fur, and there was a block between them. Their bond seemed to her to have broken.

Tamara and Mik wept, while Søren placed his arms around them both, and all three encircled the distraught cat, whose mind had nearly been destroyed. Gradually, Possum became calmer and she questioned them, one paw on Mik's knee, her eyes gazing into his, her tail draped around Tamara's ankle. She now knew they would not desert her, understood that Mik's horror had arisen from fear and alarm, not condemnation; Tamara was alive because *she* had killed the wight.

The fear threatened to return as Possum remembered how she gloated at his death, but Søren's thoughts came through to her at last. He understood, was telling her it would never happen again, that she was not mad and had killed only because there was no other choice. *Could they please take her home now?* She stood up, stretching as far as she could to place both front paws on Søren's chest. He was small like her. He understood how frightened she had been...

Søren sat down and took her onto his lap. She badly needed sleep, but he doubted whether the peacekeepers would let them take her home. Well, he was sure he could win the argument if they tried to stop them! Still, he was exhausted and realised that what they all needed was Karla's calm presence. She hadn't been involved in any of this, and he felt certain she'd be capable of taking the strain from their shoulders.

'I will call Karla,' he told the others. 'I'm sure she can help and will want to be with us. Mik, do you think she should bring the other two cats?'

Mik ran his hands over his face. He was so tired he could hardly stand. 'Sun help me, I don't know. Maybe the sight of two sane cats will convince the peacekeepers they're usually safe enough. They've got to let me take her home!'

'Do not worry, my friend. We *will* take Possum home. We will stand bail for her.' Søren smiled weakly at his own joke, but neither Mik nor Tamara joined him, so he looked away and asked his comlink to contact Karla. After several long minutes, she answered, yawning, and confused by having been woken from a sound sleep.

'Hello, Søren. You look dreadful! Have you stayed up all night drinking...or something worse?'

'Something far worse, Karla. I want you to put on some clothes and not ask any questions. Go to Mik's house, find Fliedermus and Red Matilda, and bring them with you to the Melbourne Detention Centre. Please don't lose any time. Tamara, Mik, Possum and I will all be waiting for you there. Something terrible has happened and we need your help. A patrol car will arrive for you very soon.' Søren was confident he could convince the peacekeepers to provide a patrol car – *anything* to resolve the situation!

Karla could hear the urgency in his voice, so quickly agreed and set about getting dressed. She decided not to speculate upon what could have happened, concentrating instead on the immediate task of getting to the Detention Centre. As promised, the patrol car was waiting for her when she strode through the gardens and out to the trafficway. The peacekeeper acknowledged her identification, immediately set course, and took off.

The journey was short and Karla soon found herself dealing with two sleepy but curious cats, who couldn't understand why she wanted to take them for a walk in the middle of the night. They weren't difficult to convince, bounding into the patrol car with glee, now fully awake and in high spirits. Having never flown before, they pressed their noses to the windows, fascinated by the pattern of lights below. Karla made a determined effort to prevent any disquieting thoughts from disturbing them. However, when the patrol car landed near the Detention Centre's main entrance, the cats began to growl. The fur along their backs rose and their already bushy tails fluffed out to enormous proportions. Karla doubted whether their appearance would inspire anyone with confidence, though on the other hand, she didn't know why they were needed.

'Calm down, you two,' she muttered, as they walked towards the building.

Red Matilda and Fliedermus turned to look at her, their eyes glowing greenly in the dark, but took no further notice. They were both straining at their leashes, and despite Karla being a strong woman, she needed all her strength to keep them from pulling her over. The peacekeeper offered no assistance. Completely put out by the sight of the angry cats, he was nevertheless making an effort to give the appearance of being in control of the situation. Upon reaching the entrance, the security system acknowledged his retina scan, asked for Karla's handprints, then allowed them to enter. 'Interesting,' thought Karla, 'it just ignores the cats. Someone really ought to look into that.'

Søren was waiting for them, surrounded by half a dozen agitated and slightly aggressive peacekeepers, who dwarfed him with their size. He appeared to have been engaged in a heated exchange. His golden curls were in complete disarray and an uncharacteristic flush gave him the appearance of an angel having a fit of temper.

'Karla! Convince these idiots that cats are harmless... Please!' he pleaded, turning to her as soon as they entered the room.

Karla would have laughed if she hadn't realised the situation was serious. Unfortunately, the appearance of Red Matilda and Fliedermus did nothing to help. They looked ferocious and one peacekeeper had already aimed his immobiliser at them.

'May I suggest we all calm down?' she said, looking steadily at the peacekeepers and tugging at the leashes of the two cats, who were staring intently at one of the doors leading further into the building. 'I don't know what's happened, but these two are obviously reacting to some type of threat, so would someone be kind enough to tell us what's going on?' Karla sat down on the nearest chair and folded her arms, doing her best to adopt a stern expression. 'Do us all a favour, Peacekeeper,' she added. 'Put that damned immobiliser away or I'll file a complaint.'

The peacekeeper reddened, yet did as he was asked, and the two cats suddenly flopped down by Karla's feet and began cleaning themselves.

Raising an eyebrow, she said, 'Well, as far as they're concerned, there's no problem after all. Søren, do you want to tell me what you're doing here and why *we* all need to be here as well?'

'My dear Karla, you have already worked miracles.' Søren turned to the peacekeepers, who were all transfixed by the sight of the complete change in the two cats. 'See, ladies and gentlemen, harmless.' He picked up a chair, sat down next to Karla, then took her hand in his and said, 'Tamara, Mik and Possum are in the next room. They are all fine...now...but there was an attempt on Tamara's life earlier tonight while she was out walking Possum.' He forestalled Karla's interruption by lightly pressing her hand. 'The person is dead. Possum killed him before he could touch her. So, you see, these peacekeepers aren't sure whether to let us take our little cat home. Chiu Liow, Morag and Welcome are needed elsewhere at the moment, and in any case, it's important we convince these good people that Possum acted in a reasonable manner...under the circumstances.'

Søren mentally winced at the word "reasonable", but was taking great pains to make the peacekeepers realise that Possum reacted in the same way Tamara herself would have done, given the chance. He wasn't certain, but if Tamara had defended herself by slaying her attacker, surely there would have been no question of keeping her in custody? 'I have told the peacekeepers who *I* am,' he said, 'and that cats now have legal status, but they cannot bring themselves to take responsibility for letting us take

Possum home. We are all exhausted, so I hoped you could take over the negotiations.'

Strangely enough, Karla felt neither upset nor dismayed by Søren's words. 'Must be the cats,' she thought. 'I can sense they're helping me stay calm. They've completely settled down, which probably means nothing too serious is happening to the others at the moment.'

The tension in the room was by now visibly decreasing and one of the peacekeepers even stroked Fliedermus. Karla noticed he had a fresh bandage on his hand. The cat sat up to lick his face, while Red Matilda, with all the appearance of perfect contentment, began playing with a piece of fluff on the floor.

'May we see our friends?' asked Karla, standing up.

'Sure, why not?' replied the peacekeeper who had piloted the patrol car.

He crossed to the door Fliedermus and Red Matilda were staring at a short while ago and opened it. Possum came out, her tail in the air, looking as if she'd just had a quiet nap under a rug and what was all the fuss about? Mik and Tamara followed, holding hands and appearing quite relaxed. When she saw them, Fliedermus rolled onto her back, purring. Meanwhile, Red Matilda walked confidently over to Possum to bump foreheads with her. They sat down together and Red commenced a thorough cleanup of her friend. Karla saw her hesitate when she licked Possum's face, but decided this was not the time to comment or ask questions. If the peacekeepers were prepared to release her, questions could wait. Instead, she went over to Possum and picked her up, saying, 'Well, do we all go home, or do we get to spend the night here at the Government's expense?'

One of the peacekeepers stepped forward, handing her the Detention Centre's register. 'If you'll all sign here and add your thumbprints to the record, you can go, but the cat has to stay indoors until this case is fully investigated. If she gets out, it'll be your legal responsibility, Researcher Theophanous.'

All four silently signed the register, pressed their thumbs to its surface, and just as silently, left. As one of the peacekeepers escorted them to a waiting patrol car, not one word was exchanged, and no one spoke during the short flight to Mik's home. They watched the patrol car leave, and then, as if an enormous burden had been lifted from their shoulders, started laughing.

Karla, with tears in her eyes, managed to gasp, 'What are we laughing about? Let's get inside before we're arrested for creating a public disturbance!'

Once they were inside the greenhouse, she felt a wave of complete exhaustion flow from both Fliedermus and Red Matilda, and after they had all walked downstairs to the living room, the two cats collapsed onto the floor and, almost immediately, fell asleep. Possum curled up with them, tucking her head down next to Red's, then stretched out a paw and let the night do its healing work.

As the cats fell asleep, their human friends experienced a sense of utter confusion, of unreality difficult to describe. They looked at each other warily, until Søren eventually broke the silence.

'It seems we have been cat's-paws,' he said, with a grimace. 'I don't propose to add this experience to the Judge's knowledge base until I've done some personal research into what we seem to have just discovered. My respect for our feline companions has increased, but perhaps the general population would not feel the same. In fact, I think the Breeding Centres might close tomorrow if we told anyone our suspicions.'

Karla sat down, yawning, and stretched out her long legs. 'You know, I'm not sure I minded being a cat's-paw,' she said, sleepily rubbing a hand over her face. 'An enormous area of research has opened up for you, Alfie, but the peacekeepers wouldn't be too happy knowing they've been manipulated by a pair of moggies, even if they *are* cute! I think you'll just have to leave it for a bit and then do your experiments on your own dear cat, not Mik's...and in Greenland, not Australia. Otherwise, too many people might realise the connection, because I doubt if tonight's events will be kept secret. At the very least, though, there'll have to be some sort of public education campaign to make sure cat ownership is screened in future.' She yawned again and shook her head, making an effort to stay awake.

'Like becoming parents, almost,' said Mik, managing a lopsided grin, although his face was still too pale and his hands trembled slightly.

Tamara had collapsed into an armchair, resting her head in one hand. 'Sorry, but I don't completely agree with you, Karla. I think Søren *should* do some research, in a joint effort with the staff at the Breeding Centre, but as you say, maybe not into whether the cats can manipulate us. Actually, Søren, the sooner you talk to them the better, before any public rumours of killer cats begin circulating. They'll be put under pressure to change the genetic profile if that happens...and can you imagine what they'll say when we tell them Possum drank human blood? Thank goodness she vomited! If she hadn't, I've got the dreadful feeling all the kittens would be put down.' She stared at the others, horrified by her own words.

Karla blinked. 'By the Sun, you could be right, Tamara! That would be ghastly! I wonder if Chiu Liow Jones would be prepared to order the peacekeepers and ambutechs who know about this to keep quiet? If they were able to stop any news getting out to the public – or anyone else for that matter – we'd have a better chance of preventing a general reaction against cats. Søren, what about contacting him now?'

'What do *you* think, Mik?' asked Søren, frowning. 'After all, Possum is your cat.'

Mik had been pacing back and forth, listening to the conversation. He sat down on the floor next to Tamara and took her hand in his, doing his best to think rationally. 'I expect both Karla *and* Tamara are right, Søren. We *can't* let what Possum did become public knowledge, and I'm positive the cats wouldn't have a go at anyone unless there was no other choice. When I was attacked, Fliedermus didn't try to kill whoever it was who did it. The only reason Possum did what *she* did was because Tamara was about to be murdered and there was no other way of stopping it.

'If we go back to the time when people kept pet dogs as guard animals, it's not too hard to imagine that people nowadays might be just as ready to accept the risk presented by cats – in the same way they once accepted the risk of dogs attacking when they weren't supposed to. From what I've read, dogs were incredibly dangerous, but only certain breeds were banned and only after people became convinced that the dangers of keeping them far outweighed the benefits.'

'Very well. What you say makes sense,' replied Søren, looking intently at the sleeping cats. 'Our felines are far more intelligent than dogs ever were. I think we could even convince the public that a guard cat would be a nice idea. And, yes, there *is* one thing we must keep to ourselves for the time being: I agree that *no one* would take to the idea that they can actually control our emotions, not simply influence them occasionally when we need them to.'

'It's been known for centuries that cats can affect how we feel,' said Tamara, slowly twisting one of her curls around a finger, 'but I guess that isn't the same as having them consciously change our feelings to suit themselves. I just wonder what triggers them to do it?' She got up from her armchair to join Mik on the floor, putting an arm around his waist. He kissed her on the cheek and stroked her hair, finding the reassurance he needed in the warmth of her presence.

'The peacekeepers weren't aware they were being affected, that's for sure,' said Karla. 'And there's another point that needs looking into as well. Why could Mik hear Possum screaming when neither Fliedermus nor Red Matilda reacted? I don't understand.'

'I think that while cats are bonded to us and can communicate directly, maybe they only relate to each other in a more usual way,' suggested Mik, drawing Tamara closer. She nestled her head on his shoulder, listening. 'Or another possibility is that they sometimes share their emotions with each other, but have an understanding that we're more powerful when it comes to finding help. I've noticed they seem to know when to go to each other and when to come straight to me. I've often sensed they see us as their substitute parent.'

'What you say is correct, I'm sure,' agreed Søren, finally beginning to relax. 'It's well known in scientific circles that cats do not have psychic abilities when they are kittens, and that they only develop them if they form a relationship with a human before the age of one year.'

'What happens if they aren't adopted by someone?' asked Tamara.

'They are given hormone treatment to allow them to carry embryos, and later, to lactate after giving birth,' explained Søren. 'The whole process is completely normal. The nursing cats, as they are sometimes referred to, are valuable, as you can imagine, usually living for thirty years or more. Their relationship with the staff at the Breeding Centre stimulates their psychic abilities... However, we seem to be in agreement. We must speak with Peacekeeper Jones.'

Despite the late hour, he immediately contacted Chiu Liow, who listened carefully, the strain of the night's events marked on his face.

'I am obliged to inform Parliament of the death,' he said slowly, 'but am within my rights to keep the details to a bare minimum. It is, I believe, reasonable to request that the case be kept confidential until it has been resolved, as it would be were Possum human. However, although I personally agree that cats can now be regarded as having some form of status under the law, this is something to be determined by the Judge, then Parliament, and finally, the Federation. Also, you must realise, Søren, that while it is feasible for you to conduct the research you have described – and to give your opinions to the staff at the Breeding Centre – because of your friendship with Tamara and Mik there will need to be an independent assessment of your findings. I will make a request to Parliament for an appropriate expert to be found. Meanwhile, I take responsibility for giving you and your colleagues permission to speak to the genetic engineers, but I expect to be kept fully informed of your progress.' Chiu Liow unbent a little to add, 'I hope you are all, and I include the cats, as well as can be expected under the circumstances.'

Relieved by Chiu Liow's response, Søren smiled. 'We are far more comfortable than if we had stayed longer, keeping Possum company in the Detention Centre.'

'Yes, I gather the peacekeepers were highly impressed by you all, particularly Fliedermus and Red Matilda.'

Søren's amiable expression didn't alter by even the flicker of an eyelid. 'Ah...how nice of them to say so. I must admit we were relieved to be given permission to bring Possum home so soon. They were all extremely kind to us.' He paused, then added, 'Have you managed to establish the identity of the man who attempted to murder Tamara?'

'Morag MacIain could find no trace of his identity in either the Australian or the Federation files. For all official purposes, he does not exist.'

Mik was peering over Søren's shoulder, listening to the conversation. 'So there's no doubt he was hired for the job?' he asked, his tone harsh.

'No. In view of this, your contacting me is, shall we say, timely. I planned to speak to you all later, after you had a chance to rest, but I may as well warn you now. We can assume the attack on Tamara was another attempt to sabotage the research at Willsmere. There is no other logical inference. We seem to be dealing with a terrorist organisation of some magnitude and in my opinion it is essential that none of you are alone at work, at home, or anywhere else. At the very least, you should be accompanied by one of your cats. We've had ample demonstration tonight of their ability to protect their companions. Unfortunately, Possum must remain at home. Mik, would it be possible to lend Fliedermus and Red Matilda to Søren and Karla?'

'It would,' said Mik, 'but I don't want to leave Possum without one of them for company – at least, not for the time being.'

'In that case, which of you prefers to be the one to have a peacekeeper escort you everywhere?'

Søren spoke before Mik had a chance to consider the idea. 'I think it could be most amusing. I would be happy to volunteer, but only if you find one with a sense of humour.'

'Perhaps it should be a prerequisite for becoming a peacekeeper,' said Chiu Liow, with a weary shake of his head. Before saying goodbye, he gave Søren a comlink code. 'Use this code at any time. A peacekeeper will arrive within twenty minutes. In the meantime, I hope you all manage to get some sleep for what is left of the night.'

'Thank you,' said Søren. 'I hope you do too.'

While Søren and Mik were speaking with Chiu Liow, Karla had found a bottle of whisky and was now in the process of pouring a second liberal amount for Tamara and herself, then saw that Tamara had fallen asleep. Instead, she silently handed a glassful to each of the two men, which they drank appreciatively.

Outside, the clear night sky was filled with brilliant starlight, although few were awake to appreciate their beauty. The city was sleeping. Karla suddenly shivered. It was nearly two o'clock in the morning. 'I think we should give the labs a miss today,' she suggested. 'You don't mind if I stay here, do you, Mik?'

'No, of course not. Do you want to sleep here as well, Søren?' He gently shook Tamara's shoulder and she murmured, then turned onto her other side, and woke. He held out his hand and helped her to her feet.

'I am most definitely not going home,' replied Søren, picking up the used glasses and carrying them out to the kitchen. 'I have no wish to meet further peacekeepers tonight, unless I have no choice at all in the matter. Now, Karla and I can look after ourselves. *You* should take that woman friend of yours to bed. She is making the place look untidy.'

Mik smiled, glad to hear Søren's sense of humour had returned, but Tamara poked out her tongue at him, then held a hand over her mouth to cover a yawn. 'Goodnight,' she said. 'See you both later today.'

CHAPTER NINE

That Lamesa, now the former chairperson of Myanmar's Ministry for Agriculture, felt distinctly ill at ease would have been an understatement. The sense of power he experienced while gloating over his victim, only seven weeks before, had deserted him. The sweat rolled down his face as, in a soft, toneless voice, Meng Jarrah's researcher recited his list of crimes. Meng Jarrah herself sat in the background, a formidable presence, silently condemning him, a grim smile playing around the corners of her mouth. Occasionally, Freddi rose and moved to stand behind him, as if aware that the action made the hair on his neck stand on end.

Lamesa had always detested Meng Jarrah's researcher. His constant gentleness and quiet demeanour somehow brought out in him a wish to crush, to hurt, to dominate. However, the man's artificial vision gave him a strange superiority, which, as a member of the Ministry for Agriculture, Lamesa found disconcerting, particularly during their conferences on the future directions of the laboratory's activities. Also, Meng Jarrah had at times been present at the conferences and seemed to take pleasure in the fact that when they shook hands, he was forced to squint up at her. She smiled too often as well and didn't always agree with his assessment of Myanmar's research requirements...

Despite the heat of the Myanmarian summer, Lamesa felt cold. His parliamentary privileges could not shield him from the accusations made by the Mandalay Peacekeeping Force, although they had considerably delayed his being forced to come face-to-face with the man he had tortured – and the woman whose laboratory he so enjoyed vandalising. Strange... Lamesa had been certain the researcher would have insufficient courage to name him! He was now alone and isolated. It had been made clear that should he face trial, no assistance would be forthcoming from his 'colleagues'.

His concentration was wandering. The peacekeeper was questioning him again. What did she say? Lamesa's shoulders sagged. 'I have nothing left to tell you. Leave me alone! You have your witness. You know the extent of the crimes I have committed. I cannot explain why I acted the way I did.'

'But I don't think we *do* know the full extent of your crimes, Lamesa, and in fact I am quite certain you have a great deal to say to us. We will keep you company for as many hours and as many days as seem necessary until you find your memory has returned.' Freddi leaned towards him, her tone low and insistent: 'I simply *cannot* accept your facile statement that you took the remains of extinct rainforest species because you have a penchant for antiquities!'

She swung her chair around so that she no longer faced him, folded her arms and stared out the window. The silence was profound until Freddi eventually turned to face Lamesa again. 'And it appears you have some strange fetish for sabotaging other people's computer systems.' The scorn in her voice was evident. 'Or do you persist in denying you first stole, and then attempted to destroy, valuable research data? I can assure you, it's useless to attempt to incriminate any of the other staff members or guests of the Research Centre who were there on the night you chose to indulge your sadistic desires. Our psychologists do not believe any of them could have behaved the way you did! You, and you alone, are the culprit.'

When Lamesa looked away, Freddi walked over to him and said, 'Do you realise you face permanent sterilisation as a penalty for your crime? You have an application for fertility rights, don't you? There's only one way you can hope for the application to be even considered and I think you know what that way is.'

At Freddi's mute signal, Meng Jarrah and her researcher rose and left the room. They were sure Lamesa would throw himself upon the mercy of the Court by implicating as many of his accomplices as he possibly could. He hadn't survived in politics for twenty-four years without a keen sense of self-preservation. However, his life might well be forfeit. His 'colleagues' would not be overjoyed at being named.

While Meng Jarrah returned with her researcher to his home, Freddi continued with infinite patience to question and to probe. By sunset, as the cicadas began their deafening chorus, the remnants of Lamesa's brash confidence in his own invulnerability finally crumbled. Freddi was satisfied with the list she now held in her hand. Extra proof would be needed, but with Federation assistance, it would be found.

In Melbourne, Morag MacIain waited while Chiu Liow Jones and Welcome read the report Freddi had sent them that morning. It contained a transcript of the interview with Lamesa and included the names of three people. Two of the names belonged to senior managers of a Thai timber production and research company; a company which was already known to Morag. The other name belonged to a junior member of the Myanmarian Government. Lamesa admitted to having been approached by his fellow parliamentarian about seven months ago with the suggestion that a foreign company would pay highly for certain samples of rainforest species, extinct since the twenty-first century and held in the research laboratories managed by the Australian, Meng Jarrah. It was also hinted that the chairperson's private fantasies might be indulged without any great risk to himself.

At first, claimed Lamesa, he brushed his colleague aside, but a substantial number of credits began to appear in his personal account, paid on a regular basis. Upon his request, the payments were investigated, and as it turned out, were associated with an apparent agreement that he join the management collective of a certain Thai company. The payments were legitimate and below the level at which he was obliged to declare them to Parliament. Soon after these facts were presented to him, a confirmation document, with his thumbprint and signature, arrived at his comlink, together with an effusive letter of thanks for his support.

Unable to comprehend how such documents could have been created without his agreement, Lamesa slowly realised he had no choice but to either continue to accept the payments, or face the possibility of some form of public disgrace. He also realised that any organisation capable of gaining the cooperation of senior managers of an erstwhile highly respectable company, and which was willing to forge his thumbprint and signature, also had the ability to fabricate a scandal...or for that matter, to accumulate sufficient evidence about his private peccadillos to achieve the same effect. He had chosen to do nothing until such time as it became apparent what they really wanted from him.

After a time, his parliamentary colleague approached him again, offering certain amusements arranged by the Thai company managers and paid for by their expense account. At first he refused, but as the weeks went by, his imagination fuelled his hunger. The next time Lamesa was approached, he accepted. A great sense of shame overcame him after the evening's entertainment was finished, but with the repeated reassurances of his newfound friends, he succumbed to his longings. He rationalised the conflict between his public life, his deep attachment to his bondmate, and the guilty pleasures to which he had now become addicted. Lamesa even began to develop new confidence in his ability to overcome all obstacles to further career achievements. He also felt flattered by the attentions poured on him by the Thais, and forgot to ask himself when they would demand fulfilment of his side of the agreement into which he had been implicitly drawn.

Freddi's report included a detailed psychological profile. Seemingly minor traits noted in the initial security examination when Lamesa first entered Parliament many years ago, but which had not caused any undue alarm, now dominated his personality. He was undoubtedly a sadist, yet displayed the not uncommon contradiction between this hidden part of his life and that of his more public nature: that of a caring, responsible member of his community, committed to the goal of becoming a loving parent.

Welcome grimaced in disgust, while Chiu Liow's expression remained neutral, and Morag hummed quietly to herself. For the first time, Welcome fully understood the strength of character she possessed. As a Federation Investigator, Morag MacIain would necessarily need to have a very thorough understanding indeed of humanity's frailties, as well as the ability to insulate herself from the cynicism that could so readily result from close acquaintance with their more perverse deeds.

'I've already authorised the detention of the two Thais and the junior parliamentarian,' Morag announced, her expression reflecting deep satisfaction at their first substantial success. 'I think we can expect further reports from Freddi within two days. Meanwhile, I've organised a meeting with the management collective of the Thai company for this afternoon. I'll need Rohan Maerz's approval to obtain a full disclosure of their business operations and financial circumstances before I can arrange to have their assets frozen and their business premises locked...but I prefer to talk to them first. They *may* volunteer information, and it may be revealing to hear what they have to say, given they might not realise we have the authority to take these steps. I certainly can't recall the Federation having to do so during the time I've operated as an investigator.'

'They're not an international organisation, are they?' asked Chiu Liow. 'How could they have the resources to undertake crimes on the scale we're dealing with?' He had said little while they studied the report, but could picture how well the interrogation had been handled. As a child, Freddi often play-acted such scenes with her friends, and inevitably won the subtle word games and battles of will.

'They may be acting in conjunction with other companies,' suggested Morag. 'It's not unusual for corporations to be part of a conglomerate, with its internal connections well hidden from the general public – although not from us, if we look hard enough. However, at the moment, there's a limit to how financially successful any private organisation *can* be in the timber trade, no matter how large they are, due to the massive extent of Federation-sponsored projects around the world. Therefore, it's not difficult to conceive of an attempt being made to sabotage the Federation effort in order to gain a competitive advantage – and, of course, to steal some of our latest research at the same time.' She paused to sip the tea Welcome had prepared for them earlier, then said, 'We need to review the information we've collected on Teak Australia and decide whether we treat them similarly to the Thai company. Do you agree?'

Chiu Liow and Welcome both nodded. 'We should first come to some decision about Marika and Gwenllian,' added Welcome. 'I don't think we can continue holding them under full surveillance for much longer. We have no further real evidence against either of them. I also think it'd be useful if at least one of them returned to work so we can observe their behaviour.'

'I agree,' said Chiu Liow. 'Gwenllian's brother, Owain, has contacted me once a week to protest against his sister's treatment, so I decided it would be best for me to speak with him in the hope that he'd assist us. He's been extremely cooperative, despite his hostility, which means I'm still convinced Gwenllian isn't involved, even if Teak Australia is. So, in my opinion, she's the one who should return to work.'

'Do you think Teak Australia *could* be involved without Owain knowing?' Morag reached for one of the chocolate biscuits Welcome had provided.

'The undoubted sincerity of his protests may hide guilty knowledge of some type,' said Welcome, taking a biscuit and examining it carefully before putting it whole into his mouth, 'although,' he continued, after he had chewed and swallowed the biscuit, 'I think Owain would have done his best to prevent any course of action that could endanger his sister, whom *I* don't think is involved either, Morag.'

'He might not be in a position to do anything.'

'True... Not if this operation is as big as we think it is. It's a strange situation, though. We have Marika working closely with a major shareholder, Mervyn Bradshaw, who despite being extraordinarily wealthy appears to have a perfectly clean taxation history. Then there's Gwenllian, who has a brother employed as a research coordinator with the Department of Agriculture, which just happens to be the government body with the closest working relationship to Willsmere and Lamington. Furthermore, Gwenllian works with her brother on a joint research project that's of considerable relevance to investors in the timber industry. Not only that, there's the administrator at the Central Computer Site who has a business venture with one of the directors of Teak Australia, in the form of a small furniture importing company — which, fortunately, seems to be beyond reproach.' Welcome crossed one leg over the other as if to emphasise his point, paused to brush a crumb from his vest, then added, 'So far.'

'And finally, there's the Myanmarian connection.' Chiu Liow picked up the thread of the summary. 'Myanmar has only one well-established, productive private timber company and it relies heavily on Teak Australia for its sales. It also relies heavily on the only viable transport company in the country, which in turn has recently sold a considerable part of its shares to the international giant, Wyvern Meridian. In addition, we have the unanswered question of why Wyvern Meridian's own timber plantation in Myanmar hasn't been successful, although we do have one theory.'

'Wyvern Meridian still has the application before Parliament for their Australian leasehold, too,' said Morag. 'I gather the Willsmere researchers are close to finalising their evaluation of the compatibility between the company's land regeneration and timber production proposal and Willsmere's own model. Unfortunately for us, though, in theory their conclusions must remain confidential until they've been independently validated by the Federation.' She hesitated. 'Actually, I wonder if Yuen Fong Lau would help us get just a tiny peek at the findings before they're passed on? I don't think there's any way we can access Oslo's assessment of the situation until the leasehold application is either formally accepted or rejected, so in the meantime, it'd be useful to know what Mik and Tamara have come up with.'

'Yes, I think you're right, Morag,' said Chiu Liow. 'So, until we know more, to my mind, there are only three possibilities.' He leaned forward, resting his elbows on the table in a highly uncharacteristic gesture that reflected just how relaxed he was becoming in Morag and Welcome's company. 'Given the scale of the crimes we're investigating, we can assume no single, small company is responsible on their own undertaking. Assuming for the moment that no national government or member of the Federation Assembly is involved – although we can't rule out the possibility – then either Wyvern Meridian is attempting to increase their global holdings at the expense of both the Federation and other private companies; the smaller companies have formed an informal cartel in order to compete with Wyvern Meridian; or Wyvern Meridian and the private companies have formed an alliance to compete with the Federation.'

'You seem to be excluding Rohan Maerz and other members of the FSIU from your list,' replied Morag, with a slight grimace.

'Unfortunately, if a member of the Special Investigation Unit is involved, I doubt we'll be able to find any direct evidence to convict them – at least, not within the foreseeable future. Now, we agreed to eliminate other possibilities first and I suspect that's still our best option. If we're unable to reach a convincing conclusion, we'll need to propose a defensive course of action and take the matter to the Federation Assembly.'

'That could take forever, Chiu Liow,' said Welcome.

'Better that than never.'

'Well...we still have a long way to go before we can approach the Federation Assembly,' said Morag, 'and I do agree that we should keep to our original plan. In the meantime, I think I'll take the risk of making my reports to Rohan rather brief and sending them in as late as possible. If he's involved, it could give us a small edge. He's prone to anxiety if he isn't kept fully informed, and as he's still human, I think, anxiety may make him less cautious. He'll merely set his flunkies onto me with tedious regularity.' Morag's eyes widened as she smiled, which distracted Chiu Liow for a moment when he once again noticed just how green they were.

Welcome laughed. 'Why don't you just ask your comlink to create and send standard replies? You wouldn't even have to read their rubbish.'

'Rohan knows all about automated replies because he absolutely delights in using them himself. On the other hand, he insists on having personal reports from his staff, and they in turn are required to demand a personal interview with anyone Rohan's annoyed with. But don't worry, I regard dealing with the FSIU bureaucracy as a pleasant pastime. Light relief, you might say. So, getting back to Teak Australia, and for that matter, the other private companies on our list, what have we decided?'

'I don't think we can treat Teak Australia in the same manner as the Thai company. We have no actual evidence against them,' replied Chiu Liow, and Welcome waved a hand in agreement. 'I'll arrange to meet with their Board of Directors and ask my contacts to use the information your investigators have already gathered, Morag, to begin checking the other companies on your list. I think Freddi should be able to handle the one in Myanmar. My colleague in Brazil is waiting for me to let him know of any further work we need done, so presumably he could undertake a thorough scrutiny of the research company you're interested in, which only leaves Papua and Malaysia. The investigation into the attack on Meng Jarrah's Niu Bougainville laboratory still isn't finalised, but I'm sure the local peacekeepers will be able to help us. Also, the Papuan timber operation we want to know more about is a relatively small concern, dealing mainly with recycling and restoration work, isn't it, Morag?'

'Yes,' she replied. 'The Malaysian company is small, too. They've done some genetic engineering of a local species of earthworm to increase its tolerance of high soil moisture, and hence its ability to live in some of the low-altitude forests.' Morag consulted her notes. 'I gather earthworms increase soil fertility and aeration. I'll speak to the local peacekeepers about them before I come back to Australia...the company, I mean, not the earthworms... They may be more cooperative if they receive a personal request.'

Welcome stood up to make a fresh pot of tea. 'Why *has* the Papuan investigation taken so long? You haven't told us anything about it yet.'

'I've put off telling you because the situation there is particularly serious. There was no problem tracing the security breach that resulted in Meng Jarrah's laboratories being vandalised and a valuable soil sample being stolen. One of the cleaners confessed soon after being interrogated by the peacekeepers, then cheerfully paid the fine, despite it being quite substantial. He also told them who employed him to do it. However, as in the case of the attack on Tamara, no such person exists in our records. Then, two weeks ago, faults appeared in the Papuan transport system, the library system, and the salary system. Passengers were taken to the wrong destination, libraries failed to transmit requests, and incorrect salaries were paid to all information technologists.'

'Why on Earth would anyone bother to tamper with those particular applications?!' exclaimed Chiu Liow.

'I think someone has a warped sense of humour and is playing with us,' answered Morag, her fingers lightly tapping her comlink, 'and I don't appreciate the joke.'

Reflecting upon the outcome of his work with the Breeding Centre's three genetic engineers, Søren Thorup was amused to remember how, at their first tense meeting, they each clutched a nursing cat in their laps. Also, their expressions and appearance were so similar it was tempting to believe they had all been genetically engineered themselves! If the subject of their discussions hadn't been so serious, he would have had trouble refraining from laughing out loud. Instead, he picked up a cat and began stroking it in rhythm with the others, but the satire went unnoticed.

Contrary to his and his friends' fears, the engineers' tension was generated only by their concern for the safety of their charges. They were horrified by Søren's account of Possum's behaviour, but after rushing from the room to consult each other, had been unanimous in defending the cat. They even offered to have her examined for brain damage, and it took a considerable amount of time before they accepted his assurance that she had suffered no permanent harm.

'Are you quite sure the kitty is well?' one of them had asked, earnestly leaning forward and holding the resident cat even more closely to his chest. It was purring so loudly, and in unison with the others, that Søren had difficulty making himself heard.

'She has two others to keep her company, as well as two people to take care of her,' he almost shouted. 'If there was anything to worry about, I'm sure the other cats would have let us know...somehow.'

'You didn't tell us there were two others! It makes a difference, you know.'

The genetic engineers chortled happily and the purring increased yet again. The peacekeeper who had accompanied Søren turned from his study of the closest batch of kittens and looked into the room, his face a picture of classic amazement. Søren carefully placed his cat on the floor, walked over to the open doorway and stood outside the room, listening.

'Remarkable... A cat orchestra. If only we could teach them to harmonise!' Patting the bemused peacekeeper on the arm, he returned inside.

'Is there any means of turning down the volume?' he asked, keeping his expression neutral.

The engineers, in perfect time, stopped patting their cats and the creatures obediently jumped from their laps, burbled a few times, then snuggled up together in a heap of multicoloured fur.

One of the engineers apologised: 'Sorry, we're so used to them, we forget it's a bit much for visitors.' He retrieved some knitting from a bag he was carrying and, without needing to watch his hands while he worked, asked Søren what he had in mind in coming to discuss Possum's behaviour with them.

'My colleagues and I hoped you might be willing to collaborate with me in doing some research into the way the cats choose to communicate with us...in contrast to their methods of communicating with each other, that is. We also thought you could perhaps advise us on the issue of educating the public with respect to this new behavioural trait we have discovered.' Søren chose his words carefully to ensure the broadest possible interpretation could be made.

'Ah hah! I know where you're heading! *You* think the public will demand that our cats be altered to prevent them from protecting their companions in an emergency, don't you?' remarked the knitter, wagging his head from side to side.

Søren inclined his own head slightly.

'Well, you're wrong. They'll love it! Our problem will be just the opposite. You know, we don't like people much. We prefer the cats. They're honest and reliable. Not like people... A lot of them would take the chance to train their cats to be killers. They did it with dogs in past centuries and if we let them, they'll do it with cats now. No, as far as I'm concerned, and I'm sure I speak for us all,' and he inclined his head towards the others, who bobbed theirs in unison, 'it's the people who should be vetted, not the cats.' He vigorously nodded his head this time.

Søren smiled. He had expected a colder, more objective environment at the Breeding Centre. Well, this was better, he thought. They would almost certainly put their full and considerable weight behind a public education program, as well as into the research. He decided to put the next proposition to them: 'Have any of you contemplated increasing cats' status under the law?'

He went on to outline the role Fliedermus had played in the Willsmere case. The three engineers listened in complete silence. Even the knitter stopped knitting. 'You must understand that what I have told you is strictly confidential,' Søren concluded. 'The matter is still *sub judice* and will be for some time. The peacekeepers know I am telling you all this, but you have a legal obligation not to tell anyone else until the proceedings have been completed.'

'We take it that *you* are of the opinion they already have status under the law?' said the second genetic engineer.

'Cats have *some* status here in Australia, but the matter will need to be pursued through the proper channels...the Judge, Parliament, and finally, the Federation Assembly...if it is to be confirmed worldwide.'

The engineers looked at each other and seemed to come to a silent agreement. 'Our main concern is to protect the cats,' said the third one. 'If some unscrupulous person managed to get past our future screening processes and subsequently got their cat to attack someone, the cat would need to have full legal protection.' They looked at each other again and then the third engineer added, 'And in any situation similar to the one you described earlier, the cat must be able to have its actions defended. Yes, indeed.'

The second genetic engineer added a further point: 'If the legal status of cats is to be confirmed, then research into their behaviour with respect to protecting their companions – and each other, for that matter – must be entered into the Judge. I think you realise, Søren Thorup, that *you* are disqualified from doing further work of this type due to your own personal involvement. Therefore, I think we can guess your motives in coming to us.' She smiled to make sure the last point was not taken as an insult.

Søren returned the smile.

'As to public education and a screening process, I'm sure we can collaborate with you on developing a suitable program. How long do you think we have before Possum's case is tried and made public?'

'Oh...that's hard to estimate. It *is* rather complex, and I regret to say there are other matters involved which I am not at liberty to divulge. My sincere apologies. However, I think we can safely say we have at least a few months.'

The conversation became increasingly animated and lasted another two hours. Søren left the Breeding Centre in a state of supreme contentment. No hint of his suspicion, that cats could strongly influence human emotions when they chose, had crept into their discussions. He was certain it never entered the genetic engineers' minds that their model species was even more powerful and intelligent than they gave them credit for. Did it concern him that the cats could exercise such powers if they wished? On the other hand, perhaps they could only do so under extreme circumstances, just as Possum had killed only under the most extreme provocation? Quite frankly, he wasn't sure he cared. After all, so many other factors affected emotions. Why worry about one more?

So, how should he begin finding out just how extensive their powers were? Perhaps a sociological approach might be useful? If it could be shown that cat owners – perhaps 'owners' was an inappropriate term – companions, then, were often happier with life than non-cat companions? No... This had already been shown, and besides, it didn't indicate any conscious effort on the cat's part.

The best way to at least begin, Søren finally decided, was to approach the problem by searching for anecdotal evidence involving unusual circumstances in any way similar to the incident in which Fliedermus and Red Matilda had, without any doubt at all, controlled and directed the emotions of the peacekeepers at the Detention Centre. He used the Judge's search capabilities to list any cases involving cats since its implementation one hundred and thirty years ago. There were only four. In each instance, the cat in question defended either their companion or their companion's family, yet none had needed to literally attack; the sight of the enraged creature had been sufficient to dissuade the assailant. The consistently strange aspect of each case, however, was that the culprits did not attempt to escape, but remained transfixed until the peacekeepers arrived to arrest them. So, why had Fliedermus been unable to halt Mik's attackers? Presumably because, exactly like humans, individual cats reacted differently to stressful situations and each had differing capabilities.

Søren was not at all happy with the meagre evidence he had managed to collect, but knew intuitively that Fliedermus, Possum and Red Matilda were not alone in their abilities. Still, for the time being, at least his curiosity had been satisfied, and soon afterwards, when he told Karla, Tamara and Mik what he had discovered, all four confirmed their decision not to make all their conclusions public.

Under the auspices of a public safety program, the media were invited to attend a special tour of the Breeding Centre. As a result, there had been a satisfactory amount of cooing and giggling when the kittens and nursing cats lived up to their reputation as entertainers and endearing objects of affection. The small crowd inspected the actual breeding laboratories as well, but their interest in this aspect of the Centre was relatively low.

The gentechs finally rounded up the visitors and took them for sumptuous refreshments, which were followed by a short address by the local Member of Parliament. The Member praised the work of the Centre and the contribution made by cats to the sum of humanity's happiness, *etcetera*, then told her audience that certain enquiries into records held by the Judge indicated cats had potential value as guardians of their human companions. She went on to show a recording of a recent and simple experiment where a mock attack on a cat's companion failed to arouse the cat's protective behaviour. Twitching her ears, the cat seemed more alert for a few moments, then lost interest and began cleaning herself. Finally, archival footage from the year 2056 was used to show the behaviour of dogs trained to protect 'police', as peacekeepers were once referred to. In contrast to the cats, the dogs attacked mock assailants.

The Member of Parliament explained that whereas the dogs took their cue from the actions of the attacker, the current-day cat analysed the person's emotions. No one knew how they did this, but it was slowly becoming common knowledge that they could. The conclusion was that cats would be ideal as guardians because they would only act to protect people in a genuine emergency. A patter of applause greeted this statement and then the media were sent on their way, merrier than when they arrived thanks to the generous supply of alcoholic beverages.

In this way, the campaign got off to a nice, warm, fuzzy start. The next step, however, was not so easy to stage-manage. Parliament had first to decide whether the Breeding Centre should be given the resources to undertake psychological profiling of applicants. Meanwhile, committee meetings were held *in camera* and the decision made that it was not in anyone's interest to release details to the public until the entire investigation into the worldwide series of incidents connected with the case had been concluded. Søren was amazed such a sensible decision had been made so quickly, but then, he was inclined to be somewhat cynical.

Chiu Liow Jones accompanied him to Canberra to fill in some of the more descriptive portions missing from his initial report into the attack on Tamara. A few of the honourable Members appeared ill when they began to understand what actually occurred. Fidgeting with an empty water glass, one cleared his throat a few times before hesitantly asking whether the cat in question was exceptionally large and ferocious, and were they right in understanding that its owner kept two others?

'In fact, it's unusually *small*, and spends a great deal of its time hiding beneath rugs and bedclothes,' replied Chiu Liow. 'And yes, there are two others who are considerably larger, but not in the least ferocious.' He was unable to resist the temptation to elaborate further: 'One of them often spends part of its day hanging upside-down from curtain rails. Its name is Fliedermus.'

Some of the Members tittered, while another asked, 'You're completely sure they've never been fed meat?'

'Absolutely,' answered the peacekeeper. 'Cats are unable to digest animal protein.' He refrained from telling them that Possum drank some of the blood from her victim's torn throat. They looked horrified enough as it was. Murder, and even culpable manslaughter, was rare, let alone the killing of people by either tame or wild animals...and after all, the cat *did* vomit afterwards.

'Well,' said the Chairperson, rising from her seat, 'if there are no further questions, I suggest we make a decision on this matter. As usual, I will ask for your opinions, and afterwards, we will attempt to arrive at a consensus.'

The Members gave their opinions, but after much discussion, failed to reach the desired agreement. Several were strongly opposed to any further form of psychological profiling. After all, to keep a cat was not as large a responsibility as it was to have a child, and presumably cats were never allowed to wander alone in the open? The case in question was a complete rarity, and no public threat was posed by the creatures.

While Søren listened, he began to change his original opinion as to the need for any further form of public education campaign related to the potential danger posed by cats, or even for more elaborate screening of the Centre's applicants. It appeared their fears may have been unfounded. He also realised that if funds weren't used for these purposes, more might be available for research, so he stood up, tapped the table around which they were seated, and waited until his audience took notice of him.

'I am pleased to find the honourable Members have been so wonderfully eloquent,' he began, smiling pleasantly, 'that I have changed my mind about applying for this funding, being now convinced there will be no public outcry against cats. It has also been consistently noted in scientific circles that cats are unable to bond with highly antisocial or violent personalities. I therefore withdraw my request in conjunction with the Breeding Centre for resources to establish a psychological profiling scheme for potential cat companions.'

He received a few startled looks, but ignored them and said, 'Instead, may I suggest we consider the next item on the agenda – the provision of funding for research into the circumstances under which cats communicate with humans and with each other, and how they are able to impact the human mind in the manner the cat, Possum, did. You will recall the person who attempted to murder Researcher Tamara Solanum died of a brain haemorrhage, and not from having his throat torn out. We feel we should know how cats can do this.'

'Surely an understatement, Researcher Thorup,' said the Chairperson, raising an eyebrow.

Søren raised one hand in a gesture of acceptance, but said nothing further on this particular point, until requested to do so by the Members while they deliberated.

After sitting still for so long, Chiu Liow took the opportunity to stand up and stretch a little. As he did, he made an effort to resolve what had been bothering him about the whole incident since he first read the report given to him by the peacekeepers at the Detention Centre. It escaped him yet again. Nevertheless, feeling sure the answer would come to him eventually, he sat down, and before too much longer, the Members were able to arrive at a decision: the research would be funded, although before resources could be allocated, an exact proposal would need to be submitted for further consideration.

Søren remembered how he had groaned inwardly at the idea of putting together the proposal. He was still having difficulty with it and while he was thinking about the meeting and what to write, the early morning sun had moved until it now shone in his eyes. He shifted away from the glare, and as he did, his comlink told him there was an incoming call from Karla.

'Hi, Alf,' she greeted him. 'I've just called to let you know Tamara's finished the Wyvern Meridian comparison – and I'm stunned! She and Mik found no difference at all between their model and ours as far as the long-term environmental impacts are concerned!' Karla's face clearly expressed her disbelief and she looked as if she had been awake all night. Her short hair stood up in spikes and there were dark smudges under her eyes.

'You appear tired, my friend,' said Søren, with a sympathetic smile. 'Come for a visit and let me prepare a good meal for you, then you can tell me all about these extraordinary results.'

'I hope you've got something more substantial than food, Søren. I need it!' She gave him a wry grin, and in a vain attempt to make herself look more presentable, ran a hand through her rumpled hair, then promised to see him within the hour.

Hand in hand, Owain and Gwenllian walked towards the Central Computer Site. Owain was proud of his sister's composure, but knew the effort was taking its toll. The skin of her face, usually pale, seemed almost translucent. In defiance, she wore her most dazzling garb of deep wine red, together with the silver armlet he had given her three years ago. They stopped at the security entrance, where Owain placed his arm around her shoulders. The gatekeeper smiled at Gwenllian, as he had done for so many years. His face was deeply lined and the hand he held out to her, shrunken with age. The young woman took it in both her own, tears trickling down her cheeks. Gently, the old man withdrew his hand and tenderly patted Gwenllian's face.

'Don't cry now, Gwen. There's no one but me here who knows what's happened, other than Melrose and Yilmaz. Everyone else thinks you and Mari went on a little holiday together to get over Thanh's death. Just act as if you've had a marvellous time, and if you need to cry, say it's because you're reminded of Thanh.'

Gwenllian smiled wistfully, kissed Owain's cheek, and glanced at the retina scanner. The gates opened, allowing her to enter the place that once seemed so confining yet now gave her the sense of coming back to safety and sanity. She turned and waved, her heart lighter than it had been for many weeks.

*

Marika stared at the jacaranda tree outside her greenhouse. Its blooms of sky-blue irritated her. Everything irritated her. Mervyn Bradshaw particularly irritated her. He hadn't replied to any of the messages left for him over the past five weeks. Earlier, when she told him about being placed under surveillance, expecting sympathy, he merely replied, in his typically offhand fashion, that he hoped her agreement with the Bendigo Theatre Company wouldn't be affected, and when could they expect to view her completed 'holotype'?

He was always so clever at inventing new terms. Marika had considered creating an entirely new holograph, but Bradshaw told her not to be so fastidious. Thanh, dead or alive, was still the perfect subject for their opening night. He even thought the fact that the performer was no longer alive would add a certain something to the dramatic impact of the event. Thanh had had an ethereal quality in any case, with his fine, wavy black hair, delicate features and slender frame. How suitable he should now indeed be part of the ether... Bradshaw had laughed at his own joke, but Marika glowered at him, fuming inwardly.

She turned away from the view, which had done nothing to make her feel more composed, and instead looked at her son, who was absorbed in watching a preying mantis eat a small fly. He, at least, seemed unaffected by her moods and her predicament. She wondered how long he would mourn her loss if she was found guilty of having assisted Thanh to his death. Yet, surely, it wouldn't come to that?

CHAPTER TEN

The alpine lake of Vierwaldstaattersee was calm, with only a light summer breeze ruffling its waters. The two-kilometre peak of Pilatus dominated the horizon, dark grey against a cloudless blue sky. Luzern nestled at its foot, as it had done for over a thousand years. The Swiss had preserved its monuments such that even the Chapel Bridge, built in 1333, had been retained, its timbers glowing warmly from the acrylic resins binding the fibres. In an attempt to erase the anxiety Morag MacIain's latest report had caused him, Rohan Maerz spent several hours contemplating the Federation art collection in the Kunsthaus. As he now walked past the Bahnhof and down Pilatusstrasse, he revelled in the intensely civilised atmosphere of the quaint buildings. Even the summit of Pilatus had been conquered and tourists continued to flock to its restaurants, as they had done for centuries. The steep mountainsides grew few trees and those that were there were comforting in their symmetry. Even the white swans on the lake resembled china ornaments rather than the wild birds they actually were. He slowed his pace. Walking tired him unbearably, but there was little choice. The city allowed no forms of private transport to clutter the streets, while public transport was limited to the lake and the mountain.

Usually conscientious in providing him with sufficient detail, Morag's recent reports were suspiciously brief, as well as late by anything up to four days. Granted, her time was more than utilised by the demands of her work, but surely she understood his need to be kept fully informed! His left eyelid twitched and his craving for sweets suddenly overcame his usual awareness of the social niceties forbidding overindulgence in food. He veered towards the nearest cafe to study the array of pastries and cakes before him. Throwing caution aside, he selected five and ordered a pot of Darjeeling tea. Impatiently waving away the offer to have the cakes boxed and gift-wrapped, he ignored the waiter's expression of contempt and sat down at one of the brightly decorated tables.

As he ate the cakes and drank the deliciously hot tea, Rohan avoided the scornful glances of the people at neighbouring tables. Instead, he went over again in his mind the more satisfying aspects of what Morag had written. It seemed that once their disgraceful involvement in the Myanmarian incident became public knowledge, the timber company that had operated

121

for so long and so profitably in Thailand would be on the verge of collapse. The management collective had of course denied any complicity in the activities of their two colleagues, now placed under detention. Rohan could well believe they had been kept in ignorance, but were nevertheless accountable under the collective's charter. Morag's request to have the company's assets frozen and their business premises locked, pending a full inquiry into their financial operations, had been welcome, and he granted it immediately.

Nevertheless, Morag had barely mentioned that she intended to speak to the peacekeepers in Malaysia about the follow-up examination of a local enterprise involved in genetic engineering of some sort – earthworms, that was it. Rohan wrinkled his nose in distaste. The meeting would have taken place by now, and yet he still had not been informed as to its outcome. He tapped his fingers against the side of his teacup, then winced as some of the liquid spilled, burning his hand.

Most provoking of all, however, had been the entire absence of any information regarding the outcome of the investigation into the manslaughter by that cat with the ridiculous name – he supposed it was reasonable to refer to the death of Tamara's would-be assailant as manslaughter, given that the Melbourne Peacekeepers, with due process, had released the cat into the custody of its owner, on condition that it be kept indoors, thereby implying it enjoyed legal status. In the past, such an animal would have been shot immediately!

Rising slowly, Rohan once again felt an intense desire to meet the Australians and their felines. Meanwhile, he would demand in-depth reports! Not in person, of course. That would introduce a totally unacceptable tone of confrontation between Morag and himself, and it had to be admitted, he missed her presence and her gentle teasing.

More composed than before the tea and cakes, he began to enjoy the lingering sunshine as he continued his laboured walk, turning into the Hirschmattstrasse and heading towards the Zentral Bibliothek.

The archives of the Zentral Bibliothek in Luzern held material covering centuries of scientific research and opinion. Twentieth and twenty-first century concern over the ongoing destruction of the world's soils, waterways, oceans and forests – and the very air the idiots breathed, thought Rohan – was revealing. So much of the knowledge painfully accumulated over thousands of years had been lost during the chaos of the twenty-second and twenty-third centuries, yet sufficient remained to allow the people of the twenty-fifth century to not only survive, but to make progress in restoring a great deal of Earth's ecological balance.

Leaning forward as his eye was caught by a title, Rohan gave a small sigh of satisfaction. *Medicines from the Rainforest*, by someone with the most appropriate name of 'Bird', in a magazine popular at the time: *New Scientist*. The date of the article was the seventeenth of August 1991. He scanned the pages and was gratified to find a particularly pertinent paragraph:

> Reversing the trend of destruction is now an international priority. But saving the rainforests and the plants that live in them will require global cooperation in which many conflicts of interest – notably between developed and underdeveloped nations – will have to be resolved. One strategy which is being increasingly promoted within this debate is the formation of 'extractive reserves' in the forests that can support sustainable development. The late Chico Mendez campaigned on behalf of rubber tappers for the creation of extractive reserves in Amazonia which could support sustainable exploitation of the forests. Workers within the reserves would collect rubber, brazil nuts, cocoa and other forest products and sell them to urban buyers. Sustainability would be guaranteed because workers must maintain their environments or risk losing their livelihoods. Brazil already has some extractive reserves, although there is still conflict between commercial loggers and the indians and rubber tappers who live in the reserves. The development of new drugs from the forests could provide additional arguments and incentives against the destruction of the forests by logging.

Settling back again in the comfortable armchair, Rohan played with the idea that suddenly struck him. As far as he could remember, there was a small pharmaceutical company in Brazil which had done precisely as the article of the past recommended. And if his memory served him yet again, they were on Morag MacIain's list of organisations due for their share of scrutiny.

Pharmaceutics always had been, and most likely always would be, a rich source of financial profit, and hence, power. Given that many of the drugs used in centuries past were no longer needed due to the elimination of most of the common causes of illness and disease, and that the majority of those still in use were produced by the Federation using genetically engineered bacteria or other relatively inexpensive processes, it wasn't difficult to understand that the company in question was small. Nevertheless, there was still a market for, amongst other things, painkillers, anti-histamines, and compounds to combat the side effects of the latest viral or fungal onslaught; as well as illicit drugs to delight the leisure seekers for whom the pleasures offered by an ordered society were insufficient.

He entered a comlink code and began the latest round in the series of complex negotiations that were now so necessary and which, happily, also alleviated the overwhelming boredom that had in previous years begun to creep into his role as FSIU Coordinator.

The first missive from Rohan Maerz reached Morag MacIain the next day. She chuckled as she read the terse request to send a more comprehensive account of her findings – at once! – and calculated how late her next report could safely be. Perhaps at least eight days.

Earlier in the day, Freddi had also contacted her, with the news that Lamesa, his political stature having completely crumbled, had committed suicide. Morag could not find it in herself to pity him, while Freddi regretted only that no further evidence would be forthcoming from this source.

The two had found a few minutes to indulge in a little personal gossip, having already begun to form a friendship. When Morag, with a wry smile, confessed her growing attachment to Chiu Liow, Freddi had grinned sympathetically. She loved her half-brother, yet knew that his usual cheerful reserve towards women was a significant barrier, which Morag, despite her abundant charms, might find difficult to overcome.

'Have you noticed how his speech mannerisms change when he's with people he doesn't know well?' she had asked.

'I have, I have!' Morag answered, laughing. 'But I've also noticed he's now in his relaxed mode when I'm around, which is at least encouraging. My main problem is that he seems so self-sufficient and in charge of his life, I hesitate to introduce anything that might damage his tranquillity, if that's the right word. I'd also be sorry to jeopardise our excellent working relationship.'

'He's definitely highly organised and doesn't like having his serenity, as I'd describe it, disturbed. Has he hinted in any way that he's attracted to you?'

'Well, I suppose he has. He did invite me to his home, but that was the night Tamara was assaulted, which meant I didn't have the opportunity to take up his offer. He hasn't repeated it, either.'

'Perhaps you should remind him. I don't see how it could do any harm.'

'True... He'll either retreat into formality again or take the risk of letting me in behind his defences. I must admit, though, I'd be hurt if he *did* retreat. Still, where would we be if we weren't willing to take a few risks?'

'I agree, but Morag, there are risks, and then there are *risks*! I've taken an even bigger one than you have. I think I'm falling in love with Meng Jarrah.'

'Freddi, you aren't!'

'Yes, I was attracted the first time we met. But if you think Chiu is reserved, you should try getting close to a woman who's about the strongest person I've ever met, and who, as far as I know, has never contemplated forming a relationship with anyone!' Freddi sighed in exasperation, both at her own unusual reluctance to make the first move, and at the idea that if she did, Meng Jarrah might not reciprocate.

'Meng Jarrah might be a strong woman, but I think she's also an empathic one,' said Morag, understanding Freddi's situation and wanting to give some encouragement. 'I doubt whether she'd dislike you for approaching her, even if she didn't welcome it. Any sensitive, intelligent person can only be warmed by someone else's love, whether they return it or not...and I suppose I've just answered my own doubts, come to think of it.' She shook her head and grinned.

'Morag, it's strange how people are so often threatened by love. I imagine it's because many see love as a way of meeting only their own needs, instead of it also being a way of meeting someone else's. I'm glad I'm essentially a rational person. It'd be ghastly to be the type who tries to force someone into loving them. How humiliating!'

'You're absolutely right, Freddi! And I've just thought of something. You have a cat, don't you? Wouldn't she pick up your caring for Meng Jarrah and show you in some way whether your feelings were returned?'

'Probably. It's tempting. I've only had my cat with me the once when she was around, but it's a bit of a cowardly way around the issue. It would be different if I didn't fully realise what my feelings were towards Meng Jarrah; Shela would just be helping me find out. As it is, I ought to take the conscious risk myself.'

'You're very brave. There *is* another way of looking at it, though. People don't necessarily fall in love with each other at first sight, so if you declare yourself too soon, it could put a halt to any attachment Meng Jarrah might be forming.'

'I think you've pinpointed my problem. What's the answer?' Freddi made a face, eyebrows raised, her eyes wide.

Morag laughed. 'If I knew, I wouldn't be in such a dilemma myself.'

'You've had a lot more contact with Chiu than I've had with Meng Jarrah, you realise. If he wants to become closer to you, he'll find a way of letting you know. On the other hand, even if he doesn't end up returning your feelings, I'm sure you could still manage to work together, without any problem at all on his part.'

'Though with a certain amount of suffering on mine.'

'I suppose so... Morag, sorry, my comlink has just told me it's time to go. I have a meeting with the owner of Myanmar Forest Industries. Apparently they're experiencing some production difficulties and need my help.'

'That *is* surprising. They came to you for help?'

'In a way. They were referred to me by our local peacekeepers.'

'Hmm...which would seem to indicate they're not involved in anything illegal. Unless, of course, they're playing a sophisticated game of bluff... Let me know how it turns out, and in the meantime, best of luck with your personal dilemma.'

'Thank you, and yes, I'll contact you again very soon.' Freddi smiled and closed the connection.

As she put away her comlink, Morag decided to gather her courage and invite Chiu Liow to have his evening meal with her.

Having arranged to meet for their midsun meal, Søren and Karla now sat at the dining table in his apartment, talking. Red Matilda, comfortably perched on a chair next to Karla, purred softly while she listened. The novelty of accompanying this wight on excursions stimulated the cat's curiosity. Normally, she accepted the humans with a degree of nonchalance and found their behaviour amusing. Consequently, it was rare for her to feel anxious on their behalf. They generally seemed to be self-possessed and in control of their emotions, but this had changed since the time Mik was hurt. Now, he and his friends seemed to have lost their certainty and their images were often blurred. Karla's were blurred now, so Red Matilda focused on her until her mind began to respond. Satisfied, she reached up to catch a corner of the overhanging tablecloth with her claws, gently pulling it towards her. Søren grabbed the other end as a vase of flowers teetered.

'Red, let go, you monster!' cried Karla, quickly rescuing her plate before it fell.

Staring innocently at the two angry wights, Red Matilda gave the cloth one last tweak. Then, tail and whiskers fluffed out, eyes limpid, she jumped off the chair and rolled onto her back, presenting her cream-coloured, curly-haired stomach, with paws drawn up to her chest. The distraction was complete. After a few minutes of playing with her, their minds cleared, so she relaxed her hold on them, falling contentedly asleep, with her head resting on Søren's left foot.

Karla stood up and went to the kitchen to fetch a fresh pot of coffee, as well as the cakes Søren had provided. Upon her return, she sank into an armchair, stretched her arms and laughed. 'You know what Red just did, don't you.'

'Oh yes... Now that we are aware of their abilities, it becomes quite noticeable when they choose to modify our emotions. I found myself responding as I would to a large glass of schnapps. What about you?'

'It felt like when I sit in the sunshine beneath one of my favourite trees and the warmth flows through me. I suppose each of us will experience it differently.'

'Looking back, do you think they have often affected you like this? I don't remember mine doing it.'

'No... But then again, I've never been this close to any of Mik's cats before, and I've never had one of my own. Red Matilda is obviously taking her role as my guardian very seriously. Is your peacekeeper taking *his* job as seriously?'

'He must be. Every time I join the crowds at the market, he practically has a nervous breakdown trying to keep close to me, while at the same time keeping an eye on anyone who comes near. Poor, dear man.' Søren giggled, his blonde curls forming a halo around his face. 'However,' he continued, as Karla also giggled, 'we have finished our main course, so it is time to discuss the matter at hand. Tell me everything!' Earlier, Søren refused to let Karla talk about Wyvern Meridian before she had eaten something. As far as he was concerned, nothing was serious enough to be allowed to interfere with the enjoyment of good food.

Swallowing her mouthful of cake, Karla took a sip of coffee and began: 'Our model contains projections for the next four hundred years, and so does Wyvern Meridian's, which in itself is unusual. Ordinarily, timber companies limit themselves to the minimum legislative requirement of one-hundred-and-twenty-year projections; enough time to form a semi-mature forest, but not enough to go beyond plantation requirements. However, they've put forward the same concept we have in terms of demonstrating how forest stability will be created and how it will perpetuate itself and regenerate naturally once the major tree species mature and decay. Mik and Tamara were astonished to find that Wyvern Meridian's projections even demonstrate the beneficial impact their plantation will have on the water catchment area and soil structure. On top of which, they've allowed for the colonisation requirements of the various fauna with priority status.'

'And how have they achieved this miracle?' asked Søren, frowning in disbelief.

'Ah, that's where it gets interesting,' replied Karla. 'They're using a mix of exotics introduced into Australia during the nineteenth and twentieth centuries, together with native species that became environmental weeds when they were transferred to areas where they weren't normally found. Their model shows how all the plants will initially be highly robust, but will then be limited by each other's competing requirements. So, an essential part of the management plan is a high harvest rate to create new space for regrowth, which is the total opposite to our approach of a low rate of sustainable yield. Wyvern Meridian claims that without a high harvest rate, their forest would self-destruct. Each species, being extremely vigorous, would basically try to out-compete the others, until they no longer had the space to grow and would also use up all the nutrients in the soil.'

Karla paused to drink some of her coffee, while Søren helped himself to another cake, making sure he didn't drop any crumbs. 'Oddly enough,' she said, 'I don't find any of this difficult to accept. What I do find difficult is their basis for claiming that their species won't present *us* with a problem. I mean, the plants they're using have been on our hit list for centuries! What they're proposing is to genetically engineer them all to only reproduce vegetatively. No fertile seeds, in other words. Theoretically, this means that if the plantation boundaries are patrolled and kept free of new plants, they won't be able to escape into *our* forests.'

'Their plan appears to be a highly labour-intensive method of maintaining an environment,' said Søren, after carefully wiping his mouth with a serviette.

'They're putting that forward as a *good* idea. They even have a bit of social theory to back it up.'

'Let me guess... They think there are enough people who want to leave the cities and take themselves out into the countryside during their spare time to do voluntary weeding.'

'You've got it. They're also proposing a competitive element be introduced in the form of teams being presented with an award for the cleanest perimeter section.'

'And what *is* this award?'

'Their choice of an entire houseful of hand-crafted timber furniture.'

'Do I detect a materialistic imperative creeping in?'

'I believe you do. The Federation puts enormous effort into controlling demand for timber products, while Wyvern Meridian creates demand. Wonderful, yes?'

'No. Far too insidious, I think.'

'Timber is a luxury item for the time being, so unfortunately, I think Parliament will approve the proposal if the Federation's assessment of their model verifies that it's sound, and if they accept the assumption that the spread of the plantation can be readily controlled.'

'What do Mik and Tamara say?' asked Søren, casually tickling Red Matilda's ears.

'They don't like it any more than we do, but they have to be honest and state that as long as the perimeters are strictly patrolled, there should be no conflict between Wyvern Meridian's forests and ours.'

'The idea reminds me of the old zoological gardens that were once popular... Caged wild plants instead of caged wild animals, just waiting to escape.' Søren shook his head and grimaced.

Karla agreed, then asked him how his research proposal was coming along. At this point, Red Matilda woke up and caught Søren's hand with her paws. He hastily withdrew it and she went back to sleep.

'The Breeding Centre staff are extremely cooperative, even enthusiastic,' he said, smiling. 'We've almost finished the final details. It would appear that the best approach for the behavioural aspect of the research is to call for volunteers who have cats to take part in a series of experiments designed to place some of the people in situations where they are in real, though not overly serious, danger, and others in situations where the danger isn't real, but only appears to be – the one experiment of this type already conducted is clearly not enough. We are also devising ways of testing the ability of cats to combine forces with one another to protect their companion. Of course, we should also consider situations where cats have a choice of asking for help from a human or from one of their own kind, then find out what their choices would be under the various circumstances.

'Myself, I would like to look into the interesting possibility of gathering a few people who have cat phobias and who would like to be cured. Such people never allow themselves anywhere near cats...and sometimes cannot even contemplate holding or seeing a picture of one. I wonder if a cat could affect their attitude, perhaps even permanently, if the person would let them come close enough? However, such an experiment must wait until I return home, given we have already agreed that for the time being, anything capable of showing the extent to which they affect our emotions is not for public consumption.'

As he spoke, Søren stared into the distance, becoming so absorbed by his ideas that Karla let him ponder for a while in silence, before asking, 'Do you think you'll ever be able to find out *how* they communicate with us and each other?'

Søren gave a small start. 'Possibly... Frankly, I'm not at all sure it matters. It's more important to know how they behave. Is it such a terrible thing to leave some questions unanswered? Now, to change the subject,' he continued, nudging Red Matilda off his foot, which had gone to sleep, 'how are things progressing at Lamington? Have they managed to build up their stocks and restart their growth trials?'

'Yes, thank goodness. The embryos we sent them are doing well, but unfortunately they're still at least a year behind in their schedule. Mik's still playing about with the idea of contacting that woman, Gwenllian, and her brother, Owain, to see if they'd be interested in obtaining some Federation funding in return for collaborating with us. Their research into soil restructuring sounds as if it could help the Lamington project make up for lost time, and of course Owain and Gwenllian would get the chance to speed up their own project too.'

'Gwenllian has returned to work, has she not?'

'Yes, but it seems Marika hasn't yet. What do you think? Should we talk to Coordinator Zago and find out if a formal proposal should be made?'

'Certainly. It's an excellent idea.'

As usual, Søren preferred to act immediately, so Research Coordinator Zago and Karla were soon deep in conversation and after only thirty minutes, had developed a draft contract and sent it to Gwenllian's comlink. They chatted about day-to-day things while waiting for a response.

It wasn't long before an elated Gwenllian appeared on the split screen of Søren's computer. 'I've sent a copy of your proposal to Owain and he didn't hesitate in accepting! Our only proviso is that we basically follow our original direction, with any modifications your work might require as additional features. We also wish to retain the option of operating as a commercial venture rather than as Federation employees. Whoever works with us would become part of the venture and share in any profits.'

In a dry voice, Coordinator Zago said she would put the proposition before the authorities in Oslo and request they give it priority consideration. She had no personal objection to Gwenllian's preference for working in this way, undertaking to do her utmost to obtain an endorsement within a month.

'We should have finished our field trials by then,' said Gwenllian, her startling green eyes shining, 'so we'll be in a good position to verify the value of our application before you make a final commitment to providing Federation resources.' She felt her confidence returning. This offer would not have been made if the Willsmere group still suspected her.

'Excellent, Gwenllian. I am glad we had this opportunity to speak with each other. I have heard of you, of course.'

Coordinator Zago's voice was kind, but Gwenllian winced and then blushed. 'Owain and I will make sure your trust in us is not misplaced, Research Coordinator Zago. And Karla... Thank you.' Her soft voice was warmer than usual as she said this.

'Oh, it was Mik Theophanous' idea,' replied Karla, smiling. 'It'd be such a waste for your research and ours to continue in isolation from each other. The only problem I can think of is that from Mik's account, you'll need to learn to get along better with cats than you do now.'

Gwenllian blushed again. 'Was it really his idea? I didn't feel his cat liked me at all when we met.'

'Under the circumstances, you couldn't expect her to. It'll be different next time, I'm sure.'

'I hope so,' said Gwenllian, with a shy smile, then with the usual farewells, the conversation was concluded to the complete satisfaction of all concerned.

With a grin, Karla turned to Søren, put her hands on his shoulders and waltzed him around the room. Red Matilda woke up and pranced with them, tail waving to and fro. After a while, they collapsed into each other's arms, gasping and laughing. When he recovered his breath, Søren decided they should give Mik and Tamara the good news in person. He spoke to his comlink and within the promised time, his guardian peacekeeper was at the door, ready to fly them to Willsmere.

High above the tree canopy, storm clouds were forming as the charcoal gatherers walked swiftly, but with great care, through the Papuan rainforest. The air was still and hot, the humidity rising rapidly, forewarning the workers of the tumult to come. When the rain began, it was almost a relief, despite the deafening drumming of the drops. The temperature began to fall, but they were familiar with the rapid changes of the tropical weather and so donned their thin, waterproof jackets. The ground, always soft beneath their feet, became slushy; they would need to be more careful than usual to examine their bodies for leeches. A sharp cracking sound warned them of a branch about to fall and small scurrying noises signalled that other forest creatures were also hurrying to take shelter from the anger of the heavens.

The charcoal gatherers had been lucky of late; several forest fires had given them a rich harvest. The traditional potters of the district, who used their produce to fire kilns, would pay well. The workers began to sing in quiet harmony with the steady downpour. Each looked forward to the companionship they would share whilst preparing the evening meal once they reached their temporary forest home.

After a time, the wind changed direction and the rain began to ease. When it stopped, the temperature began to rise, and soon steam issued from their clothing and from the forest floor. Dry and cheerful, they reached the campsite. Sunbeams shone through the gap in the canopy, highlighting the chaos they found, increasing their sense of unreality and confusion.

The storm could not have done this damage. Only humans could so spitefully have scattered their stores and destroyed their sleeping places. Bewildered, the charcoal gatherers wanly picked up the remnants of their belongings, finding no words to express their dismay. Eventually, one of them contacted their transportation unit. By dusk, the last traces of their activities had been erased.

In Niu Bougainville, the peacekeepers were equally puzzled when they received the news of the sabotage. Forest workers harmed no one, surely? Chiu Liow's friend, the peacekeeper now assigned to delve further into the financial and business operations of this minor recycling and forest restoration company, added the incident to his collection of facts.

The Papuan company had operated for nearly seventy years and during that time its workers had given their full support to all Government and Federation initiatives designed to protect the forest while at the same time developing small and medium-scale sustainable industries. The ownership of the company remained in the hands of the workers themselves and its financial basis was sound. The turnover amongst them was low, there having been no new members of the collective in six years. The situation was therefore beyond comprehension.

Could it be coincidence? Vandalism wasn't entirely unknown and usually occurred as sporadic outbursts, which soon settled once the public were informed and the offender brought forward, usually by angry parents. Charges were rarely laid, as the culprits were often very young and somewhat maladjusted. In these cases, the parents were counselled and the youth placed under stricter supervision, with a busier study and social schedule.

Nevertheless, this act of vandalism was admittedly different. Access to the highland forests was difficult, almost impossible without air transport. It was hard to imagine that any youngster would have the resources to commandeer an airjet, let alone pilot it, then land safely in such a tiny clearing. The destruction had also been highly systematic and thorough, and therefore not characteristic of juvenile acts of spite.

Unfortunately, for the time being, the only assistance he could give the company was to issue them with official confirmation that they hadn't destroyed their own property in an attempt to gain compensation – and to send a report to Chiu Liow.

CHAPTER ELEVEN

Steam rose from the deeply furrowed clay soil as Freddi and the plantation manager of Myanmar Forest Industries toiled up the newly created scar on the landscape. It was close to the middle of the afternoon and the daily tropical downpour had recently finished. The plantation manager stopped, removed her hat and wiped a grimy forehead with it. Having reached the crest of the hill, they could now look down upon the entire scene. A stretch of forest had been reduced to a tangle of shattered trunks and branches, interspersed with great clods of earth and the twisted remnants of the fleet of logging jinkers. Deep holes that were already filling with water marked the places where the explosions originated. Dejected workers stood silently by and stared. They had waited for several hours while the peacekeepers inspected the damage.

'That mess represents over one third of our transport company's vehicles, and all but one of their loggers. They've already sent someone over here and are claiming this is all our fault because *our* security isn't good enough! Who on Earth would patrol a logging site twenty-four hours a day? No one's ever heard of such a thing happening before!'

The plantation manager sat down wearily on a tree stump and gazed up at Freddi, eyes narrowed against the glare of the sun. 'We'll be forced to use our own capital reserves to invest in a fleet of jinkers. Wyvern Meridian has cancelled their transportation contract with us.'

'Did one of their people come over to assess the damage?' asked Freddi, likewise taking a seat on a stump.

'Oh no... From what I've heard about them, they just sit back and rake in the profits! No, the former owner came. She's a changed woman. Used to be good to deal with, but she's a real bully now.'

'I see! What a shame... So what did you make of their ten percent decrease in charges when Wyvern Meridian bought the controlling interest?' Freddi picked up a twig and drew a few designs in the wet clay.

'That was just fine, except what people didn't get to hear about was the trade-off. We had to agree to cover any loss of business they suffered if something went wrong and we were at fault. It meant we were forced to increase our insurance premiums, so overall, gained only about a one percent decrease. Very magnanimous, I'm sure!' The plantation manager clenched her fists and scowled bitterly.

'Which means you now need to prove to the insurance company that there was no negligence on your part.' Freddi indicated the disaster area with a broad sweep of her arm.

'That's right, which is why we've come to you for help. Anything at all you want to know, or see, just ask. Now that Wyvern Meridian's made a claim on our insurance company, we can't continue production until we get a clearance certificate, and if their claim succeeds, we won't be able to get affordable coverage on any logging jinkers we buy. Without transport, we might as well say we're out of business.' She wiped her face again, this time with a soil-encrusted hand.

'I know it's asking the obvious, but can you think of any reason why Wyvern Meridian, or anyone else come to think of it, would want to do this to you?'

'It hadn't even occurred to me that Wyvern Meridian could've done this!' exclaimed the plantation manager, startled by the question. 'Why would they?'

'We can think of a number of reasons, though I'm afraid I can't share them with you. I don't want to give you the impression we think they *are* responsible, it's just one of several possibilities.' Freddi was careful to keep her voice neutral. She didn't want to start any rumours.

'Honestly, I can't think of *any* good reason... Their own plantation isn't anywhere near the harvesting stage, so it's not as if they were wanting to remove us as competitors. Anyway, there's such a demand for hardwood that the market could easily carry both *our* products and theirs. As to anyone else, unless it's something to do with one of our workers, I can't think of a single business enemy we've ever made.'

'I'm sure a lot of people wish they were as fortunate.' Freddi smiled for the first time since she arrived. 'I'll do my best to get things moving. The area will need to be kept isolated until we've examined everything. We'll also need to interview all your employees. Can you reassure them we're taking an open and unbiased approach, and that they've nothing to fear? I expect they've had little to do with peacekeepers before.'

'Sure, let's go down now. You'd have the right to access all our data, wouldn't you, so I won't have to arrange much in that way?'

'No, just introduce me to your computer. It should recognise me.'

The plantation manager blinked. 'Ah...it should?' she managed to say.

'Sorry,' said Freddi, 'it's not a good time to make silly jokes.'

The two women walked carefully down the slippery hillside. As they approached the forlorn and dazed workers, many stared at Freddi, as they had done when she first arrived. None of them had ever seen a woman with ebony skin and golden eyes before. Her hair too was unusual – a mass of long, shiny black curls interspersed with intricate plaits. She stood a full twenty centimetres above the tallest of them, yet despite her powerful build and the black uniform of the Mandalay Peacekeeping Force, none found her intimidating. Instead, they instinctively crowded near, asking questions, creating a chattering confusion of sound. Freddi held up her hand and they were silent. The small, ever-present noises of the countryside crept into their consciousness, and for a short while, they seemed suspended in time, within the glow of the warm, humid sunshine.

When the plantation manager began speaking, the workers shifted their fascinated gaze from the peacekeeper to their colleague, listening as she explained that while the peacekeepers were investigating the sabotage of their forest and workplace, they would be required to remain away from work. The worksite was to be regarded as strictly off-limits. They would, of course, be paid their usual salaries and would be kept informed of any progress. Freddi and her team intended to call upon them individually to obtain whatever information, or even ideas, they could provide. The workers were assured they would be treated with respect and courtesy.

Once the manager had finished speaking, she turned to Freddi, who stepped forward and smiled reassuringly. She began by saying, 'I have an important request to make of you all. Until this investigation has reached a conclusion, it is vital you do not discuss the events with anyone, not even your closest family. This is a great deal to ask, but I do ask it, and am sure my confidence in you will be repaid.' Many heads nodded, intrigued by the unusual lilt in her voice, although no one interrupted with questions. 'We won't interview you in your homes, but instead will appreciate your returning here when required. For the time being, though, I would appreciate you all waiting a few minutes longer while I consult further with your plantation manager. Afterwards, we will speak with some of you, while the remainder leave the site.'

More heads nodded, in understanding and willingness to cooperate. Freddi scanned the crowd. A few had overcome their awe and were whispering to each other. She decided to select them first, then turned away and walked with the plantation manager to a relatively small, compact building which housed the administration and facilities complex. When they entered, Freddi was aghast to find there was no security scanner. The plantation manager immediately noticed her expression and grinned, relaxing for the first time that day.

'I know what you're thinking, but we're really not that naive. Our workers don't like retina scanners, or any of the other recognition systems. They take immense pride in working the required number of hours without having anyone keep track. After a while, we managed to convince everyone that scanners and suchlike aren't always used for timekeeping and when one of them came up with a new idea, we funded its development. They keep trying to find ways of fooling it, but up until now it's worked beautifully.'

'So what is it?' asked Freddi.

'You're standing on it,' replied the plantation manager, laughing.

Freddi looked at her feet. 'Not a foot odour system, surely?'

'No, they were tried last century, but they're not one hundred percent accurate. This one recognises the way each individual walks. It can gauge a person's weight, the exact size of their feet, their actual walking pattern...such as the way their weight is distributed while they walk and the way they stand when they're not walking. It's an ancient idea, you know. It's been used by trackers for thousands of years, and I gather some work was done on it during the twenty-first century.'

Freddi was impressed. 'Does anyone else know about this?'

'No. The workers like keeping it secret because they get a laugh out of visitors thinking there's no security system. We don't tell new workers about it until we're sure they're trustworthy... So, if they enter any of the areas they've been told to stay away from, we know immediately, which is useful.'

'And sneaky, too. Sorry, I've done it again, haven't I...'

'Oh, don't worry, I'm a lot better than I was an hour ago, and I can appreciate a good pun. Anyway, the computer is through here, and it does have its own retina scanner. We use it in case we're working on something and get called away without much warning. The computer switches to low power mode and then if an unauthorised person approaches, turns itself off. The security list is local, so you'll have to speak to it or use the ID pad to get it to recognise you.'

Freddi walked over and placed her right hand onto the pad. The computer turned itself on and said, 'Good day, Peacekeeper Freddi. What can I do for you?'

'My goodness, you're the politest machine I've ever met! I'd like you to send all your plantation personnel records, work schedules, contract histories and site plans to my comlink.'

'Certainly. Please wait one moment... There you are, all completed successfully. Is there anything else you require?'

'Thank you, but no.'

'Any time,' the machine replied, before displaying a complex and accurate rotating pattern of the southern night sky.

'Who programmed this?' asked Freddi, turning to the plantation manager.

'One of our workers did it in his spare time. He makes a fairly decent income from creating personalised operating environments and various bits of peripheral software.'

'You must have a great deal of trust in him. Is that wise, given what's happened here today?'

'We all have to trust someone, Peacekeeper Freddi. He's my son, you see, so I don't worry too much.' The plantation manager smiled.

Freddi's eyes widened in surprise. 'In that case, I'd better interview *him* as soon as possible. Do you think he'd be upset if a Federation investigator was present as well? I don't have sufficient knowledge to deal with a computing expert, but this other woman has, and anyway, I think she'd find a trip here useful.'

'He might even enjoy it. Shall I ask him now?'

'No, I need to consult my colleague first. She's in Australia at the moment, so it might not be until tomorrow, or the next day, depending upon her other commitments. I think we can start with some of the bolder workers today and schedule the rest after I've read their work histories.'

Freddi suddenly realised she hadn't eaten anything since very early that morning. 'Actually, would you mind if we stopped for a short meal break? Perhaps we could use your facilities and reimburse the expense?'

'I'd like to say you could all be our guests and not pay, but I know that isn't legal. I'll just say you're very welcome,' replied the plantation manager, bowing courteously. 'I'll show you where the food hall is.'

'Oh no!' Morag stared at her screen in horror and felt her hands begin to tingle, as if the blood had been drained from them. She stood up slowly, leaning on the desk for support, then walked once around her borrowed office in the Rialto tower. Standing in front of the computer again, with arms folded in a gesture of self-protection, Morag took a deep breath and sat down to check the results one more time, even though it was hardly necessary.

Her in-depth study of the Papuan transport, salary, and library systems had taken far longer than she expected, but eventually the changes which caused the malfunctions were found. Each individual application was logged as having been modified at precisely the same time and using the same identification: her own.

A full search of the preliminary routines that recorded the transaction details made it very clear it would be impossible to demonstrate this was not her work. To her best knowledge, no one else, other than the FSIU Coordinator, had the necessary authority, as well as the expertise, to have made the amendments simultaneously, which meant that either Rohan Maerz had put her in this position, or...the other possibility was worse. Someone, about whom they knew nothing, had access to the lattice security overlay and had broken its barriers.

Shaking her head, Morag did the only thing possible and called Chiu Liow. 'May I come to see you...now?' she asked him, making an effort to keep her voice steady.

'Yes, please do. I've just made a pot of tea. Would you like some?'

'Lovely, thank you. I won't be long.'

Chiu Liow carefully put the steaming cups of tea onto the low table that stood between the soft, dark red armchairs strategically situated near the windows to take best advantage of the view. The door chimed and Morag walked in, her face paler than usual. For once, she hesitated before taking a seat. When she picked up her tea and looked at him, the welcoming smile he had come to expect was missing and her hand trembled briefly as she brought the cup to her mouth.

'What's wrong, Morag?' Chiu Liow sat down in the chair next to her instead of the one opposite, as he normally would have.

'I've found the bugs in the Papuan systems, but unless I've become some bizarre chameleon who does things in her sleep, it appears someone has used my ID to insert them...and I can't prove otherwise.' Morag put down her cup before she spilled the hot liquid, trying yet again to control her voice. 'Would you please call Welcome?'

Staring at her, Chiu Liow nodded, then ran a hand through his hair, saying nothing, simply giving himself time to take in what she had said. Morag's head was bent over her hands as she toyed with the teacup, but she suddenly met his gaze.

'You *know* Welcome and I will support you,' he said slowly. 'He should be in the building; I'll call him now.'

They waited in silence, each with their own thoughts. When Welcome entered the office, he stopped, and then, frowning, sat down. 'I can see something has upset you both. What is it?' he asked.

'I suspect I'm about to be recalled to Luzern,' answered Morag, attempting a smile. 'Here, I'll show you.' She brought out her comlink and displayed the results that were still making their mute accusations on the screen in her office.

Welcome took the device and read, one finger playing with his bottom lip. He scrolled up, read the previous two screens, and handed it back. 'Apparently someone believes you're becoming a nuisance, Morag MacIain. What do you want to do?'

'I need to call Rohan. I've asked Chiu Liow to be here when I do, and wanted you here as well. I'm sure you understand why.'

'Of course. Do you want to do it now?'

'Yes. There's no point putting it off, is there.'

Morag stood up and went over to Chiu Liow's computer, placing her hand onto its ID pad, then entered Rohan Maerz's comlink code. The two men joined her. Welcome put his arm around her shoulders, but stood aside when the call was answered.

'Good morning, Morag...and Welcome and Peacekeeper Jones... What special occasion brings you all together to greet me at this time of night?' Rohan was eating his last pastries of the day and fastidiously brushed a small crumb from his chin as he waited for their reply.

'Rohan, I'm sorry to interrupt your evening, but this can't wait. I seem to be guilty of having had more involvement with the Papuan lattice than I should. You'll see what I mean when I send you this.' Morag transmitted the final results of her analysis. 'If you want more, I can send the full catastrophe for you to examine and verify.'

The FSIU Coordinator's eyes narrowed while he read. When he looked up again, a small smile played around the corners of his mouth. 'Well,' said Rohan, his voice low and soothing, 'it does appear as if you've taken your responsibilities somewhat less seriously than you should. Still, unless Welcome is there to let me know you've been taken in charge for psychiatric treatment, I can only assume we have a mystery to keep us entertained for a little while... I apologise, Morag, but I must insist you return to Luzern by this evening's flight and will arrange for an escort to meet you at the airport. I'm sure you understand. We can have breakfast together on Thursday after you've had a chance to rest. That will give us an opportunity to exchange our views on the situation.'

Teak Australia's Board of Directors had delayed making an appointment with Chiu Liow Jones for as long as possible. They now sat in their small yet well-furnished conference room, faced by the solemn peacekeeper. Silently, he cursed them all for preventing him from sharing Morag's last few hours in Melbourne. The shock of this morning's revelation remained, although he flatly refused to accept she was in any way implicated. Wrenching his thoughts back to the present, he managed to focus on the question being put to him:

'May we have your personal assurance there will be no attempt to freeze our assets? We are strongly of the opinion there can be no possible justification for doing so.'

'Before answering your question,' said Chiu Liow, 'perhaps you can give me some explanation for the way in which Teak Australia appears to be implicated in a series of attacks on Federation research centres?'

He held up his hand for silence as one of the directors began to protest that they had no knowledge of any such crimes being committed. 'Please do not be afraid to acknowledge your awareness of these attacks,' he continued. 'Owain is one of your major shareholders, and I am sure will have passed on all the information he has obtained during the time his sister, Gwenllian, has been under suspicion.' He forced himself to smile in order to allay their understandable nervousness.

The directors glanced at each other and seemed to arrive at an unspoken agreement. 'It's true. Owain has kept us up to date, but as none of the events have been publicised, we should not, perhaps, be in possession of as much information as we actually are. It's a relief, I must admit, to speak openly at last. Some time ago, we began to realise there were too many connections between Teak Australia and these events for our comfort. If I attempt a summary, you could see if there's anything we've missed?'

Chiu Liow agreed, so the director continued: 'Owain has told us that his sister's colleague, Marika, is also under suspicion of having helped engineer the attack on the Willsmere, and possibly even the Lamington, research centre, and that she is a close friend of another of our major shareholders, Mervyn Bradshaw, a wealthy and influential man. I might also say a somewhat unscrupulous one, but we've no real evidence his other business dealings are not what they should be. Call it intuition if you will.' She smiled briefly. 'I put great faith in intuition. Our subconscious minds are much more efficient than our conscious ones. However, I am digressing. To continue... I have a business colleague by the name of Vensor, who has a small furniture importation company in partnership with myself, and he also works at the Central Computer Site as an administrator. Were you aware of this?'

Chiu Liow nodded, but said nothing, not wishing to interrupt.

'Owain himself is a research coordinator with the Department of Agriculture, and in turn, this department has joint responsibility with the Federation for Lamington and Willsmere. Together with his sister, Owain is also doing valuable research relevant to the timber industry.' The director paused. 'Did you know Gwenllian and Owain have accepted a proposal, authorised by Federation Research Coordinator Zago, that they collaborate with Willsmere and Lamington in return for funding of their project?'

Chiu Liow forgot himself and exclaimed, 'No, I haven't heard of this! When was the offer made?'

'Don't be too upset at not knowing. It only happened yesterday. Frankly, we're delighted. Owain hasn't been his usual self since these events began, but since yesterday has regained much of his confidence. He has assumed this display of trust in his sister must mean she's been presumed innocent. I didn't wish to disillusion him, but I do hope it's true?'

'I am unable to comment, but I can certainly hope, along with you, that it *will be* the case. Gwenllian is a talented woman, and I imagine the collaboration will be of great benefit to the Federation effort.' Chiu Liow paused to pour himself a glass of water, took a sip, then said, 'We are particularly interested in Mervyn Bradshaw, so if you find yourselves in possession of any facts likely to assist us in learning more about him, they would be most welcome. In the meantime, as a matter of routine, we will examine your company database.'

He quietly wondered how they would manage this feat without Morag's specialised help. 'Meanwhile, should anything at all out of the ordinary occur that affects your business, either beneficially or adversely, please inform me at once. Also, I assume you *have* received the latest news from Myanmar?'

'Yes, we have. The situation is extremely serious for them, as it is for us. We were at first reluctant to assist you with your inquiries because we felt unable to offer any information of value and, to be blunt, resented the implication that our highly reputable organisation could be stupid enough to involve itself in any form of unethical business practice.'

The director drew herself up to her full height, brushing a stray lock of silver hair from her forehead. 'However, the situation has changed. In fact we now ask for your assistance in resolving the Myanmarian incident. We've only a three-month supply of raw material left, and although our capital reserves, sound reputation and insurance contracts should allow us to survive one poor financial year, and possibly even a second, we prefer not to be put into such a situation. We offer you the full resources of our company, if this can be of any assistance in avoiding undue delay.'

'I thank you and appreciate your offer, but we cannot accept private resources. Nevertheless, we would certainly benefit from both full information disclosure about your company's operations and assets, as well as any other information you are able to glean and pass on. Now, to answer your earlier question, this latest crime indicates your company is unlikely to have been involved in any of the previous ones – unless you are being subjected to some form of extreme pressure that has forced you to sabotage your own source of timber. As this seems a remote possibility, I can at this stage assure you that there are no plans to freeze your assets.'

Chiu Liow drank the remaining water in his glass, stood up, shook hands with each of the directors in turn, then left the building with a strange sense of disorientation. Morag's recall to Luzern would severely deplete their resources and his growing fear that Rohan Maerz was somehow at the centre of the assault on the Federation – and now private research and forestry enterprises – created the nauseating picture in his mind of floundering in a quagmire. Having removed one Federation investigator, would he send them another? And if so, would they be just a pawn, or would they too be discredited if 'overly efficient', as perhaps was the case with Morag?

Chiu Liow checked his comlink. He had almost an hour before he was due to meet Morag and Welcome at the transport exchange; they had arranged to eat their evening meal together at the airport. Well, in the meantime, he would quite simply keep working and contact Coordinator Zago for her belated account of the extraordinary offer made to Gwenllian and Owain.

Situated on the site of the original Melbourne City Baths in Swanston Street, the new bathing centre dwarfed the old red brick building, which now stood in its new position at the heart of the complex. Its interior had been painstakingly cleaned of the mould and dirt accumulated during almost two centuries of neglect and partial submersion. The decorative tiles of the restored pools gleamed and Welcome could almost imagine himself back in the nineteenth century – when he would have been sent to gaol for not wearing a suitable bathing costume, or, as in this instance, not wearing one at all. He floated contentedly on his back, the self-discipline of years exercising itself, rendering his mind calm and uncluttered.

This was the quietest time of day to spend here and he usually preferred to have the pool to himself to relax and indulge his daydreams. Today, however, instead of dreaming about rare and beautiful wines – his private passion – he mulled over the morning's latest developments. The case was far bigger than any he had been involved with before and many of its features were outside his considerable experience. He was beginning to perceive the influence of a single malignant mind, or at least a single group of minds working in consort. The confidence of that mind was extraordinary. Anyone of reasonable intelligence, which literally meant most people, could readily perceive the overabundance of coincidences.

He paddled his feet, then abruptly turned and swam the length of the pool. For a few moments, he had been afraid. Hoisting himself up onto the edge, Welcome vigorously applied his towel, ruefully regarding his stomach and muttering to himself. It was definitely growing a bit too large; something would have to be done about it – one day.

Dressing slowly, he decided to re-read the latest reports. There were two, one each from Papua and Malaysia. The Malaysian research company had worked steadily and methodically for a number of years, but received only limited funding from the sale of shares. Three days ago, Wyvern Meridian had offered a substantial grant, in addition to a generous payment for a thirty-percent shareholding. There was little doubt the offer would be accepted. Apparently the scientists were still recovering from the effects of their celebration.

The content of the Papuan report made him think that one of the incidents it described could only be regarded as harassment, as little real damage had been done to the charcoal gatherers' collective and no one was injured. However, Welcome doubted this would be the last act of malice they would experience.

He checked his comlink. There were just forty minutes left before he needed to leave to meet Chiu Liow and Morag at the Parkville transport exchange.

The transport exchange was crowded with a large number of excited students, who were milling around swapping travel stories and exchanging comlink numbers. A few over-anxious parents had arrived to meet their youngsters, rather than waiting patiently at home for their return. Morag welcomed the noise and laughter as a distraction from the gnawing pain that accompanied the growing certainty that Rohan Maerz had embarked upon a deadly game in which she had become his chosen and unwilling adversary. Having examined every known possibility, she had arrived at the conclusion that no one else could have used her identity to sabotage the Papuan lattice. That any of her fellow Special Investigators could have done so seemed improbable: the precautions surrounding their access to the global lattice simultaneously used several forms of identification, not just handprints. Stealing and reproducing a set of prints, or even retina patterns, was relatively simple, but reproducing voice and keystroke patterns too? Well, on second thoughts, Morag had to admit voice would not be that difficult either, and presumably a neuralnet temporarily inserted into their operating environment in Luzern could have captured her keystrokes, allowing selected sequences to be replayed as required. Still, forging all the necessary forms of identification and using them at the same time would have taken considerable skill and ingenuity. Damnation! She had trusted Rohan!

When Welcome's voice interrupted her thoughts, Morag turned away from her gloomy contemplation of the sunlit reflections in the still water surrounding the landing bay.

'You look as if your mind is already back in Luzern, working out the next move. You're sure it's him, aren't you.'

He had so closely read her thoughts that she shivered. 'I wish you were coming with me, Welcome. I think he'd find you wonderfully disconcerting.'

'So why don't I? You'll need a defence if you stand trial, and who would be better than the criminologist who's had more than enough opportunity to study your very soul, did such a thing exist.'

His eyes crinkled with laughter as Morag clasped him by the shoulders to give him a quick hug. 'Watch it, Chiu Liow might be envious,' he added, then quickly sidestepped before her playful blow could land on his button-like nose.

'You're the very devil, Welcome! I must admit to wishing he *would* be envious, though how we can joke, I don't know. You do realise I face a very long sentence if this comes to trial and I'm convicted?'

Welcome took her hand gently in his and stroked its short, smooth nails. 'I know. But you wouldn't be. You're one of the sanest people I've ever had the privilege to meet – next to myself, you understand – and the Judge would know that only someone who isn't quite sane could have taken part in this fiasco.'

Chiu Liow had been standing at a distance, watching, unwilling to interrupt. He now approached, wishing he could take Morag's hand as easily as Welcome had done. Why was he unable to overcome his fear of rejection, even under circumstances where it was the most natural thing in the world to comfort someone, who at the very least had become a dear friend?

'Just in time, Peacekeeper Jones!' Welcome called out. 'I've decided to accompany our friend here to Luzern. We have two perfect excuses: firstly, she must have a guard because she's such a dangerous criminal, and secondly, she may require a good defence psychologist. Can I take it you agree?'

Chiu Liow laughed in relief. 'Agree? Of course I do! I can manage here for a while without you, though not for long. Morag, I don't suppose I'll be allowed to communicate with you directly once you're undergoing preliminary examination – Rohan Maerz will see to that! Welcome, you can be our go-between, can't you?'

As Welcome smiled and patted Chiu Liow on the shoulder, their transport arrived, so they quietly took their places. The journey was short, and since the railcar was crowded, all three remained silent. Sitting next to her, almost touching, Chiu Liow realised he could not risk losing Morag. If necessary, he would bend or break every regulation he knew in order to obtain evidence to prove her innocence and convict Rohan Maerz – or, as inconceivable as it was, whoever else had put her into this position – even if it meant spending the rest of his life paying off the fines! In the meantime, he needed someone with whom he could discuss the case and who was neither a peacekeeper nor an investigator. Someone he could trust and who would help him maintain perspective – someone who the FSIU Coordinator would not be aware of. Karla's face, with its blue eyes and strong, determined features, appeared in his imagination. When they reached Tullamarine, he rose and, without hesitating, took Morag's hand in his.

PART II

CHAPTER TWELVE

Five minutes before Karla was due to rise, the overhead lamp switched itself on and then gradually increased the light until the room glowed pleasantly. The previous night, she had chosen to wake to the melodious warbling of magpies. When it began, Red Matilda's tail and whiskers twitched in curiosity. Half opening her eyes, she stretched out her legs and rolled over to touch Karla's face with one paw. Karla mumbled and drew the blankets over her head, so Red Matilda stood up and planted both front legs on her middle. 'Her' Wight woke abruptly and the birdsong ceased as Red licked Karla's face, purring noisily. Yawning, Karla reached out to cuddle the warm, furry body, then rubbed her forehead against the cat's, enjoying the cosy comfort of her company for several minutes until they both got out of bed.

Before doing anything else, Karla combed Red Matilda's long fur. The cat arched her back in typically feline pleasure, then turned and grabbed the implement with both paws, chewing it until Karla, laughing, gave in and played with her for a short time. Afterwards, she left Red Matilda to her own devices while she took a bath.

Emerging from the water, Karla looked critically at her body. Small signs of age were beginning to appear, but it would take at least another twenty years before any of the youthful lustre of skin and hair was lost. She vaguely recalled reading that hundreds of years ago people usually showed signs of ageing at around forty and often worried themselves silly attempting to delay the inevitable. Sad, thought Karla, recalling the beauty of Research Coordinator Zago's ancient, wrinkled face. She pulled one of her favourite tunics over her head, luxuriating in its softness. The rich brown colour suited her. It had cost more than she would have liked, but never creased and had lasted for many years. Next, a pair of loose, dark green trousers and lightweight, matching socks were added to the ensemble. Admiring herself in the full-length mirror, she decided to be extravagant and put on her precious Swedish clogs. The warm glow of the polished wooden soles complemented the tunic. The clogs were a luxury given to her by Søren for her last Namingday, and knowing she loved bright colours, the fabric uppers were a brilliant red.

Running out of patience, Red Matilda padded into the room and wailed. 'Yes, puddums, I'm ready now. Don't I look beautiful?' Karla pirouetted around the room, but Red swished her tail and wailed again, loudly. 'Okay, cat, so you don't have any sense of aesthetics. Come on, let's find something to eat.'

Before they left to walk the short distance to the communal area, Red Matilda tugged her leash from its hook and gave it to Karla. Most of the other residents had quickly become used to the sight of the huge animal sharing their domesticity, but a few still held reservations about having her in the dining room. However, none of them were willing to question Karla's judgement in bringing the cat with her. Occasionally her friends asked how she came to acquire an adult, but were satisfied when told she was just cat-sitting for a work colleague on leave. This morning, no one interrupted her preferred solitude at breakfast. Once they finished eating, Karla collected their dishes and carried them to the washer.

Outside, the day was overcast and cooler than usual, but the brightness of the red-flowering surface of the trafficway compensated for the lack of sunshine. They waited only a few minutes before a railcar stopped at the callstation and Karla laughed when Red Matilda assumed her now customary pose: paws on the windowsill, tail erect and whiskers twitching as she watched the scenery pass by. The other passengers smiled and pointed, but the cat ignored them. Karla thought this was just as well; Red Matilda's sense of humour could simply not be trusted on unsuspecting humans!

The day promised to be a stimulating one. Coordinator Zago had obtained approval for Gwenllian and Owain to join forces with Willsmere, Lamington and Serro do Cachimbo in the Federation's ongoing effort to rehabilitate the world's rainforests. Some preliminary discussions had already taken place, with excellent results, and the morale of the Lamington researchers improved dramatically at the prospect of making up some of the time they had lost through the disruption of their plant trials.

At Mik's request, Zago had also obtained Meng Jarrah's agreement to explore the possibility of a cooperative effort between her laboratories in Myanmar and Papua and theirs. Coincidentally, it appeared Meng Jarrah, being of Aboriginal descent, had ancestral ties to the Lamington region and its Yugambeh people, so Karla hoped this would give her even more reason to collaborate. A meeting had been arranged and Meng Jarrah was due to arrive at Willsmere at 17:00. Not having previously met the famous woman, Karla greatly looked forward to doing so.

When the railcar reached its destination, the two alighted within short walking distance of Willsmere's ironwork gates. Karla's clogs crunched pleasantly on the gravelled path as they walked up to the massive front doors. She had entered Red Matilda's retina pattern and paw prints into the building's security database, partly as a joke, yet also with a sense of achievement. Mik had joined in and entered Fliedermus', although, on Søren's advice, refrained from doing the same for Possum, given she was still under 'house arrest' – Søren was intent on treating her case in the same way as that of a human.

It hadn't taken long to train Red Matilda to use the retina scanner. In fact, it seemed to amuse her and Mik was convinced that if he didn't supervise her closely, the cat would spend half the day letting herself in and out of the building, just for the joy of having the door open and close at her command. Fliedermus also entertained herself by exercising her newfound powers, wandering throughout the building, yet wisely ignored the front entrance, as well as the room containing the central building maintenance and security systems, which was off-limits to the cats anyway – though how she knew this was a mystery.

This morning, as the doors opened, Red scampered down the length of the hallway, while Karla followed at a more sedate pace, going over in her mind the arrangements they needed to put into place before their guests arrived later in the day.

The tall, slender, brown-skinned woman sat towards the rear of the international airjet, enjoying the sight of the vast red sand hills of central Australia below, safe in her air-conditioned comfort from the scorching heat of the waterless dunes. A host waited politely to gain her attention before offering yet another refreshment. Although the flight from Mandalay lasted only five hours, this was their third meal. Perhaps some of the passengers are nervous, she thought, leaning closer to the window to gain a better view. Or perhaps they aren't able to cope with the sight of the empty desert, being used to more populated, or 'civilised', expanses?

Turning to the host, Meng Jarrah accepted the small plate of food, then ran a hand through her thick, dark brown curls to roughly comb them into place. She felt grimy, despite the luxurious appointments of the aircraft, and disliked the feeling of being cooped up for any length of time, much preferring the sharp cleanliness of uncrowded open spaces and forests.

Many years had gone by since her last visit to Australia, and several more had passed since she had returned to the lands of her ancestors in Queensland. When Coordinator Zago contacted her two days ago with Mik Theophanous' request that she consider joining her research with the Federation's, her first reaction, upon Lamington being mentioned, was a sudden wish to re-establish the link with her people. She simply had to find time to do that...somehow.

While she finished eating, Meng Jarrah thought about her departure from Myanmar, and the image of Freddi returned, as it had done many times during the flight. The peacekeeper had appeared forlorn when they parted, which seemed a total contradiction in terms: Freddi, forlorn? She had accompanied Meng Jarrah to the airport, yet was unusually silent until they arrived. The two women had seen a great deal of each other these past few weeks and normally had little difficulty finding something of interest to talk about.

Eventually, breaking the silence, Freddi suggested they stay in contact so that any developments relevant to their investigation, scientific or otherwise, could be discussed and taken into account. She was fully aware of recent events in Australia because whenever possible she communicated with Chiu Liow on a daily basis, and although Freddi never underestimated her brother's abilities, she knew he would have limited understanding of the technical implications of the attacks on Willsmere and the other research centres.

In response, Meng Jarrah tried to explain that she wasn't travelling to Australia to look into anything other than the possibility of a joint research project, but Freddi had insisted that the opportunity to 'dig around', as she put it, was too good to miss.

'You're aware of everything that's happened here, which means you'll be able to relate it all to anything you learn about the situation there.' Freddi frowned as she spoke, and her usual, even-tempered tone of voice had changed to one of frustration and irritation. 'We've lost two investigators for the time being, Welcome and Morag, and the investigators Morag appointed have been withdrawn. All of which means, I am now up to my neck in work! Chiu's having trouble finding the time to liaise with me, too, and has the added worry of trying to find evidence to clear her.'

Realising Freddi was behaving out of character, and not wishing to upset her further, Meng Jarrah had agreed, without further hesitation. 'Alright, I'll do what I can...although there isn't the remotest chance of Morag being guilty. I'm sure of it, and no doubt you are too?'

'Of course I am! We've worked far too closely for me not to have noticed something odd about her. By the way, did you know they haven't even arranged for her replacement yet?'

Freddi had sworn and thumped the nearest piece of padded furniture, which happened to be where her cat, Shela, was sitting, meticulously cleaning her sleek black fur. When the cat leapt off, staring at her companion in surprise, Freddi, her ringlets more ruffled than usual, crouched down to take the cat's face in her hands. 'Sorry, sweetie, I know I don't usually take it out on the furniture.' Shela licked her nose, then jumped back onto the chair.

'The FSIU really are a bunch of bureaucratic ninnies!' exclaimed Meng Jarrah. Noticing that her airjet had moved into position on the runway, she swung her travel bag onto the waiting baggage transport.

'Well, who knows if that's what's wrong, or if it's deliberate?' replied Freddi, standing with arms folded, glaring at the aircraft. 'It's one of the things we need to find out.' She turned to face Meng Jarrah. 'It's time for you to go. Call me when you can?'

As the airjet began its descent, Meng Jarrah remembered Freddi's golden eyes, rare and beautiful, as were her fine-boned, yet immensely strong, hands. Most people's personalities were reflected in their hands, she thought. The brief anger hadn't made Freddi any less attractive, either, or even less dignified. An unaccustomed tingling sensation flowed through her arms when she realised just how much she would miss her.

Having hardly noticed the time passing, it was with a sense of joy that Meng Jarrah saw the gum trees surrounding Tullamarine airport below. While the airjet circled widely over Melbourne, waiting for instructions to land, she basked in the sensation of coming home. The blue reflections of the Rialto, the yellow-brown waters of the Yarra River as it snaked its way to Port Phillip Bay, and the bluestone walls of Saint Patrick's Cathedral were all still there.

Characteristically, she had asked that no one meet her, either at Tullamarine or at Parkville, preferring to take her time exploring a little before making her way to Willsmere. Her first stop would be the Melbourne City Baths. She wanted to wash and then refresh both body and mind with a vigorous swim in clean, clear water.

Meng Jarrah slipped off her clothing, took a brief shower, and entered the gloom of one of the centre's saunas. As her eyes grew accustomed to the dim light, she could make out the shapes of three others, lying in a heat-induced stupor on the wooden benches. A brazier burned, and from time to time someone roused themselves sufficiently to pour lime-scented water onto the coals. They hissed and a cloud of steam wafted its way over as she stretched luxuriously and lay down on a soft towel. The heat was just short of unbearable. Her lithe body relaxed, and with it, her mind. She was sinking into a gentle doze when a smooth, warm hand stroked her shoulder then continued down towards the small of her back. Startled, Meng Jarrah raised her head, to see the delicate features of a small, black-haired woman, whose dark brown eyes crinkled in amusement.

'You look almost like a cat taking a nap. I couldn't resist stroking you, and apologise if I've upset you. I am a masseur by profession... Would you like some soothing?'

The woman's voice had a delicious lilt and the last phrase an almost musical quality. Meng Jarrah mumbled her agreement, since it was not uncommon for masseurs to be attached to public saunas. She lay down again and the small woman began to massage the soles of her feet, finding the tender points and gradually easing the pain she initially induced. A flow of energy coursed throughout Meng Jarrah's body, but as the masseur slowly, and with great skill, worked her way along the outside of her legs, kneading the strong, fine muscles, easing their tension, she relaxed deeply, until the woman found her customer had fallen soundly asleep, dreaming of someone else's touch.

When Meng Jarrah awoke, almost an hour had passed. She rolled onto her side and savoured the warmth and comfort of the sauna for just a little longer, then smiled and rose to take the promised swim. As the water streamed over her head and body, this highly independent woman found herself thinking of Freddi not just as a friend, but as someone with whom it might be possible to share more. She recalled how well they worked together, how they could laugh and relax in each other's company, and how much they seemed to trust each other. As she emerged from the pool to dry off, Meng Jarrah came to a decision.

A cool wind had sprung up, rustling the oaks. Leaves scurried across the brilliant blue-green lawns, while in the background, thunderclouds gathered on the horizon. The light had developed that unique quality which precedes or follows a rainstorm, when all things are brighter and more golden than usual. Willsmere seemed a fairytale place as Meng Jarrah walked towards its gates, which opened smoothly for her, as did the massive front doors. She recognised most of the faces of the small group waiting for her in the great reception hall. At one time or another over the years, and particularly more recently, she had been told who each of the researchers were, so felt comfortable assuming the woman standing close to a young man and holding his hand was Gwenllian, while the man was her brother, Owain.

They were a striking pair. He was dressed in a knee-length white robe embroidered with silver thread, his blonde hair falling in waves to his shoulders. His sister was clad in a body-hugging, one-piece suit of emerald green that matched her eyes. The fabric sparkled when she moved forward with the rest of the group to shake Meng Jarrah's hand.

Clearly delighted by her arrival, they all seemed to be speaking at once. Søren Thorup bowed when he introduced himself, then took her hand and kissed it. Did he always do such unusual things, she wondered, accepting the gesture. The woman called Karla had a large, golden-red cat twining itself around her legs, while Mik Theophanous carried another over his shoulder, supporting her weight with one hand while using his other to emphasise everything he said in a series of wide, flowing gestures. Standing next to him, Tamara Solanum's clear grey eyes, friendly mouth and air of complete honesty attracted Meng Jarrah immediately. She was certain they could work well together. Meanwhile, Martha, Lamington's research coordinator, stood to one side, weighing the situation and waiting for a quieter moment to make herself known.

Eventually, with the introductions completed, the general merriment subsided into a more serious, work-like atmosphere. Nevertheless, Meng Jarrah gave in to temptation and placed her arm around Søren's shoulders while they walked towards the centre's dining room. This seemingly angelic creature had indicated that the next two hours would be dedicated to the civilised activity of eating excellent food, drinking fine wines, and discussing their work, all the while insisting that nothing helped the efficient working of the mind as much as fine dining.

In the end, they occupied the dining room for almost twice as long. Gwenllian and Owain enthusiastically described the success of the field trials of their soil analysis method, as well as the purchase by the Australian Government of their intelligent decision-making systems module, which, when integrated, allowed applications of certain types to self-diagnose their own functions and give early warning of any imminent problem. They had decided to invest half the proceeds from the sale in this joint Federation venture.

Pleased with their discussions, Meng Jarrah felt confident in offering her centre's resources, particularly since her Myanmarian researcher had now almost fully regained his health and composure: 'Though I have to say that due to the continuing instability of the lattice in Papua, and despite our labs there being fully functional, I suspect we'd be taking an enormous security risk if we included them in this project.' Meng Jarrah frowned for a moment, then looked directly at each of them in turn. 'As I assume we all know, Morag MacIain has been placed under house arrest, pending her trial. I'm sure none of us believe she was involved in the sabotage of the Papuan information systems, but without her input, we can't trust that any communications we have with Niu Bougainville won't be intercepted.'

'Nothing we do is fully secure, as far as I can make out,' ventured Martha, and then blushed at having become the centre of attention. 'I mean, we have to go on as if we're alright, but I think we should realise we might not be...and take whatever precautions we can think of. I'd like to suggest that our research not be left on either our computers or the lattice. We should do our work on back-up drives instead and take them home at the end of every shift. We can ask for local versions of our software to be installed on our computers, too, and that way we won't need to stay connected to the lattice, unless we want to.'

Everyone gazed at her, impressed. Such an obvious safety precaution had escaped them all.

'What do you think about comlinks?' asked Mik. 'Maybe we should avoid using them to discuss our work.'

'Well, I for one would be happy to spend more time having discussions in person, rather than using a comlink or computer,' remarked Søren, grinning as he pictured the increased level of stress such a step would engender in his guardian peacekeeper.

Karla laughed, knowing full well what made Søren grin. 'I'm sure Red Matilda wouldn't mind going out more, either. Perhaps we should meet at Mik's place when we can, to keep Possum company?'

'*Who* is Possum?' asked Meng Jarrah, wondering at anyone having chosen such an odd name.

'Mik's other cat,' answered Tamara. 'Possum was the one who saved my life.'

'What under the Sun do you mean, Tamara?!' exclaimed Owain.

'Oh, that's right, not all of you know, do you?' Tamara paled, and gave an abridged version of the night she had nearly been murdered in the park, and how Possum prevented it.

Gwenllian, Martha and Owain looked sick and rose from the table.

'So what will happen to the cat?' asked Martha.

'Possum will actually be placed on trial in about two months time,' replied Mik, scowling, his eyebrows bristling. 'In the meantime, she has to stay at home.' In disgust, he crushed his serviette into a ball and threw it onto his empty plate. 'Still, at least the Breeding Centre is helping us with her defence. They're conducting research into cats' protective behaviour and Søren's spending most of his spare time working with them. He's looking into the way cats communicate with us and with each other. Because of the importance of this case to the future of cats in general, Parliament has commissioned an independent behaviourist to evaluate all their findings and enter everything known about the modern day cat into the Judge.'

'What do you mean, she'll be placed on trial?' Gwenllian couldn't believe she had heard him correctly. 'A cat being tried, just like a human?!'

Angry, Mik began to stand, just as Fliedermus snarled, thrashing her tail, eyes huge, glaring at her. Gwenllian jumped in fright and Mik made an effort to control himself, placing a restraining hand on Fliedermus' head.

'It may interest you to know, Gwenllian of the green eyes,' drawled Søren, 'that the Melbourne peacekeepers themselves afforded our dear little Possum legal status by allowing Mik to bail her out of the Detention Centre, rather than shooting her there and then. You, I think, would be wise to find out a little more about cats. *We* are all very fond of them.'

His voice held a dangerous edge, which Gwenllian was quick to notice. She moved over to Mik and touched his arm. 'I'm sorry I offended you. I didn't mean to. It's just that I don't know much about them, and you must admit, it isn't exactly common for a nonhuman...' she chose her term with care '...to be afforded the protection of the law to such an extent.'

'Yeah, sure,' Mik replied, managing to relax slightly, although he didn't smile. 'I tend to forget the majority of the population don't have cats and actually know very little about them. I guess I'm just lucky to have three.'

The atmosphere rapidly improved and soon everyone, except Fliedermus and Red Matilda, had chosen to forget the incident. After tidying up the dining area, and although the evening was late, they moved off to the laboratories. Meng Jarrah wanted to see at least some of their work, and spoke about her plans for her precious twentieth-century soil sample to be sent to Myanmar for full structural and microbial analysis. The sample, as it turned out, had originally been taken from the Lamington region, a factor which played a significant part in Meng Jarrah's decision to join the others in this venture.

Gwenllian and Owain had already arranged to travel to Lamington in three days time. They would both take leave of absence from their usual workplaces in order to determine the composition of a widespread number of soil samples. These were to be compared to the analysis of Meng Jarrah's ancient specimen in the hope that recommendations could be made for an accelerated reconstruction program for Lamington's depleted soils. Meng Jarrah was willing to then examine the idea of re-creating any extinct micro-organisms that might appear essential to the success of the enterprise.

'In theory, I'm reasonably confident we could succeed in doing this,' she said, 'but without knowing the quality of the soil sample, it's impossible to say whether we'll have sufficient intact material to base our work upon. As far as I'm aware, there are no surviving records of the genetic profiles of these types of organisms. Have any of you heard otherwise?'

All of them shook their heads, but Karla was optimistic there would be enough information from which they could extrapolate, using Gwenllian and Owain's application if necessary: 'Assuming you *are* able to re-create even a small number of micro-organisms, we should be able to determine how they would affect the soil composition in the short, medium, and long-term.'

'I agree,' said Tamara, brushing a few curls away from her face. Mik placed an affectionate arm around her waist and she smiled up at him. 'Our reforestation model's based on a massive amount of information about ecological relationships, so that'll help too.' She turned to Gwenllian and asked, 'Do you think we'd be able to run a comparison between your modelling techniques and ours? I gather you've used a totally different approach, so it'd be great to know how they fit together.'

Owain and Gwenllian glanced at each other, coming to a quick, unspoken agreement. 'You'll be happy to know we were planning to make that suggestion ourselves, although the results would need to come under the commercial agreement we've all signed. If your application is improved as a result of the exercise, it would mean we'd have to negotiate a fee, over and above the Federation funding we're already receiving. On the other hand, if *our* model's improved, the Federation would be entitled to recoup a proportion of its funding and even receive an additional payment from us if the improvement appeared to have the potential to produce significantly greater profits. Mind you, the fees could cancel each other out if both our applications are improved.' Gwenllian smiled, then said, 'I hope this sounds fair?'

The other members of the group seemed uneasy, but given they had agreed to the commercial nature of the joint venture, they needed to come to terms with calculating payments. So, once the matter was disposed of, they were soon involved in a highly technical discussion about the methods used by Karla and Søren in their genetic modelling, and those used by Tamara and Mik in their work with Lamington. Meng Jarrah also had many questions for Martha about the nature and progress of the Lamington growth trials.

'The embryos we sent to replace the ones they lost are doing well,' said Tamara, a hint of pride in her voice, 'and the older, outdoor trials are growing according to our model's predictions. I guess you know that a great many of the Station's plants were destroyed?'

'Oh yes. Morag MacIain kept me well informed, as did Research Coordinator Zago.' Meng Jarrah paused, then said, 'It's been a long day and a marvellous one, so I think I'd better ask you, Karla, to settle me into one of those bedrooms in your communal dwelling. I feel like I need to sleep for a solid ten hours!'

She stood up and stretched, while the others rose to walk with them to the callstation. As Gwenllian picked up her parasol and bag, Red Matilda pounced on her hand, scratching it. Gwenllian cried out and snatched it to her mouth, and when Karla turned around to find out what had happened, she saw Red Matilda sitting two metres away, innocently cleaning her tail, while Fliedermus was still curled up by Mik's feet.

'What on Earth...?!' She walked quickly over to Gwenllian to examine the scratch. It was deep, and Karla didn't believe it had been accidental. She turned angrily to Red Matilda, demanding an explanation, but for the first time since living together as constant companions, the cat's mind was closed to her. Astonished and annoyed, Karla rummaged in her bag, then applied antiseptic to Gwenllian's hand, followed by a small bandage.

Mik turned to Søren, saying, 'What's happening with those two? I don't understand why they're reacting to Gwenllian like this, damn it!'

Fliedermus tried to wind herself around his legs, but he brushed her away. In dismay, she turned and fled down the corridor. Søren took Red Matilda's furry face between his hands and stared into her eyes. Although she met his unflinchingly, Søren couldn't receive anything from her, either. He stood up and followed Fliedermus down the corridor. When they came back, the cat's tail was well down.

'For some reason I find difficult to understand, these two do not like you,' he said, frowning and pointing a finger in Gwenllian's direction. 'Can it be that you do not like them?'

She had begun to cry. Her brother held her close against his chest, glaring defiantly at Søren, his face red and twisted in rage. 'And just because two cats don't like my sister, does this mean the rest of you think she's guilty of being involved in everything that's happened lately? Because if you do, I want to know about it, now! Either you trust us and we go on, or you don't, and that's the end!'

Karla took a step towards him. 'Owain! Please... We like and admire you both! If we thought either of you had anything to do with it all, we would never have suggested you join us. I know we're a bit obsessed with Mik's cats, but they really are special. There's also a lot we still don't know about them, even though Søren's working hard to find out more. Please...'

Gwenllian stopped crying and wiped her eyes. Karla reached a tentative hand towards her, but pulled back when Owain clasped his sister even closer and she turned her face away.

'The only suggestion I can make,' Karla said instead, 'is that we take as little notice of their peculiar dislike as we can. They won't be happy, but perhaps they can't have it all their own way.' She placed both hands on Gwenllian's shoulders this time and turned her around so they were face to face. Surprised, Owain let go of his sister and stepped back. 'Who knows why the cats don't like you, Gwen! I know *I* do,' said Karla, smiling, 'and so do we all.' She gave Gwenllian a quick kiss on the cheek. 'Come on, let's walk to the callstation. Would you all like to come home with us and watch the storm from the observatory? It should be spectacular.'

Everyone, except Owain, smiled, although rather weakly. He hesitated, and watched while Fliedermus and Red Matilda waited quietly for the leashes to be attached to their collars. Knowing her brother would still be angry, Gwenllian turned and linked arms with him, touching him gently on the cheek. 'Come on... Let's trust them... Please?'

Owain, face less red, nodded abruptly, and they went with the others to the door. Just as the group reached the callstation, the first heavy drops of rain spattered down. The fruit bats feeding in the nearby bushland stopped their chattering, waiting for the lightning. The air was completely still, until a distant rumble of thunder broke the silence.

*

As he made his call, to Chiu Liow's surprise, the computer screen initially blanked for a few seconds, but when Freddi's worried face finally appeared, he greeted his sister as usual.

'Well,' she replied, 'what do we do now?'

'I'm taking the first flight to Myanmar so I can speak with you in person. I've become paranoid. With the lattice having been compromised, even comlink calls might be unsafe! The next flight is in fifty minutes, so I'll see you around midnight.'

At midnight, as promised, Chiu Liow was waiting at the Mandalay airport. They embraced warmly, then walked to the nearest callstation, not speaking again until they were seated in the parkland outside Freddi's home. The night was hot and humid, but they wanted to be sure they were alone, and somehow the darkness gave them the comforting illusion of security. All Chiu Liow's public composure was gone. He spoke as he felt: unhappy, yet relaxing as best he could for the first time in many days, more at ease in Freddi's company than anyone else's.

'You care for her, don't you, Chiu,' said Freddi softly, touching his arm.

'Yes, Freddi, I do, very much. The only comfort I have is that Welcome is with her. We're communicating using our maximum-security lines, in the hope they're safe, even though they might not be. There's nothing else we can really do. I'm prohibited by my duties here in Australia from going to Luzern, and while Morag is under house arrest, I can't even speak with her in the usual way.'

Freddi put an arm around her brother's shoulders and gave him a sympathetic hug, saying, 'What did you want to talk to me about tonight?'

'I wanted to tell you about an idea that came to me. As you know, we can't trust anyone Rohan Maerz sends to replace Morag, so I've decided to bend the law slightly and ask some private individuals to assist with the investigation. You might be able to find someone to help in a similar way.'

He stopped and waited for her to say something. Several seconds went by before she simply asked, 'Who?'

'Karla, from Willsmere. She can assist with the scientific aspects of the case...and help keep me sane; I've enjoyed talking to her.' He managed an uneasy smile. 'Lance Melrose Naylor from the Central Computer Site will help too. I need a computing expert and they have to be someone who isn't with the FSIU. Melrose is good, and he's willing to help. He's been hit hard by all this, and still can't cope with the possibility that Marika was involved in the sabotage of Willsmere, maybe even more. It seems they've been close friends for years.'

'I gather Morag is certain he isn't involved in any way?'

'Yes, or I wouldn't have asked him.'

'No, I suppose not. Sorry... Anyway, it's a good idea.'

Chiu Liow took a deep breath and nodded. 'Tell me more about the explosions at the logging site. If you want, I'm sure Melrose could take a short period of leave and give you a hand as well.'

Freddi considered the offer for a moment. 'I've put off interviewing their security expert because I needed Morag's help, but I doubt if the security officer could possibly be involved. He's the plantation manager's son. Still, it's got to be done, so, yes, I could use Melrose for a day or two. Thank you, and we should make all the arrangements now. That way, I won't need to contact him myself, which could be risky. I suggest he meet us at the local dance being held next Friday... 20:00 would be good. The crowd's not too thin or too great at that time. It's not unusual for men to dance together in groups, and sometimes even in pairs, which means he and the young man can dance and talk to each other to their heart's content without anyone overhearing them. I think it might be hard for the security officer to lie while being held close to someone's chest! Afterwards, Melrose can dance with me and pass on what he's discovered.' She grinned, hoping Chiu Liow would see the humour in the plan. He did.

'I've always liked your imagination, Freddi. I can't guarantee Melrose will *enjoy* dancing with a man, but I'm sure he'll manage. I'll give him instructions on how to get there. He'll need to dance with you first, though, to get a better idea of what you want him to find out. Perhaps you could bring one of your other peacekeepers to keep the plantation manager's son occupied before he has his little tête-à-tête with Melrose.'

'Yes, I can arrange that.' Freddi went on to give a summary of her interviews with the other plantation workers, as well as a basic analysis of the data obtained from the site computer. She told Chiu Liow about their security system and how polite the computer had been, and was pleased to see him smile again. 'What we need to admit, though, is that almost anyone could have walked in, laid the explosives, then walked out again, without being noticed. There aren't any fences, and no reason for having any. These sorts of crimes just don't normally happen, and Myanmar Forest Industries wouldn't ruin their own business, particularly given the contract they had with Wyvern Meridian. Besides which, their record is exemplary. I think the fact that Teak Australia deals with them is in their favour too, don't you?'

'Indeed, and I'm almost certain Teak Australia isn't implicated in any way. They've nothing to gain and everything to lose. But what was the contract with Wyvern Meridian about?' Chiu Liow raised an eyebrow, prompting Freddi to explain the terms of the insurance arrangement they forced the timber plantation to accept.

Chiu Liow frowned. 'Meaning it was essentially a public relations exercise on their part when they announced a ten percent decrease in transport charges. Interesting... So, will you be giving Myanmar Forest Industries a clearance certificate so they can restart production?'

'I fully intend to, but can't officially until we've interviewed their security officer. Even so, I imagine they'll take at least two years to recover.'

'That fits in with Teak Australia's assessment of their own situation. They've been badly affected by the loss of their raw materials. Have you managed to find out how Wyvern Meridian has been affected – if in fact they have?'

'No, I can't get a word out of them. I've applied to Parliament for access to their business records, but as I've no evidence to incriminate them in any way, I doubt whether it'll be granted. That's where Morag could have helped. In these particular circumstances, she would automatically have been entitled to the information.'

Freddi looked down, clenched her fist and swore under her breath. Chiu Liow briefly clasped her by the shoulder and said, 'Yes, Freddi, I know, but somehow, we have to manage. I obtained a small amount of information from Yuen Fong Lau. You remember him? Our illustrious Member of Parliament, who was Thanh Fong Lau's father? It turns out that according to Mik Theophanous and Tamara Solanum, Wyvern Meridian's model for an Australian timber plantation creates no conflict with the Willsmere approach to reforestation. The Federation has already begun its own independent evaluation of their work, although it could be some time before they announce their conclusions.'

Freddi shook her head, but allowed him to proceed uninterrupted: 'Overall, Wyvern Meridian seems to be in reasonable shape as a company and they're on good terms with the Malaysian Government because they've recently bought a major shareholding in one of their soil reclamation companies. I would think the Myanmarians regard them favourably as well, despite the lack of success of their local timber plantation.'

'Yes, I'm sure they do,' said Freddi, thoughtfully. 'By the way, did you know the international director of Wyvern Meridian is an Argentinean-born person of Japanese descent named Kenjiro Kakura?'

'No, I haven't had time to trace through the maze of business connections. I gather you have?'

'No, I didn't find out by doing any digging. It appears he's taking a grand tour of Myanmar. More public relations, I expect. Do you think I should meet him?'

'Yes, I do, and take your cat.'

'Why?'

'I'm beginning to trust their assessment of people's characters. It would be useful to see how Shela reacted to him.'

'True...it would. Oh, and before I forget... Did you know Meng Jarrah left for Australia this morning to meet with your researchers about a cooperative effort to speed up their work?'

'No, I didn't. This is the second time I'm the last to know what's going on at Willsmere!'

'Well, from now on, hopefully you won't be. Once you've spoken with Karla, I'm sure you'll be kept up to date. I'd be surprised if she refused to help.' Freddi grinned again and added, 'By the way, *I've* asked Meng Jarrah to give me her impressions of the setup down there, which means we'll each have our own private sleuth and we'll be able to compare notes. She and Karla may pick up on different things.'

Her brother returned the grin, feeling a great deal better than he had since Morag left for Luzern. They spoke together for a little while longer before he made his way back to the airport. There were only a few minutes to wait before boarding the airjet. It rose above the city of Mandalay, circled once, then flew high into the night sky. Chiu Liow willed himself to relax by remembering Morag as he last saw her. He could still imagine the velvet touch of her lips on his before she left, and soon fell into a light, dreamless sleep.

CHAPTER THIRTEEN

Two impassive guards waited stoically as the interview dragged on. One of their duties was to provide an independent account, should it ever be called for, of the intricate verbal game between the two occupants of the room: former investigator Morag MacIain and Rohan Maerz. At least the room was pleasant and the food excellent. The guards winked at each other when the third order went out for sweets: the FSIU Coordinator's habits were well known. That was two hours ago, and now it was almost dusk. The lighting and heating adjusted itself as the day darkened and the late winter temperature dropped dramatically. Moments after the first moonbeam crept in from the night outside, dark red curtains silently swished together to block out the cold creeping down the stairway from the greenhouse above.

Morag's home was classically Swiss, although with less ornamentation than usual. A vase of bright yellow chrysanthemums from her greenhouse graced the black, polished surface of the dining table at which they sat. The delicate fifteenth-century Norwegian chairs had diplomatically been replaced with sturdy modern ones capable of bearing Rohan's massive weight. He sniffed the piece of honeyed pineapple he had carefully selected from the array before them. Before popping the sweet into his mouth, he held it up to the light to admire its pale translucent colour. To be polite, Morag chose a cherry and slowly ate it, feeling slightly ill. She had eaten more in this one afternoon than she usually did in a whole day.

Suppressing an increasingly urgent desire to walk out of the room, Morag forced herself to continue answering his questions. From the very first, Rohan had adopted a gentle, slightly bemused tone, behaving as if he had no doubt of her innocence, yet insisting that the evidence against her gave no other option than recall and house arrest. He apologetically explained that official charges were to be laid the next day, and as Morag had never been in any doubt this would happen, she was at least relieved to have an approximate date for the trial.

After wiping his fingers on a red linen napkin, Rohan sipped his tea, then, leaning forward as far as his expansive waistline would allow, said, 'Morag, before your trial, you will have a full three months to prepare your case. I hope this will be sufficient?'

'Oh yes, Rohan, quite sufficient, thank you. I hope it will be enough for you too.'

Rohan could hardly fail to understand the ambivalence of Morag's words. He had already noticed a disquieting tendency for her Australian psychologist to appear at frequent intervals and in unexpected places when he left his high-security office complex. Ah well, chess would be a boring game without a challenging opponent!

'The prosecution's case is almost fully prepared,' he replied, with a kindly smile. 'I can assure you that you'll have the full transcript within days. There'll be no last-minute disclosures as in a pre-twenty-third-century melodrama...*and* you'll have the advantage of not being required to provide me with *your* transcript if you prefer not to. I look forward to seeing you released, of course, although I must admit I've enjoyed your company. I missed you while you were in Australia, and even more when your reports became so infrequent. Oh, and do you know, there must be something wrong with the lattice. For the past few days there haven't been *any* comlink calls, other than the most brief, between our young friends. How odd... I must have it looked into.' He tilted his head to one side and paused, considering. 'Perhaps they'd rather their conversations were kept private. What a frightful thought. Do you think someone could be listening in on them?'

'I'm sure of it. Aren't you?'

'I respect your opinion, my dear Morag, but as far as I know, such a thing would be virtually impossible.' Rohan smiled complacently.

'I'd be interested to know what the fault was, if you find there is one,' she replied calmly. 'I also have a favour to ask. Would you be prepared to meet my defence psychologist? I'm sure he could entertain you far better than I.'

'What a dreadfully nasty thing to say, Morag. I don't find your situation the least entertaining. Surely we've been friends far too long for you to have such a hurtful opinion of my interest in your predicament? It is highly distasteful to me that I must be the one to assume the role of formal interrogator, but there quite simply is no one else qualified to take it on. That's a compliment, you know...and I'd be charmed to meet your colleague. His name is Welcome, isn't it? Marvellous sense of humour he must have...'

Rohan eased himself out of the well-cushioned chair, patted his stomach and burped gently, his hand over his mouth. 'Forgive me, I must leave. Shall we make an appointment with Welcome for a midsun meal at one of our better restaurants? Oh! My apologies. Well! It will have to be here. Shall we say 13:00 tomorrow?'

'That would suit very well. I look forward to it.' Morag picked up his enormous purple woollen cloak and handed it to him. He retrieved the matching wide-brimmed hat and carefully placed it at just the right angle on his head. The outlandish effect was given its finishing touch by a pair of fine maroon leather gloves. Rohan Maerz had a penchant for the rare and beautiful, as well as the extravagant. The gloves alone would most likely have cost him two full months' credits.

The curtains drew aside when he approached and the two guards followed him patiently up the staircase to ground level. Outside, the snow piled thickly against the greenhouse walls, glimmering in the starlight. The night was still and their footsteps marked the fresh fall as the three walked towards their waiting airjet. Morag watched while it rose and flew off towards Luzern, far below her home on The Rigi. Shivering, she hurried down to the warmth of the main house.

When Morag spoke to her computer, Welcome's cheerful face soon appeared on the screen. He was relieved to hear of her success in arranging a meeting with the FSIU Coordinator. 'Although, I can't help noticing you seem a bit weary,' he added. 'Has he only just gone?'

'Yes, and he's been his usual considerate self the entire time. I'm finding it harder and harder to imagine he's behind all this, despite the evidence. He even apologised for having to treat me as the prime suspect, and for having to be the one to interrogate me.'

'When is the trial to be?'

'He informed me it would be towards the end of May or the beginning of June. There was something else he said that intrigued me, although I think you should come over here to discuss it.'

Welcome looked puzzled, but refrained from asking any questions. 'Right. I'll commandeer an airjet from one of the local peacekeepers. Defence privilege. See you in about half an hour.'

The screen blanked and Morag considered its slim, black form before absentmindedly playing her fingers lightly over the matching keyboard. The computer beeped and asked if she wanted anything.

'Yes, I do,' she replied. 'Please copy the notes for my defence case to the back-up drive.'

Morag put the copy away safely then curled up in an armchair to wait for Welcome.

At precisely 13:00 the next day, the household security system announced the arrival of Rohan Maerz and his two guards. To give themselves a psychological advantage, Welcome and Morag had decided to provide a sumptuous midsun meal. They would also avoid any discussion of the case or the trial until the meal, which was planned to last for around two hours, was over. Rohan, whatever his role in the series of crimes, clearly preferred to play-act. So be it.

The previous evening, Welcome had been staggered by Morag's assertion that Rohan was tapping into the lattice. The implications were that they would be forced to resort to manual methods of communication with Chiu Liow, although it appeared the Australians were already avoiding the lattice whenever possible. It was a most peculiar and difficult situation. 'Postage' was generally used only for freight, which meant requests to send letters would inevitably be met with amused disbelief. Still, given that freight handlers tended to be intensely proud of their ability to guarantee delivery and to safeguard their goods, the letters would almost certainly arrive safely. Their first would contain the substance of today's meeting.

Welcome and Morag both stood to greet Rohan as he, with some difficulty, descended the staircase. When Welcome reached up to help him down the last few steps, Rohan scowled for an instant at the implied insult, but managed to smile as he accepted the offered hand.

'Morag MacIain, whatever will I do if you're found guilty?' he said. 'There's no one else I know who has the ability to provide an outstanding table together with sublime company!' Removing his coat, hat and gloves, which today were deliberately black, he handed them to Welcome, saying, 'Would you be so kind?'

Welcome bowed, ran lightly up the staircase and placed the garments on the simple coat stand near the greenhouse entrance, where most guests would have left them before entering the main abode. When he returned, they seated themselves at the table, which was decorated with a red hand-embroidered tablecloth, green napkins, and white arum lilies. Rohan touched one of the lilies. 'Are we celebrating a death today?'

'We gambled on your appearing in black, so chose the lilies to complement your attire,' explained Welcome, smiling broadly, the small crinkles around his eyes and mouth giving him a homely appearance.

'Entrancing!' replied Rohan, returning the smile. 'I would have brought a posy with me if I'd known you'd be going to this much trouble. Perhaps forget-me-nots would have been appropriate?' He tucked a corner of the napkin under his chin and surveyed the table.

'Please, do start,' invited Morag, handing him the basket of black rye bread. Rohan took two slices and spread them liberally with vegetable butter. After the others followed suit, the remaining dishes were passed around in silence. Once everyone had helped themselves, Morag stood up to pour the pale pink, plum champagne commonly served on such occasions. Glasses were raised in salute and then drained. A second glass was poured, and with the ceremony over, Welcome began the conversation.

'I understand that amongst other things, you're the author of several works on subjective reality, covering a number of fields, such as belief in an afterlife. I've read all your books and I'm impressed.'

Rohan coughed in surprise just as he was about to swallow a morsel of pickled cucumber, almost choking. Welcome patted him firmly on the back until the fit subsided. Red in the face, Rohan turned to look him straight in the eye. Welcome's warm brown gaze met the icy grey stare with equanimity. The seconds passed slowly before Rohan answered.

'Many read the works,' he said, hesitating slightly, 'but few bother to research the identity of the author. When did you come across them?'

Welcome waved his hand in a vague fashion. He had spent two weeks researching the private occupations of his adversary, and was intrigued to learn what they were. He'd then spent ten hours a day for five days re-reading Rohan's – or Martyn Steinberg's, as he termed himself – seven published texts, despite having already read them during his studies towards a degree in criminology.

'I am, as you know, a psychologist specialising in the study and apprehension of criminals,' he replied. 'It would be strange if I'd *not* read your books. Perhaps we can spend some of the time I'm here in Luzern discussing them?'

'Do you understand why I use a pseudonym?'

'I think *I* do,' interrupted Morag. She had a quiet smile on her lips and rested her chin on clasped hands. 'Authors explain not only the behaviour of others, they reveal a great deal about themselves. As Federation Special Investigation Unit Coordinator, you'd prefer people to know as little about you as possible. You surround yourself with barriers and enjoy creating mystery.'

Rohan poured himself a third glass of champagne before replying: 'You are, as usual, correct.' He twiddled the stem of his crystal flute. 'I create mysteries, as well as solve them... In fact, I use a pseudonym because I prefer to retain credibility. Do you seriously believe the texts would *have* any credibility if the academic world knew a *fat* man had written them? And do you think they would feel safe if they knew I held such views? The world accepts the power of the Federation Special Investigation Unit, and my position in it, because we're anonymous and supposedly impartial. Once our innermost thoughts and values became known, they'd fear and resent us, and me in particular.' He sat back from the table and carefully dabbed his mouth and chin with the napkin.

'How have you managed to maintain your pseudonym all these years?' asked Welcome, managing to convey an apparently genuine ignorance of what he had already discovered for himself.

'I have a representative. Martyn Steinberg does exist, and is sufficiently learned and plausible to present my theses to the public. He receives the payments and I receive little 'presents' from him to mark special occasions. Simple... It would hardly be in his own interest to expose me,' he added, answering Welcome's unspoken question.

Rohan suddenly found himself yearning for the opportunity to discuss his work with this funny little man. 'Indeed, how lonely I am,' he realised.

Morag broke his reverie by suggesting she bring the next course. Rohan and Welcome stood up to help carry the emptied dishes to the kitchen, while the two guards remained seated, one at each end of the table, innocuous witnesses to what had been said. Their duty was to ensure no pressure was brought to bear on either the accused or the accuser, as well as to answer direct questions at the trial, should any matters of procedure be brought into question. Nevertheless, they were enjoying themselves and brightened even further at the wonderful aromas that greeted them as the main meal was set on the table.

Welcome lifted the lid from one of the larger pots to sniff appreciatively at the chicken soup, which was garnished with fresh parsley and contained tiny dumplings and diced carrots. A second dish held a delightful assortment of golden, roasted vegetables, accompanied by a steaming jug of rich chicken gravy. Amidst these delicious aromas, rather than talking, they all paid attention to their food. The light in the room became dimmer as the afternoon passed, and when conversation began again, the cosiness of the atmosphere was reflected in the subjects chosen: the earlier sparring was left behind. When the table was finally cleared, they moved away to make themselves comfortable in the soft, grey armchairs.

'I have decided to take over the Australian side of the investigation,' announced Rohan. 'Until this matter is resolved, I'm not inclined to trust anyone else in the FSIU. I *am*, however, tempted to put off my departure so I can take up your desire to discuss criminology, Welcome, but sadly, my personal wishes must be put aside.'

His announcement had the desired effect. Both Morag and Welcome were good actors, but their dismay was clear.

'I'd prefer you didn't report my intention to Peacekeeper Chiu Liow Jones,' Rohan continued, waving a hand in Welcome's direction when he seemed about to protest. 'Oh, I've no knowledge regarding the subject of your conversations with your colleague, but as an intelligent person, I must assume you *are* in contact.'

'Naturally,' Welcome replied, wondering if they had been recorded. 'I'm here in a formal capacity, and Peacekeeper Jones has a duty to provide evidence for Morag's defence...as he must also provide evidence of her guilt, if he finds any. When will you leave?'

'Tomorrow, I think, or even the next day. My case against you is progressing well, Morag. I apologise for what this implies, but we must be realistic... Still, there is always the possibility you'll be found innocent. We must all maintain hope, and as the Judge will present the facts, there's no reason for me to be present at the trial. We can at least spare each other that.' He rose and took her hands in his, pressing them gently. She did not draw away, instead standing to look into his face: Morag saw nothing but the kindly expression she had always seen.

Red and yellow lanterns shone gaily on the dancing couples and circles of friends. It was now just past 21:00 in Mandalay and Lance Melrose Naylor was thoroughly enjoying himself. The trip to Myanmar held sufficient novelty to temporarily take his mind away from the continued, gnawing grief over Marika's predicament. He *still* could not bring himself to condemn her. Instead, he toyed with all the possible motives she might have had for involving herself in Willsmere's sabotage, and possibly even Lamington's: blackmail, threats? Who knew what lurked in her past? He had never been able to find out, and certainly did not believe she had anything whatsoever to do with Thanh Fong Lau's tragic death.

For the moment, however, he was occupied with the entertaining and enlightening conversation of the young man with whom he was dancing. He was almost, although not quite, sorry when the music ended and he transferred himself over to Freddi. Laughing, he told her the experience had been unique, and perhaps she should try interrogating her female suspects in a similar way? Melrose was surprised to see her appear only fleetingly amused, but thought no more about it as he launched himself into an abbreviated account of what the plantation manager's son had told him about their security system.

'He's brilliant, you know. Their system is an improvement on ours, even. I've convinced him to write a paper on it and send it to me. I want to get a similar one installed at the Central Computer Site at home.' The Senior Systems Technologist was clearly overjoyed at the concept of introducing something so simple, and yet previously unheard of – or at least, not heard of in recent times. He was drifting off into a pleasant reverie when Freddi reminded him what he was there for.

'Hmm...what? Yeah, you're right. Business... Look, I'm sure the little guy's not involved in anything he shouldn't be. He was completely relaxed and not in the least show-off about his invention. He adores his mother and is totally loyal to Myanmar Forest Industries. I tried the trick of insulting them a bit to see what he'd say and he trod on my foot – heavily, too – and didn't apologise. Nice...very nice person,' and Melrose once again wafted away into technical permutations.

He winced when Freddi punched him lightly in the ribs. 'Ouch! Okay, I'll concentrate... Will you want me to give evidence if and when this all goes to trial?'

'Yes...assuming we get that far some day. For now, I'll just ask you to make a sworn statement, tomorrow, so we can give them a clearance certificate. I must admit, I'm pleased to hear we can at least do that much.' Freddi frowned, then said, 'You could take a copy of the statement back to Chiu for me, if you don't mind. He'll be wanting your help too, won't he?'

'Oh, yes. I'll be going through Teak Australia's database for him tomorrow. I've already said not to put any of his personal ideas on the lattice and to use a back-up drive instead. He probably would've thought of it himself, but it's important to make sure. I also offered to install some local software for him, which he was pleased with, but said he didn't particularly mind handwriting when that would do the job. Strange man! It's a pity in a way that he has to put all his official stuff through the lattice, though. You'd think he could delay it a bit.'

'We'd like to, but that would involve an even bigger risk. We can't afford to allow the slightest lapse in providing information to the Judge, otherwise we could appear to be suppressing evidence and end up with a null verdict...' Freddi paused at the startled expression on Melrose's face. 'Didn't Chiu tell you we'd begun inputting?'

'No...and I didn't think you had permission yet from the FSIU to go to trial.'

'Not yet, no, but formal charges were laid against Morag MacIain two days ago, so now everything relevant to *her* trial – which means virtually everything we have from the time of the first security breach – has started going in. Let's just hope no one's capable of corrupting the Judge's knowledge base!'

Melrose blanched, and Freddi could feel his palms begin to perspire. She felt a bit sick herself at the idea and wished she hadn't mentioned it. They danced in silence for a while then joined in with some of the other revellers.

The voice on the other end of the comlink rose and fell in waves of anger. Chiu Liow listened, as he had done for the past hour or so. Marika's father, a South Australian peacekeeper, had belatedly taken an interest in his daughter's welfare, and if this conversation was typical of the man's style, Chiu Liow was grateful, to some extent, that he hadn't taken an earlier interest. He even began to think Marika might have some excuse for having behaved in an aberrant fashion, if indeed she had. When the peacekeeper paused for breath, Chiu Liow took the opportunity to break into the monologue:

'She *is* going to trial. Wasn't that clear? I acknowledge Marika has been under surveillance for a substantial period of time and is now under house arrest, but it's unavoidable, given the seriousness of the charges. There will be absolutely *no* problem incurred by your visiting her...if she wishes to see you.'

As the angry voice interrupted, Chiu Liow over-rode it. 'May I ask when you last paid her a visit, or she you?'

The voice blustered, then fell silent, embarrassed.

'Yes, I thought so. Three years is a long time for a parent not to have seen their child. I suggest I contact her now to obtain permission for your planned visit. Your daughter is undergoing a great deal of stress since having been informed only yesterday of her impending trial. Perhaps she would prefer not to add to it.'

This last comment was cruel, but Chiu Liow couldn't resist indirectly reprimanding the man for the neglect of his daughter. He didn't bother waiting for the peacekeeper to agree, instead keeping him on hold while he made contact with Marika.

The young woman's face had lost its normal healthy tan and there were smudges of fatigue below her dark eyes, otherwise her appearance was unaltered. The shoulder-length brown hair swung in silky waves, framing a broad face with high cheekbones and bird-wing eyebrows. A dimple in the middle of her chin gave Marika an endearing quality, despite the severity of the overall impression.

Chiu Liow chose not to insult her intelligence by wasting time on preliminaries. 'Marika, I have your father on comlink. I gather this may be the first contact he's made in some time? He demands to be given permission to visit. Do you want him to?'

Despite her strained composure, Marika was caught off-guard, and with a sharp intake of breath, hesitated. Chiu Liow wondered at the extent of her father's neglect; her mother had died many years ago. However, in a calm voice she said, 'By all means, let him speak to me.'

Chiu Liow made the connection, then watched as Marika coolly greeted her father. After all, he had little to say beyond conventional queries after her health and standard expressions of anger at her situation.

'You *know* I don't think you had anything to do with breaking into Willsmere or Lamington. And didn't you always say you were fond of that young bloke...Tim was his name, wasn't it?'

'No. It was Thanh, Dad,' his daughter replied, weariness creeping into her voice. 'Would you like to come to midsun tomorrow? I could put something special together. It's a long time since we shared a meal.'

'Sorry, do you think we could put it off until Thursday? I'm in the middle of a big case right now. Have to give evidence to the prosecutor tomorrow and there's a chance the verdict will be given the day after. I'd hate to miss it.'

'Sure, Dad, that'll be fine. I'll see you about 11:00 on Thursday, then.'

Marika broke the connection. Chiu Liow did the same. He no longer wondered at the affection Lance Melrose Naylor felt for her; she had immense depth of character, if not much in the way of human empathy.

While he was thinking about Marika and her father, the computer beeped, and when he answered the call, Melrose appeared on the screen, obviously pleased with himself.

'I've got something for you, Chiu Liow. Would it be alright to come over with it now?'

'Certainly. In about twenty minutes?'

When he arrived twenty-five minutes later, Freddi's letter in hand, Melrose sat down and waited impatiently while Chiu Liow read it, then launched into ecstasies about the security system he had heard about while in Myanmar. After some time, Melrose realised Chiu Liow was barely listening. 'What's happened?' he asked.

'I have just spent the past hour listening to Marika's father rabbit on about how much he cares for his daughter. To say the least, I am very, very angry. I suppose you can see that!'

Melrose nodded, and looked apprehensive. 'She's going to trial, isn't she.'

'Yes, in three months, at the same time as Morag MacIain. The two cases are being tried simultaneously. They're now seen to be one and the same.' Chiu Liow touched the young man sympathetically on the forearm.

'May I visit her?' His voice faltered for an instant.

'Yes, I think you should. Her father will be there on Thursday for midsun. May I suggest you join them? It would help her if you could.' Chiu Liow spoke gently, not wishing to push him into too difficult a situation.

Melrose nodded again. 'I'll speak to her as soon as I leave here.' He made an effort to control his anxiety, then said, 'I've gone through Teak Australia's database, and they're clean – I'm sure of it. Anyway, Vensor, one of the administrators at the Central Computer Site, wouldn't have anything to do with them if they weren't. He couldn't afford any dubious connections or it'd mean his job – which, by the way, he's extremely good at. As far as I'm concerned, I think there's been a deliberate attempt to implicate Teak Australia. The situation is ludicrous! No successful company would be stupid enough to forget the connections they have with the Site! Mind you, following up on all these links has taken up a fair bit of time...which might just be the motive, you know. After all, anything illegal Marika may have done could just as easily have been undertaken from Luzern.'

Chiu Liow studied him for several seconds. Morag had already discussed this possibility, but he wanted to know what the systems technologist knew. 'What exactly do you mean?'

'All the local sections of the lattice are backed up by the Federation network. There are incredibly complex manoeuvres to perform if the network administrators don't have a verified local request to modify, or even use, these overlay systems, but that doesn't mean it can't be done.'

'How many people normally have access to these 'overlay' systems without having received a local request?'

'Only Rohan Maerz, certain members of the Federation Assembly, and the FSIU security investigators.'

'Of whom Morag MacIain is one.'

'Yes... I just assumed she'd checked out the possibility already. It would've been the most incredible cheek for me to ask her about it.'

'She did,' replied Chiu Liow, resting his forehead on a clenched fist. He knew it opened the way for Marika to be cleared, but it also opened the way for the Judge to find Morag guilty. He raised his head and looked at Melrose again, who said nothing; his thoughts mirrored those of the peacekeeper. While they stared at each other, the door chimed annoyingly and displayed the vast form of Rohan Maerz, waiting politely to be given permission to enter.

Chiu Liow stood and immediately felt dizzy, as if he were suffering from an hallucination. His reflexes allowed him enough control to maintain a bland voice and expression as he greeted the Coordinator and invited him in. The door to the office slid aside and Rohan appeared in person, dressed in cool, flowing green appropriate to the hot, humid weather of Melbourne at this time of year. As Melrose stood up to be introduced, Rohan held out his hand to be briefly grasped, then, without saying a word, went over to the window to observe the view.

Turning around, he addressed Melrose: 'Morag has mentioned your fine work.' Rohan waved his hand when the young man began to speak. 'I remember faces. Yours was in her files... No mystery.' Walking over to Chiu Liow and clasping his shoulder, he laughed. 'And it's a pleasure to meet you at last, a man of great determination and imagination.'

Chiu Liow flinched, and Rohan withdrew his hand.

'No doubt you were discussing the impending trials and I've interrupted. My apologies. Could I be importunate enough to ask for some tea? It was abominably hot out there, and I'm completely unused to such weather.' He sat gingerly on one of the desks, as none of the chairs in the office seemed large enough to take his bulk. 'I appear to be the only one with anything to say. How strange...' and he looked at each of them expectantly.

'How do you take your tea?' asked Chiu Liow, at a complete loss.

'Oh, your servery will have taken care of my order. The computers here know me quite well.'

Melrose had taken a seat again, and for a moment, put his head in his hands. He was caught between an overwhelming desire to giggle hysterically and to burst into tears. The most powerful man in the world had just walked in...and asked for a cup of tea? And not only did he ask for it, the servery had responded to his voice and was currently complying with the request, presumably from details Maerz had amused himself in supplying. Well, blast it, he would serve the damned stuff as if it were the most natural thing in the world. Maybe that would give Chiu Liow time to think of something more intelligent to say! He got up and arranged Rohan's order on a tray.

Rohan gratefully accepted the tea and apple pastries, spooning custard onto them with avid greed. The trip had stimulated his appetite enormously. The others joined him. Why not? There was little the man could do here that he couldn't have done from Switzerland. At least they now knew who would be replacing Morag MacIain.

CHAPTER FOURTEEN

The soft creamy paper covered with Meng Jarrah's untidy scrawl seemed an artefact from the past. Having never received a 'letter' before, Freddi held it to her nose, imagining she could detect the warm scent of the writer, then sighed and read it again. Without the use of the comlink, Meng Jarrah seemed too far away.

Shela jumped onto the dark pastel-blue couch and buried her head in Freddi's lap, sensing her friend's sadness. Freddi smoothed back the cat's tufted ears, then picked up her newly acquired pen and began a reply, frowning at first with the unaccustomed effort of writing at length, but eventually beginning to enjoy the novel exercise. The report was written with her brother in mind, as the one letter would do for both he and Meng Jarrah, she decided, sternly pushing away sentimental alternatives. Her news consisted mainly of the formal clearance of Myanmar Forest Industries from having sabotaged their own plantation and the transport fleet, as well as her meeting with Kenjiro Kakura.

With his permission, she had recorded their entire conversation, a copy of which was being sent with the letter. Watching it for the third time, she skipped through the preliminaries to the point where Shela had intervened by howling and screaming, straining at her leash in an attempt to flee the reception area of the hotel where Kakura was staying. Freddi could still recall how her breathing suddenly became laboured, and how she almost collapsed when the cat's mind impacted upon hers...

As Shela strained and bit at her leash, Freddi staggered and fell to one knee. Kenjiro Kakura gasped and stretched forward to steady her, gesturing to one of his bodyguards to take hold of the restraint. When the man backed away, reluctant to intervene, Kakura snarled a command. The bodyguard blanched, then moved forward, but leapt aside as the cat attacked. Screaming, he covered his eyes, blood trickling from beneath his fingers. Freddi pushed Kakura's hand from her arm and stood up, while Shela whipped round to circle him, ears flattened, the hair on her back an upright brush of rage. The second bodyguard began to draw his laser, but

172

before he had the chance to shoot, Kakura stopped him, by placing himself between them.

Freddi's astonishment at his behaviour brought her out of the shock that had, for an instant, rendered her incapable of doing anything. 'Shela,' she called out, 'come here at once!' then knelt down and held out her hand. The cat slunk to her feet and crouched there, trembling, while Freddi gently stroked her head.

Before turning his attention to his bodyguard, Kakura gave Freddi a strange look of admiration, combined with a challenge. He then searched through the guard's emergency kit, found what he wanted, and administered a mild sedative. Afterwards, he examined the man's face and eyes for any serious damage, his movements precise and effective. Luckily, the claws hadn't reached the eyes themselves and the scratches were superficial. While Kakura cleaned the wounds and applied a coagulant to stop the bleeding, Freddi watched, impressed by his cool efficiency and by his foresight in having his guards carry an emergency kit.

'You have an unusual protector, Peacekeeper,' remarked Kakura, after he had finished his ministrations and sent the guard away to recuperate. 'Did you think I was dangerous?'

'No, and I must apologise for Shela's behaviour, to say the least. This has never happened before.'

'I am, fortunately, unhurt. It may be best, however, if we speak together without your pet present.' He bowed slightly.

Shela growled, but kept her place at Freddi's feet.

'I'll send her home. It won't take a moment to arrange.'

Before long, another peacekeeper arrived to take charge of the cat, casting an inquiring look at Freddi, who raised her eyebrows in an 'I'll explain later' manner. Turning to Kakura, she looked directly into his dark brown eyes and said, 'I trust Shela's instincts implicitly, and believe we have a great deal to discuss concerning your company's likely involvement in criminal activities in this country. I formally request that you accompany me to our Reconciliation Centre.'

'Of what am I accused, Peacekeeper?'

'Sabotage of Myanmar Forest Industries.'

Kakura smiled and waved away his remaining bodyguard, who had moved protectively towards his master. 'Really? I would be honoured to accompany you,' replied Kakura, and bowed again.

Freddi, intending the irony, returned the bow before escorting him to her airjet. During the short walk, Kakura remained entirely at ease, his broad shoulders relaxed, lean figure erect and dignified. Only his thick black hair was ruffled as the breeze brought the scent of frangipani to them from the nearby foothills.

The subsequent interview had been conducted formally, with Witnesses present to ensure the proceedings were held according to law. Throughout,

Kenjiro Kakura displayed complete control of his features and words, expressing himself dismayed at the accusation against himself and his company. To Freddi's total amazement, he even offered to provide the Myanmar Peacekeeping Force with complete access to his business and private databases.

Smoothing a small wrinkle in his slate-grey, immaculately tailored jacket, Kakura then said, 'I can offer no proof my company was not involved in the sabotage that has so regretfully occurred, yet it seems to me you have no evidence whatsoever to implicate us. A cat's behaviour cannot be used as such, I am sure. The animal may not like me...many people do not...but you have been hasty in basing this interview on its reactions.'

Freddi prevented a smile from reaching her lips, satisfied he had no knowledge of the work being done in Australia to give cats legal status, both in terms of protection by the law and as witnesses. Still, she admitted to herself that Shela's reactions were not enough to bring this man and his company to trial. The only way to do that, it seemed, was either by a process of elimination or through an eventual mistake on the part of Wyvern Meridian. Freddi was sure they would find nothing in the company's databases, given they were provided with such alacrity...

'Stop!' Freddi exclaimed, and the computer was silent, the images frozen on its screen. Now why had she jumped to the conclusion that Wyvern Meridian's Director was connected with the damage to Myanmar Forest Industries? She really did have almost no evidence. Rohan Maerz was now their prime suspect. Wyvern Meridian was, in all likelihood, his victim. It would have been entirely possible for him to set up a conspiracy to discredit the international giant, although why he would want to was at present beyond her. Frowning, she picked up the jade and silver pen and wrote for the next half hour, describing how Kakura was now under surveillance and outlining the results of Melrose's examination of the company's records.

Melrose had used one of the more sophisticated forms of software that searched for, amongst other things, patterns of investment, employment and growth. His findings were inconclusive. It was clear Wyvern Meridian was associated in some manner with several of the private companies involved worldwide in various forms of lucrative forest industry, but had no apparent links with the remainder.

Freddi's own investigations had established that Kakura himself had no known criminal or other dubious connections or background. His one peculiar trait was the style of his personal business methods: highly centralized and authoritarian. He involved himself in most major corporate affairs on a worldwide basis, and employees unwilling to adapt themselves to his regime were promptly sacked. Rather than keep them in his employ one minute longer than necessary, Kakura preferred, apparently, to give them the financial compensation the law demanded.

An examination of meeting schedules showed that he seemed to have exceptional stamina and often slept only a few hours each night. Freddi recalled the strength of his handshake when they first met and the firmness of his grasp on her arm when she fell to her knees. There were also few people tall enough to gaze directly into her eyes, and she was sure even fewer would be willing to place themselves in the path of an enraged cat the size of Shela. He was, without doubt, imposing.

As she sealed the letter, Freddi found herself wondering which of their two suspects was the greater threat: Kenjiro Kakura, or Rohan Maerz?

South Yarra retained many of its highly decorative nineteenth and twentieth-century buildings. It had remained an affluent and distinctive area of Melbourne for six hundred years, and had managed to avoid the trend to place dwellings underground. Residents successfully argued that their homes were of national significance, despite the periodic restoration work required over the centuries which in some cases had changed the buildings to such an extent their original owners would hardly have recognised them.

Mervyn Bradshaw enjoyed living in this little pocket of nostalgia and ostentation. He especially enjoyed viewing the Yarra River as it meandered along at the bottom of his garden, and loved the way it flowed backwards when the tide came in. Occasionally, he spent his mornings rowing with the flow and imagining the banks as they must have appeared before the old eucalypts drowned beneath the tide of salt.

On this particular morning, the sun poured onto his balcony as he polished his rifle. Its outward design was early twentieth century, but its abilities were definitely modern. He admired the gunmetal finish of the long, elegant barrel and the way the wood glinted in the light. Delicately touching the trigger, he sighted a magpie two hundred metres away, across the river. But the bird was not in any danger. The weapon was not to be despoiled by such petty use. Bradshaw examined its settings and chose one with great care, considering the circumstances and the distance required. Satisfied, he placed the rifle in its case and checked the time. He would wait another thirty minutes, then make his call.

On this same morning, Marika was considering her preparations for the midsun meal she was to share with her father and Melrose, and felt intensely grateful her friend would be there to help her cope. Impatiently wiping away a tear, she chose a yellow tablecloth that would be perfect with the silver cutlery given to her by her mother before she died. It looked lovely, gleaming luxuriously in the sunlight. The meal was to be in the greenhouse, surrounded by lightly scented flowers and the butterflies she nurtured. Her father had few gentle emotions, but he did love her plants. At least they would be able to talk about *them* without animosity.

When the security scanner chimed, Marika turned to see Melrose waiting at the door, so pressed the entry key. He seemed oddly shy as she impulsively embraced him, placing a kiss on his forehead, yet held her longer than usual. She could feel his heart pounding and looked up into his grave, troubled face.

'What's this, Melrose? I'm not dead yet, you know. It's a beautiful day, I've prepared a wonderful meal, and I don't want your long face to spoil it. Come on, let's have some wine while we wait for Dad. He shouldn't be too long.'

She took his hand and gently pushed him down onto a garden seat surrounded by red and green orchids. He tried to smile, but couldn't.

'Marika...' he managed to say, his voice filled with yearning, 'I love you.' When Marika's eyes widened in astonishment, he hesitated, then said, 'I think you probably *were* involved in breaking the security system, but I simply can't believe you knew what would happen. Please, tell me the truth!'

Holding the bottle of wine, Marika gazed silently at her friend. Wishing she knew what to say, she turned away and walked over to the plastiglass wall, hardly noticing the bright, warm sunlight. While Melrose watched, waiting for her to speak, the wall suddenly shattered and Marika fell to the floor without a sound. The bottle smashed and red wine flowed around his feet as Melrose leapt towards the still form. In desperation, he fought to revive her, after wasting precious seconds calling the ambutechs, not realising the surveillance system had already alerted them. When they arrived, only minutes later, Melrose stared in horror as they confirmed his own ghastly verdict: Marika had been murdered.

Just as the ambutechs were lifting Marika's body onto a hoverbed, her father walked in. He dropped the box of sweets he had brought as a gift for his daughter, hurling himself at Melrose.

'You bloody butcher! What've you done to her! You're covered in her blood, you bastard!'

The burly peacekeeper struck Melrose full in the face, then dropped to his knees by the hoverbed, covering his own face with his hands and sobbing loudly. Then, without any warning, he leapt to his feet again and grabbed Melrose by the throat.

Melrose, his nose broken and bleeding, clutched at the ambutech who rushed over to help, but fell backwards, smashing one of Marika's orchids. It was red, like her blood. Melrose found himself staring at it stupidly. The other ambutech, taller and stronger than the almost hysterical peacekeeper, expertly overpowered and sedated him, while the first one briefly clasped Melrose by the shoulder, then carefully examined his face. After he had administered a painkiller, his patient attempted to stand, but the ambutech prevented him. 'Please, just keep still until the bleeding stops. Does it hurt much now?'

Melrose shook his head slightly, then noticed, as if in slow motion, that a butterfly fluttered around Marika's face – they hadn't covered her.

The ambutech noticed too. 'Was she your bondmate?' he said softly.

'No...but she should have been...' Melrose began to weep, grieving for the life that ought to have been his to share, the tears containing all the pain he had suffered for so long.

Meanwhile, as the sedative did its work and his years of training and discipline re-asserted themselves, Marika's father relaxed and the ambutech tentatively released his grip. Melrose glanced at him, flinching when he saw the look of hatred. 'I loved her!' he cried. 'It wasn't me! She's been shot and I was trying to help her!'

Marika's dead eyes stared up at them. The butterfly had gone. Her father slowly wiped his face with a shaking hand.

'It's true,' said the ambutech who had held him. 'We've taken a quick look at the security records. The shot came from outside, and this man was in here with her when it happened. She was under surveillance... Did you know that?'

'Yes, I did.' He gave a great sigh and straightened his shoulders. 'Peacekeeper Chiu Liow Jones has told me what's been going on, which is why I'm here.' Looking straight at Melrose, he said, 'Who are you, anyway?'

'My name is Lance Melrose Naylor. I worked with Marika at the Melbourne Central Computer Site. We were friends for a long time.' His muffled voice was strange even to his own ears; his nose was beginning to swell. 'I've been helping the peacekeepers with the IT side of this investigation, so I know what she's been going through, and why.'

As he spoke, two MPF peacekeepers walked in through the open door, immobilisers ready. The women stopped to survey the room before speaking to the nearest ambutech. 'You can take Marika to the morgue now,' said one of them. 'The Coroner will be waiting. We've seen the surveillance records and know what's happened, except for the last couple of minutes. Melrose, do you need any help getting home? I think you should leave now.' She took a step towards him, holding out her hand.

Unsteadily, Melrose stood up and was taken by the elbow, not ungently. 'Yes,' he mumbled, suddenly exhausted. 'I'd like to go home. Will someone be able to take me?'

'Yes, we have a patrol car ready. Just come outside with me.'

'I want to say goodbye first...' He stumbled over to the hoverbed and, despite the pain, kissed her on the lips for the first time, but drew back almost at once. The Marika he loved was no longer there.

Meanwhile, all traffic leaving Australia had been halted and all incoming travellers detained at arrival points. Within twenty minutes of the murder, Chiu Liow had instigated a national population location census. He had never expected the procedure to be used, even though the ability to carry it out was put into place one hundred and forty years ago. Every person had a comlink code, which was the same as their Federation identity number, and everyone over the age of seven was expected to carry a comlink. At any point in time, it was possible to establish the whereabouts of virtually all citizens by broadcasting nationally the requirement that they activate the emergency signal built into their unit and then, as near as practicable, stay where they were until a final broadcast allowed them to change their location.

Within ten minutes of the broadcast, the Central Computer Site had created two listings. One gave the names and IDs of all citizens who hadn't responded to the broadcast. The other gave the identity of everyone who did respond and were within thirty minutes travelling distance of Marika's house.

From his office in the Rialto, Chiu Liow could see the swarm of airjets patrolling the city and could imagine the terror his order had created. He began to perspire as a second broadcast was transmitted, and a second set of reports generated. The procedure was then repeated at ten-minute intervals until virtually the entire population had been accounted for – allowing for those who might not necessarily be in a position to respond. Chiu Liow compared the final summary report to the file containing all the people associated in some way with the Willsmere-Lamington case. The overlap was almost complete, and all of them had responded to the broadcast. He sent out the order to release those who were outside the travel time limits.

Swearing in exasperation, Chiu Liow pushed his hair back from his face, then settled back in his chair to think, gazing absently out the window. Fifty minutes later, the Coroner delivered the preliminary autopsy results. They showed that a long-range ultrasound weapon had been used to kill Marika: highly lethal and totally illegal for civilians to carry.

Chiu Liow called his most senior peacekeeper and together they made the short trip to Marika's home. The place from which the rifle was fired had readily been identified by their forensics team, but so far, apart from a slight disturbance to the ground, nothing helpful had turned up.

'The place *is* relatively isolated, which means the likelihood of finding anyone who's seen something is low,' said Chiu Liow in frustration, after they had searched the area for more than two hours. 'I don't even think we'll gain anything from transport records. The killer could have walked here and then waited for as long as they needed to before shooting her, or for that matter, used a landjet if they had access to one.'

'We'll have to speak with everyone who lives or works around here anyway...*and* check the Computer Site's transport records. I'll organise it now,' replied his colleague, running a hand over his face.

'While you're doing that, get them to check the national weapons database as well.' Chiu Liow dusted his knees. They had spent time crawling beneath overhanging shrubs, double-checking some of the work already done by forensics. 'What have they found out?' he asked, when the peacekeeper put his comlink away.

'Nothing! Nothing at all! No one on our list has made a transport call to this area within the past forty-eight hours, other than Lance Melrose Naylor and Marika, and no civilian is registered as owning an ultrasound rifle. The only people who have them are all accounted for...and far away from here. Still, we should question them, as well as anyone who *has* travelled here by public transport and doesn't live or work in the area, particularly if we can't establish their exact whereabouts at the critical time.'

'Yes, I agree. In the meantime, a physical search of nearby homes and workplaces would most likely be useless. It goes without saying that anyone with a weapon like this would hardly advertise it, particularly not now. The only way of finding it would be to use an aerial scan, which could take a while. In the meantime, there are thousands of people, most likely angry and frightened, still waiting for my order to let them go about their business!' At least it wasn't raining, he thought gloomily. Otherwise, anyone caught outside by the broadcasts could hardly have been expected to remain where they were for so long.

Chiu Liow straightened his back and gave the order to release everyone, then put the scan into effect. He could expect results within the hour, but wasn't optimistic. The assassin could now leave the area, if they were still in the vicinity, or someone could meet them and remove the weapon if they did it quickly and were lucky enough to avoid the search. He pushed aside the question of how it would all be explained to the nation. Thankfully, this was the responsibility of the Speaker. Nevertheless, Parliament would not react well to the mass of minor accidents which had arisen due to the alarm created by the census. Unused to draconian measures, many had panicked.

Fortunately, none of the reports flowing into his comlink indicated any serious injuries. Chiu Liow forced himself to relax, to breathe quietly and deeply, to simply focus on the next step in their investigation.

Rohan Maerz entered the office and sat on the edge of Chiu Liow's desk, smiling. Chiu Liow faced him, not returning the smile. 'I assume you already know what we are doing. I do hope it meets with your approval,' he said, trying, without success, to keep the sarcasm from showing in his voice.

'Oh...quite, though you might have consulted *me* before instigating the census procedure. But please, don't be embarrassed. After all, I'm only here to assist, not to dictate.'

'Assist whom?'

'Now you *are* being disagreeable. Assist *you*, my dear man. You aren't suggesting otherwise, I hope?'

Chiu Liow ignored the question. 'If you do wish to assist, please take a seat other than on my desk and give some thought to the subject of how an ultrasound rifle could have found its way into the hands of someone on this list.'

Rohan delicately eased his bulk from the desk, sat down in front of one of the other computers and began rapidly entering commands. He soon turned around and waved his hand at the display. 'Here's your man: Mervyn Bradshaw, lately of South Yarra, now located within a mere two point four kilometres of your Detention Centre. How convenient for you. I expect you'll find his rifle quite close by. From his personal details, I can see he's not so terribly stupid...just somewhat.'

Chiu Liow walked mutely over to look at the screen, annoyed by his own sudden confusion. If Rohan Maerz was at the centre of this complex series of crimes, he wasn't behaving as expected. He earnestly wished Welcome was here to discuss it all with, yet felt unable to take the risk of speaking openly with any of his other peacekeepers. Who knew where Maerz had spun his web?

What Chiu Liow read on the screen was remarkable. He glanced at Rohan's smug expression, then ignored him while he gave instructions for Bradshaw's immediate arrest.

'You *are* about to ask me how I obtained this little gem, aren't you?' said Rohan, as soon as Chiu Liow stopped speaking.

'Will you tell me if I do?'

'No. If you could access the information I can, the FSIU wouldn't be required, now would it?'

'Bradshaw cannot be tried by the Judge unless the evidence is entered and verified. You know that, so stop playing silly games!' Chiu Liow was having difficulty with his temper. The man was almost unbearable.

'I doubt Bradshaw will ever come to trial.'

'And why not?'

'Because,' and Rohan tilted his head to consult the computer, 'I predict that within a very short space of time, he will no longer be alive. The Judge is not the only arbiter of justice.'

After briefly glaring at Rohan, who stood up and moved a short distance away, Chiu Liow took his place and spoke urgently to the computer. The peacekeeper he was now dealing with moved aside to allow Chiu Liow to see the scene behind him. Mervyn Bradshaw lay crumpled on a soft carpet of green moss surrounding the small water garden located at the bottom of his property. An envelope lay on the ground beside him, together with an open container.

Rohan peered over Chiu Liow's shoulder. 'It appears someone has sent Bradshaw a poison pen letter. How unusual...'

Marika's father spent the rest of the day, and most of the night, in the Melbourne Detention Centre. Despite there being no charges laid for his assault on Melrose, no one trusted him enough to allow him to leave. He had shouted at the peacekeepers that he wanted to be part of the investigation: 'She was my daughter, damn you! It's my right to find out who killed her!'

He kept arguing while they patiently told him why he couldn't be part of the team – he was her father, exactly, and therefore *could not* be involved any further. Eventually they called Chiu Liow Jones, who bluntly told him to shut up.

'Instead of taking up our time, may I suggest you do something useful, like apologising to Melrose and finding out where Marika's son is? No one has told him yet that his mother has died. We actually thought it might be something you'd want to do. Well?'

Marika's father had the grace to blush, although he was still angry. 'Alright,' he said brusquely, 'I'll speak with Melrose. He may know where the boy is, and I suppose you're right. It'd be best coming from me, though we're not as close as we probably ought to be.'

Chiu Liow watched in disgust, yet also with pity, as the man made the call, suggesting they meet at Marika's house. Melrose looked as dreadful as he felt, although the swelling in his face was less than before. He accepted the apology and reluctantly agreed to the meeting.

They both arrived at the house just before midsun. The peacekeepers had finished their work, so the two men were allowed to do as they wished.

The hole in the greenhouse wall had been temporarily patched and there was little left to see of the previous day's tragedy. Melrose waited while Marika's father walked around the deserted house, touching some of his daughter's belongings with more tenderness than even he had expected to feel. Before long, he returned to the greenhouse and sat down on the garden seat.

'Marika must have had a key role in this whole mess, otherwise she wouldn't have been killed,' said Melrose, sitting down as well, 'but I can't believe she was fully aware of what she was getting herself into.'

The peacekeeper startled him by taking his hand in a firm grip. 'Thank you,' he said in a harsh tone, as if the words were being forced out. 'It might sound strange, but I'm glad she died here, with her friend and in her own home, rather than spending the rest of her life in prison. I think I want to stay here for a few days. I've not been the father Marika wanted, and it's too late to do anything about that, but before I go back to South Australia, I want to know whether her boy's being properly taken care of by his father.'

'As far as I know, his father has him now.' Melrose had difficulty controlling his voice and turned away.

'I think it'd be best if we both go and tell them what's happened, instead of leaving it to the MPF, but before we do, is there anything here you want to keep to remember her by?'

'I only want to sit here for a while, if you don't mind.' Melrose wondered at his offer, but had no need of any mementos. He would never forget Marika.

Her father heaved a sigh and stood up, then looked around and began tidying the smashed orchids and other greenhouse plants. Melrose found himself envying him his apparent absorption in the simple task, yet was unable to stir from his seat. He felt utterly and completely depressed.

Three days later, still unaware of Marika's death, the companionable silence in Søren and Karla's laboratory at Willsmere was disturbed only by Red Matilda when she made periodic attempts to gain their attention. She wasn't the type of cat to settle down quietly and dream, or to chase her own tail unless someone was looking at her and laughing at the antics. Fliedermus, meanwhile, preferred to keep Mik and Tamara company, and could not be persuaded to stay merely to keep Red Matilda entertained. As a result, she was bored and irritably flicked her tail.

Noticing the cat's mood, Karla took pity on her. 'Alright, Reddles, let's go visiting. Do you want to walk for a bit, or go to the nearest callstation?' Red loved the public transport system, so enthusiastically projected images of fascinated people watching her while they travelled. Karla grinned, knelt down to attach her leash, and said, 'Søren, we're going to see Chiu Liow and we'll be out for about two and a half hours.'

Without turning around, Søren absentmindedly nodded, lost in his work. He didn't want anything to interfere with his research into the behavioural psychology of cats and visited Possum nearly every day, spending long periods of time attempting to communicate images and to receive specific responses. He decided it was time to have one of these regular sessions, and also to borrow Fliedermus, so sauntered into Mik and Tamara's laboratory. He halted just inside the doorway, leaning against the frame, his arms folded, while he waited until they became aware of his presence. Fliedermus was sprawled on top of a storage cupboard, head tilted back, yawning widely. She sprang down from her perch and rubbed herself against his legs.

Deeply involved in his work, Mik muttered, 'Yeah, Søren, you can take her with you. I expect we'll be here for quite a long time yet.'

Tamara looked at him, head to one side. 'He hasn't said anything. How did you know what he was going to ask?'

'Intuition, I s'pose. Søren doesn't usually come in here just to gossip, does he?'

'That's true,' replied Søren, before Tamara could answer, 'but I have never asked to borrow your Fliedermus before, have I?'

Fliedermus adopted a smug expression and twined herself around his ankles, purring contentedly. Realising what had just happened, Tamara came over to them, crouched down, and scratched the cat's head. 'Let's see if she'll do what *I* visualise her doing,' she said, with a grin.

Tamara concentrated and Fliedermus stood up, butted her forehead, then sat down again, tail neatly tucked around her body. 'That's not what I asked you to do, Fliedermus. Let's try again.' The cat looked at her, pupils narrowing, then walked over to Mik and planted one foot on his knee. Tamara sighed. 'No, still not right.'

'I'm not so sure,' said Mik, stroking the cat's soft black nose and finally giving them his full attention. 'I've got the definite impression she knows you want something, but isn't sure whether to do it. What if you write down what you tried to say to her and then I give it a go? She could be asking my permission.'

Trying hard not to giggle, Tamara scribbled a few words on the screen of a hand reader and passed it to him. Mik put a hand over his eyes and laughed. Immediately, Fliedermus tore out of the room and they could hear her pounding into Søren and Karla's laboratory. Søren threw them a look of astonishment before he too disappeared into the corridor. There was complete silence until Søren returned, a gleeful expression on his face.

'Come and see, you clever people!'

They all went back to the lab, where they saw Fliedermus sitting on Søren's chair in front of his computer. She had one paw delicately placed on its identity pad and was gazing intently at the screen as it confirmed her security profile and asked, in its usual bland voice, whether she wished to initiate the creation of her new operating environment. When the machine received no answer, the request was written to the screen. They continued to watch as the letters grew larger and the colours changed to give greater contrast.

Fascinated by the display, Fliedermus lifted her paw to touch the screen, but when nothing happened, jumped from the chair and onto Karla's. When the cat placed her paw onto the identity pad, the computer switched on and asked if she wished to close the previous session. Receiving no response, it went through the same procedure as before. With the final colour change, the computer bleeped several times and displayed a "No response" message, together with Fliedermus' security details. Meanwhile, Søren's computer shut itself off and Fliedermus stayed where she was, but turned to look at the delighted humans. Purring, she licked one paw and began cleaning her face.

'Can I assume this is what you wanted her to do, Tamara?' asked Søren.

Tamara grinned and passed him the hand reader. The scribble confirmed Fliedermus had done just as requested, but only after receiving permission from the person she viewed herself as belonging to: Mik.

'Wondrous little Spud! I love you!' Søren hugged Tamara and kissed the tip of her nose.

Fliedermus leapt down from Karla's chair, pattered into the other lab and returned with a leash in her mouth, completely satisfied with herself.

Søren was practically dancing on the spot with enthusiasm. 'Come with me to try this on Possum,' he pleaded. 'We really *must* see what will happen!'

Possum was waiting for them at the door of Mik's greenhouse. She stretched, meowed softly, then turned and walked elegantly down the staircase to the main living room, her slender tail waving and curling. Fliedermus headed straight for the kitchen to sit by her bowl, so Mik gave in, rummaging through the cupboards for something tasty, which the cat devoured as if she were starving. The others followed Possum. Søren made himself a generous glass of whisky and lemon before snuggling down into Mik's favourite armchair, earning himself a glare from the owner when he joined them.

At first they gazed at each other in silence, until eventually Søren spoke: 'For all their remarkable traits, the cats are still cats, only more so,' he said, sipping his whisky. 'I feel strongly that there should be a limit to the type of behaviour we attempt to have them exhibit. If they become stressed by moving beyond the boundaries of what is normal, it's possible they could become neurotic, and therefore, potentially dangerous. I suspect the boundaries of normal behaviour are reflected in the amount of effort it takes to have them understand and cooperate.'

Tamara perched herself on the arm of his chair and began playing with his curls. 'In other words, Alf, to avoid a potential paradox we'd have to demonstrate repetitive, normal behaviour occurring at our direction.'

'Will you be so kind as to stop that!' He pushed her away. 'You seem to be learning to behave like a cat. Is that why they like you, hmm?'

Tamara made a face at him and went to sit on Mik's lap instead.

'It'd have to be something that didn't bore them, too,' said Mik, as he made Tamara comfortable, 'which I think could be a problem with Red Matilda – she's the most wilful of the three. Possum would usually be the most cooperative.'

'We could ask her to crawl under the rug and only come out when we say to. I think she would find that amusing, don't you?' suggested Søren.

Possum turned and blinked at him. Tamara agreed: 'Yes, and I think *you* should try it first, followed by me, and then Mik. She won't need permission to do it, so if she understands, should react. On the other hand, if we asked Fliedermus to do the same thing, she might need prompting because she doesn't normally crawl around under rugs. Then, if we asked Possum to climb up onto the curtain rails, she probably wouldn't, unless it was you who asked her, Mik, given she never has.'

Mik laughed. 'Maybe we should lay odds on who does the best! What do you say, Søren? A bottle of your best cabernet shiraz to me if I win, and a bottle of my best whisky if you win?'

'And what about me?' objected Tamara. 'I might win. Does that mean I get to have both prizes?'

Søren shook his head. 'This isn't quite fair. Your cats may *choose* who *they* want to win! No, my friend, we had better take this seriously; we can gamble on something else another time.'

In the end, none of them had any difficulty persuading the cats to repeatedly crawl under the rug, one at a time, and Fliedermus was only too pleased to hang from the curtain rails at anyone's unspoken or spoken suggestion, but when it came to convincing Possum to even climb up there, they all met with complete resistance.

'This, to my mind, Tamara, demonstrates the extremity of her rage when she killed your would-be assassin,' concluded Søren.

Tamara grimaced, walked over to the staircase and sat down, chin in hand. It did, but they would need to come up with a far more sophisticated demonstration for the trial; it could simply be claimed they had trained the cats using conventional techniques. Also, *they* might be able to make the deductive leap from Possum's polite refusal to act in an unusual manner to her behaving in an extreme way only under extreme circumstances, but this could hardly be expected of anyone else.

'I think one way would be for the prosecutor to try to communicate with Fliedermus,' she said eventually. 'Possum would most likely be too nervous to cooperate and Red Matilda would be just as likely to either ignore the suggestion or do the exact opposite. However, we'd still have to work out some way of testing Possum's reactions in front of Witnesses, not just those of our reliable Fliedermus. So, given there are only six weeks to go before her trial, we really do need to put her defence together.'

Søren and Mik agreed. With the cooperation of the Breeding Centre, which had decades of knowledge about cats, the entry of data into the Judge was progressing well. Therefore, the Centre's staff should, they all thought, be in a good position to act as witnesses to their more elaborate experiments with the cats. They put together their plan, working well into the evening, until Søren insisted they stop and have a civilised meal break.

Just as they were sitting down to eat, Mik's comlink signalled an incoming call. When he reluctantly answered, an angry Karla appeared on the screen. 'Where have you been all day?' she accused them. 'I returned to the labs to find you all gone, with no messages left for me, nothing tidied away...and my computer telling me Fliedermus had attempted to initiate a personal environment! Some joke!'

Mik held out his hand to the screen in dismay, saying, 'Karla, it wasn't a joke... It was an experiment that worked and we were so excited we forgot you'd come back and get all upset.'

Søren peered over his shoulder and said, 'If I make a personal promise never to become excited again in my whole life, will you forgive us and come over to share our excellent dinner? Please?'

Karla glowered at them. 'What do you mean, it was an experiment that worked?'

'Using her mind, not her voice, Tamara asked Fliedermus to go to my computer and touch the ID pad with her paw, which she did, but only after Mik gave her permission by laughing. She then repeated this with your computer...on her own initiative.'

'You've just said that Mik gave her permission, but how did he know what Tamara asked Fliedermus to do?'

'Oh... Yes, of course... She wrote it on a hand reader for him to see after Fliedermus failed to act on her suggestion.'

Karla immediately forgot her anger and for the time being, her dismay over the news Chiu Liow had given her during their visit. She laughed, in both relief and amazement. 'That's wonderful! Are you working on Possum's defence now?'

Søren and Mik both nodded. 'Do you want to come over and help?'

'Of course I do! I'll see you soon...'

*

Almost three weeks had now gone by since Chiu Liow told Karla about Marika's death and the subsequent murder of Mervyn Bradshaw. That ancient tool of assassins, cyanide, had been used to kill him. A beautiful, delicately engraved, pressurised cylinder containing the gas was put into an envelope, together with a handwritten note of congratulation, created using brush calligraphy. It would have been surprising if he hadn't opened the cylinder to see what it held.

Unaware of Red Matilda's ability to influence Karla's emotions, Chiu Liow was surprised, although relieved, when she seemed less upset by his news than he would have expected. He could only assume that the rapid sequence of violent crimes had numbed her to some extent. Nevertheless, he took care to remain with her while she spoke to Gwenllian at Lamington.

When Gwenllian first appeared on the screen, her face was clear of worry and she greeted Karla with happy surprise. Before Karla had the chance to tell her the news, she called to Owain for him to join her and say hello. He too seemed more relaxed than when they last saw him, but before long, both regained their earlier tense, nervous expressions, even though Karla carefully avoided either giving too much detail or commenting unnecessarily; there was still the chance they could be 'overheard'. The two researchers had subsequently travelled to Melbourne for Marika's cremation, though stayed for only two days before returning to Lamington.

Chiu Liow kept his promise to the ancient gatekeeper by telling him about the death of Mervyn Bradshaw, together with the manner of it, knowing the old man would keep it to himself. The gatekeeper also attended Marika's cremation, saying little to anyone else, but giving Melrose and Gwenllian as much comfort as he was able.

'There now, my dears, you mustn't break your hearts. Mari wouldn't have wanted you to do that, would she? We all know death is part of life, though it's hard when someone goes too soon. One day, Melrose, you'll find another young woman, that's for sure, and Gwen, you've already found some new friends. I'm sure they all know how unhappy you are and will want to help.'

Melrose had taken the old man's hand in his own. 'How did you know about my feelings for Marika?'

'Ah, well, I see a lot of things. So will you, once you reach my age.' The gatekeeper put his other hand over Melrose's and pressed it. 'Now, it's time we all went inside to say goodbye.'

As the calm, warm beauty of Lamington eased their minds, Owain and Gwenllian were able to recapture their earlier enthusiasm for their work. Even the absence of Mik's cats helped Gwenllian overcome her recent doubts regarding the trust the Willsmere group had in them. She remembered Marika and Thanh with great sadness, yet was determined to put her energies into the present and into the future. Before long, their daily routine re-established itself, as it did at Willsmere.

Meanwhile, Meng Jarrah spent time familiarising herself with the work being done by both groups, and had recently received encouraging preliminary results from the analysis of her soil sample. Consequently, the combined research effort was progressing well and an air of quiet optimism soon returned.

Karla maintained regular contact with Chiu Liow, which, when she passed on what he told her, helped the group deal with their situation. They were, however, no closer to discovering the reason behind the series of crimes. It seemed that both private and Federation-owned timber and forestry-related industries were being targeted, yet no clear purpose behind the attacks made itself apparent – although the magnitude of the operation implied the participation of an immensely powerful organisation.

Freddi's first report to Meng Jarrah and Chiu Liow had been illuminating, insofar as the personality of Kenjiro Kakura was concerned, although they could only share her inability to decide whether Rohan Maerz, Wyvern Meridian, or some other unknown, was implicated; those who knew Morag MacIain all steadfastly refused to accept she was guilty of anything.

On the other hand, it seemed highly likely to everyone that Marika had engineered the initial security breach that allowed the attacks on Willsmere and Lamington, but it seemed less likely she was directly involved in any of the other incidents that occurred before her death.

Whether Thanh bore any responsibility, they would probably never know. His murder, and those of Mervyn Bradshaw and Marika, had been callous and effective. It seemed they had served their purpose and were quite simply no longer required.

CHAPTER FIFTEEN

The afternoon downpour had turned the forest floor to slush, as it usually did at this time of day during summer in Papua. The peacekeepers waded through the mud, persistent in their search for even the tiniest clue to the identity of those responsible for this latest outrage. It was hot, as humid as a sauna, noisy with the chattering of birds and other wildlife – and dangerous; the slightest scratch could turn septic. Chiu Liow's colleague had immediately sent out his forces once the news came in informing them of the death of one of the charcoal workers. Her body had been found skewered in a pit dug into the forest floor and then carefully disguised; an ancient and vicious form of trap for the unwary animal, or human.

The peacekeeper leant back in his chair and drummed his thick fingers against the desktop. There was no doubt in his mind that this incident was yet another designed expressly to harass and dishearten the small recycling company, as well as the international team of investigators. Such traps had been outlawed centuries since, and there were no tribes left in the highlands who still depended on hunting for their food. In any case, the charcoal workers gathered their wares with great care, and only after the area was fully surveyed for unsuspected dangers.

Three hours had passed since the search began, but he expected it would be nightfall before hearing back from his taskforce. It was therefore a surprise to hear his computer's discreet bleep and then his team leader's voice. Her face was streaked with grime and her hair hung in limp curls because of the humidity. She was holding a small emblem between her forefinger and thumb for him to see. Its gleam contrasted strongly with the warm pink and brown tones of her hand.

'Where did you find it?' he asked, staring at the peculiar design of the object.

'About two hundred metres from the pit. We think it was dropped accidentally and not left for us to find on purpose. Look, the pin's broken.' She turned the emblem over for him to see.

He realised the object was a form of brooch, and appeared to be made from silver, in the shape of a two-legged winged dragon with a barbed serpent tail. It had an old-fashioned fastener made of metal and the pin was indeed badly bent, with soil adhering to most of the surface. The ornament looked as if it had fallen from its wearer before being trodden into the mud.

'Did you find anything else in the area?'

'Certainly did!' She grinned, her large white teeth glinting in the sun. 'A full set of landing and takeoff marks from an airjet. Once we knew what to look for, it was easy to find the footprints leading to the pit. They'd done a good job of trying to hide their traces, but there's enough left to show there were three of them.'

The smile left her face as she remembered the murdered woman. One of the stakes had pierced first an eye and then her brain. At least the charcoal gatherer died quickly. Otherwise, she could have lingered for hours.

'Keep searching as long as there's light. Is there anything you need that you haven't taken with you?'

'No, we're fine. We'll concentrate on collecting the evidence and trying to determine whether they've left any other lovely little presents for someone to stumble into. I hope the charcoal workers have taken out insurance!'

'So do I!' replied the peacekeeper, clenching his teeth. Sometimes it was difficult not to hate.

In Brazil, Federation Researcher Eduardo Arreza had taken a break and was browsing though the day's news items. When his colleague, Sirinya, heard his gasp of surprise, she looked up from her microscope then stood and crossed the room to where he was sitting. As she peeked over his shoulder at the article he was reading, he turned to face her, saying, 'This has to be some fool's idea of a joke!'

'Let me read... I can't see if you jiggle it up and down like that!' Sirinya snatched the hand reader from him, pushing him away when he tried to retrieve it. 'I don't think it *sounds* like a joke,' she said slowly. 'No, this is definitely serious. Six cases so far! What a hellish thing to happen to someone.'

Sirinya wandered over to one of the windows and gazed out. The panorama of the forest lay before her. Serro do Cachimbo was the only place she had ever lived, and the forest the only place she ever wanted to live. She had many friends who felt the same and one of them worked for the small pharmaceutics company who were the subject of the controversy in the news item. She would have to talk to him. Strange, why hadn't he told her what was happening? He should have known she would be interested and willing to help.

Eduardo joined her at the window. 'What are you thinking? Will you call Erminio?'

'I think I should. I can't understand why I haven't heard from him. We're talking about a lot of cases in a very short space of time. You would've agreed to help them, wouldn't you?'

'Of course! Their own database should be good enough to let them find an antidote if one already exists, but they might not have some of our newer material on file. Come to think of it...' He went back to his computer and began scanning their most recent entries. 'Got it!'

'What've you got?' Sirinya asked him, peering over his shoulder again.

'We've got an entry on one of our newest fungi that says more research is needed to find out how safe it is. This little beauty is one they bought from us eight months ago. Our description of its probable psychotropic qualities had them interested, but they weren't supposed to go and use it!'

'Their contract with us specified they'd be buying the fungus for further medical research only, didn't it?'

'Oh, I'm sure it did. Let's have a look.' Eduardo opened a copy of the Federation contract. It showed that Epsilon Pty Ltd had bought the rights to perform a five-year study of *Claviceps atropurpurea* and its likely effects on patients suffering from certain visual delusions associated with extreme phobias.

The news items had described the apprehension over a period of time of six individuals who were found naked in a variety of public places attempting to burn their clothing, screaming that they were infested. The type of infestation was slightly different in each case. Each person, after being sedated, treated for shock, and put into the care of their medical practitioner, approached the media with their stories, claiming they wanted to make sure no one else suffered the same way. They all appeared to have been treated with a new drug that was meant to ease their morbid fears of creatures ranging from snakes, toads and spiders, through to cats. Instead, they became overwhelmed by equally strong fears, but of different objects: generally some type of stinging or biting insect. They all produced partially empty containers of tablets, each bearing the manufacturer's name: Epsilon.

The media attempted to question their practitioners, but after receiving little in the way of response, approached Epsilon directly, who were only too eager to save their reputation. Epsilon acknowledged the release of a new drug, but only after having conducted full laboratory and clinical trials, and with Federation permission to release it to the public. The description of the trials, together with the properties and ingredients of the drug, were also published, as was to be expected. Those adversely affected by their product were not, however, satisfied and demanded compensation. Epsilon in turn requested that the tablets be independently tested in order to verify their composition. The results showed they contained an extract of *Claviceps atropurpurea*.

The news of a previously unheard of species of fungus being sold to the public as a medication, without adequate trials and without Federation permission, was too good a story not to publish. From this point onwards, the case was taken up by the Office of the Attorney General and the media were excluded from any further involvement. The article left the reader in no doubt that they, the media, regarded this outcome as highly dubious.

'So *is* there an antidote listed?' asked Sirinya.

'Umm...no...but our preliminary studies suggest the effects are short-term. That'd be why we haven't heard from Erminio yet. Epsilon would be fairly confident that the people who were given the drug had it out of their system by the time they contacted the media... I mean, if it wasn't, they wouldn't have been in a fit state to contact them, now would they?'

'No, I s'pose not. Still...I think I'll have a talk to him. I'd like to know if they've come up with an explanation for how the wrong product managed to get onto the market.'

'Do you honestly think he'll *want* to talk to you, given the Attorney General's Office is involved? That's pretty serious stuff!'

'Can't hurt to try, can it?'

Sirinya sat down at her computer and before long her friend, Erminio, appeared on the screen. His usually cheerful countenance was strained, his eyes a pair of dark smudges. 'Hi,' was all he had to say.

'We've read the news...so you can guess why I've called.'

Erminio grimaced.

'We'd like to offer our help,' continued Sirinya, not having expected any other reaction. 'I'm sure Research Coordinator Zago wouldn't object, if we asked her.'

'She'll end up being involved anyway, Sirinya. The Attorney General will want to see your records, plus the copy of the Federation contract of sale for this wretched thing.' Erminio made an effort to wipe the sour expression from his face. 'Anyway, it's good to see you. Is Froggy there with you?'

Eduardo made a rude gesture at the screen. 'I shouldn't be associating with crims, but I'll talk to you because I'm so benevolent.'

'Good of you, Fred. How's it going over there?'

'Just great, until you gave one of our pets a bad name. Is this a talent you've been cultivating, or what?'

'Oh yeah, love giving you lot a hard time... Got any other duds for sale, while we're at it?'

'Hang on, I'll check out our garbage bin.'

'Don't stress yourself. Sirinya, why do you keep working with this mediocrity?'

'Well, not for love, that's for sure. Talking of mediocre, how did you lot manage to stuff up?'

'Oops?'

'I'm sure the Attorney General will love *that* answer. Seriously, what's happening?'

'Seriously, I can't tell you. The only thing I *can* say, because it's going to be obvious soon anyway, is that all production runs are stopping as of tonight. No more Epsilon products on the market until we find out how Claviceps got out of control. Which also means everything of ours gets withdrawn.'

'How long can you survive that?'

'We haven't been told yet. A general meeting has been arranged for this afternoon. Still, it shouldn't take more than a few months to work out how it happened, and I'm fairly sure we can carry that amount of time.'

'Assuming you can clear yourselves.'

'True...but the worst that can happen is we find out someone got the wrong model into production and our insurance premiums go up for a few years. We're not looking at anyone having suffered permanent damage, thank the Sun. What's more, the compensation won't be contested from our side, I wouldn't think.'

'Even so, it's going to take a long time for your reputation to get back to what it was.'

'Yeah, that's the main problem. We'll have to rely on people remembering our major successes. Getting something big onto the market as soon as we can would help too.' Erminio turned away for a moment, as if someone had called him. 'Sorry, I have to get going.'

'Okay, but let me know if you think we can do anything.'

'Sure. See you.'

Sirinya turned to Eduardo. 'What do you think? Is there anything we can do?'

'I'd say the best thing would be to mention it to Zago. She mightn't have read the news report yet.'

'The Attorney General's Office may have gotten to her by now.'

'Yes, maybe... She'll want to talk to us though, so we might as well contact her first.'

'Alright, I'll do it now.'

Sirinya spoke to her computer and found that Research Coordinator Zago was in Oslo for the Federation Herbarium's annual 'open day', the only time when the public was allowed to enter its sacred portals. As usual, her expression was relaxed, but her voice held a tinge of agitation; Zago did not overly enjoy playing host to large numbers of people.

'Sirinya, you appear to be perturbed. What can I do to help you?'

'I *am*. Has the Brazilian Attorney General's Office contacted you yet?'

Zago shook her head.

'We've got some interesting news that was published this morning, to do with one of our recent discoveries, *Claviceps atropurpurea*. Do you remember us selling the development rights to the company, Epsilon, a while back? Apparently a product containing it was put on the market by accident, and up until now, six people who took it have reacted badly. I've sent the article to you. Have you got it yet?'

'It is just arriving now. Thank you, yes, I have it.' Zago paused to read, then looked up. 'Hmm, I can see this *is* quite serious. You have my permission for everything we have on the organism to be made available to the Attorney General. We do not want the matter to take longer to resolve than necessary. Also, it would be best not to discuss the issue with anyone else...and once I finish with this circus here, I may pay you a visit.' She was interrupted by a small child tugging at her cloak. Zago smiled apologetically, then closed the connection.

'That was a bit enigmatic, don't you think, Eduardo?'

'Yes, I do, as a matter of fact, but I don't know why. Do you?'

'No, but I think anything that goes wrong and is connected even indirectly with our laboratories is something Zago's going to treat with suspicion. It'll be interesting to hear what she has to say if she *does* come here.' Sirinya folded her plump arms and frowned. Eventually, she sighed and went back to her microscope to continue her interrupted work.

The defence case for Morag MacIain was progressing well, thought Welcome, as he settled himself more snugly into his soft, well-padded armchair. Rohan had hand-delivered the prosecution case to him only two days after their meal with Morag, and since then, the only reports of his activities had arrived in the mail from Chiu Liow.

It had been a surprise to Welcome that the prosecution did not attempt to establish a motive, and even admitted they were unable to postulate one. Nevertheless, the issue would inevitably arise, although he was sure they would find it difficult to say she had any. Her psychological profile established her as realistic, well-adjusted, socially motivated, *etcetera, etcetera;* in fact, everything anyone could wish for in terms of personality. Her professional life contained a few bumps and blotches, but nothing that hadn't readily been resolved. In a sentence, Morag had everything in life. Why would she want more?

Welcome rubbed the tip of his nose then scratched his ear. He contemplated the hypothetical possibility of her having become bored with 'having everything'. No, it didn't fit. Her job as an investigator led her around the world and into almost every corner of life. She didn't even have an additional, voluntary career. Instead, Morag donated at least fifteen hours a week to the FSIU.

He scribbled a few doodles on the screen of his hand reader, then erased the curved lines. What other motives could she potentially have? A practical joker on the grand scale? Ridiculous! Welcome couldn't imagine the Judge accepting that proposition. Had she become an egomaniac? Did she see herself as so clever that she felt compelled to test her skills against the FSIU? No, that seemed more in Rohan Maerz's line. Still, it wasn't impossible for someone in Morag's position to develop this type of personality. A very carefully prepared line of reasoning would need to be presented to refute the possibility. So, could it all have been a blind to monetary gain? Yet Morag's financial situation was transparently innocent. No unusual expenditures, no extra income. Either the banking records were correct, or they'd been altered as well. But if this line of reasoning was followed, what hadn't been? He shuddered, yet hopefully the uncertainty that was part of almost every aspect of this case was in her favour.

Welcome continued to write for almost an hour, then yawned and wriggled his toes comfortably inside his slippers before standing up and stretching his back and arms. The computer showed it was almost 17:00. He should make up his mind what to do for dinner. Go to a restaurant, visit Morag, or stay quietly here? He walked over to the window and looked outside. Snow was still falling heavily. He was having trouble adjusting to the cold and even more trouble adjusting to the lack of public transport. The thought of having to trudge to a restaurant on foot ruled out that option, which left two. However, a quiet evening would allow him to concentrate on the final section of his submission to the Judge. Welcome laughed. He would jolt these parsimonious people by having an ostentatious dinner sent up to his room, without even the tiniest pang of guilt.

As he stood at the window contemplating what to order, the door chimed. It was a remarkably genteel little sound, he thought absentmindedly as he padded over to answer it.

'Another parcel for you from Australia,' announced the messenger standing patiently outside.

'Thank you, thank you. Tell me, do many people send personal parcels or letters these days?'

'No, you're the only one for a long time. But don't let that worry you,' and the messenger winked.

Welcome winked back. How nice to think he would be remembered by at least *one* person in this city! He opened the package, expecting a report from Chiu Liow. It was there, together with a copy of a news item and a note from Research Coordinator Zago:

> On Karla's advice, I have recently taken up the art of letter writing – quite a novelty. She and I have 'discussed' the enclosed article, and at her suggestion I am now sending it to you, together with some relevant bits from our research database in Serro do Cachimbo, Brazil. They should be self-explanatory. Chiu Liow Jones – who already has a copy of

everything – believes your input is essential in terms of deciding whether this latest event is part of the overall pattern or merely coincidental. You have my permission to use this information in any way you think appropriate.

Welcome read the news item, then turned to the letter Chiu Liow had written, humming and nodding his head occasionally while he read:

...Once the news reached me I immediately contacted our colleague in Brazil, who promised to do everything he could to speed up the investigation. To say the least, he was surprised by my request to send the more 'interesting' details of his inquiries through the mail. However, knowing me as he does, did it, even if he couldn't resist adding that he didn't relish the idea of writer's cramp if he ever needed to send more!

By the way, do you realise that if we disconnect our computers and hand readers from the lattice, we don't have anything to record or write with unless we go to the trouble of either applying for software to be directly installed on their drives, requesting specialised equipment, or using our comlinks? The problem is, though, if we use our comlinks, our material isn't completely secure, because as far as I know, there's no way of turning them on without being immediately connected to the lattice. Have you ever considered that before? I haven't.

Still, if he wants to, I'm sure Maerz will be able to access the main details of what we're doing, but at least we can keep his knowledge to the absolute minimum – to irritate him, if nothing else. Although, up until now, I haven't even succeeded in doing that. He just keeps smiling at me!...

Setting the letter aside for the moment, Welcome read the report from Brazil, which told him that someone had substituted the model of the active ingredient of *Claviceps atropurpurea* for the one actually designed to be used in Epsilon's new product. The substitution occurred during the third production run. Two limited releases had been sold successfully to the medical world, so the third one – far more extensive in light of the high initial sales – was expected to establish the drug's reputation.

The package also contained the official, and hence recorded, interviews, most of which were only mildly interesting. After listening to them, Welcome was sure none of Epsilon's employees could be responsible. He also felt certain that an outsider hadn't physically bypassed their tight security measures. As a result, it didn't take long for him to reach the same conclusion as that of the Attorney General's Office: Epsilon's section of the lattice had been broken into and their database tampered with.

The one positive outcome was that this particular crime occurred while Morag MacIain was under house arrest. Not that this meant it could be said she was innocent of having engineered the crime. It just indicated there was a formidable 'other' person still at large who might, or might not, be working with her.

Returning to Chiu Liow's letter, it finished with an outline of the most recent events in Papua. He pointed out – although Welcome had already realised it – that with Epsilon's reputation in jeopardy, all private companies who had invested significant resources into their own original research and whose main source of income was from some form of forest industry, were now either suffering market setbacks or were in the hands of Wyvern Meridian.

Welcome stared at the handwriting for a few minutes without seeing it, then asked his computer for the daily stock market report. He was not a follower of share prices, but the format presented was straightforward enough for him to understand. It appeared that Wyvern Meridian was trading strongly overall but was making significant losses in their Southeast Asian subsidiaries. He requested a comparison between private and Federation trade in forest products worldwide, as well as a detailed breakdown by company. The computer gave the comparisons by volume and by monetary value, then asked Welcome if he wanted trends over time to be displayed. Why not, he thought, and said, 'Give me the patterns for the past ten years.'

'For each product, or overall market share? There are 2,542 possible product comparisons.'

'Overall market share.' Welcome sighed, shrugging his shoulders in annoyance. He would need to ask for an automated analysis. Looking through thousands of graphs and tables would hardly be useful.

One and a half hours later, Welcome realised he was hungry. As far as he was concerned, the information had been of interest mainly to a prospective investor. It was clear the Federation was the dominant supplier of all essential goods, as well as a significant number that could only be supplied at an overall loss, yet which were considered socially useful – Welcome had chuckled when he noticed cocoa and chocolate on the 'socially useful' listing. Private companies, on the other hand, tended to stay within the realm of 'optional' goods and services, or else competed with the Federation where it was unable to meet demand.

The report did at least tell him that aside from the companies which they already knew were suffering market setbacks, the remaining smaller concerns all had stable investment profiles and robust market share values; he had asked for this additional information as an afterthought. Wyvern Meridian, on the other hand, appeared to be the only significant speculator.

They were large enough to absorb losses, so seemed prepared to take bigger risks. The analysis of their performance gave the only trend Welcome found useful to the case: Wyvern Meridian invested a large proportion of their funds on goods that competed with those produced by the Federation, and were, in many instances, highly successful. It wasn't the competition he found odd, it was that they appeared to have *chosen* this direction in preference to easier markets for luxuries.

Going back to Epsilon's problem, he simply could not see why Wyvern Meridian would want to become involved. Whilst they manufactured pharmaceuticals, there was no financial dependence on any that competed with those marketed by Epsilon. Welcome wondered, therefore, if Epsilon was on the verge of bringing something to fruition that the international giant was also working on? Without a great deal of exceedingly clever, and totally illegal, espionage, of which he was unfortunately not capable, it would be impossible for him to find out.

Thinking along these lines brought Welcome back to Rohan Maerz. If *he* was involved, rather than Kenjiro Kakura, it would be far easier to put forward some plausible theories, but without supporting evidence, it was hardly possible for him to present them in Morag's defence. On the other hand, he could draw a picture of the type of person likely to sabotage a company such as Epsilon, then demonstrate she did not have this type of personality. Reasonably satisfied with his work, he finally ordered his belated dinner.

The following day, Rohan Maerz was thoroughly enjoying his own evening meal as he sat in his newly refurbished Melbourne apartment. It now held an air of personalised luxury. The brocade curtains were of gold and red, the carpets of handmade wool; they alone had cost half a year's salary. His favourite item was a mahogany dining table with an inlaid design depicting a stylised owl. The tablecloth of fine white linen bore at its centre a single red camellia floating in a Stuart crystal bowl: his tribute to Morag.

As no further dramas had occurred since Marika's demise, there was ample time for him to monitor events and explore the city. The restaurants were far better than those in Luzern and there seemed to be less emphasis on eating as little as possible. In fact he felt happier here than ever before. The transport system even seemed to be designed for people who didn't like walking! As a result, he was able to go anywhere he pleased without the unpleasant physical exhaustion he normally associated with life.

The tendency of Jones, his fellow investigators, and the Australian researchers to avoid the lattice amused him, yet Rohan felt sure there was little happening that required his immediate attention. Nevertheless, there were other developments to intrigue him, related to those cat creatures he now longed to meet. To find out more, he decided to arrange a visit to the Breeding Centre and suggest he be present while their experiments were conducted prior to Possum's trial. He couldn't conceive of anything to prevent him, and perhaps he might even adopt a cat? He needed a companion... If Morag MacIain was found guilty and incarcerated, there would be no one left to whom he could so easily relate.

Setting this thought aside, he poured himself another glass of wine and finished eating his entrée of tender buttered asparagus, scalloped potatoes, and grilled salmon.

CHAPTER SIXTEEN

Since 06:00 that morning, Meng Jarrah had wandered along the walking trails threading their way throughout the forests of Lamington. The region had been protected as a national park since the twentieth century, so here in the centre of the forest, there was no discernable loss of the species needed to maintain its complexity, although weeds and alien pests had invaded the borders. The air was hot and humid, but she breathed it in with delight. The humidity felt different from that of Myanmar and the forest scents were quite different too. A few drops of water trickled down the back of her neck as her hair brushed against an overhanging twig. She looked up at the tiny blue opening in the canopy. It would be even hotter outside the forest.

Deciding it was time for a break, Meng Jarrah searched for a dry place to sit. The log she chose was almost a metre in width. It had fallen long ago and was now home to dozens of different ferns, mosses, fungi and insects, as well as the odd seedling. She wriggled her toes inside the heavy walking boots and stretched luxuriously, although before eating her midsun meal, she inspected her legs for leeches. Unusually, there were none.

There were still another ten kilometres to go before the circular route that started and finished at the research station was completed. Walking steadily, it would take at least two hours over the rough terrain. Two more hours of gorgeous solitude! She promised herself there would be other days like this.

Surrounded on all sides by seedlings and saplings at various stages of growth, the research station occupied the smallest possible cleared space. Each test plot was neatly marked with the species it contained, the date of planting, and a code designating the trial conditions. Martha was inspecting the older plots, close to the forest edge, when Meng Jarrah rounded the last mature silky oak, raised her arm and called out a greeting. The salute was returned by the younger woman, who smiled shyly as Meng Jarrah approached.

'Gwenllian's been waiting to talk to you,' said Martha. 'She's got some great results.'

'What, from the stuff she was working on last night?'

'Yes, and Owain was looking pleased with himself too.'

'Great! I want to take a shower, so meanwhile, if you see them, you could say I'm back. See you later,' and Meng Jarrah continued her casual stride towards the main house.

Martha went back to her careful measurements, pausing now and then to compare her results with the previous week's. Content, she decided they were doing better than could be expected, given the setback they had suffered.

After a deliciously cool shower, Meng Jarrah rubbed her curls dry with a towel, roughly brushed them into shape with her fingers, then examined herself critically in the mirror. She eventually chose a grey silk dress that matched her eyes. The slippery fabric settled into elegant folds when it was drawn over her head and tugged gently into place. She didn't bother to put on shoes as the slate tiles of the floor felt smooth and clean to her feet. Finally, pleased with her appearance, Meng Jarrah walked barefoot through the house to meet Gwenllian and Owain, who didn't hear her silent approach.

Not normally an easy woman to shock, Meng Jarrah was nevertheless astounded by what she saw. The brother and sister were sitting close together on the floor in a bright patch of sunlight streaming in from the open window. Gwenllian was turned away from Meng Jarrah, but Owain faced her, eyes shut, his whole body completely relaxed. His sister's arms were raised, with the tips of her fingers resting lightly on his forehead. This might have been a simple form of meditation were it not for the delicate phase shift in the light that surrounded Owain's whole form – all the colours of the rainbow created a narrow outline.

Meng Jarrah tiptoed back to the doorway then ran lightly down the corridor to her room. Once there, she put on a pair of sandals with solid heels and walked briskly back. This time, Owain and Gwenllian were sitting motionless in the window seat, the sunlight still shining on their fair hair. They gazed at her for a few moments, as if at a loss for words, before Gwenllian stood up, walked over to Meng Jarrah and placed her fingertips on her forehead.

By reflex, Meng Jarrah raised her hand in an attempt to take Gwenllian's wrist, but found she had no will to complete the action. There was no fear, just warm contentment and a languorous calm. After a few moments, Gwenllian removed her hands from Meng Jarrah's face and stood before her, waiting. The two women gazed at each other without saying a word, then turned to Owain. He was still sitting by the window, but had leaned forward, eyes wide, amazed by what he had seen.

'Forgive me, Meng Jarrah,' whispered Gwenllian, 'but I had to know. What did you see, Owain?' she asked, moving closer to her brother.

'I saw Meng Jarrah relax, just as I did, and the light around her seemed to shift, forming a rainbow silhouette. Is that what happened to me?'

'I don't know. My eyes were closed.' Gwenllian timidly touched his arm.

'It *is* what happened to you, Owain,' answered Meng Jarrah. 'I came in earlier to see you because Martha said you were waiting. I didn't have any shoes on, which is why you didn't hear me. I was so shocked by what I saw, I went straight back to my room and put some on so you'd notice when I came back in again. I didn't want to alarm you.'

Meng Jarrah was still standing where she had been when Gwenllian touched her. Although she spoke rationally, a strong sense of unreality seemed to prevent her from being able to move. She suddenly felt weak, and attempted to walk over to join Owain, but stumbled. Gwenllian immediately came back to put an arm around her shoulders, then helped her sit down, taking a seat beside her. They sat there for several minutes, trying to absorb and make sense of this unknown power Gwenllian had discovered. The sun warmed their backs and the room seemed remarkably peaceful. Eventually, Gwenllian broke the silence.

'I honestly don't know what I've done. We were just sitting on the floor talking about today's work and waiting for you to return. Then, when Owain said he had a headache from having stayed up late last night going over our results, I offered to massage his temples. I'm not sure what the time was, but when we heard you walk down the corridor, it seemed as if we were waking from a pleasant dream...and something like half an hour had simply disappeared. As soon as I saw you, I had to find out if what we experienced was real or not... I'm sorry if it's upset you, but I *needed* to know.'

'I'm not in the least upset, Gwen, but I *do* feel confused,' replied Meng Jarrah. 'This *is* quite bizarre, you realise!'

'No more bizarre than being able to communicate with cats.' Owain was beginning to recover and to think more clearly. 'We should contact Søren. He would definitely want to know about this.'

'It might help solve the puzzle of why Mik's cats don't like me.' Gwenllian glanced first at Owain and then at Meng Jarrah, a vulnerable expression on her pale face.

Although Meng Jarrah had limited experience with cats, she remembered how Red Matilda deliberately attacked Gwenllian during their meeting at Willsmere, and also Søren's amazement at the way in which the cat shut her mind to him afterwards. 'Well he'll certainly be interested,' she agreed, raising her eyebrows. 'Shall we call him now?'

Owain reached for his comlink and after a longer than usual delay, Søren appeared on the screen, his expression grumpy. 'I take one day to sleep late, relax, then cook something very special for my dinner and someone has to call me just as I am about to sit down to enjoy it! Really, it is too much!' He glared fiercely at them.

'We'll let you get back to your dinner if you want, Søren, but I think you might prefer to hear what we have to tell you,' said Owain, tapping his fingers impatiently against the edge of the window seat. He sometimes found Søren's humour trying.

Søren quickly realised the call wasn't a social one and abandoned his ill temper. 'What has happened, my friend?'

'We think Gwenllian has developed some type of telepathy. She's been able to affect both Meng Jarrah and I, just through touch. When it happened the first time, to me, she didn't even realise it would, so deliberately tried it on Meng Jarrah, who was affected the same way.'

Søren gaped at them. Not usually someone who had difficulty finding something to say, this became one occasion on which he was literally speechless. He listened carefully while Owain described the aura he saw surrounding Meng Jarrah, explaining that she had seen the same thing enveloping him while he was being influenced by Gwenllian's mind.

'I gather you have called me before Gwenllian has tried it on anyone else?' asked Søren, still looking dazed. When Owain nodded, he said, 'This could explain why Red Matilda and Fliedermus disliked your sister. They may well have detected the great difference between her mind and all the others they have come across and might not have known what to make of it. It occurs to me that they may even have been unable to read her mind, or to influence it, which I am sure would not have amused them.' He shook his head and smiled gently. 'I think sometimes they are far too pleased with themselves.'

Gwenllian held out her hand for the comlink, which Owain gave her, then set it to speaker volume so the others could listen to the call. She stared at Søren for several seconds, attempting to calm herself, before saying, 'Søren, I need to find out more about this...what I can and can't do, and if I can actually control it. At the moment I have no idea at all how I did what I did, and whether the effect I had on them is the only type of effect I *can* have. I assume from your surprise that you've never heard of this type of thing before?'

'No, never,' he replied, 'but that doesn't mean it hasn't happened before. There has always been a great deal of speculation and many reports over the ages of people having telepathic abilities, although never any scientifically proven ones. We need you to come back to Melbourne, if you can, to look into this further. Would that be possible?'

'No... I'm sorry to say no, but I just don't want to leave our work here at Lamington. We're getting some wonderful results, and anyway, I've gone through too much lately to want to come back. I'm thoroughly enjoying the change of scenery here, too...and really need to take things a bit quietly at the moment.' Søren was about to interrupt, when she said, 'I won't pretend this didn't happen, and as I said before, I *will* try to work out what I can and can't do, but I want to take this slowly. It *is* rather frightening!'

Owain placed a hand on her shoulder, as if to protect her from Søren.

'Owain,' said Søren, 'I have no intention of hurting your sister. I am only trying to help, and can easily imagine that having this ability is frightening, but I can also imagine that once she develops and understands it, her powers will be an extraordinary asset.' He spoke carefully, smiling and doing his best to charm them. 'Would you allow me to visit Lamington instead? There is much we could do to test your newfound abilities without in the least interrupting your workdays, if you prefer not to. There are, after all, the evenings. I cannot stay long, though, because Possum's trial is in two weeks.'

Meng Jarrah liked Søren a great deal and thought his suggestion excellent. 'Come on, Gwen, you must let him come here and help look into this, you really must. He's had so much experience with cats, you'd be in good hands.'

Gwenllian saw only sincere concern in Meng Jarrah's face and an honest wish to help. Meanwhile, Owain said nothing, not wishing to put more pressure on his sister. She sighed, turned back to the comlink, and nodded.

'I *am* glad,' responded Søren. 'I will see you tomorrow at midsun. I do hope you'll have a lovely meal waiting for me... Oh, and make sure you have enough food for a very large and hungry peacekeeper, as well as a bed for him to sleep in.'

'What under the Sun do you mean?!' exclaimed Owain. 'Surely you're not *still* being escorted everywhere?'

'Yes, indeed, and enjoying it too!' Søren laughed openly, his perfect features becoming even more beautiful in the process. 'I think, to flatter myself just a little, they like escorting me here and there. They will fall over themselves to be the one who visits Lamington with me. A nice little holiday.'

'How long do you think you'll want to stay?' asked Gwenllian, beginning to smile.

'Oh, at most a week. It depends on how well we can begin to understand your fascinating new powers...and also upon how well you manage to take care of me,' he teased, then grinned, waved goodbye, and terminated the connection.

Meng Jarrah placed her hand lightly on Gwenllian's arm, wondering what would happen, but felt nothing unusual. 'Gwen, what do you want to do now?'

'Honestly?' replied Gwenllian. 'Not a single thing. I need to think, and I want to be alone to do it.' She glanced apologetically at Owain, who gave her a brief smile and nodded, fully understanding.

They left Gwenllian sitting in the sunlight by the window and walked silently to the kitchen, where they sat down at the old wooden table standing in the centre of the tiled floor and stared at each other.

'I think she'll want to wait until Søren gets here to really do anything about all this,' began Owain, 'and in the meantime will sort it all out in her own mind and try to decide how best to begin when he arrives. We were planning to tell you all about our day's work, you realise, but I guess we got a bit sidetracked.' He grinned. 'She really is special, isn't she?'

Meng Jarrah smiled in agreement, deciding simply to let him talk.

'We've always been close and always wanted to link our professions, so being here together like this is wonderful. I don't want our work to be delayed because of what's happened, but on the other hand, we have to deal with it systematically. We'll need to know if she can control this power and also how much more can be done with it.'

'That could take a long time... It's a complete unknown.' Meng Jarrah regarded him earnestly, resting her chin in one hand. 'Gwen received no warning of this. Who knows what might happen next? Still, I'd say the first thing to do is to find out if she can will it to happen.' She stood up and stretched, realising she was hungry. 'Do you want to help cook something? Martha must be getting hungry by now too. I'll go and ask her, but I don't think we should tell her about Gwen, do you? I think it would be best if we just say that Søren's arriving tomorrow for a short holiday.' Meng Jarrah flexed her strong shoulders again, and then, when Owain agreed, walked out to the forest clearing.

Søren arrived the next morning, not long before midsun, his guardian peacekeeper contentedly in tow, as predicted. They were conducted to the specially prepared table set in the shade of an ancient, moss-covered Antarctic beech growing near the edge of the forest. Søren gazed in satisfaction at the dark blue tablecloth, the bowl of white orchids at one end, the red linen serviettes and the highly polished cutlery, all complementing the white bone china tableware.

'I am greatly impressed,' he said, and bowed to each of the researchers waiting expectantly.

The peacekeeper put a large hand to his mouth to hide a smile, although he was pleased to have the chance to relax a little and to enjoy the generous effort everyone had made. Søren had briefly filled him in on the reason for the occasion, but his role was to guard, not to participate, or so he assumed.

Martha bustled around arranging for the food to be brought out from the kitchen, while Søren seated himself at the head of the table, correctly assuming the place of guest of honour. The table gradually filled with the delicacies they had taken all morning to prepare. The day had become an excuse for a brief respite from work and worry, to be savoured and remembered. Small creatures from the forest crept out to beg for scraps, and from time to time, a curious bird hopped down to perch nearby, head to one side to see better and often becoming bolder when they were given small pieces of food. Yellow robins darted down to gather crumbs, oblivious to the laughter and conversation, while a small crowd of rosellas paced about, waiting to be noticed and comical with their antics. The treetops were filled with birdsong, sometimes tuneful, often raucous when flocks of white sulphur-crested cockatoos circled overhead, finally settling down to idly strip bark from the trees as the afternoon became warmer.

For the time being, Søren refrained from discussing their research, his own work, cats, or even the reason why he came to Lamington. However, once the meal was finished and the table cleared, and all the dishes washed and put away, he gathered Meng Jarrah, Owain and Gwenllian, as well as his guardian, and walked away from the main research station. He led them to a small, sunlit area, comfortably furnished with handmade chairs and a beautifully aged cedar table. Søren was fond of this hideaway, having discovered it during an earlier visit to Lamington, but also wanted to ensure their discussion was neither overheard nor interrupted.

'Gwenllian,' he began, 'I am almost certain you have spent all of yesterday afternoon and a good part of the evening deliberating upon your newly discovered talent. Would you like to tell us what you want to do?'

A small group of scrub turkeys wandered out from the forest and scratched around in the leaf litter by their feet, hoping for a free meal. Finding nothing, they wandered off again. Gwenllian watched them for a while before replying: 'You already seem to know me very well, Søren.'

Smiling, Søren shrugged, his hands folded in his lap, quite relaxed.

'I want to see if I can cause the effect at will, not just by chance. I think the best person to try it on is yourself, Peacekeeper Sullivan. I've never met you before, so have no mental link whatsoever.' Gwenllian moved her seat closer and he turned crimson, never having conceived of being part of this discussion, let alone part of any experiments. He even stuttered a little as he answered.

'Well, well, of course, of course... Whatever you think is best. What...what am I supposed to do?'

Søren, who was sitting next to him, took his hand and the poor man blushed an even darker scarlet. 'You can see that when I hold your hand, nothing whatsoever happens to you,' said Søren, an amused yet sympathetic expression on his face, 'but if our beautiful Gwenllian can control her ability to affect someone telepathically...that is, anyone, not just someone special...you *may* experience something unusual, although we don't know what, if anything.' He gently let go of Sullivan's hand and the peacekeeper sighed in relief.

Gwenllian moved her chair again – this time to sit directly in front of Peacekeeper Sullivan – then placed her fingertips on his forehead and closed her eyes in an attempt to clear her mind. The others watched, keeping as still as possible to avoid disturbing her concentration. Minutes went by and nothing seemed to happen. She shifted slightly and the peacekeeper nervously shuffled his feet. A small wallaby hopped over to them, sniffed at Sullivan's hands, then hopped away again. No one stirred, waiting. The peacekeeper stopped shuffling and relaxed.

Gwenllian dropped her hands, sighed, and straightened her slender back. 'I don't think I've managed to do it again... At least, not this time.'

The peacekeeper didn't move, so she looked at him more closely. His eyes were shut, his breathing deep and even. Gwenllian touched his hand, but he took no notice at all. Meng Jarrah slowly stood and tiptoed over to see. Peacekeeper Sullivan was fast asleep! When Søren leaned over to touch him firmly on the shoulder, he started and woke up, blinking and confused.

'My goodness, I don't know what came over me... I've been asleep, haven't I? I'm really sorry,' he apologised, embarrassed at having ruined their experiment. 'Must be all the good food and hot sun. I truly am sorry, indeed I am.'

Owain laughed, patting him on the back. 'Do stop apologising, Peacekeeper Sullivan! We've simply chosen the wrong time of day to try this. Would you mind if we returned to the house and made another attempt in about an hour, and after some good strong coffee? It might even help if you went for a walk to wake up properly.'

Peacekeeper Sullivan ran a hand over his face and nodded several times. 'Yes, yes, good idea. I'll do that. See you in half an hour,' and he strode off along the nearest walking track.

With Martha and the other staff working some distance away in the forest, at the appointed hour, and after several cups of coffee to keep him awake, Peacekeeper Sullivan once more subjected himself to Gwenllian's delicate touch. As before, the others sat quietly and watched. Yet again time passed and nothing seemed to happen. But as the sunlight crept towards them from the nearby window, small motes of dust at first formed delicate random patterns, then little by little, a slender silhouette of light formed itself around the peacekeeper. Gwenllian appeared to notice nothing as she continued to concentrate. Gradually, the light shifted and the silhouette took on all the colours of the rainbow, beginning with red and ending in violet. It grew, widening, until he was enveloped in colour and radiance – and then the silhouette disappeared. Gwenllian cried out and fell to the floor. The peacekeeper fell forward as well and the two stayed where they were until the others collected themselves enough to react.

Owain was the first to reach his sister, gathering her into his arms and holding her to his chest like a child, his face buried in her pale golden hair. Distraught, he called her name and she woke, gently pushing herself away.

'I'm fine. I'm not hurt at all. It was just a shock! What's happened to Sullivan?'

Gwenllian crawled over to the peacekeeper, who was now sitting up, his head in his hands, totally confused. She brushed a lock of hair away from his forehead, peered into his face and murmured, 'How are you? Are you all right?'

Peacekeeper Sullivan rubbed his eyes then looked up at them all, dazed, but himself again. 'Well, I guess if I ever have trouble sleeping, I'll know who to call,' he said, with a slight, but good humoured, grimace. He carefully stood up, bracing himself against Gwenllian, who had already risen to help him.

Silently, they all looked at each other, not knowing where to begin. 'What did it feel like this time, Gwen?' asked Meng Jarrah at last, as she sat down again.

'Almost like the first time, but *this* time, I willed it to happen and didn't lose track as much. I can vaguely remember being aware of Sullivan's reactions – not in any specific way, just a sense of connection. I really think that with practice I could control this.' Gwenllian was walking back and forth now, excited.

'You have never communicated with a cat, which is a great pity,' said Søren. 'If you had, it would be fascinating to hear your thoughts on the matter. Perhaps if you attempted to connect with me, I might be able to compare the two sensations. Are you well enough to try? However, this time,' he added, with a comical downturn of his mouth, 'it would be wise to seat ourselves more securely.'

'Yes, that's true, it would!' agreed Gwenllian, smiling, although Owain appeared dubious. She briefly clasped his hand, so he said nothing.

Søren and Gwenllian sat down opposite each other, well braced in their chairs. Within only moments this time, Søren was illuminated by an aura of colour. He had closed his eyes and appeared fully relaxed. Gwenllian maintained the contact for almost a minute, and then, voluntarily this time, withdrew her hands from his face. Søren shook his head before opening his eyes. He appeared quite alert.

'You are most definitely not a cat, Gwenllian, even though you have such beautiful green eyes,' he told her, settling back into his chair.

She did the same, a strange, satisfied expression on her elegant features. Bent forward, his elbows resting on his knees, Owain peered anxiously from one to the other. Meng Jarrah and the peacekeeper remained silent, waiting for them to say something further.

Søren stared at his loosely folded hands for a few seconds while he put his thoughts together, then looked up and said, 'Cats seem to take images from us and can project them to others. We believe they are also able to influence our emotions, which is not something many people know, and at present, perhaps it would be best if we leave it that way. However, I have never felt anything like this before... There is always a sense of separation to some extent. With you, Gwenllian, the connection was quite direct. I had some idea of what to expect, of course, so was not as overcome as you, Peacekeeper Sullivan. As a result, I retained a degree of control. *You* did as well, did you not?' He stood up, then bent down and took Gwenllian's hand in his.

Startled, she almost pulled away, before accepting the gesture for the compliment it was. 'Yes,' she agreed, 'I did feel I could control what happened, just a little, but it still took a lot of effort. I didn't try to control *you* in any way, Søren. I just tried to sense who you are, if that doesn't sound silly?'

'No, that is exactly what I felt. There were no images or other unusual sensations coming from you, but there was a strong feeling of calm and reassurance. As a result, I am still puzzled as to why Mik's cats find you threatening. Perhaps they are annoyed at finding a human with similar abilities to themselves!' Søren laughed, and the others joined in, glad to find something to laugh about. 'Well, now, I do think we should leave this and have something to eat,' he suggested, ready to head for the kitchen.

Smiling, Meng Jarrah shook her head and went with him. She was rapidly becoming used to Søren's universal panacea for all things doubtful! Gwenllian and Owain linked arms and, with the peacekeeper following close behind, joined them.

While they were eating, Søren's comlink chimed, and when he reluctantly answered, to his astonishment, Rohan Maerz appeared on the screen.

'My dear young fellow, forgive me for interrupting, but I've wanted to speak with you for some time and decided not to delay the pleasure any longer.' He smiled graciously, inclining his head.

Søren hid his surprise well and returned the smile with an equally gracious expression. 'What a pleasure it is indeed,' he replied. 'I have anticipated our meeting for some time...or at least, our speaking together. What may we do for you?'

'I've a large favour to ask. I'd like to be present at Possum's trial, and intend to pay a visit to the Breeding Centre to find out more about cats. I'm hoping to be of some assistance. My input as the Federation Special Investigation Unit Coordinator might be useful, who knows?'

Søren's hair prickled on his scalp and he was momentarily unable to answer. The others were staring at him. Meng Jarrah, who sat close enough to hear, frowned and shook her head, as if to say, 'No!' Søren collected his wits and said, 'My dear Maerz, it would depend upon how well this visit to the Breeding Centre you so wisely intend, turns out. If the cats react badly to you, or if the Breeding Centre's genetic engineers consider you to be a disruptive presence, it would be impossible.'

'Ah, I see. I'd not considered that aspect,' replied Rohan, an extraordinarily sad expression on his face. 'Well, one can hope to be accepted,' he added wistfully.

Søren knew little of Rohan's private life, but wouldn't have thought being accepted by cats would matter in the least to such a man. Putting the thought aside for the moment, he said, 'If you do go, let the genetic engineers know you wish to be present at the trial. They will soon give you formal notice as to whether you are...acceptable...or not. If you are, they will give you the time and place and you will then be able to discuss with them as to whether there is anything relevant you could contribute. With the help of an independent expert, the Breeding Centre is coordinating the input to the Judge, as well as the conduct of the trial. *I* do not have any rights in this respect as I am too closely involved.'

'Very true, Søren Thorup, but given your status as a zoologist and the close ties you have with the cat – as well as, if I may describe it as such, her family – I believe I owed you the courtesy of this call.'

'That is kind of you, Rohan Maerz. Would you like to call again once you have spoken with the Breeding Centre staff?'

'I would...but perhaps I'm keeping you from something more important. I'll leave you to get on with it.' Rohan smiled one last time before cutting the connection.

'How extraordinary!' exclaimed Meng Jarrah. 'Why on Earth does he want to involve himself with Possum's trial?'

'Simple curiosity,' replied Søren, continuing his meal. He said very little for the remainder of the evening, which was a highly unusual occurrence.

They all retired early for the night. Gwenllian found herself to be exhausted, while the others had a great deal to think about and preferred to do it alone.

CHAPTER SEVENTEEN

Melbourne was at its sunlit best on the morning Rohan Maerz strolled to the nearest callstation and requested transport to the Werribee Breeding Centre. Having just spent part of the morning thoroughly enjoying the food hall at the new Victoria Market, he gazed in delight at the bright yellow flowers of the trafficway, savouring their delicate aroma while he waited for his request to be answered. When the railcar arrived, a number of passengers were already seated and, to Rohan's additional delight, not a single one noticed him any more than was normal, despite his size and highly colourful clothes. The trip lasted only twenty minutes, but was long enough for him to relax and happily consider what type of cat he might have. Long marmalade fur, he thought, and green eyes, just like Morag MacIain, with a sense of humour, if that was possible in a cat?

When a voice announced their arrival at the callstation nearest his destination, Rohan carefully alighted, balancing his weight with the handrail. He managed to take pleasure in the short walk to the breeding centre, for the ground was level, which meant his arrival was not accompanied by the usual wheezing and overheating that were his almost constant, highly unpleasant companions in the streets of Luzern. Not for the first time, he seriously contemplated making Melbourne his home.

As Rohan glanced at the building's security scanner, the double doors slid aside and he entered. He immediately noticed the floor, which consisted of multicoloured terracotta tiles laid in a complex mosaic depicting cats in a wide variety of charming vignettes. The spacious foyer also had a domed ceiling made entirely of plastiglass and was wonderfully warm and light, while ferns, native orchids, various rainforest plants and a tinkling fountain created an enchanting indoor garden. Decorative seats were placed here and there, inviting visitors to make themselves comfortable. There was even a discreet servery offering refreshments, which, judging by the delicious aroma, included fresh coffee. Rohan resisted the temptation to help himself, preferring to meet the cats first. Instead, he gazed appreciatively at the well-disguised surveillance cameras that appeared to encompass the entire area. Apparently the staff here wished to be prepared before meeting their visitors.

Accordingly, a door opened several minutes later and a tall, slender, silver-haired man entered, gracefully extending a hand in greeting. 'Welcome, Coordinator Maerz,' he said. 'We've been expecting you. My name is Smith, and I'm pleased to be the one who will introduce you to our cats and explain our work here. Would you like something to eat or drink before we go in?'

'Most kind of you, but I'm eager to see your cats, if you don't mind. No doubt you'd first like to find out more about me?'

Smith smiled. 'Oh, we already know a great deal about you, rest assured.'

Rohan returned the smile and said, 'Well, in that case, let us proceed.' But how did they know anything about him at all, other than the little he had told them and whatever was on public record? Surely they hadn't discussed him with Søren Thorup?

Smith led the way out of the foyer and into the Breeding Centre itself. As they walked, Rohan became increasingly aware of a multitude of cat voices – burblings and purrings in what seemed to be all the notes of the musical scale. The voices rose and intermingled, becoming louder and louder as they approached the main living areas.

'Are they always this vocal?' he asked.

'No, no,' said Smith. 'Only *some* visitors have this effect on them.'

'But they haven't even seen me yet!' Rohan exclaimed.

'Oh, they don't need to. In extreme circumstances, we estimate their transmission and reception range extends to approximately one and a half kilometres, possibly even further, but it's usually around five hundred or so metres. They appear to like you.'

Rohan stopped in his tracks, while Smith continued on a short distance before realising his guest was no longer with him. He turned and laughed, not unkindly. 'Yes, they like you. Do you find that so difficult to accept?'

For the first time in his adult life, Rohan Maerz was close to tears. He put a hand to his eyes for a moment, then controlled himself. This simply would not do! He must not give in to such extreme sentimentality. Although he wanted a cat, he certainly did not want to be mastered by one. 'To be quite honest, I know almost nothing about them,' he replied. 'Before coming to any final decision about applying for one, I'd prefer to study the background and profiling material which I gather the Judge now contains.'

'Well, well, I'm sure that would be most wise of you,' said Smith, his eyes crinkling in amusement. 'However, the cats are looking forward to meeting you. We mustn't disappoint them.'

He led the way to the adoption centre via a long corridor lined with artistic drawings, paintings and photographs of all the various breeds and types of cats available. Rohan would have liked to have taken time to appreciate them, but after only a quick glance, followed his guide. The corridor led to another spacious garden room, similar to the foyer though much larger. It also had a transparent dome to let in sunlight. In addition to the seats, this room contained furnishings specifically designed for cats to sleep in and upon, to sharpen their claws on, and to play with. They were everywhere, and they were all watching him, yet now, silently. Tails twitched and ears listened. Occasionally some would stretch themselves then settle back down to watch. Smith said nothing, simply observing the cats and observing Rohan.

Rohan hardly knew what to do, so did the obvious. He walked slowly towards the nearest cat and stretched out his hand to pat it. The cat, a large white one with short, thick fur and blue eyes, rubbed her head against his hand and purred, then went away, tail in the air. After glancing at Smith for his approval, Rohan approached another cat, and this time, held out his hand for it to sniff rather than attempting to touch her. The cat did so, carefully and thoroughly, before giving it a quick lick and also walking away. Looking around, Rohan decided it might be best to take a seat and see if any of the cats wanted to approach him. He found one large enough to accommodate his girth and sat down, taking care not to crease his cloak. Smith followed suit a short distance away, still watching.

As time went by and none of the other cats approached, Rohan began to feel uneasy. He didn't want to seem worried, but was having difficulty preventing himself from fidgeting and even began to perspire. It was rather too warm in here, he thought, and longed for a cool drink. Still, it was also pleasant, in a way, just to sit, to relax, to think of very little, which in itself was a novel experience. He found himself becoming calm again, and studied the cats more intently. Some appeared to have gone to sleep. A few were playing with their toys or using their scratching posts. Others were cleaning themselves, no longer taking much interest in him. He visualised his Melbourne apartment and how even more pleasant it would be to have a cat to take care of, and for her to sleep on his bed each night.

After a while, a cat with long golden fur, dark golden eyes and huge paws came up to him and rubbed herself against his legs, purring loudly. Rohan tentatively stroked her head and she jumped lightly onto his lap, placing her paws on his stomach, kneading happily and gazing lovingly into his eyes. He gathered her into his arms and held her to him. Tears ran down his face unheeded. When the cat licked his cheek, Rohan unashamedly wept.

*

Kenjiro Kakura was gratified by his tour of Myanmar. The government officials assigned to ensure his stay was pleasant and productive had treated him with respect and courtesy. He had been entranced by the carefully preserved pagodas they visited and was pleased so many thousands still remained in this beautiful country. However, as entertaining as it might be to play the tourist, this was not his main objective. He needed to consolidate his gains, confirm the allegiances owed him, and review his plans for the future. Wyvern Meridian was gaining ground in world markets for forest industry products of nearly all types, except within Southeast Asia, which, to his mind, included Australia. Well, the application for the Australian lease was progressing and should make a difference in the long term. The competition from other private companies, where critical, was gradually being eliminated, which left only the Federation, and he was confident he could succeed in his plans in relation to *their* global markets. Kakura smiled grimly.

Meanwhile, he was due for his training session. Kendo was one of his passions. He regarded its strict code of honour as the basis for all his actions, and its simple, but honest, social ideals as on par with his own. Picking up the bag containing his uniform and practice sword, he called his bodyguard. An hour later, he entered the dojo in full uniform, bowed, and commenced training. After three hours, elated by the physical and mental exertion, Kakura returned to his hotel, and before returning them to their rightful place, meticulously cleaned his armour, helmet and sword.

When a soft tap at the door told him that the simple meal he had ordered was being served, he thanked his host and sat down, giving his full attention to the food, as always. Kenjiro Kakura was efficient in all that he did and was able to devote himself fully to any activity in which he chose to participate. After the meal, he spoke to his comlink and was soon deep in conversation with his bondmate and their three children.

Freddi walked slowly down the slope towards the wreckage the workers of Myanmar Forest Industries were clearing away. Her investigations had discovered nothing further, even after all this time. Consequently, there was no reason to delay their efforts to remove all traces of the events that had so disrupted their lives. Detailed records had of course been made and entered into the Judge for future reference, should they be fortunate enough to track down the culprits. However, she wanted to take one last look, just in case anything occurred to her that hadn't already.

It had rained heavily during the night, so the mud was deep and the workers were straining to keep their balance. Freddi walked towards them, watching her feet so as not to slip. Noticing something glinting in a puddle, she stooped to pick it up, then examined it closely. The object appeared to be made of silver, depicting a winged serpent, beautiful and unusual. Perhaps it belonged to one of the workers? Freddi placed it in a transparent envelope and then into her breast pocket, stepping around a pile of rubble as she went on. One of the men stopped work and approached, smiling courteously.

'Good morning, Peacekeeper. It's kind of you to visit us again. You can see we're doing our best, despite the rain. We want to get back to normal as soon as possible.'

'Good morning to you too, Tuan,' replied Freddi, bowing slightly. 'I'd like to take a look around while you remove the wreckage, just in case anything turns up in the mud underneath. I'll try not to hinder you. By the way, I've just found this. Does it belong to anyone here, do you think?' She showed him the silver earring she had found.

Tuan examined it, but shook his head, then turned away to call out to the others. They stopped their machinery and came over. Each looked at the earring in turn, but also shook their heads, then went back to work. Freddi returned it to her pocket and continued picking her way around the cleared areas. Finding nothing more, she went back to the administration complex, hoping to show her discovery to the plantation manager.

As before, the building's security system recognised her authority to enter, although Freddi found only the manager's son. He was sitting at the kitchen table thoroughly enjoying himself as he munched his way through a particularly large bowl of noodles. Freddi's stomach growled, reminding her it was midsun. 'Hi!' she greeted him. 'Is your mother not at work today?'

'She's gone to check out possibilities for our new transport fleet. Thanks to your prompt handling of the clearance certificate, we can obtain insurance for them, although the premium is still a bit higher than we'd like. We should name a jinker in your honour!' He grinned broadly.

Freddi laughed. She liked the young man's spirit. 'I wanted to show your mother something I found in the mud outside, but perhaps you could tell me what you think instead. Just don't touch it.'

Setting his bowl of noodles aside, he stared at the small serpent sitting in its protective envelope. 'Why, that's a mythical creature called a wyvern!' he exclaimed. 'I design jewellery based on dragons and suchlike, so just happen to have seen one of these creatures illustrated, though I've never used one quite like this.'

'Have you noticed anyone wearing this type of thing around here, or anywhere else, for that matter?'

'Oh, lots of people like wearing dragon art, especially earrings. Otherwise, I wouldn't make good earnings from it, would I?'

'I suppose not, though I've never really noticed whether people tend to wear these particular designs,' admitted Freddi, with a smile. 'I want to track down who made this, so do you have any suggestions for a good starting point?'

'The metal itself should tell you a lot, and the artist is often named somewhere on the actual piece, usually woven into the design. Your labs will find it if they look hard enough. Silver of this quality isn't something that's mass-produced either and the work is excellent. Someone will be sorry to have lost it.'

Freddi was quietly satisfied that somebody as forthcoming as this young man truly had not made the earring, and also had no idea to whom it belonged. Naturally, she knew perfectly well how to track down its manufacturer and, if luck were with her, the person who had worn it: a DNA analysis would soon show whether any of the minute fragments of tissue that usually clung to ornaments such as this still remained. Freddi thanked him and returned to her office, elated at the possibility of having found a lead. She then contacted the Mandalay forensics team, who confirmed that if she brought the earring over immediately, they could complete a full analysis by early the next day.

Wyverns were also occupying Chiu Liow's thoughts. His Papuan colleague had sent the forensics report on the brooch found at the site of the murder of the charcoal worker, but as yet, he hadn't passed it on to anyone else. It appeared that although DNA analysis had not been possible due to the torrential rain having washed away any trace of human tissue, the silver itself was informative. Being of the highest quality, it could be traced to a mining company in Patagonia, which also produced finished products, such as fine jewellery. The item, described in their catalogue as a sleeping wyvern, had indeed been sold by them, although the name of the buyer did not appear in any Federation records. That in itself was, to his mind, an indication the wearer may well have been involved in the hideous crime.

Frustrated at being unable to readily discuss this development with a fellow investigator, he decided instead to call Freddi and suggest she visit him in Melbourne, where they could exchange information without the chance of being 'overheard'. At the same time, he knew she could give him some much needed moral support.

Until Chiu Liow could meet with his sister, he felt unable to progress further with the case, which bothered him intensely. Even worse, Morag's trial was looming closer, and his hands were tied there as well! Frowning, he left a message with Freddi's comlink to call him in the morning, then decided it would be best to have an early night. He tidied his workstation, collected the few things he needed to take with him, and before leaving, walked out onto the balcony to admire the sunset over Port Phillip Bay. Resting his arms on the railings, he savoured the fresh sea breeze, the salt tang stimulating on this cool evening. A few early stars were already out and it was possible to see the lights on the cruise ships as far away as the Docklands and Williamstown. The view inspired him to be less gloomy, and as a result, thought that if Freddi did come to Melbourne, they could treat themselves to a trip around the bay before she returned to Myanmar.

Despite the situation, Chiu Liow slept well that night and thoroughly enjoyed his breakfast of mango juice, fresh pancakes and coffee. Taking time for a bath, he was deliberating whether to work from home or from the office when his comlink beeped. Sighing, he got out of the tub, wrapped a towel around his waist and answered the call. It was Freddi.

'I gather I'm too early,' she said, laughing at his attire.

He smiled, always glad to see his sister. 'Thanks for calling. I was hoping you could come to Melbourne for a short visit.'

Freddi said nothing for several seconds, thinking about her workload. 'Yes, I can,' she said at last. 'How about tomorrow evening? I'm off tomorrow and Thursday, and could apply for Friday as well, if you'd like.'

'Wonderful! I'll meet you at the transport exchange. What time should your flight arrive?'

She consulted her comlink. 'About 18:00. Allowing for travel time to Parkville, I should see you at around 18:45 at the latest.'

'Until then,' he replied.

Freddi arrived appearing harassed, which was an unusual state for her to be in. The weather was appalling – windy, wet and cold – one of the sudden changes Melbourne excelled at providing. Fortunately, having brought an umbrella, she remained relatively dry, but had failed to dress for the cold. Sympathising, Chiu Liow grimaced, and when they arrived at the Rialto, decided to be extravagant, heading for the nearest boutique to buy a warm, knee-length woollen cloak of darkest emerald green, something Freddi would be glad of for many years to come.

'A present,' he said, when Freddi tried to pay for it. 'I'm just so very glad you're here!'

Freddi kissed him warmly on the cheek and adjusted the cloak to fit her shoulders. 'Let's get some dinner at a restaurant. Consider it a small present in return.' She grinned, then added more soberly, 'I suspect you miss Morag, don't you?'

Chiu Liow blinked, then stared at her in surprise. 'Yes, I do,' he acknowledged, 'and it's terrible not knowing when, or even if, I'll ever be able to speak with her again in person.'

'I understand,' said Freddi softly, linking arms with him. They walked on in silence until they reached a nearby establishment offering a wide range of international dishes. Once seated, she picked up the conversation where they left off.

'Some time ago, Morag and I had an honest talk about certain personal things. She told me about having become very attached to you. You need to hold on to that, Chiu, and you *know* Welcome will do everything he can to put together the best defence possible.'

'You're right,' he replied, looking down for a moment, 'although I was hoping the charges would be dismissed once all the preliminary evidence had been entered into the Judge. Apparently not... Her trial is to be in a month's time. I'll have to go, you realise?'

'I expect you've only to be there in case the Judge needs you to answer any questions that come up.'

'Yes, I've entered everything I know that's relevant. I would hope nothing is missing, but it's possible something may need further explanation... But Freddi, I want to be there in any case. I want to be there no matter which way the verdict goes, although I don't for one minute think she's guilty, do you?'

'No! Of course I don't. It's totally out of the question!' Freddi was adamant. 'By the way, isn't the trial of that cat, Possum, coming up soon?'

'Oh yes, so I gather. There's no reason for me to attend. The evidence I had to offer was very straightforward and I've put in my own recommendation, which is justifiable manslaughter.'

'It's pretty amazing to treat a cat in the same way as a person would be treated in a court of law. Are you happy with that?'

'Yes, I am. I've become quite close to Karla and her colleagues over the past few months, and their respect for these creatures and belief in their capacity to communicate with us, almost as equals, is so profound, I've learned to accept them on that basis. It would be illogical not to. The cat had no real choice but to kill, and didn't turn into some type of monster afterwards, which means there's no reason to treat her any differently, in a legal sense, than if she were human. There *is* one thing that's bothered me all this time, though.'

'And what's that?' asked Freddi, tweaking her new cloak a little and once again noticing just how deliciously soft the fabric was.

'Let's order first, and then I'll see what you think,' replied Chiu Liow, picking up the menu.

They were seated at a small table near the windows, away from the other customers. The place was warm and cheerful, with most people exchanging brisk conversation after their day's work. After choosing what they wanted, and indulging themselves by ordering a fine verdehlo from Western Australia, Freddi and Chiu Liow sampled the fresh fruit that had been placed on the table, together with a flask of ice-cold water. Freddi drank some of the water, then asked, 'Well, what is it that's bothering you?'

Chiu Liow swallowed his mouthful of pineapple and slowly wiped his fingers with a serviette. 'If Possum were human,' he said, 'she wouldn't have recovered so quickly from having killed someone. Yet when they left the Detention Centre that evening, she walked out of there fully at ease and with her tail in the air. Under the circumstances, I don't think the peacekeepers would have allowed a human out on bail, either, but they gave no opposition at all to letting Possum go. From the report they gave me, confirmed by the surveillance records, everyone was tense and visibly upset until shortly after the time Karla and the other cats arrived. Almost immediately, everyone calmed down. Also, apart from when they first entered the building, Fliedermus and Red Matilda behaved as if nothing whatsoever was wrong, whereas previously, they appeared ready to attack someone themselves. At first I put it down to them simply reacting to the reassurances of their human friends, but I'm no longer sure. *You* have a cat, what do you think?'

They were interrupted by the arrival of their meal. Both ate in silence for some time, listening to the rain outside and enjoying the warmth of each other's company. The darkness outside seemed only a pleasant contrast. Freddi answered the question once she had finished most of her fragrant risotto.

'I think they can influence our emotions, but I'm not sure whether it's an indirect effect or one they consciously control. I've never discussed this with anyone, but from my experience with Shela, I do know she sometimes has a soothing effect on me that seems more than just the result of my love for her and the type of comfort another warm presence brings. So, yes, overall, I suspect they *could* choose to effect our emotions. However, I've never had more than one cat, and don't know anyone other than Mik who has. I've no idea what they could manage to do with each other's thoughts...or feelings. Søren would be the one to ask. He's the local cat expert. Does it matter very much?'

'In terms of Possum's trial, no, it doesn't,' agreed Chiu Liow, 'but if they can act with this degree of purpose, it's possible the Detention Centre's peacekeepers were unduly influenced, so to speak, and might otherwise not have agreed to give her bail. Not that any harm was done, although obviously it did set a legal precedent with wide ramifications for cats. Speaking of which, did you know that Karla has entered Red

Matilda and Fliedermus' retina patterns and paw prints into Willsmere's security system?'

Freddi burst out laughing, so loudly that some of the other diners stared, but then smiled and politely turned away. Chiu Liow couldn't help but laugh himself. He had to admit, it definitely was funny.

'Does Rohan Maerz know they've done it?' Freddi used her serviette to wipe her eyes and managed to keep a straight face while he replied.

'He hasn't mentioned it, but probably does. It couldn't bother him too much, or I expect he'd have arranged for the records to be taken out again.'

'How are you managing to work with him?'

'Well, it's actually a relief to have him here, which amazes me. Maerz has a total grasp of the case and nothing happens that he doesn't know about almost immediately. At first I was horrified when he appeared as Morag's replacement, but I've become used to his flamboyant ways and even find him quite charming. He's certainly entertaining, although I still don't trust him. I'm also annoyed to say that I haven't progressed much further with the case. Have you?'

'Before we go into that, I think I'd like some tea. What about you?'

They entered their request into the menupad and waited a few minutes before the tea was served, deliciously hot and fragrant, with lemon wedges on a plate.

'I have something to show you,' replied Freddi, after drinking some of her tea. She gave him a hand reader displaying an image of the silver earring she had found, together with the results of the forensic examination.

Chiu Liow gazed at the image, stunned, then summarised what he had read, staring at Freddi as he spoke. 'It's a wyvern, made from silver mined in Patagonia and with the designer's initials hidden in the folds of its wings: 'MY'. The designer in question is Michiko Yamada, who is the bondmate of Kenjiro Kakura, and neither the DNA analysis nor the purchase records could match anyone in the Federation database.' He leaned towards her across the table, his golden eyes wide, his pulse quickening, and a fierce expression on his dark features as he told her of the Papuan find.

CHAPTER EIGHTEEN

Søren was packing his few things to take back to Melbourne after 'his' peacekeeper had dutifully reminded him it was nearly time to leave. He tucked the last piece of clothing into his bag, pleased everything fitted neatly – despite the considerable amount of space taken up by the collection of beautifully pressed flowers Martha had presented him with as a farewell gift. 'How are you feeling now, Gwenllian, about these powers of yours?' he asked.

'I'm over the shock, but still don't think I want to use them. I'd hate to put people off, and I don't want to invade anyone's privacy...which would be so easy to do, without even realising. If there was some *practical* use, it might be different, but I can't think of any, can you?' When Gwenllian's voice faltered and her mouth trembled, Søren took her hand in his and pressed it gently.

'You didn't *intend* to develop these powers,' he reminded her, 'and may not have full control for quite some time. Nevertheless, when you feel more comfortable with the idea, you *should* gradually explore what you can do with them...and please, don't forget, you will always be welcome to talk to me. As you know, I adore cats!'

Gwenllian carefully withdrew her slender hand and attempted to smile. 'Thanks for not being frightened to touch me, but it might be best if you didn't... At least, not until I'm more certain of myself. Sorry.'

'Think nothing of it. One day, I am quite sure you will find some practical use for your abilities...and learn you have been given a remarkable gift.'

As Søren met Gwenllian's eyes and smiled, Peacekeeper Sullivan appeared at the door and tapped politely, saying, 'Are you ready? Our transport is due in about ten minutes.'

'Yes, yes, I'm ready, and as my colleague here prefers not to shake hands at present, we will satisfy ourselves with a simple farewell.'

Søren picked up his bag, and before leaving, blew Gwenllian a kiss, which made her laugh, just a little.

After he had gone, Meng Jarrah diplomatically decided not to raise the telepathy issue, unless Gwenllian wished to. Accordingly, they spent the rest of the day and most of the following three days going over the new soil models and structural analyses, then giving their initial proposals to Martha.

'Our recommendations will, as I think you'd agree, depend upon comparisons with my twentieth-century soil sample,' Meng Jarrah reminded the others, 'although it appears the innermost Lamington region is in remarkably good health. Only its outer perimeter needs to be modified, either by short-term addition of suitable micro-organisms and nutrient substrates; long-term rehabilitation using a variety of reintroduced indigenous species and organic matter; or a combination of both.'

'I tend to prefer the long-term approach,' said Martha, having at last lost her earlier shyness. 'It's safer, but I must admit that if your models have as high a probability of success as these results indicate, it's tempting to use them. My doubts arise from the difficulty of avoiding harmful mutations, particularly if the biological controls are initially missing. What guarantee can you give, Gwenllian, that any particular mass-produced bacteria, for example, won't produce a harmful mutation that succeeds in establishing itself?'

'I can't give a one hundred percent guarantee, no one could, but we're predicting the odds against it are high enough to warrant the risk and to reap the benefits through much faster land regeneration. I could ask you a similar question: what's the probability of your current method succeeding, given the extent of degradation around the perimeter, together with the fact that it appears to be creeping inwards at an unacceptably high rate?'

Having left a great deal of the discussion to his sister, at this point, Owain joined in: 'I can only suggest we compromise by taking all three approaches and monitoring the progress of each. If we leave large enough buffer zones between the three test areas, the chance of overlap should be reduced, and it would be even better if we declared a quarantine around them. We could do that, couldn't we, Martha?'

'We could, and in a sense we already have a limited form of quarantine. The entire test region is only open to authorised traffic, but it could easily be tightened to full quarantine. Come to think of it, it's a very good idea. So, with the proviso that Meng Jarrah's sample can provide more information about suitable micro-organisms, I'd agree with you, Owain.'

Satisfied with their compromise, they discussed the practicalities until a definite plan was finalised and recorded.

Meanwhile, in Melbourne, Possum's trial began. Mik and Tamara's home was full to overflowing with all those who needed to be present:

Witnesses, the Court officials, various consultants, and Possum's friends. Rohan Maerz was also present. All the evidence for the trial had now been entered into the Judge. The Defence and the Prosecutor, as well as the registered consultants, had read the evidence, confirmed it was sufficient and complete, and had notified the Judge that they required no further additions.

The Court was silent while the Prosecutor identified herself to the Judge. Each person gravely followed suit, until it was the turn of the Accused. Everyone watched intently as Possum was coaxed to walk across a newly designed identification 'path', which registered her physical characteristics and paw prints. She walked gracefully, with tail erect and ears pricked, whiskers fluffed out and a smug expression on her face. Mik held a hand across his mouth to hide a grin.

Red Matilda and Fliedermus looked at him, asking permission to do the same, and were clearly delighted when the Prosecutor gave them the opportunity. Red bounded across the identification path as she had been taught to do by the Breeding Centre staff, but Fliedermus walked slowly and sedately – then spoiled the effect by rolling onto her back in front of one of the Witnesses, begging to be stroked. The Witness ignored the cat, who then sat on his feet and refused to move until Mik called her back. The Prosecutor shook her head, amused, yet determined not to let these creatures reduce the solemnity of the occasion.

'Now that all present have been properly identified,' she began, 'the trial of Possum the cat can commence. Possum is charged with having caused the death of a person, whose identity is unknown, on the night of the third of January 2451, in the Melbourne suburb of Glen Iris. She is currently residing in the house of her companion, Mik Theophanous, having been bailed from the Melbourne Detention Centre at 0:50 the same night.

'At the time of the incident, Possum was in the company of Tamara Solanum, who is a colleague and close friend of Mik Theophanous. Shortly after sunset, they were walking through an area of parkland approximately six hundred metres from the home of Mik Theophanous, when Possum allegedly detected the presence of a stranger whose intent was to harm her friend. She attacked the stranger, biting and tearing his throat, while Tamara Solanum lost consciousness, due, it is believed, to the impact of Possum's rage upon her mind. Mik Theophanous arrived at the scene shortly afterwards, having 'heard' Possum's distress via their telepathic link. He immediately called for medical assistance and also contacted the peacekeepers. Tamara Solanum was taken to the nearest medcentre, in company with Mik Theophanous, while Possum was taken to the Melbourne Detention Centre, where she remained until given bail.

'While Possum was being held in custody, arrangements were made for Søren Thorup, a zoologist working at the Willsmere research centre, to attend and attempt to communicate with her. He is a colleague of both Tamara Solanum and Mik Theophanous and well known to the cat. At first, his attempts failed due to her severely traumatised state. However, he eventually contacted Mik Theophanous, who was able to bring Tamara Solanum to the Detention Centre as she was by then well enough to leave the medcentre. Once they arrived, Possum calmed down to the extent that she was able to telepathically relate her version of events. Shortly afterwards, she was released into her companion's custody, on condition she be kept at home until further official notice.

'All evidence relating to these events has been entered into the Judge. The Summary of this evidence will now be given to those gathered here today. Anyone wishing to provide or request additional evidence or explanation will then have an opportunity to do so, having previously registered their interest in being present, or having been called by the Defence or the Prosecution. Silence will be maintained while the Summary is read.'

Red Matilda and Fliedermus sat quietly, their tails twitching, but otherwise they appeared unconcerned. Occasionally one of them licked Possum as the impersonal, neutral tones of the Judge gave the Summary of evidence, the text of which appeared on each person's comlink:

'...Having evaluated the details of the forensic examination of the deceased, designated as 'unknown male', the Coroner has concluded that he died of the immediate effects of brain haemorrhage and not from the actual physical attack made by the Accused. It is therefore necessary to determine, if possible, whether or not the Accused, Possum, caused the brain haemorrhage, and if so, whether by accident or intent. It is also necessary to establish whether or not the attack by the Accused was justified.

'Since the death in question, the Werribee Breeding Centre for Cats has conducted extensive experimentation into the abilities of cats and into their liability to attack when companions are threatened. These experiments have demonstrated that cats, including the Accused, are capable of discerning a mock attack under a wide variety of conditions, and do not react aggressively to such attacks in order to protect their companions. It may therefore be concluded that in all likelihood the Accused genuinely believed the unknown male intended to injure her companion, Researcher Tamara Solanum. The Court will now view portions of the two most relevant experiments that were conducted with the Accused and her feline companions, Red Matilda and Fliedermus, and which were undertaken in the presence of the Prosecutor, the Defence and Witnesses.'

*

Possum waited for the wight whom she had never met before to do something. The cats were now familiar with the other wights and knew they were harmless, although Possum could sense they wanted to surprise her. She glanced at Red Matilda and Fliedermus for reassurance: her friends were settled comfortably, tails tucked in and paws neatly folded under their chests. Without warning, the stranger leapt forward and attempted to grasp Fliedermus by the scruff of her neck. She twisted sideways to escape, hissing and flattening her ears, then backed away, settling down to watch – wary, yet not frightened. Red Matilda also leapt away, but when the immediate surprise was over, bounded over to the stranger, stood up, and placed her paws on his stomach, purring loudly. In the meantime, Possum watched, her eyes half closed, with tail moving slowly from side to side, only her curiosity aroused.

When the wight tried to roughly push Red Matilda to one side, she simply wound herself around his legs and continued to purr, while Fliedermus pranced over to join the game, tail in the air. She sat down in front of him, delicately placing one paw on his foot. He knelt down to pat them both, enchanted by their interest in him.

'Jonathan, you're meant to be aggressive towards them! What are you doing patting them?!' exclaimed the Prosecutor.

'Uh, I don't know!' he answered, hesitating, then standing up, bemused. 'I don't seem to be able to pretend any longer. How very strange.'

One of the Breeding Centre's genetic engineers covered his mouth and laughed. 'They have that effect on most people,' he said, 'but we wanted you to see it for yourselves. We believe an attack would need to be sudden and entirely genuine for the cats to react in self-defence. They could most likely sense that you weren't serious. Do you want to try again another day?'

'No,' replied the Prosecutor, 'I think we should proceed to the next test tomorrow.'

Possum gazed at them all. She could tell they planned to surprise her yet again. This could be interesting!

Tamara walked through the crowded plaza with Possum on her leash, enjoying the afternoon sunshine after the heavy rain earlier in the day. There was a cold wind, but she was dressed warmly. Possum sniffed the air: eucalyptus; late roses from the display beds; a multitude of scents from the cheerful, busy wights going about their business; the occasional unique smell of another grimalkin, and the salt smell of the sea. She happily followed Tamara on this wonderful long outing, unusually far from home.

Suddenly, a small dart embedded itself in Tamara's cheek. She cried out and staggered, then collapsed onto the pavement, unconscious. Possum frantically licked her face, calling out to the wights who were beginning to gather around. So many faces... Couldn't they hear her? She stared at them. Who had done this? Possum whirled around and found him, only metres away, checking to see if his target had fallen before he escaped. No, he would not escape!

Her ears twitched and she sat down. This was not real. Tamara wasn't really hurt. Was *this* the surprise?

Tamara sat up, rubbing her cheek where the tranquilliser dart had pierced. It still itched, but otherwise, she was unhurt. Possum glowered at her, sulking, and projecting a strong protest at being treated to such a *very* nasty surprise. Tamara mentally apologised and put her arms around the slender grey cat, kissing her head and holding her close, while the gathered crowd sighed in relief. Her 'attacker' came over to help Tamara rise to her feet, reassuring the onlookers that it was just an accident and no harm had come to anyone.

One elderly woman moved closer to peer at her. 'Are you sure you're all right?' she asked, then looked at Possum. 'Your cat is still angry, isn't she?'

'Yes, she is,' answered Tamara ruefully, 'but she'll be fine after she's had a chance to make certain we all know, though I'm sure she'll hide for a few hours once we're home again.' Tamara smiled to show the elderly woman she had fully recovered.

'Well, you're lucky to have such a nice cat. I used to have one, but she died three years ago. I thought perhaps I shouldn't have another one at my age.'

'I'm sorry,' said Tamara sincerely. When Possum nuzzled the woman's hand, she gave her a gentle pat before slowly walking away.

Once the recordings had finished, the Judge continued its Summary: 'Various other experiments have shown that the abilities of cats are extensive, in that they are able to follow spoken and unspoken commands and requests consistent with their basic natures, and are capable of exercising judgement. On the other hand, they are unlikely to follow suggestions or commands fundamentally contrary to normal cat behaviour. They are, for example, unable to digest meat, and to date, have not been induced to eat it. However, for reasons that do not require further explanation, it is not possible to reproduce an unexpected and genuine attack upon a person, so there is still a high degree of uncertainty as to what their behaviour would tend to be under extreme circumstances. Similarly, at this point in time it is not possible to establish beyond doubt whether the Accused caused the brain haemorrhage responsible for killing the unknown male. Nevertheless, as no other medical cause has been ascertained, it is more likely than otherwise.

'Only four other incidents are known to have occurred where cats defended their companions, or immediate family, against attack. In each of these cases the cats used no physical violence, yet the assailants were unable to escape, having been sent into a form of trance and then kept in that state until arrested. Based upon extensive feline psychological data resulting from studies conducted by the zoologist Søren Thorup and staff of the Werribee Breeding Centre, the logical inference is that in all probability, the cats induced these trances, presumably using some form of telepathy. This same ability may explain how the Accused potentially caused the assailant to suffer a brain haemorrhage.

'In a recent, and potentially related, case – that of the assault upon Researcher Mik Theophanous at the Willsmere Research Centre on the thirteenth of November 2450 – his cat, Fliedermus, was unable to physically defend her companion due to having been confined in a cage at the outset. To date, no information is available to explain why Fliedermus did not, or could not, use her psychic powers to either prevent herself from being confined, to defend him, or to prevent the assailants from leaving the premises. Her distress was, however, transmitted to a fellow researcher, Karla, prior to her entering the centre the next morning and while she was still some distance away. This, together with the other information provided, appears to imply that cats are capable of intentionally communicating with human beings in a highly intelligent manner.

'Considerable information has been provided by the Breeding Centre strongly indicating that cats are unable to bond with highly aggressive people, or people with marked antisocial tendencies. This reduces the likelihood of them being used as weapons by those with unstable personalities, or persons of criminal intent. Hence, it is improbable that on the night of the attempted assault, Researcher Tamara Solanum intentionally caused the Accused to attack, with a view to kill. Instead, it is likely that her extreme fear of the assailant, combined with the cat's ability to understand his intent, caused Possum to not only immobilise the unknown male, but to then physically attack him.'

Tamara gasped, her eyes opening wide. She hadn't considered the possibility that she might be suspected of having urged Possum to kill her attacker. Everyone stared at her, then quickly looked away as the Judge continued:

'It is therefore my initial determination that the Accused, Possum, is not guilty of murder. Before giving a formal verdict, is there anyone who wishes further explanation of this Summary, has additional evidence to enter in the presence of Witnesses, or wishes to challenge this initial determination? The full transcript will be made available to the public once the final verdict has been delivered.'

Throughout the trial, Red Matilda had carefully watched Rohan Maerz. Despite not having met before, she had a sense of knowing him, and associated her feelings with Søren's, who had recently returned from somewhere warmer than here. She fluffed out her fur, thinking it was time someone turned up the heating, and continued watching, concentrating more deeply in an attempt to penetrate his thoughts and feelings. When he turned around and their eyes met, the cat entered a mind so different from any she had ever experienced that she withdrew, startled. As Rohan raised his eyebrows at her, Red Matilda blinked and turned her back on him. She would sneak up on him later, when he was more fully occupied...

Rohan felt a presence like that of his darling golden cat, Aurora: alike yet unlike, probing, not bonding. He had never met any other cats than those in the Breeding Centre and consequently had little idea of what to expect – although he realised Mik's 'family' would inevitably want to find out more about him. It was a risk, yet one Rohan was perfectly willing to take, so he concentrated on Red Matilda, realising the presence was hers and not either of the other's. How he knew, he wasn't sure, but it was something to do with her size and colour, as well as her eyes. Green eyes and long marmalade fur – the type of cat he had visualised before Aurora chose him.

A slight sense of shock when Red Matilda retreated disconcerted him and he wondered whether either of the other two would attempt to communicate. Time went by and neither did. He eventually concluded that a dinner might be a pleasant way of having closer contact with these extraordinary creatures, as well as giving Aurora a chance to meet them. If he invited Mik and Tamara, they would of course bring Fliedermus, and perhaps even Possum, and as Karla was still escorted everywhere by Red Matilda, he should invite her as well. It might seem odd not asking Søren, but the presence of a peacekeeper would be so very tiresome! Of course, with all the cats present, he might not need to bring a guardian. Still, better not take the chance.

Rohan smoothed the fabric of his fine, woollen cloak. The weather had become colder, almost overnight, which was a pity, and also wetter. The rain, to his great distaste, had stained his new boots. Ah well, at least he wasn't forced to walk everywhere! He turned his attention back to the Judge.

Since no one required further explanation of the Summary or needed to provide additional evidence, the Judge delivered its final verdict: on the balance of probabilities, Possum was found to have performed justifiable manslaughter.

The Defence solemnly shook hands with the Prosecutor, then both shook hands with Mik, who was still seated, holding Possum on his lap and feeling light-headed with relief. Meanwhile, Possum gazed at them all, eyes wide and pupils dilated – no one blamed her for having killed the wight who wanted to attack her friend, Tamara, and she would at last be free again! Leaping down from Mik's lap, she bounded joyfully up the staircase to the greenhouse above, immediately followed by Red Matilda and Fliedermus. They ran about and tumbled over each other, hid in amongst the plants, then rushed out again in ambush. To Mik's dismay, some of the plants were shredded in the process, but this was a small price to pay after all these months of suspense.

Caught up in their happiness, everyone joined the cats to watch their play. They smiled at each other, shook hands with those whom they hadn't previously met, and even Rohan Maerz forgot himself for a while, chatting about his own cat to one of the consultants – a forensic pathologist, and normally an introverted fellow who rarely found anything to discuss with anyone other than colleagues.

Having arranged for refreshments, Tamara approached with a tray of glasses and a decanter of wine. 'To celebrate our success,' she announced, with a wide grin on her friendly features.

Rohan and the pathologist each accepted a glass and toasted first Tamara and then each other, before looking around to find Possum and toasting her as well, although *she* didn't notice; she was too busy chasing her own tail.

'To life and to freedom,' replied Tamara, raising her own glass, 'and may we hope for as good a result when it comes to Morag MacIain's trial.'

'Yes, indeed...' said Rohan, serious again. He regretfully decided it was time to leave. Still, at least Aurora would be waiting for him.

Crouching behind a large peace lily, pretending to hide from Fliedermus, Red Matilda watched Rohan prepare to go. She inserted her mind into his and gently probed, careful this time not to alert him to her presence; he was *so* sensitive. A large golden grimalkin was uppermost in his mind:

good...this was a *very* good thing. She delicately reached below the images. A woman was there, with wavy red hair, a freckled nose and a broad smile: an alert, intelligent face – someone whom he loved even more than he loved his own grimalkin. Yet he was cruel, and had hurt this woman. Red Matilda snickered softly. How could he hurt someone he loved? This wight was strange, she thought, but then he was gone and Fliedermus had pounced, distracting her for the moment. But she didn't forget what she saw, and the next day, showed Karla an image of Aurora asleep on Rohan's bed, curled up beside him, her head resting against his shoulder.

They all celebrated that evening, far into the night. Everyone avoided discussion of work, research, the ongoing investigations, and even the impending trial of Morag MacIain or any other ills of the world, for just this one night. Chiu Liow called by to find out what the verdict was and took the opportunity to join in. He was sure Freddi would have enjoyed the company as well, but she had already returned to Myanmar.

Søren, for once, left the catering to Mik and Tamara, which was an indication of just how tired he felt now that the worry of Possum's trial was over. He didn't insist that the table be cleared or the dishes washed, or even that the room be left tidy before they retired for the night. All he wanted to do was sleep, so as soon as everyone left, he dropped into bed in one of the spare rooms. Possum came in, leapt up beside him and snuggled down, warming herself against his slender form. He put an arm around her, caressing her soft fur, and slept soundly, without waking, the whole night through.

The next morning, when he was woken by a bright beam of sunshine coming in through the skylight above, the cat was still curled up against his back. Søren felt completely refreshed and anticipated with pleasure a good day's work at Willsmere. He rolled over and stretched, revelling in the simple feeling of being alive. Possum, however, was now wide awake and ravenously hungry, persuading him to get up, put on his dressing gown, and wander into the kitchen, yawning and thinking of hot, strong coffee to start this beautiful day.

That same morning, Meng Jarrah received a call from her Myanmarian researcher – the final outcome of the analysis of her soil sample was now available. She had the choice of having the results sent to her in the mail or going to Myanmar. Deciding it would be best to discuss them with her colleagues in person, and at the same time obtain their help with any further work required, Meng Jarrah made a booking on the earliest available flight. She took the preliminary results from the testing done on the Lamington region's soils with her so they could be used for further modelling before returning to Australia.

Meng Jarrah arrived in Mandalay late in the afternoon and was met by Freddi at the airport; a comlink call during the flight had proved irresistible. They hugged enthusiastically, then, laughing, kissed each other on the cheek. Freddi picked up half the luggage to carry to the nearest callstation, and while they walked, it seemed natural for them to link arms. Passers-by smiled at them, seeming to share their obvious pleasure in each other's company.

Freddi had finished work for the day, and since it was a little too late for Meng Jarrah to disturb her researcher, they decided to make good use of the remaining daylight by taking a trip to Mandalay Hill. Once there, they thoroughly enjoyed the splendid view and fine dining facilities, and then at dusk, the sunset, made enchanting by a flight of birds forming a delicate silhouette against the sky as it changed colour. Afterwards, while they talked about their lives and laughed at each other's stories, both women felt increasingly sure they wanted to share many such evenings, and perhaps a great deal more.

CHAPTER NINETEEN

'Are you staying long?' Meng Jarrah's researcher asked her, head tilted to one side, a wistful expression on his fine features.

'No, I'm rather sorry to say that I have to return to Australia with the soil sample, together with the micro-organisms we hope to develop from it. I'm hoping to take back some new ideas as well. I'll be here for a little while though,' replied Meng Jarrah, smiling and putting her hand on his slim shoulder.

'Good,' he said briskly, returning the smile. 'In that case, we should start work and make the best use of the time we have. I gather you brought the test results and models with you?'

'I certainly did, so let's run the comparisons and find out what we need to do to Lamington, if anything. We'll have to take into account changes in climate since the original specimen was collected, as well as small geographic differences. There'll obviously be a margin of error, which means any modifications to the experimental areas should be conservative. It's much easier to add than remove.'

They began the first of an extensive series of simulations aimed at predicting how they could achieve stable, productive soils that would allow a return to the most viable indigenous ecosystem in the shortest possible time. Towards the end of a long day, a walk around the gardens of the research centre refreshed them both.

'You're fully recovered now, aren't you?' asked Meng Jarrah.

'Oh yes, I am quite myself, but it did take a long time. It helps to have you back, even if only for the time being. Are you staying with Freddi?'

Meng Jarrah laughed and turned to him. 'How did you know?'

'She has often been in and out on short visits since you left and always asked after you. I could tell by the tone of her voice that she was unhappy at your not being here.'

Meng Jarrah was aware her researcher was very fond of her, as she was of him, and knew the earlier wistfulness in his voice reflected his strong desire to see her fulfilled and content in both her private and professional life. He could not understand why she lived alone, and, since completing her university studies, had always lived alone, while he shared his life with a bondmate of some fourteen years standing, as well as a much beloved child of eleven. She was glad to be able to ease his mind just a little.

'Freddi and I have become very dear to each other these past few months, so I'm staying with her until I go back to Lamington. After our work there has finished, we'll decide whether I return to Oslo or not. It's too early to know what the outcome will be, my friend. I'm simply glad to enjoy what the present holds.'

The researcher considered her carefully, then simply nodded. They resumed working for a while longer, until it was time to leave for their respective homes and their evening meals, happy with the day's progress.

Managing to arrive home early, well before Meng Jarrah was due back, Freddi had time to prepare eight easily served savoury dishes, as well as a truly luscious dessert. After tidying the kitchen, she set the dining table then cast a quick eye over the rest of the house to make sure everything looked its best. The small house was uncluttered and elegantly furnished, with subdued pastel colours and simple, yet comfortable, furniture. She left the windows open, giving the rooms a delightfully fresh and cool ambience.

Freddi was fond of music of many different types, as was Meng Jarrah, and had one of her favourite pieces playing when her friend returned. She could see her as she walked up the few steps to the door, which immediately opened for her. To Freddi's eyes, Meng Jarrah was beautiful, which indeed she was, and seemed even more so this evening. As the two women embraced, with renewed pleasure at their growing love for each other, Shela immediately wound herself around their legs, trilling her approval. She was soon given a cuddle, then sensing their happiness needed no enhancement, leapt onto the nearest armchair to sleep while they ate the meal so lovingly prepared.

Meng Jarrah tasted each of the dishes in turn. 'Mmm... I think I like the grilled fish with cashew sauce the best, but they're all wonderful!' She helped herself to another serving of the seasoned basmati rice and also a few more spoonfuls of mango salad. 'I hope you know how glad I am to be here,' she added, then laughed, 'and how much I enjoy your cooking!'

'Yes, I think I do, and it's great to hear you say so...but wait until you see what I've made for later!' Freddi smiled, heaping her own plate as she said, 'I gather from your generally serene expression that your work went well today?'

Shela woke and came over to nudge her knee, asking to be patted, then curled up to sleep again, satisfied everything was still as it should be.

'Yes, it did,' replied Meng Jarrah, grinning broadly. 'Once allowances are made for climate change, former pollution levels, and the normal forest lifecycle fluctuations, our soil sample is highly similar to the current soils from the innermost parts of Lamington. It was just pure luck the specimen was originally taken from the same general region, otherwise it might not have been as useful. So, what this basically means is that we can be confident the central area's in as good condition as we thought it was, and that we can use its soils to repopulate the perimeter. A small number of micro-organisms are missing, but only three appear to be essential. I'll be working on modelling what their addition would do over time, and if they appear beneficial, we'll start reproducing sufficient quantities to bring back to Australia.'

'How long do you expect it to take?' asked Freddi, in an uncertain tone.

'Oh, I would think about three or four weeks, but don't worry, I don't intend to go back to Lamington and not visit you again for ages. I couldn't bear that... Don't you know by now how much I care for you?'

Freddi reached across the table and took Meng Jarrah's lean brown hand in her own, caressing it tenderly. 'Thank you. I couldn't bear it either, particularly since we can't use the comlink for anything important. Letters are all very nice, because they're a novelty, but it's not the same as seeing your face and hearing your voice.'

Meng Jarrah raised Freddi's hand to her lips, kissing the fingertips. 'One of these days the work there will finish and I'll be able to return for longer. But what about you? Do you intend to extend your placement here, or return to Jamaica?'

'Well, it depends upon this case...and whether we'll still be talking to each other in six months time.' Freddi smiled to make sure her words could not be misunderstood. She was hopeful that not only would they be talking to each other, they would be thoroughly enjoying each other's company, no matter where in the world they ended up living.

Meng Jarrah returned the smile, kissed Freddi's hand one last time before releasing it, then said, 'In that case, we'll have to make sure we don't argue too much!'

Freddi laughed, and they continued eating in companionable silence, until she told Meng Jarrah about their one real piece of evidence now linking Wyvern Meridian to the series of murders and sabotage attempts. Freddi hadn't dared to commit such things to paper, for even the postal service wasn't immune to corruption if the stakes were high enough.

'Has Kakura left Myanmar yet?' asked Meng Jarrah, finishing her dessert and regretting she was too full to eat any more.

'Yes, he's in Malaysia. I suspect he bought a substantial shareholding in the local soil reclamation company in the hope their research would improve Wyvern's own techniques, which, as we already know, have generally been poor up to date. Also, I imagine that if they *are* connected to these crimes, as we now strongly suspect, they'd be extremely unhappy at the progress being made by the Federation through the cooperative venture with Gwenllian, Owain, and yourself. What are the chances they've heard how far it's progressed, do you think?'

'It's a matter of public record that Gwenllian and Owain joined forces with us, but nothing's been published yet, either about their work or what we've done at Lamington. It's far too early.'

'But if Wyvern Meridian somehow had access to Federation records, or even our earlier comlink calls, they'd almost certainly know what our current plans are. I think we need to assume they *do* have access, because I'm fairly sure they did in the past.'

'I gather you've ruled out Morag MacIain as having a role in their schemes, and that whoever is working with them is still out there?'

'Yes, I have. Rohan Maerz is still one of our main suspects, and we believe it's possible he could be assisting them.'

Meng Jarrah stared at Freddi in horror. This was something she hadn't been aware of. 'What! Do you really think he and Kakura could be in this together?'

Shela woke up, flattening her ears and growling softly. She knew her two Wights were no longer happy, and received strong images of a very large, powerful man, with enormous influence over their lives, as well as the lives of countless others. If she ever met this wight, she would protect them from him – with her life, if necessary!

Meng Jarrah was driven by a new urgency for her work to succeed and to return to Lamington. The news that Rohan Maerz might be involved made it clear her friends were at risk and she needed to warn them. Freddi needed her too, but was more than capable of taking care of herself. Also, whereas the Willsmere researchers already understood their situation and had precautions in place to protect them, Gwenllian, Owain and Martha were vulnerable.

She wondered what was happening in Papua and Serro do Cachimbo. Her Papuan laboratories had little to do with the current work as it was considered far too dangerous for them to be involved. Instead, once the investigation into the theft of her soil sample was concluded, if unsatisfactorily, they had continued with their usual research. Meanwhile, the Papuan salary, transport and library systems had returned to normal – or so she gathered from reading the global news reports. However, within the country it seemed there was still a lingering lack of confidence in their section of the lattice. As a result, security procedures were being even more closely examined than before.

'Just how security conscious does one have to be?' she asked herself. It seemed to be a never-ending spiral. Shaking her head, Meng Jarrah returned to their most recent simulations, poring over them until her researcher tapped her on the shoulder and suggested they have their midsun meal. Sighing, and stretching her arms to relieve the cramp in her neck and shoulders, Meng Jarrah stood up and followed him out into the warm sunshine.

Research Coordinator Zago was shocked. After a lifetime of one hundred and seven years, it was difficult to shock her, but nevertheless, she was. Since her visit to Serro do Cachimbo, it seemed wise to keep an eye on any applications made to the Federation for either the public release of new medications based on rainforest products, or research into rainforest species. She was not privy to Epsilon's scientific agenda, or their list of pharmaceutics due for commercial release, but was usually able to gauge fairly accurately what they were doing because they needed to apply for right of entry to protected areas, as well as the right to harvest. This meant her laboratories were required to evaluate their applications, which, in turn, made it relatively easy to foresee where the interests of this highly imaginative group of scientists might lie. As far as she could see, there were no ethical problems in doing so since Epsilon rarely attempted to compete with the Federation. Even so, occasionally it was tempting to follow up on what they were planning.

How, therefore, had Sirinya missed the similarity between the Epsilon application for access to Tumucumaque and the one made by Wyvern Meridian only fifteen months later? Both companies should not have been given the same harvesting rights unless Epsilon failed in its objectives, which to date, it hadn't, even though Epsilon's operations were struggling under the adverse publicity of the Claviceps affair. Therefore, Zago needed to consider the possibility that Sirinya had in fact not missed the similarity and that one of the entries was false, perhaps having been deliberately inserted into their database during the first security breach last year.

She accessed the Federation pharmaceutics knowledge base and began an extensive search. One and a half hours later, she had a list of the likely ingredients contained in the plants both companies were interested in and which appeared to warrant medical investigation. Next, Zago cross-referenced this list with existing medications and found an antifungal preparation with the greatest similarity. The drug was currently produced by the Federation and distributed at low cost when recommended by a medical practitioner. However, if a far more powerful variant with less potential side effects was produced for a reasonable price, the financial gains could be massive.

Tired and apprehensive, she closed her eyes and covered her face with both hands, then sighed and stared out the window at the twilight outside. She urgently needed to speak with the Brazilian Attorney General. It was vital he be informed and that an inquiry was initiated immediately, yet Zago could not trust the lattice. There was no option other than to ask for an appointment and travel there in person – again – so she entered the relevant comlink code and waited. Several Secretaries later, an appointment had been made for two days time.

'What is this urgent matter you wished to see me about, Research Coordinator Zago?' said the Attorney General, after they had shaken hands. He politely offered her an armchair and urged her to have some of the aromatic coffee being prepared. Zago accepted a cup and sat down, leaning on her staff as she did.

She had handwritten a detailed account of her findings and silently passed it across the table to him. The Attorney General read the summary on the first page and looked up, raising an eyebrow. Zago returned his gaze without comment, so he continued to read in silence for some time before sitting back and tidying the pages into a neat bundle.

Straightening the edges of the paper as he spoke, as if glad at least *something* could be made tidy, he said, 'If I understand correctly, you wish me to look into this further in order to find out which of these two companies does in fact have right of harvest and research into the plants listed, and what, if any, progress has been made?'

'Yes, I do,' replied Zago. 'There is nothing in the least wrong with either of them competing with the Federation to market this or any other type of medicine. However, within the context of the earlier effort to discredit Epsilon, it is reasonable to suggest that this situation could be yet another attempt, by either someone unknown or this second company, Wyvern Meridian. To begin with, I would like to know how far both companies have progressed as this may throw some light on the matter.'

The Attorney General reached for his comlink, but before he could place the call, Zago raised a warning hand, saying, 'I don't think you should use the lattice for this. We have avoided it for some time now for anything significant associated with the various sabotage attempts on government research centres and private forest industries. We believe all these crimes are interconnected and that our calls are being monitored.'

He put down the comlink and stared at her. 'Oh! Yes, I see. It's a hard habit to break. This will certainly test our resourcefulness.' The Attorney General shook his head in frustration. 'Are you able to remain here in Brazil until this investigation has produced results, assuming we *can* produce results?'

'I think it would be advisable,' agreed Zago, 'otherwise it will be hard to collaborate. I also think we should avoid calling on the FSIU, given their possible involvement.'

'I hadn't considered the possibility that they were involved!' The Attorney General's expression showed his dismay. 'Why do you say that?'

'It is not yet public knowledge, but one of their most senior investigators, who was assigned to help us look into the earlier sabotage attempts, is about to be placed on trial. She has been charged with having extensively interfered with the Papuan lattice. However, it is possible she is innocent and that someone else within the FSIU contrived to implicate her. We came to this conclusion some time ago, although I am sure you will understand why we have chosen not to publicise our views. The FSIU Coordinator, Rohan Maerz, has taken her place and is currently in Australia. The problem is, one must suspect that if anyone else *is* involved in this incident, it could be him...or otherwise, another FSIU member with high-level access to the lattice and sufficient expertise to make the required changes to both its software and its information stores.'

The Attorney General's eyes opened even wider as he fiddled nervously with the handle of his coffee cup. 'What you have said,' he concluded unhappily, 'means we should avoid using their databases, some of which we'd normally access in a case like this. Really, this is all becoming remarkably difficult. I can think of only one way to approach the problem and that's through our Parliamentary resources, which have the highest levels of security. I'll make a confidential approach to my colleagues...and assume *they* can be trusted!'

'Yes. It seems a great deal of trouble to go to in order to look into a case which might normally be assumed to have resulted from an innocent error, but given the circumstances, I simply cannot rule out an association with past events. Our problem, though, will be how to pass on whatever information you do obtain to the peacekeepers in Australia and elsewhere. Perhaps it had better rest with me to do that.' Zago was quite willing to accept the risk.

The Attorney General held her in the highest esteem, which now rose even higher. She was a formidable woman. They stood up, and before parting, solemnly shook hands.

*

Erminio read his screen again, just to make sure he'd understood. The report was so unexpected and improbable that his mind felt as if it had ceased to function.

Tumucumaque was a priority reference area, having one of the most diverse ecosystems in Brazil, with many species still unidentified and even more insufficiently studied. Epsilon had progressed steadily with their harvesting program and were now beginning to feel optimistic that their efforts would produce a new, cheaper, and more effective antifungal medication. Once its merit had been established and production methods were fully trialled, they intended to offer it to the Federation on a royalty basis. Erminio himself had taken the scientific notes for almost two years and transcribed them into this report. He last accessed the file only a few weeks ago, and yet now, it was completely different!

The report stated that the clinical results indicated the new medication was insufficiently free of serious side effects to warrant further development. The cost of production had also been altered to show it was not as commercially viable as existing medications, and was therefore unlikely to appeal to the Federation, even if the undesirable side effects could be overcome. Unbelievably, even the chemical composition of their product had been subtly changed, taking on an altogether different mode of action.

His heart rate had increased noticeably and his palms were sweaty as he accessed the file's security details. He hadn't manually recorded the exact time and date of his last entries, but they seemed about right. Frantically searching for his back-up copies, Erminio found his hands were trembling. When the young man finally located the copies, they were the same as the current version. Impossible!

He sank back into his chair and tried to breathe slowly and deeply, eventually managing to think clearly enough to realise that the report could be re-created. The original data still existed. It would just take time. Meanwhile, Erminio asked his computer for a high-priority broadcast to be sent to all the researchers involved, as well as to the company directors. The report was attached, with the changed sections highlighted. As responses to the broadcast came in, he set up a virtual group meeting.

'Have you looked at any of the original notes or pricing data yet?' asked one of the researchers.

'No,' replied Erminio, 'I wanted to speak with everyone first in case this becomes more serious than it already appears to be. So, while we're all present, I'd like to suggest that you each, in turn, access your own data and notes to check the key features. Do you agree?'

Everyone nodded. Even though it was time-consuming, it seemed a sensible way of ensuring they were all witness to one another's reactions. Over the next three hours, each scientist found key changes had been made to both their data and their conclusions. Even worse, in all cases back-up files reflected the changes. There were in fact no original records left. The situation was a disaster.

'We *know* we were successful, but we can't prove it!' cried one of the botanists, in tears, while another held his head in his hands, also close to weeping.

The directors were prepared to do whatever was necessary to salvage the situation. 'We have no choice but to contact the Federation and tell them what has happened. They would have no reason to disbelieve us, particularly when they take into account the problems we experienced due to the Claviceps incident. Someone is trying to kill off our company! There's simply no other explanation, so we *must* keep going! Each of you knows what you did to obtain your results and can do it again, isn't that true?'

Everyone looked miserable, but after a certain amount of muttering and head shaking, they all agreed. 'Who do we contact?' asked one of the pharmacologists.

'We have the choice of dealing with Research Coordinator Zago or taking the case to the Attorney General,' replied Erminio, blushing slightly as he pre-empted a reply from the directors.

'That's true... Given a crime has been committed, it might be more convincing if we approached the Attorney General. I suggest we do it immediately. Do you all agree?'

The directors waited until the scientists reluctantly gave their approval, although Erminio tended to favour contacting Zago. However, he pointed out that if they failed to obtain a useful response from the Attorney General, they could still do so.

'I think we should ask for a time when we can all be there,' suggested one of the biochemists. 'That would emphasise our unity, while showing this isn't some plot to fool him into allowing further access to Tumucumaque because of a failed first attempt.'

Once again, everyone agreed, then waited nervously while Erminio made the call. Before long, a secretary's face shared the screen, uncomfortable at suddenly finding himself in the middle of a conference of such proportions. 'Yes?' he asked, blinking. 'How may I help you?'

'We urgently need to meet with the Attorney General. Our most important research project has been compromised and we want to show him what has happened and ask for help,' replied the current spokesperson.

'Before I can allocate a level of priority to this request, I need a little more information, please,' answered the secretary.

'Certainly. Around two and a half years ago we applied for permission to harvest a specific variety of plants from Tumucumaque with a view to developing a new medication. We were progressing well, to the point where we were soon to offer the Federation joint commercial rights, but have just discovered that all – and I do mean *all* – our research data and reports have been altered. The findings now in our database contradict our real findings. According to the changed reports, our new product is a failure...which is most definitely *not* the case! It was a complete success!' The spokesperson became more and more agitated as she spoke. The enormity of the situation was incomprehensible.

The secretary considered her words for a few moments. 'How many of you wish to be at the meeting with the Attorney General?' he said at last.

'All of us!' stated the spokesperson flatly. 'We want to make sure he understands the full extent of our total commitment to this project, as well as the effort we are prepared to make in reproducing our results. Unfortunately, we *must* have access to Tumucumaque again for more plant samples. We simply *don't* have enough left for another research effort.'

'Ah...yes...I understand... This is an extraordinary request, but there are new circumstances which make it important that you do indeed speak with him as soon as possible. I do not wish to discuss the details now, but may I suggest 14:00 tomorrow as a suitable time?'

They all stared at the secretary, amazed a meeting had been arranged this quickly, although unsettled by there being "new circumstances" involved.

Once the appointment had been accepted, the secretary left the meeting and one by one, so did Epsilon's members, each still deeply troubled. Alone again, Erminio shook his head, still unable to comprehend how their database and back-up systems could have been accessed by an outsider without his knowledge.

PART III

CHAPTER TWENTY

The boardroom of Wyvern Meridian was decorated in pre-twentieth-century splendour, with an ornate ceiling, a massive chandelier suspended from its centre, and dado panelling of darkest mahogany. A black marble fireplace of gigantic proportions dominated one wall and on this cold, wet day, filled the room with warmth and flickering firelight from the wood burning within. The carpets were of dark green silk, rare and precious, and of an antique design not made in Middle Eastern countries for centuries. The floor itself was an intricate parquetry of dozens of different hardwood timbers, while in each of the corners of the room sat a bronze wyvern cradling a globe of the Earth in its claws. The wyverns gazed malevolently at the board members seated around the oval table.

The large, central table, made from Australian blackwood, was a rarity from the nineteenth century, inlaid with delicate traceries of silky oak depicting the floral emblems of each of the original States. Each matching wooden chair was a masterpiece of comfort, with maroon leather upholstery and delicately crafted, openwork backs. A sideboard of eighteenth-century oak completed the décor. Decanters containing a variety of fine malt whiskies stood ready on its ample surface, complemented by glasses of the most exquisite Swedish design.

The comfort of the room was not reflected in the expressions on the faces of the board members. Not a single word had been spoken for more than ten minutes, nor did they dare meet Kenjiro Kakura's dark eyes.

He looked at each of them in turn, then finally spoke: 'I will ask you once again. Why was Epsilon's original application for entry into Tumucumaque left in Serro do Cachimbo's database?'

The silence continued. None of the board members so much as glanced at each other, until one of them eventually found enough courage to answer.

'You *must* believe me, it was taken out as you ordered. All trace of their application was removed at the same time as the changes to the research database were made. There should not have been *any* proof they were conducting legal or productive research.' The board member slowly wiped the palms of his hands on a pristine white kerchief.

'You do understand this mistake has cost us one of the most lucrative pharmaceutical products of the past decade? Do you also realise this mistake may cause the FSIU to take even more notice of us?' Kenjiro Kakura's gaze took in all the board members and every one of them flinched; mistakes were not tolerated by Wyvern Meridian.

Kakura stood and walked over to the sideboard, where he helped himself to a whisky, then offered the decanter to the board members, placing a glass before each of them in turn. They passed the decanter around the table and filled their glasses.

'Skål,' Kakura toasted them, as he raised his own glass to his lips.

Slowly and unwillingly, the board members drank.

The apartment obtained for Rohan Maerz during his stay in Melbourne was situated in Bourke Street, on the sixteenth floor. As such, it commanded a fine view over the city and he was able to admire the Rialto while contemplating the next step in the complex web of events that contributed to making his life worthwhile. Boredom was now a thing of the past.

The evenings had become colder and darkness now fell earlier, so he closed the rich brocade curtains to keep in the warmth. The oak dining table was without a tablecloth this evening, as he preferred not to hide the intricate inlaid woodwork from his guests. Instead, richly embroidered placemats of deep red protected its surface. A large blue and white antique Chinese vase adorned the centre, containing an elaborate bouquet of deep yellow roses, the last of the season. White candles in elegant Florentine candlesticks were placed at each end.

Rohan stood back from the window, checked the table one last time, and then, satisfied with the effect, glanced at the clock for what must have been the fifth time this evening. Aurora watched him from her place in front of the glowing electric heater he had purchased, at great expense, especially for her. She yawned, stretched contentedly and rolled over, the better to warm her creamy stomach. Rohan could almost feel himself purr as he watched her for a few moments, before hastily going back into the kitchen to check the progress of the dinner he had spent all day preparing and most of the previous day shopping for. He was stirring the delicately flavoured orange sauce and adding a final touch of freshly ground cardamom to it when the security system announced the arrival of his guests. After carefully turning down the heat and then checking the oven, he answered the call, allowing Karla, Mik, Tamara and their three cats to enter.

*

Earlier, when they first received the dinner invitation, Mik immediately contacted Chiu Liow Jones, wanting to know whether they should accept. All the surprised peacekeeper could do was caution them not to be inveigled into discussing any aspect of their work, or the case, and once the evening was over, for them to let him know how it went.

Naturally, the invitation was also discussed with Søren, together with the fact that Rohan now had a feline companion. Upon hearing this, Søren became uncharacteristically quiet and brooded for some time, before concluding that perhaps cats *could*, after all, bond with unsavoury characters, as he put it, but which he struggled to comprehend. So, either the FSIU Coordinator was *not* involved in any of the recent crimes, despite the overwhelming indications to the contrary, or Maerz *was* involved, but for reasons this cat, Aurora, could understand, perhaps even accept and forgive?

'There *is* another possibility,' said Karla. 'Rohan's personality may be so complex that the cats find him intriguing. Whatever reason he might have for involving himself in these crimes, perhaps it's unusual enough for it not to prevent them from being able to bond with him?'

'Well, I suspect your Red Matilda, who finds him so fascinating, will tell us more after you consume what will almost certainly be a very fine dinner, and which *I* will not have the privilege to partake of.' Søren sniffed theatrically as he wiped away an invisible tear.

They all chose to ignore Søren's complaint. Instead, with a wry smile, Mik glanced in his direction and said, 'I think it'll be Fliedermus who'll tell us the most, given she was there when I was assaulted, and afterwards, present for so many of the interviews. I'm hoping she can remember it all, so if there's anything in Rohan's mind that's related, she'll most likely react. I wish Welcome was here, though. His opinion would've been useful.'

'No doubt Chiu Liow wishes he was here too,' said Tamara, 'but since he isn't, I guess the only thing to do is write and tell him what's happened then see what he says. It shouldn't take long to hear back from him. By the way, when does Morag's trial begin?'

'In two weeks, I gather,' answered Karla. 'The third of June. Afterwards, Welcome may or may not come back; it depends upon the verdict.'

After handing him their heavy coats, Rohan's guests now gazed in awe at his apartment. He had placed a ceramic container for umbrellas in the entrance hall and took the dripping items from them before the water could damage the floor. The rain had been heavy for at least half an hour.

'Welcome, welcome,' he said, eagerly shaking their hands. 'Aurora is looking forward to meeting you, and dinner is ready and waiting. Come in, and find a place at the table, if you like. I've put something together for the cats too, if they want to come into the kitchen.'

Fliedermus, Red Matilda and Possum found their own way, sniffing the air cautiously and followed by a curious, but friendly, Aurora. Four bowls were placed on the floor instead of the usual one, and each was full of cheese pasta. Possum sniffed suspiciously, but tasted a small sample and decided it was acceptable. Fliedermus dabbed at it with a paw, then threw a piece into the air and chased it around the legs of the nearest chair.

Mik, who had followed them into the kitchen, with the others close behind, turned to Rohan, shrugging his shoulders in embarrassment. He picked up the pasta and put it into the recycling chute, then waggled an admonitory finger at Fliedermus, who merely sat prettily, waving her tail at him. Aurora touched noses and licked her forehead, before turning to her own bowl and eating heartily. More interested in the company than the food, Fliedermus flopped onto her side, watching. Red Matilda, on the other hand, inspected each bowl in turn, butting in on Aurora and Possum and pushing them away, until she finally crouched down by one of the other bowls and attacked the food with relish – Mik received a distinct image of cheese pasta being served at home, thank you very much!

Karla turned to Rohan, smiling warmly. Despite her deep suspicions, she intuitively liked him, and sniffed the aromas in the kitchen appreciatively, thinking it a great pity Søren hadn't been invited, although she had no trouble guessing the reason. Pleased, Rohan returned her smile, then left the cats to their meal and ushered his guests into the dining room.

'Your home is absolutely lovely,' said Tamara, noticing the carpet in particular. 'Is this woollen?'

'Yes, from Australian alpaca,' he replied, delighted by her honest appreciation. 'All the colours are natural. It's a wonderful pattern, isn't it?'

Meanwhile, Mik admired the roses, leaning over to find out if they had any scent, which they did. 'You're lucky to find these so late in the season,' he remarked, and was surprised by how at ease he felt.

'I wonder if it's his cat?' he thought. Reminding himself to be cautious in his conversation, he put an arm around Tamara's waist and gave her a quick kiss on the cheek. Raising an eyebrow, Tamara glanced meaningfully at him. 'The cats are much happier tonight than they usually are, don't you think?' he said, hoping she would understand.

Tamara hesitated for only a moment. 'Yes, they are,' she replied, with a slight smile. 'They're most likely enjoying Aurora's company. They don't often get the chance to meet another cat.'

As she sat down at the table, Karla noticed her friends' odd expressions. Fortunately, Rohan had by now returned to the kitchen to finalise his preparations, prior to serving what promised to be a truly magnificent meal. She tilted her head to one side and silently mouthed, 'His cat?' They quickly nodded, before taking a seat opposite. Karla grimaced and shook her head, now on guard.

Soon afterwards, Rohan came in with the first course, which consisted of a cauliflower soufflé, Danish cucumber salad, carrots in an orange sauce, and small caramelised potatoes, all accompanied by a fine sauvignon blanc.

He had consulted each of them on their taste, and found, to his satisfaction, that they shared a common interest in early chamber music. Listening to the music, and to his young guests as they exchanged light-hearted conversation, he was relieved that the evening seemed to be progressing well. For one of the few times in his adult life, Rohan was content to relax and listen, rather than being the centre of attention and constantly in control of the situation.

When Aurora rubbed herself against his legs, he realised it was time to present the next course. He stood up to take away the used dishes and Mik immediately jumped up to assist.

'Can I help with anything else?' he offered, with a grin.

'No, no, you go back in and enjoy the rest of the wine. I'll bring in another bottle with the next course.' Rohan gave a brief stir to the sauce on the stove, then lifted the lid on one of the other pots and gave the contents a quick taste. Everything seemed perfect. Returning to the dining room, he deftly placed the next set of plates and cutlery on the table, together with fresh wine glasses and a bottle of cabernet merlot. 'This is from the Yarra Valley. It's nicely aged and has an excellent colour,' he said, smiling as he poured a little into each glass for them to first taste.

'I may as well enjoy it,' thought Mik, as he read the wine label. The man was clearly going to a great deal of expense to give them a meal!

The second course consisted of seasoned wild rice, handmade potato gnocchi with finely chopped sautéed mushrooms in a pure cream sauce, a mango and tow salad, and snow peas with a light honey glaze. Very little was said for some time while they ate the food and savoured the wine in all its subtle complexity. Rohan was pleased when they all took extra helpings.

'I myself have an overwhelming fondness for food,' he said, after they finished eating, 'so I do hope you all have good appetites. Perhaps we should wait before we have the third course?'

Karla carefully wiped her mouth with the soft napkin provided and settled back in her chair. 'To be honest, I haven't eaten this much in a while, although Søren sometimes insists on feeding us more than we can possibly want. He'd be annoyed to know this exceeds even his standards.'

Rohan smiled. 'Søren is fond of food, I gather?'

'Oh yes,' said Mik. 'He spends a significant proportion of each day thinking about what he'll eat next and who he'll share it with. His global solution for all emotional upsets is fine food and plenty of it.' He laughed at the memory of his friend's frequent, elaborate meals.

'I'm astounded,' remarked Rohan, quite genuinely. 'He's tiny! How can he be so small and eat so much?'

Tamara looked embarrassed, as did the others. It was clear Rohan might have issues in some circles due to his girth and, as it appeared, his massive appetite. Søren was fortunate in not having the same problem, yet what could be said in reply? People like Rohan were a small minority, who no doubt suffered as a consequence.

Mik broke the silence by replying, in his usual good-humoured way, 'Well, keep in mind that all small creatures eat a lot and eat often because they lose heat at such a high rate. Søren is a zoologist, so has to behave like the animals he studies... Marsupial mice, for example. He frequently jumps and skitters around, just like them.' He waved his hands to demonstrate, quirked his eyebrows at Rohan, and grinned.

Rohan laughed. He couldn't help himself, and the others joined in. 'Perhaps I should have invited him after all, even if it did mean a peacekeeper at the table.'

'Maybe another time,' said Mik, hoping there would be another time if this meal was typical of his host's hospitality. He was also intensely curious to know the man better and wondered if Søren, like him, could overcome his suspicions long enough to actually enjoy such an occasion.

Rohan appeared gratified. 'Yes, another time would be most enjoyable. Perhaps when he no longer requires an escort. One can indeed hope this will soon be the case.' No one could disagree.

'I'll miss Red Matilda,' said Karla, glancing at the cats. 'It's wonderful having her with me. When the day comes that I won't need her and have to return her to you, Mik, I might just apply for a cat myself. How did you find the application process, Rohan?'

All four cats were snuggled together in a heap of multicoloured fur in front of the radiant heater. Aurora rested her chin comfortably on Possum's stomach, while Red Matilda lay partially on her back, with her hind legs pressed against Fliedermus' flank. Aurora raised her head to look directly at Karla, who gazed back at her, struck by the image the cat projected.

'Why, Rohan,' she exclaimed, 'Aurora selected you!'

Rohan's mouth opened in surprise. 'Isn't that usual?' he asked. 'How did you know?'

'She just told me!'

Rohan turned to his companion, a bewildered expression on his face. 'I was under the impression she would only talk to me now. Apparently not!'

The cat calmly regarded him for a few moments, then stretched and padded over to place her head on his knee, her eyes meeting his. Rohan fondled her silky, golden ears. 'You're my darling, aren't you? She thinks I'm very special,' he crooned, without looking up. Aurora rubbed her head into his hand then rolled onto her back, purring while he stroked her stomach.

His guests were enthralled by his behaviour. He was obviously as much in love with his cat as they were with theirs. Rohan had passed the 'cat test' in quadruplicate!

Eventually, after giving Aurora one last pat, their host announced it was time to serve the third course. 'I thought we should keep this simple,' he said. 'Would fresh oysters with Australian lime, followed by lightly grilled marinaded prawns with shredded lettuce, be to your taste?'

They all nodded, amused he had chosen to have seafood now, rather than at the start of the meal, as most people did. Then again, why not?

A fresh bottle of wine was opened, this time, a mature chardonnay from the Mornington Peninsula. The warmth and elegance of the room, as well as the fine food, contrasted cosily with the sound of the growing storm outside. Forgetting Chiu Liow's warning, they spoke of their passion for the work they did and of the reasons for having entered their chosen profession. Rohan listened, occasionally agreeing with their ideas and elaborating a little with his own. Mostly, he just allowed them the pleasure of sharing their thoughts with him and with each other. The evening soon passed, and as the old clock in its wooden case chimed midnight, Rohan announced the final course.

'I have an assortment of the most delicious Greek pastries and cream cakes I've seen in years, as well as Belgian truffles and a fine botrytis riesling from the Yarra Valley; a region, it appears, that makes the most excellent wines.'

Rohan headed back to the kitchen, once again accepting help with the empty dishes. 'Thank you so much, Mik. If you just put everything over there, I'll rinse them. They can be washed later. I do hope you like Greek pastries? Perhaps they're not much of a novelty for you?'

'Oh, I love them, but there aren't any pastry shops near where I live, so I don't actually have them very often. This'll be a treat.'

Rohan beamed as he presented Mik with a large tray to carry into the dining room, following closely behind with the chocolates and the bottle of sweet wine. He then placed yet another set of glasses on the table, together with dessert plates, clean serviettes and silver cake forks. He had the air of a maitre d'hôtel, thought Karla, as she selected a cake made from a chocolate shell containing mousse, fresh cream and sugar-glazed fresh strawberries. It was absolutely delicious! The others were absorbed in their selections too. For several minutes, no one said anything as they savoured the delicacies.

After a while, Rohan elected to have a second pastry, but before choosing a piece, offered the tray to his guests. Having so far eaten only a simple, yet delectable, shortbread, Mik was able to manage one more, this time choosing a confection of finely chopped walnuts and filo pastry, steeped in honey and coated in chocolate. Karla, on the other hand, laughed and waved her hand to decline. 'As much as I'd like to, I can't fit another thing into my stomach this evening. Everything has been wonderful... Though I might just get a glass of cold water, if you don't mind?' Rohan immediately pressed her shoulder and insisted he get it for her, soon returning with ice-cold filtered water from the unit he'd had specially installed. She drank appreciatively.

Meanwhile, Tamara ate a third truffle and sipped her wine, enjoying every mouthful of the excellent vintage. However, feeling slightly tipsy, she was thankful the glass was small, and even though the dinner was superb and the apartment somehow reassuring in its opulence, she nevertheless felt uneasy. How could it be forgotten that their host was most likely either responsible for, or at the very least, somehow connected with, the attack which nearly cost both her life and Possum's? Twisting one of her curls around a finger as she drank another mouthful of wine, she made an effort to move away from the darkness of the memory and to relax. After all, they were here to get to know Rohan Maerz better and to report back to Chiu Liow Jones. She looked at Possum and silently asked her a question, but the cat ignored her, which seemed strange. Did Aurora's presence limit what their own cats were prepared to do, or could do? They would need to wait until they were home to find out.

Fliedermus' whiskers twitched as she attempted to probe the wight's mind without his grimalkin noticing. The cats had rapidly established a companionable feline relationship, doing nothing all evening to alarm Aurora in any way. She was now asleep, snoring and lying on her back, her head resting on Red Matilda's ample tail. Red Matilda and Possum were also sound asleep, basking in the unaccustomed heat of the radiator. Good... This meant they would not accidentally wake Aurora. Fliedermus tickled the surface layers of Rohan's thoughts, finding only simple contentment – enjoyment of the good food, the music, and pleasant company – as well as...gratitude? She probed deeper, very careful not to startle him. Ah... He was grateful that her Wights seemed to like both his company and the meal he had given them. Fliedermus was familiar with normal gratitude of this type; Søren often projected it when he visited and brought food for them all to share. Mik felt something similar when Tamara said she loved him, only more so, but this wight's feelings weren't quite like theirs: they held a strong element of surprise and of deep sadness.

She briefly touched Aurora's mind. Finding the grimalkin still asleep, Fliedermus delved deeper into Rohan's. What the cat saw was beyond her comprehension. There was an image of a dead wight in a mossy garden by a small pool of water. A piece of paper lay near him. The death was associated with an intense feeling of satisfaction, as well as achievement. She withdrew in fright. Aurora woke up and hissed, staring at her, pupils huge and black. Red Matilda and Possum woke up as well, startled, springing to their feet, tails swishing from side to side, ears back, ready to either attack or defend.

The noise brought the others to their feet. They rushed over to the cats and when Rohan put out a hand to touch Aurora, Mik stopped him. 'Don't... Not yet... Wait a moment. She might scratch if she's frightened.'

Rohan withdrew his hand and straightened up. Confused, he stared at Mik in surprise. He sensed his cat had been deeply disturbed and his strongest impulse was to comfort her.

While Mik and Tamara crouched down by Possum and Fliedermus, Karla slowly approached Red Matilda, knelt, and attempted see what was in her mind. All four cats were still agitated, sitting straight and still, ears pricked, paws and tails tucked in, watching each other with half-closed eyes. None of them allowed the humans to see their thoughts. Time went by without anyone saying a word. The cats still did not move, although Red Matilda and Possum began to focus on soothing Aurora and Fliedermus' distress. Aurora eventually folded herself into a more relaxed position, but continued to gaze at Fliedermus, who slowly began to clean herself. The other two followed Aurora's lead and lay down, content now to simply watch.

Despite his deep interest in them, Rohan had made an effort during the evening not to dwell too much on Mik's cats. Now seemed the right moment to gain a better understanding of these strange creatures. 'Mik,' he said softly, 'what do you think occurred just now? Is it simply a minor upset that can happen when cats are together?'

'Oh yes, they sometimes dream and become frightened, just like us,' Mik replied, looking at Rohan and smiling. 'I suspect Fliedermus half-awoke and, without meaning to, sent the last of her dream to the others.' However, Mik knew full well there was no evidence whatsoever that cats projected dreams. Instead, he had a very good idea of what actually happened. Making an effort to appear normal and cheerful, he added, 'I suggest we give them all a cuddle, then finish our dessert.'

Stroking his chin, Rohan nodded, then caressed Aurora's golden head until she purred softly and nestled back down, nevertheless with eyes narrowed, studying the other cats without blinking.

The remainder of the evening passed pleasantly in a general exchange about cats, their individual personalities, their amusing antics, and how Mik acquired his three: 'While I was at university, I spent some time working at the Breeding Centre during my holidays. I'd always wanted to know more about cats and thought it'd be fun to look after the kittens. At first it never occurred to me to have one of my own, then one day, when I saw a funny little grey cat who was often alone, I began to give her a bit more attention than the others. After a while, she let me pick her up, and that was that.'

'I gather the Breeding Centre staff felt you were responsible enough to have her?' asked Rohan, with a touch of envy.

Mik laughed. 'Oh yes, otherwise they wouldn't have let me work there. The problem was, I *kept* working there, and just couldn't resist applying for another one who took my fancy. That was Fliedermus. She started off as the skinniest little thing, with a curled tail and long, silky fur. She loved climbing into ridiculous places and had that peculiar ability to use her tail to hold on to things. A genetic oddity, I suppose. I hoped she and Possum might be good company for each other, and happily for us, the Breeding Centre agreed.'

'So how did you become fortunate enough to be given Red Matilda as well?'

'Ah, that's a different story. She was returned after her companion met with an unfortunate accident and died. The poor thing was so unhappy and lonely the Centre thought it'd be best if they gave her to someone who already had another cat. That way, if anything else happened, she'd at least be able to remain with her friend. Not that anything was about to happen to *me*, but it was better to be safe. Anyway, it's probably why she's sometimes a bit aggressive. Compensating...' He turned to look at the cats, as did the others. 'I'm incredibly lucky to have them.'

As the old clock struck two, Rohan rose and quickly made coffee, providing a fine cognac to finish the repast. 'I don't know that I've spent a more delightful evening in years,' he assured them, when they finally made ready to leave. 'Thank you all so much for coming and for bringing your cats with you. I hope you'll come again another time. May I even be so bold as to suggest I visit you and bring Aurora?'

They each shook his hand, telling him warmly he was welcome to visit them any time at home and that they'd be more than happy to receive any further invitations. Afterwards, they made their way out of the building and into the cold silent street, then walked quickly to the nearest callstation. The cats padded alongside them on their leashes, unusually subdued. Since it was late, there were no other passengers on the railcar when it arrived. Fliedermus sat next to Tamara, pressing against her, but the cat's mind was still closed, as were those of the others.

'What's wrong with them, Mik?' Tamara drew his arm closer. 'I've never known them to shut off like this.'

'They might tell us once we're home. Karla, do you want to come back and stay the night?'

'Yes, I think so. Despite being such a wonderful dinner, I feel strange... Perhaps it's because the cats aren't behaving normally.' She stroked Red Matilda, who pushed her head into Karla's hand, trilling softly. 'I've become used to an undercurrent of communication with Red and feel weird having it suddenly cut off. It happened as soon as we entered Rohan's apartment.'

'They all did it,' said Tamara. 'Other than when she spoke to you, there was nothing coming from Aurora the whole evening, either, though that could be normal, given she hasn't met us before, but I'm sure Possum and Fliedermus were positively blocking us out.' She hugged the brown tabby, peering into her face. 'When are you going to talk to us again, eh?' Fliedermus licked her nose, but didn't answer.

'What did you think of Rohan?' asked Mik.

'Would you believe, I really liked him?' replied Karla. 'I'm dying to talk to Chiu Liow about tonight. From everything he's said about Rohan, I was sure I wouldn't enjoy his company. I expected him to have a slightly sinister undertone, but I felt nothing, absolutely nothing of the sort. Perhaps Aurora is having a good influence on him.'

'I liked him too,' said Tamara, 'which is a surprise. We should invite him to visit, maybe after Morag receives her verdict. Whichever way that goes, I'm sure he'll want company, either to celebrate or commiserate. Of course, he may return to Luzern.'

'Or he'll stay here,' suggested Mik. 'His place is amazing and he seems happy. I'd say Melbourne agrees with him. I wonder how Chiu Liow would cope if he does, though. I'd lay odds he wouldn't!'

Karla laughed, but wryly. 'I think Chiu would apply for a transfer! He's still convinced Rohan's the one who supplied the expertise for the attacks on our labs, as well as for many of the other crimes. It *is* logical, and have you noticed how quiet it's been on that front since he came to Australia? I wouldn't be surprised if it's because he wants to get to know us, our cats, and our work better before planning something else!'

'Well, I hope not,' said Tamara. 'I'd hate to like someone so awful!'

As she spoke, they arrived at their destination and the front door opened for them as they approached the house. They were all happy to get inside as quickly as possible, into the warmth and light. After removing their coats and leaving them in the greenhouse, everyone followed the cats to the kitchen, staying with them until all three finished eating their bedtime snack. Meanwhile, Mik closed the door to make sure none of them left the room. 'Fliedermus,' he said in a low voice, 'I insist you talk to me. What happened tonight?'

Fliedermus sat at his feet, staring up into his face, then sighed and sent him the image she had seen in Rohan's mind.

'Sun help us, he's killed someone!' exclaimed Mik. 'That's what Fliedermus saw!' He began pacing back and forth, a hand to his forehead. 'We've got to tell Chiu Liow, but we can't call him! Rohan would know we'd found out something. I think he's been *sweet* all evening to try and make sure none of our cats could detect anything, not just because Aurora's having a good influence on him!'

Tamara began trembling, but made an effort to stop. She crouched down next to Possum, willing the cat to talk to her. When Possum sent her the same image Mik was shown, Karla picked up the details as well. She also saw Rohan's satisfaction at having caused the man's death.

'That's Mervyn Bradshaw,' she stated flatly. 'I recognise the scene from the case files. He's the one who murdered Marika. Chiu Liow never could find out how Rohan located him so quickly, or who killed him. Now he'll know, but won't have enough proof to do anything about it. I doubt whether the Judge would convict Rohan on Fliedermus' testimony alone.'

Frowning, she stared at the cat, who returned the stare, burbling an inquiry, but Karla merely shook her head in frustration, while Red Matilda hunched her shoulders and growled.

'It's a start!' Mik replied angrily. 'We'll have to call Chiu Liow tomorrow and make a time to see him. I think it's best if only I go, Karla. It'll be less conspicuous that way. I'll take Fliedermus with me.'

Outside, high overhead, the moon shone full and white. Winter was fast approaching and the cold air held the promise of early frost. Frogs croaked in the small wetland nearby, while a bird, disturbed from its rest by a possum, flew up, called out, then settled back down when the possum went on its way, seeking food, its paws damp from the dew on the grass. The night spiders were busy spinning their webs between the shrubs of the parkland. In the morning, these delicate creations would shine with myriad rainbows as the sunlight fell onto the dewdrops, gathered into intricate patterns – transient beauty, noticed only by the very few.

CHAPTER TWENTY-ONE

When he was at home, Kenjiro Kakura and his bondmate, Michiko Yamada, kept each other company almost every evening. They had a purpose-built room where they often spent their time together. It was below ground, well away from the main house and forbidden to their children, while the household servants were under strict instructions not to enter other than at specified times. This was their private domain and where Michiko did her best work.

The walls and ceiling of the room were painted pale cream, with heavy, darkest red, square-cut wooden beams forming panels of elegant dimensions. The floor was made from warm, gleaming, golden timber, and at one end of the room, a large sunken bath provided a restful place to finish their evening's work or entertainment. A brazier of coals was kept nearby for perfumed oils to be burnt if they desired.

An antique wooden cabinet of exquisite Japanese design was placed at a convenient location to Michiko's workbench and each of its many drawers contained various instruments and other items related to her artistry. As a special service to his bondmate, Kakura meticulously cleaned and put away the instruments after they had been used. Tonight, while she gave the final touch to an ornate silver gryphon that was part of the hilt for a ceremonial dagger, he carefully polished the finely etched bronze handle of a long, black, single-thonged whip. The metalwork, which depicted a snarling wolf, was also Michiko's design. Holding it up to the light, he sighed in satisfaction at its masterful workmanship, then placed it into its presentation box and closed the lid. Michiko put down her tools and turned to him.

She was slender, almost childlike, and tonight was dressed in colourful green, red and gold robes embroidered with silver thread. Her feet were bare and her long hair flowed luxuriously around smooth shoulders then far down her back in a glowing black cascade. Kakura stroked it lovingly, caressing her cheek when she gently pressed his hand to her face. Her long eyelashes were dark against her warm skin. He removed his own crimson and blue robe, to stand before her with bare, finely muscled chest and arms, then slowly drew Michiko's robe from her shoulders, just a little, kissing her tenderly as he did. Picking her up, he carried her to the bath, then set her down, and together they entered the steaming water.

While Michiko washed his body and thick black hair, Kakura revelled in a sense of profound ease, which deepened further as first his hands and then his feet were expertly massaged. He took her hands in his and kissed one small ear, then helped wash her heavy hair, which spread out into the water in dark, rippling waves. Time seemed to stop in this peaceful place, but eventually Michiko kissed him on the forehead and left the bath to make tea. He studied her every elegant movement while she heated water on the brazier and made sure that each detail of this special ceremony was correct. When the pale green liquid, in its dainty cups, was almost ready, Kakura rose from the water, dried himself, and once more put on his robe. The room was warm and quiet while they drank their tea. Not a single word had been spoken this whole evening. Words were unnecessary.

The third of June was warm and sunny, and the citizens of Luzern strode about their sumptuous city taking full advantage of this first summer day that finally brought an end to a long, cold spring. Chiu Liow had little time for either the sunshine or the cloudless blue sky. Not a man easily rattled, he couldn't help but feel nervous as he sat in the city's law courts waiting for Morag MacIain's trial to begin. The ponderous entrance of Rohan Maerz and his choice of seat next to him didn't help, despite the presence of his impressive cat.

Chiu Liow edged himself away from Maerz as unobtrusively as possible. He was sitting next to a killer! A murderer he could not arrest! The peacekeeper seethed, and had been seething ever since Mik gave him the account of their evening's dinner with the man...*and* his cat! How could the creature have bonded with an assassin! Did Maerz see himself as a justifiable executioner, and did his cat agree?

The question ran through his mind for what must have been the hundredth time. Perhaps the FSIU Coordinator's power had finally caused him to lose his mind. This seemed the only possible explanation. However, in other respects, Maerz behaved in a completely normal way; that is, if alternating sincere kindness and subtle forms of sinister intrigue could be called normal. The more he thought about it, the more Chiu Liow was convinced that this was all a game; a game Rohan Maerz wanted to play with Morag MacIain, his only worthy opponent. A pity people died in the process!

'Damn it, he's been talking to me and I didn't even notice,' he thought, forcing himself to listen.

'I'm overjoyed to see you here today, Jones. Have you seen Welcome yet? I was sure he'd be here already, but presumably he's still helping Morag deal with what must be an exceptionally trying time. I'd thought not to be here today... In fact, I virtually promised I wouldn't be, but find I really must be present. Moral support, you understand, nothing else, though I haven't been allowed to see her yet, have you?'

The peacekeeper made an effort to speak in an even tone. 'No,' he replied. 'As I am sure you know, other than the Court officials, Welcome is the only person allowed to be with her now. I can look forward to speaking with her once the trial is over and she has been proven innocent.'

'My dear man, of course she's innocent! We all know that, but the evidence may not agree. The Judge doesn't know her as we do and can only base its verdict upon the evidence. No other culprit has been found in all this time, despite our best efforts to find one. You must admit, the case does look very bad.'

It was all Chiu Liow could do not to throttle him, metaphorically speaking. Instead, he simply shook his head and glanced at Maerz's cat, only to find himself transfixed by her golden eyes. She was the most remarkably beautiful creature, even more so than any of Mik's cats. The courtroom and Rohan seemed to disappear as he became lost in the image Aurora was projecting: an image of Morag.

Morag stood up as she heard her name being called. It was time to enter the courtroom. Welcome squeezed her hand before taking his place at her side.

The last few weeks had gone by so tediously that she longed for the verdict more fervently than ever and dreaded to think what life would be like if the trial went against her. Welcome had tried his best to take her mind away from such a negative possibility, but in the end Morag could think of little else.

With the aid of all the official case notes already accumulated before her arrest, together with the report relating to the death of the Papuan charcoal worker, the results of the Brazilian inquiry into the Epsilon-Claviceps affair, as well as the conclusion that lattice security had been broken, Welcome had presented the Judge with a complex defence based on three premises. Firstly, that Morag had neither motive nor the psychological traits necessary to commit the crimes with which she was charged or of having masterminded the attack on Epsilon prior to being placed under arrest – although it was conceded she possessed both the expertise and the required security clearance. Secondly, if all the incidents in Papua were related, and existed within the wider context of

Morag's earlier investigations, the logical conclusion was that the culprit could well be the private company that stood to benefit: Wyvern Meridian. Finally, there was also the possibility that an as yet unknown other person or organisation was at large and were capable of high-level security breaches.

Both Morag and Welcome had fully expected the prosecution to launch an attack on their defence and to call in new evidence for entry into the Judge within the two-week period allowed. They became more and more nervous as time went by and nothing was entered. They had even predicted Rohan Maerz would call for an adjournment to allow direct questioning of the board of management of Wyvern Meridian, as would normally have occurred when a second party was accused. Although an adjournment would have prolonged the suspense, they were sure a more detailed examination of the affairs of Wyvern Meridian would have exonerated Morag and brought Kenjiro Kakura to trial. However, no such adjournment eventuated, and they were now at a complete loss as to how the Judge would view the case.

When Aurora abruptly released him, Chiu Liow felt dizzy at the suddenness of it. He realised Rohan was speaking to him again.

'Have you heard that one of the board members of Wyvern Meridian has died of heart failure? He was healthy one day and dead the next. Most peculiar, don't you think?'

Chiu Liow felt as if he would almost choke with anger at having to speak to Maerz, but managed to say, 'Most people *do* die of heart failure, one way or another, unless they become brain dead first. What did the autopsy find?'

'Well, nothing whatsoever to explain it. That's why it's odd. According to his family, he'd gone to a board meeting only the evening before, then suffered quite extreme pain in his chest before dying some hours later in the nearest medcentre. He was in too much pain to say anything at all, so despite the autopsy being unable to find the cause, there was obviously something wrong. We just haven't found out what. His body won't be released for cremation, of course.'

Aurora stared up at Rohan, the merest hint of distaste on her features. He noticed, and fondled her ears. 'I'm sorry, my love. It's a horrid topic of conversation. I'll stop thinking about it.'

The cat put her paw on his massive thigh, very, very slightly digging in with one claw. When Rohan winced and carefully removed it, Aurora twitched her tail, settled down at his feet and began cleaning her face. Chiu Liow was intrigued. He had never seen any of Mik's cats so much as hiss at their companions, let alone use their claws to produce pain, no matter how little. He wondered if Aurora was attempting to modify Rohan's behaviour. If so, it could only be for the better, he concluded, and mentally congratulated her. She rolled onto her side, purring gently.

His thoughts were interrupted by the sound of a door opening, followed by the entry of the Court officials and then the Accused, all in silent procession. The Prosecutor, Welcome as the Defence, Morag, the Witnesses, and all the consultants used in the preparation of the cases, stood before the assembled participants. Morag held her head high. Her beautiful auburn hair was arranged in a more formal style than usual, lending further dignity to her severe suit of dark grey. Welcome was also dressed in a grey suit, but had placed a small posy of bright yellow daisies above his breast pocket. He surveyed the Court, seeking Chiu Liow, and was startled to see Rohan Maerz. Morag had already noticed him, and Welcome was relieved to see that Rohan's presence appeared to have been expected, for she was smiling in his direction.

Chiu Liow glanced at Rohan to see his reaction. He appeared to be returning her smile. The peacekeeper made an effort to retain his composure and smiled as well, although his heart began to race when Morag inclined her head in acknowledgement. Forcing himself to remain calm, he continued to send her his silent support. Meanwhile, the Prosecutor identified himself to the Judge, then waited while the other Court officials and the defendant did the same. For the first time since they parted at the Melbourne airport, Chiu Liow heard Morag's voice. His throat constricted with the pain of it.

The trial began with the customary statement from the Prosecution: 'Now that all present have been properly identified, the trial of former Federation special investigator, Morag MacIain, can commence. Morag MacIain is charged with sabotage of the Papuan lattice – in particular, the sabotage of the library, salary, and transport systems, having implemented the unauthorised and illegal changes at 21:08 on the third of February 2451. She is currently residing in her own home on The Rigi, Switzerland, after being placed under house arrest by Federation Special Investigation Unit Coordinator, Rohan Maerz, on the twenty-first of February 2451.

'All evidence relating to the crime has been entered for the Judge to consider. The Summary of this evidence will now be given to those gathered here today. Anyone wishing to provide or request additional evidence or explanation will then have an opportunity to do so, having previously registered their interest in being present, or having been called to be here by the Defence or the Prosecution. Silence will be maintained while the Summary is read.'

The Judge began with a brief description of Morag's professional career, followed by her academic qualifications and specific areas of expertise, and finally, the level of security clearance her work with the FSIU gave her. The fact that the Prosecution could ascribe no motive for the crime was also noted. An outline of its repercussions was then given, together with the direct evidence that lead to charges being laid:

'...The Papuan transport, salary, and library systems were altered so as to cause passengers to be taken to incorrect destinations, library requests to be ignored, and for information technologists to be paid incorrect salaries. The changes to these applications were discovered by the Accused and duly notified to, initially, the Melbourne Peacekeeping Force, and later, to Federation Special Investigation Unit Coordinator, Rohan Maerz. As the identification used to gain access to the systems was ostensibly that of the Accused, Coordinator Maerz recalled Morag MacIain to Luzern, placed her under house arrest, and immediately put into place the required investigative process.

'At the time these changes became apparent, Morag MacIain was undertaking an investigation into various crimes that had earlier taken place in Australia, Papua, Brazil and Myanmar. Based in Melbourne, she was working in collaboration with the Melbourne and Brisbane Peacekeeping Forces, as well as with peacekeepers from each of these latter three countries.

'The Prosecution case rests upon the elimination of all other possible suspects for the crime, which the Defence refutes. Nevertheless, while it would not have been impossible to forge the identity of the Accused, it would be extremely difficult, and in all probability beyond the capacity of anyone other than very senior FSIU employees. Taking this into account, the Court concludes that there are in fact only two persons known to have had both the required security access and the level of expertise needed to implement the alterations to the applications in question at precisely the same time, as appears to have been the case. They are Morag MacIain herself, and Rohan Maerz as having potentially forged her identification.'

Chiu Liow glanced at Rohan, expecting him to be surprised and upset, but instead, with a doting smile on his face, he was looking at Aurora, while his cat gazed back adoringly. Meanwhile, the Judge continued:

'The pattern of events prior to the arrest of the Accused, and relating to the investigation she was conducting on behalf of the FSIU, indicates that the sabotage of the Papuan systems exists within a wider context. This context includes the theft of information and samples associated with scientific research being conducted by various governments into crucial aspects of reforestation and land reclamation; the direct hindrance of private companies involved in forest industries; the assault of company and government employees; as well as the murder and attempted murder of certain people connected with this situation. Since the arrest of Morag MacIain, three more murders have taken place: that of a charcoal worker, who was a member of a forestry collective in Papua which had previously suffered from an earlier sabotage attempt; and those of two others already associated with the broader inquiry.

'Rapid and significant changes within the structure of private sector forest industries have also taken place within the past eight months, generally through changes in ownership patterns – although the Court notes that these changes may or may not be related to the crimes under investigation. Furthermore, Brazilian inquiries into the recent release of contaminated pharmaceutical products by the company Epsilon Proprietary Limited, concluded that their section of the lattice had been illegally entered and misused. At the time, Morag MacIain was already under house arrest and without normal access to the lattice, so although this event may have no bearing upon the overall investigation being conducted prior to her arrest, it does indicate that another person exists who has the expertise to compromise highly secure information systems.

'While there is no direct evidence to date of the guilt of any particular person or organisation in relation to the wider series of incidents, there is some considerable basis for concluding that the party most likely to benefit financially from the outcomes is the private company, Wyvern Meridian. Having this motive in mind, and given the extensive nature of the crimes committed, it may also be reasonably conjectured that the only body, other than the Federation, with sufficient resources to undertake them is, in all probability, also Wyvern Meridian. While of itself this conclusion does not form grounds for the detention of any person, it does provide a strong foundation for further deliberation.

'It is therefore my initial determination that the Accused, Morag MacIain, will be held for a further period of time under house arrest, pending a wider examination of the activities of Wyvern Meridian, within the scope of the questions currently under consideration. In addition, given the possibility that he is also implicated, FSIU Coordinator, Rohan Maerz, is hereby suspended from duty on full salary. He will remain within Australia and, until this case is reviewed, his FSIU identity chip will be monitored at all times.

'Meanwhile, the entire matter will be referred to the Federation Assembly. An independent person will be appointed to the role of interim Federation Special Investigation Unit Coordinator, and as such, will coordinate the ongoing inquiry on their behalf. A review will be mandated in eight months. By that time, if conclusive evidence of the guilt of Morag MacIain has not been obtained, she is to be released, but will continue to be suspended from duties on full salary until such time this Court is satisfied of her innocence. The guilt or innocence of Rohan Maerz will also be reviewed in eight months.

'While the matter is subject to Assembly jurisdiction, no person assisting is to discuss its details with anyone not formally and directly associated with the case unless given specific permission to do so. Also, until their innocence is proven, or the matter is resolved, the Accused and Rohan Maerz are to have no access to any material produced as an outcome of the ongoing investigation. Nor are they to communicate with each other in any way.

'Before giving a formal verdict, is there anyone who wishes further explanation of this Summary, has additional evidence to enter in the presence of Witnesses, or wishes to challenge this initial determination? At this point in time, the full transcript will be made available only to the Federation Assembly and its appointees. The public will have access to the transcript once additional and conclusive evidence has been obtained, allowing the case to be concluded.'

At first no one moved or spoke. Morag stood up, then sat down again, transfixed and horrified at being condemned to suffer another eight months in virtual limbo. Welcome heaved a profound sigh and patted her shoulder. He had at least obtained a reprieve, and, he thought, to his own credit, had managed to implicate both Rohan Maerz and Wyvern Meridian. It was an achievement to be proud of and he profoundly hoped she would see it that way. Unfortunately, he wasn't sure Chiu Liow would cope at all well with Morag's continued absence. Glancing at his friend and colleague, he shrugged his shoulders in sympathy. However, sitting with his head bowed, Chiu Liow did not see the gesture. Welcome noticed that Rohan Maerz stood beside him, with one hand on his shoulder, while his cat briefly licked Chiu Liow's face. He shook his head in sheer disbelief at the sight, then turned his attention back to Morag.

Chiu Liow ignored both Aurora and Rohan. He wanted to think, and then talk to Welcome; at least he could now do that. He wondered if he would be allowed to visit Morag just once before she returned to her lonely house on the mountain?

There was nothing further he could place in evidence before the Judge. It was too early. They first needed to have a complete case and couldn't risk yet another inconclusive verdict. There was a great deal to consider, not the least being that Rohan Maerz was now a suspect and no longer part of their team. To a certain extent, this was something to be grateful for – and also that Morag had not been found guilty, or at any rate, not yet.

Hardly hearing the Judge as the final verdict was given – confirming the earlier finding – the peacekeeper raised his head and then abruptly stood. Rohan and Aurora quickly moved out of his way. Their eyes followed him as he strode over to Morag's guards and asked for permission to speak with her. They gave him fifteen minutes, indicating the Court antechamber was available if they wanted privacy. He raised an eyebrow at Welcome, shook his hand, then turned to Morag, who appeared just the same as ever. She was a strong woman, thank the Sun!

Morag smiled at him, calmer now in the knowledge that Chiu Liow cared a great deal for her – it was there for anyone to see in the way he held out both his hands to her: beautiful, fine, strong hands, with a personality to match. She clasped them in her own and Welcome briefly placed his hand on her shoulder, before leaving them to have their short time together.

CHAPTER TWENTY-TWO

While he waited for Morag to return, Welcome read a letter which had arrived only that morning from Karla – he'd not had time to deal with it before the trial. It gave a full account of the dinner they shared with Rohan Maerz, and also that he'd obtained a cat. She described the image Fliedermus saw in his mind – that of the murder of Mervyn Bradshaw – and finished by telling him that Chiu Liow was familiar with the entire letter's contents.

Welcome put a hand to his forehead and shook his head, relieved the Judge had consigned Morag and Rohan to different continents. However, he could not divulge the letter's contents to anyone, particularly not to Morag. The knowledge that Rohan had murdered Mervyn Bradshaw would hardly benefit her anyway. Nothing would benefit Morag now, except to be found innocent by the Federation Assembly. In order to do their best for her, the logical course of action was for both he and Chiu Liow to return to Australia as soon as possible.

An additional page had been written by Søren. He told Welcome that, if he had time, he would appreciate him reading the transcript of Possum's trial, which was now available to the public. Taking into account the evidence provided by the new research into cat behaviour, could he please give an opinion as to how Aurora could have chosen Maerz as a companion? Even more remarkable, wrote Søren, the Breeding Centre's charges apparently all liked the man!

Stroking his chin in thought, Welcome looked up to find that Chiu Liow and Morag had finished saying goodbye to each other. They both appeared somewhat agitated as they emerged from the antechamber to walk slowly over to where he was sitting. The guards were standing a short way off, chatting quietly. Being patient men, they had allowed more than the fifteen minutes granted, but still had their duty to do. As they approached, Morag gave Welcome and Chiu Liow a quick hug each, then turned away and nodded briefly to them.

Rohan was pleased with the verdict. For the first time in almost a decade, he was now able to relax, and with a small thrill of joy, he realised there was no immediate need to take responsibility for anyone but himself and his beloved Aurora. Morag was quite safe for the time being and the FSIU monitoring didn't worry him in the least. In fact, he welcomed it – so gratifying to feel secure at last. Of course, with Aurora to accompany him everywhere, he had already been sure of that. How long it would be possible to relax depended upon Welcome and Chiu Liow's ability to put together a case against Wyvern Meridian, no doubt with the help of Research Coordinator Zago and Freddi. They now had a vital piece of evidence linking the company to their investigations. He trusted it would be sufficient to allow them to find more. If not, his period of relaxation would be over and with his usual patience, he would watch and wait, and if circumstances dictated, act.

In the meantime, unable to even say goodbye to Morag, and having no sentimental reasons for staying in Luzern, Rohan wanted to return to his home in Australia and visit his new friends. Perhaps he could even take the initiative and call Søren Thorup to have a long conversation about cats? Søren had tried hard to hide how distasteful and intimidating he found him. Well, so much better the challenge! At least they had a love of food in common... Mulling this over, he made a booking for the next flight to Melbourne, due in three hours. This left him with just enough time for coffee and cake at one of his favourite cafés – one of the few places Rohan would miss, although he most certainly would not miss trudging there!

Aurora looked up at him, her ears forward. 'Yes,' he said to her, 'we're taking a walk, and we'll get you something to eat as well.'

She gazed lovingly back at him and projected an image of creamed potatoes with cheese topping. He doubted a pastry shop could provide such a dish, but perhaps an inn might? They would stop at one on the way. Naturally, Aurora should be fed before he indulged himself. Having agreed on this, they happily left the Court precincts and took their time to amble along the footpath, standing aside for other pedestrians when necessary and warming themselves in the summer sun. Since the cat stopped occasionally to sniff at things she found, it was some time before they arrived at their first destination.

The innkeeper sourly regarded Rohan's cat, not used to providing meals for animals in his establishment, yet unwilling to forego the payment. Aurora adopted her most appealing expression and for an instant, he actually thought she was speaking to him. Deciding it wasn't possible, not having met a cat before, the innkeeper found himself whistling while he prepared her food and searched through his cupboards for a suitable dish. How peculiar, he thought, feeling much happier than he had all day as he placed the bowl on the hearth of the old fireplace, then watched while the cat ate with relish. When Aurora finished, Rohan paid him, bowed slightly, and wished him a good day.

They finally reached the pastry shop, opened the door – to the sound of an old-fashioned tinkling bell – and found a seat by the window. The same family had owned the shop for almost five hundred years, which was quite an achievement and may have accounted for the exceptional quality of their cakes and handmade chocolates, as well as the old doorbell. A fine array of teas was kept, together with a wide range of different styles of coffee. The shop also held a limited licence for the serving of alcohol and provided superb liqueurs for customers to have with their coffee or cake. Rohan sighed with relief as he sat down. He would definitely miss the place, particularly on a day like this when the bright sunshine filled the interior, glinting on the warm woodwork of the tables, chairs and wall panelling. The aromas were heavenly and uniquely European, as was the décor. Small pots of bright red geraniums took pride of place on each table and the wooden floor gleamed from centuries of polishing, while the lace curtains that brightened the mullioned windows were freshly washed and pressed.

Aurora was once again sniffing assorted table legs and corners, as well as the feet of other patrons. Rohan was mildly surprised to see that none of them were annoyed by her presence, although he had never seen a cat in here before. Perhaps the novelty outweighed the usual objections to having animals in food shops?

His pleasant reverie was interrupted by the cheerful, plump woman who waited on the customers. She was short, broad, and well rounded in all respects, with a small nose, dark friendly eyes and curly white hair. Her kind nature and ample proportions were another reason he thoroughly enjoyed the shop.

'It's a long while since we've seen you,' she said, her eyes crinkling with good humour when Aurora came over to be introduced. 'I see you have a new friend. Have you had her long?'

'No,' replied Rohan. 'I hope you don't mind me bringing her?'

'Not at all. My daughter has one, and I know how well behaved and clean they are. As long as the other customers don't mind, which they don't appear to, I'm very happy to have her here. Now, what can I get you?'

Aurora placed a large paw on Rohan's knee, met his eyes and meowed a soft inquiry.

'I'll have a piece of shortbread and a bowl of water for my little friend here, whose name is Aurora,' he answered, 'and for myself, I'll begin with a chocolate cream slice and Russian Caravan tea. I might have a small Drambuie afterwards, although we'll have to watch the time. I have a flight to catch.'

'Where are you off to, then?' she asked, genuinely curious.

'I've been in Australia since you last saw me and need to return there today. I may be gone for some time, so please don't be concerned if you don't see me again for a while.'

'Well, I'll be sorry not to have you here. You've been one of my best customers. May I ask what you're doing in Australia?'

'You must forgive me, but I can't give you any details about what I've been doing up until now, but henceforth, I am taking a holiday!'

She laughed and patted him on his broad shoulder, saying, 'And about time too! I'll get your order for you.'

A few minutes later, the shopkeeper came back to lay out a crisp white serviette, the beautifully presented cake on a blue and white plate, a matching cup and saucer, a gleaming silver cake fork and teaspoon, and a pot of tea decorated with a hand-knitted cosy. She stood back to watch in satisfaction while he tasted the cake and then saluted her good work.

'Excellent, as always,' said Rohan, as he cut another piece and poured the steaming tea.

While she bustled off to fetch the shortbread and water for Aurora, he added milk and sugar to the cup, then stirred it well and savoured its fragrance as he drank. While doing so, he realised not a single other customer appeared to notice him. From past experience, this was, to say the least, unusual. Rohan was accustomed to people staring at him, before quickly turning away in embarrassment, particularly if, as was sometimes the case, he asked for a second pastry or more than just a few chocolates. There was no other explanation, he realised, looking at Aurora. She was either consciously, or unconsciously, influencing people's behaviour – for the better, as far as he could see. Well, well, another thing to discuss with Søren, if the man would deign to talk with him.

It then occurred to Rohan to wonder if Aurora influenced his own behaviour. Well, without doubt, she did. For the first time in his long, lonely life, the FSIU Coordinator now had a real companion – anyone would be happier. How far it went beyond this was difficult to tell, but the possibility needed further consideration. Although not now, he decided, and concentrated instead on enjoying the last morsel of cake.

The house on The Rigi was colourful, warmly inviting and elegantly designed, but also isolated. Normally, Morag enjoyed the isolation. However, with the end of this first court proceeding, she was more alone than ever, now that Welcome had returned to Australia. There was little choice, unfortunately, as he needed to assist Chiu Liow and they couldn't continue to communicate only by letter or take the ongoing risk of using their high-security lines. The problem was, what to do with herself? She was used to working and not fond of being idle. To make matters worse, the people she normally associated with were now out of bounds. Having no direct family left and no other friends, Morag was for all intents and purposes without company. Even a skirmish with Rohan Maerz would have been welcome, yet now he too was gone.

Wandering over to the side of her greenhouse with the best view of the valley below, Morag considered whether he had planned for her to be isolated like this. In hindsight, the Judge's decision wasn't difficult to predict, so wouldn't he have realised there was a high probability of being implicated himself? Frowning, she tweaked a curtain into a more pleasing fold, irritating herself in the process. As much as Morag loved her home, it would be very hard to spend her whole life here, with nothing to motivate her to even get out of bed!

Having been busy thinking about the verdict, Chiu Liow, and her own predicament, it had taken her until now to realise that Rohan hadn't left the courthouse alone. He was accompanied by a cat! How could this be possible? Could it be that Rohan was someone's intended victim, just as she herself appeared to be? If only there had been more time to notice and to ask Welcome about it...

Morag longed to talk to another human being, but there was no one, and the house seemed so empty. To survive the next eight months, or even longer, a solution had to be found. The memory of Chiu Liow's face, his hands, and final kiss before they left the antechamber, returned yet again and helped give her the strength to face this silent life. Somehow, she *would* find a way back!

Several days later, when the household security system chimed and Mik Theophanous looked up from the book he was reading, he was horrified to see Rohan Maerz looming large at the door, filling the entire screen. Leaping to his feet, he paced the floor, then called Fliedermus. She came bounding in, but stopped short, concerned at his indecision, as well as the trace of fear. Mik finally made up his mind and climbed the stairs to open the door. He definitely did not want that man walking anywhere in his house alone, not even down the staircase!

Fliedermus reached the door before him and stretched up to touch the handle, turning around and meowing impatiently. Surely not! She *wanted* to see Rohan – or did she want to see Aurora? He gently pushed her aside. Once the door was open, Rohan held out his hand, which Mik instinctively grasped, then, feeling faintly sick, quickly released.

'Come in,' was the only response that occurred to him after Rohan apologised for having arrived uninvited, meanwhile taking off his latest extravagant hat, full-length artificial fur coat, and heavy gloves. Mik placed everything on the coat rack and gestured for Rohan to precede him. Meanwhile, Fliedermus and Aurora pranced and capered about, chasing each other around the small fountain gracing the centre of the indoor garden.

'They seem to have forgotten the fright they suffered when you came to dinner. I'm glad, aren't you?' remarked Rohan, as he made his way carefully down the staircase, which was a touch narrow for someone of his size.

What could Mik possibly say but a rather pale, 'Yes, I am.' To be polite, he added, 'Fliedermus is a natural clown. It would take more than that for her to lose the chance of a new playmate.'

Noticing its warmth and colour, Rohan surveyed the living room, which was very different from his own, yet pleasing nonetheless. 'It's lovely and cosy in here. Do you have additional heating, or is it all self-sufficient?'

'It's all self-sufficient,' Mik replied, inviting him to sit. 'Most houses in Australia are. Aren't they in Switzerland?'

'No, the terrain and climate make it more difficult, but efficient centralised heating systems overcome the problem, and the houses are well built and well insulated. I imagine this house would be cool in summer?'

Both of them knew they were making polite conversation to overcome the initial unease of a first visit by an uninvited guest, although Mik had given in to the inevitable and was making an effort to appear friendly.

'Yes, it's very cool. If you'd like, I'll show you around,' and he led the way back to the greenhouse, with its extraordinary display of flowering and ornately-leaved plants that provided a riot of colour, even at the beginning of winter.

The two cats stopped their play and bounded towards their companions, cavorting and leaping around their legs. Rohan bent down to pat Fliedermus and, to Mik's astonishment, she not only allowed him to, but pushed her head into his hand, pressing herself against his legs. Fondling her fluffy ears, Rohan beamed, then ran a finger around the inside of her curled tail. As he did, Fliedermus' tail tightened around his hand and she sat down by his feet, staring into his face, her black pupils dilated.

Time disappeared. It was as if Rohan was seeing a reflection of himself in the cat's mind. Not a physical image, but an image of how he occasionally saw himself in dreams: younger, slimmer, and agile, with a close friend who loved him, but whose face he could never see. Overwhelmed, Rohan put his free hand to his eyes and swayed. Mik instinctively grasped his upper arm, then jerked away in shock when he saw the same picture of longing. Fliedermus released Rohan, moved away, and began cleaning herself.

Mik hardly knew what to say, so simply led him to the nearest seat and put a hand on his shoulder. Tears were now streaming down Rohan's face. Aurora, who had watched with interest, came up to him and raised one golden paw to gently place it on his knee. She meowed, low and urgent. He stirred, and then lifted her onto the seat, hugging the big cat to him as if she were his last and only friend. Mik sat down next to them and waited, while Fliedermus fastidiously continued to clean herself. When he sent her an inquiry, she didn't answer, except to project a general sense of wellbeing. At last, Rohan wiped his face with a neatly pressed, finely embroidered kerchief, and sighed.

'Please forgive me for embarrassing you like this,' he said. 'Apparently your cat...' and he paused, taking a deep breath, 'can even see my dreams. It was extremely disconcerting. I really don't know how to explain.'

'You don't need to. I'm not embarrassed; I saw the same image when I held your arm. I've found that the cats don't always play by our rules. They have their own ideas about a lot of things and often know more about us than we do ourselves. I suppose Fliedermus wanted you to think about what she showed you, and wanted me to understand as well. If it'd been something I *shouldn't* know, I don't think Aurora would have let her do it. She's not angry with Fliedermus at all, but I'm sorry you're upset.'

Despite himself, and despite all his suspicions of Rohan – and even the dire knowledge that he had murdered someone – Mik found himself warming to him and actually wanting to get to know him better. 'Maybe it's the influence of the cats,' he thought, 'but they seem to think he had a good reason for killing Mervyn Bradshaw. How could they accept him otherwise?' In spite of this, he didn't dare tell Rohan what they knew. It was far too soon and far too dangerous. After all, despite their extraordinary powers, cats were not omniscient. Instead, Mik stood up, holding out his hand to Rohan, who accepted it, and then, with some difficulty, rose.

'Come on,' he said, 'let's get a good strong cup of coffee, maybe even a stiff shot of whisky. Afterwards, if you want, we can talk about it. If you'd rather not, you can tell me what you *did* want to talk about when you decided to pay a visit.'

Mik smiled winningly at Rohan, who was shaken by just how uncertain he had suddenly become and how vulnerable he felt, feelings he was not at all familiar with. Nodding, he negotiated the staircase again and followed Mik into the kitchen. The cats came with them only as far as the living room, where they jumped onto the couch, curling up together to sleep.

His visitor watched silently while Mik prepared the coffee and found a bottle of best malt whisky, as well as some macadamia nut shortbread biscuits.

'I'm sorry, I don't have much in the house to give you to eat,' Mik apologised, waving a hand in the general direction of his pantry. 'I was planning to do some shopping tomorrow.'

Rohan accepted the coffee and carefully tasted the scalding liquid, then complimented him on how good it was before helping himself to a biscuit. 'It's me who should apologise for not letting you know I was coming. You might have found an excuse for not being home, you see. And besides, Aurora deserved a trip and a walk. If you weren't home, it would have been worthwhile just to see your garden. It's very impressive.'

Genuinely pleased, Mik smiled again, but his response was interrupted by another chime. When Søren's face appeared on the security screen, Mik almost jumped in horror. He definitely did not want to be in the middle if Søren chose to practice his wit on Rohan while he was feeling so uncertain. However, to his surprise, Rohan sat straighter and appeared pleased.

'Well, well,' he said, 'I did so much want to speak to our cat expert. I *am* in luck today!' Taking another biscuit, he turned expectantly to the door.

Søren came in and stared, open-mouthed, when he saw Mik's other guest. He hadn't noticed the two cats on his way in, as they were sound asleep and hidden from view. He knew Rohan had been suspended from duty because Chiu Liow still kept Karla fully informed, ignoring the Judge's strictures regarding communication about the case with outsiders.

However, Mik's entire body language warned Søren that he needed to behave himself. He could also see that Rohan had been made welcome and was eager to meet him. The situation called for diplomacy, so he held out his hand and they greeted each other gravely.

Sitting down next to Rohan, he said, 'Do you have any more coffee, Mik? The coffee is most definitely why *I* am here – I could smell it all the way from Willsmere – and a whisky as well, if you please.' Søren smiled winningly at them both. 'Now, what brings *you* here, Rohan Maerz?' His grey eyes looked deep into Rohan's, but the effect was still one of honest friendliness.

'As you say, it must be the coffee,' replied Rohan, keeping his tone light and pleasant. He knew full well that Søren didn't trust him, which he also knew was understandable. 'However, to be honest,' he explained, 'I enjoyed our dinner together with Mik and his other friends so much that on a beautiful day like this, I thought it would be a good excuse to take Aurora outside. I've looked forward to meeting you again, Søren, so your coming here today is most fortunate. We had little chance to speak to each other at Possum's trial.' Tilting his head to one side and meeting Søren's eyes again, Rohan paused, then added, 'You don't appear to have a peacekeeper with you. May I ask why that is?'

'Ah well, I escaped. The poor man will be wondering where I am. I really will have to put him out of his misery quite soon. He'll be putting in an emergency call any time now if I don't, yet perhaps he can suffer a little while longer before I let him know it's safe for me to be here.' Søren laughed, his usual mischievous nature reasserting itself. 'After all, there are two cats in the house. What more could I want?'

Mik frowned in disbelief. How *could* he have just left Willsmere and travelled all the way here alone! 'Søren,' he said sternly, his arms folded, 'I think you should call *now*. Did Karla or Tamara know you were coming to see me? What if they're worrying too?'

'I told Red Matilda where I was going and to let the others know if they needed to,' replied Søren peevishly. When Mik glared at him, he added, 'Oh well, if you insist,' and turned on his comlink.

'You're incredible sometimes, Søren!' said Mik sharply. 'You even turned off your comlink! Why?'

'I just wished to delude myself for a little while that the world was as it should be and that no harm would come to me or anyone I care for. It sounds silly, but I simply *could not* resist.' A genuinely plaintive note had entered Søren's voice, but he made the necessary call. Peering over his shoulder, Mik could see an exceedingly angry, red-faced peacekeeper on the small screen.

'Where are you?' said the peacekeeper, despite clearly wanting to say a great deal more.

'I'm visiting Mik Theophanous and it appears I am in very good company. There are two cats here, as well as one former FSIU coordinator by the name of Rohan Maerz.' Søren winked at Rohan, his good humour restored. 'You don't need to fetch me. I'm sure I can find an escort back to Willsmere.' He looked meaningfully at Mik, who nodded. 'Yes,' Søren confirmed, 'Mik and Fliedermus will come back with me, so you can take a rest, if you like. I will be about an hour and a half, I think.' He looked quizzically at his friend again, and also at Rohan. This time, they both nodded.

The peacekeeper shook his head in disgust, but agreed to "take a rest" at Willsmere until Søren returned. There was little point going anywhere else in the meantime, unless an emergency arose.

'You ought to take your situation more seriously,' Rohan told Søren, when the call was over. 'You *are* in danger, you know.' Mik and Søren both stared at him, startled at such an overt admission.

'Chiu Liow Jones is a highly competent peacekeeper and would not have made sure you were protected at all times if it wasn't necessary, and if you recall,' Rohan continued, a deliberate edge of patience to his voice, 'I was, until recently, in charge of the investigation into your Willsmere incident, as well as all the others that are so patently related. I most certainly wouldn't have sanctioned the expensive use of a dedicated peacekeeper, Søren Thorup, if it wasn't important.' He waggled an admonitory finger in Søren's face and couldn't help feeling pleased at the disconcerted expression on the elfin features. Neither Mik nor Søren uttered a word.

'You must forgive me for not being able to enlighten you further,' said Rohan. 'That's forbidden by the Judge and its verdict, but take my word for it, you must not give in to this temptation again, no matter how understandable it might be.' He waited while they considered what he had said. Mik was the first to speak.

'I think we may have become a little complacent, because since Marika's death, nothing much else has happened in Australia while you've been here.' This statement was not entirely honest, but Mik wanted to know what the response would be.

'Very true,' replied Rohan, 'and for good reason, though now that I've been suspended, the situation could change. We can hope it won't, but there's still a possibility further developments, if you like, will occur. With both our dear Morag and me out of the picture, there's a certain...vacuum. It remains to be seen whether the Federation Assembly can fill it.'

'Well,' concluded Søren, 'on that decidedly ambiguous note, I think you and I, Mik, should return to Willsmere, but perhaps just another cup of coffee and another of those delicious shortbread biscuits before we do?'

'Why not. Do you want some more too, Rohan?'

When Rohan held out his cup and saucer, Mik gave him the last of the coffee then made another pot for Søren and himself. At this point, the two cats ambled into the kitchen, having received a clear indication they were soon to be leaving for a walk. As they did, the atmosphere in the kitchen began to grow more relaxed, almost cosy.

'Do you know,' said Rohan, 'I really would like to come to Willsmere with you. I can't come inside, not anymore, but at least I could accompany you and take a tour of the perimeter. I understand it's quite impressive and that the landscaped gardens and nearby river are worth seeing.'

The two cats projected enthusiastic agreement, so they could hardly disagree.

Mik and Søren walked slowly, for Rohan's sake. Once they reached the callstation, it wasn't long before a railcar arrived and they were on their way. Aurora had the same habit as Red Matilda of standing on the seat to watch the passing scenery, tail twitching, snickering at any people she saw, whereas Fliedermus sat with her tail wrapped around Søren's wrist, as if to make doubly sure he would not 'escape' again.

'Not much gets past these cats,' thought Rohan, noticing. They weren't even in the kitchen when Søren's lapse of common sense was being discussed. He turned to him and asked, 'I've wanted to talk with you for some time about cats and their behaviour, if you don't mind?' then continued without waiting for an answer: 'My most recent observations lead me to conclude that they can influence our emotions, and as a result, possibly even our behaviour. What do you think?'

This was not something either Søren or Mik wanted to become common knowledge, but on the other hand, it was only a matter of time before it did. Since Possum's trial, the legal status of cats was now firmly established in the Judge's knowledge base. Perhaps a moderately honest answer might be warranted? Much to his own surprise, Søren made a quick decision to trust Rohan for the time being.

'Yes,' he answered, 'we think they can, to quite a significant degree, although not in trivial ways. It seems as if they only make the effort when something out of the ordinary and quite important to their companion has occurred. We became aware of what they could do only very recently and are still not sure how widespread the ability is amongst cats. As you may be aware, there is little data in the Judge or anywhere else on this particular point.' Rohan murmured his agreement, so Søren elaborated further: 'Our only direct experience is with my own and with Mik's beloved cats, which, of course, isn't a representative sample. What have you discovered about Aurora?'

Rohan described his recent experience in the Luzern café. 'The event wasn't unusual at all, you see. When I lived there, I frequented the shop regularly and became inured, or so I'd hoped, to the reaction most people have to me. Mind you, they don't seem to react the same way here in Melbourne, which I must admit is a pleasant surprise.'

Puzzled, Mik said, 'What reaction, exactly, do you mean?'

'I like good food and eat a lot, but that's not the reason why I'm this large,' and Rohan looked meaningfully at Søren. 'Genetic screening has its limitations, and this is a trait I was born with, so I can't see why I shouldn't take the opportunity to indulge in eating whatever I like. It will hardly make me any bigger than I already am. I also admit to provoking people on occasion, such as dinner guests whom I was obliged to entertain but didn't especially like. However, many people frown at what they see as overindulgence, particularly in public places. When I order a second, or even a third, serving in this café...or anywhere else for that matter...they look down their noses at me and are sometimes even rude enough to comment amongst themselves, making sure I can overhear.'

Despite Rohan's serious expression while he told them this, Søren burst out laughing, and received a few smiles from the other passengers as a result. 'I really am sorry,' he gasped, 'but I know exactly what you mean. I am fortunate in that respect in being small. When *I* eat a great deal in public places, I merely receive looks of bewilderment. I have also been fortunate enough in my profession not to be forced to suffer fools at my dinner table. My friends and colleagues find me provoking enough on a daily basis, so my eating habits, and what I serve *them*, are no cause for additional comment. Still, as you say, people seem to be much more tolerant and sensible here in Melbourne than in some other places I've lived. So, I gather you will be staying with us?'

'Yes, I hope to. But getting back to the café in Luzern, what I meant to say was, I thought Aurora influenced the other customers. It was the very first time no one so much as gave me a second glance. Why would she do that?'

'I think it's because, to her, the event *was* unusual, and also I've noticed how protective they tend to be.' Mik waved a hand to emphasise his point. 'Considering she's never been anywhere other than Melbourne, taking a flight with you for the first time – and to something as important as a trial, where the verdict affected you as well – would make her even more alert than usual to anything that might hurt you. She probably picked up on the negative reactions of people in the street as you walked to the shop. In other words, Aurora was well prepared before you even entered the café.'

Glancing at Søren, Rohan carefully considered Mik's words.

'Oh yes, I agree,' said Søren. 'I would think she knows precisely how vulnerable you are and is on the watch for anything preying on this vulnerability.'

Mik recalled the image Fliedermus had projected a while earlier and lowered his eyes, saddened. Raising them again, he saw both Rohan and Aurora looking pointedly at him and realised they understood what he was thinking and wanted him to keep the revelation to himself. However, at that moment, having reached their destination, the railcar chimed, interrupting further discussion. They walked the short distance to the perimeter of Willsmere in silence, each occupied with his own thoughts.

At the main entranceway, Rohan, smiling, held out his hand, first to Mik and then to Søren. 'Thank you for allowing me to come this far. I'll leave you both to your work now as I don't imagine the security scanners would recognise me any longer. I'll just take the opportunity to have a look at the outside of the building and perhaps walk down to the river. I haven't seen a natural forest in a long while, and I'm sure Aurora hasn't explored one like this before.' Sitting neatly by his feet, Aurora purred her agreement.

After the gates opened for them, Mik and Søren walked along the pathway to Willsmere's magnificent front doors, and before entering their workplace, turned to wave goodbye. Rohan watched until they were well inside, then looked down at Aurora, who continued to purr in approval. Reaching into his voluminous pocket, he withdrew an electronic device – obtained some two months before Morag's trial – checked to make sure no one was nearby, and pointed it at the security scanner. The readout, as well as a low click, reassured him that the device was operational. Satisfied, Rohan put it back into his pocket and began his leisurely tour, taking time to enjoy the scenery and the last of the daylight. As he walked through the nearby bushland, Aurora ran ahead, picking up and playing with small twigs and leaves. At one point, the cat stopped to dab a paw at a spot on the ground, then brought him the object she had found, making sure not to damage it. He put his hand down to accept the gift and saw it was a complete cicada case from last summer, brown and fragile. Rohan turned it over, studying it curiously, never having seen one before, then carried the small treasure all the way back to their apartment, where he placed it into an ornate box for safekeeping.

CHAPTER TWENTY-THREE

While Red Matilda slept by her feet, Karla sat with elbows on the table, chin resting in her hands, and Søren sat opposite, coffee cup raised to his lips. 'Do you realise we're now halfway to Armageddon?' said Karla, looking straight at him, her expression serious.

Søren stopped drinking his coffee and stared at her. 'Have I missed something I shouldn't have?' he asked, blinking a few times.

'That's very likely. Most people have. It's lucky our astronomers haven't – or so I gathered from an article I read this morning. It seems there's a thirty-kilometre-wide meteor still headed towards Earth and due to hit in approximately another four hundred years. It was discovered almost four hundred and fifty years ago. They say it could be nudged out of our way if we remember it's there and launch something to provide the nudge early enough. Makes you put things into perspective, doesn't it?'

'What type of perspective were you thinking of, Karla?'

'Oh, we all work hard to preserve our natural environment and to bring back as many endangered species from the point of extinction as we can, and meanwhile, a stray meteor could come along and wipe us all out, together with nearly everything else on the planet. This particular meteor isn't the only one out there, either. And then, of course, a massive volcano could erupt and there'd be yet another catastrophic set of mass extinctions. There are so many possible scenarios. In my view, we should appreciate what we have all the more because it's so fragile, so transient. I simply can't understand why anyone values enormous wealth and vast material possessions above the natural wonders all around us...free to anyone prepared to just look and appreciate.'

'People lose perspective far too easily,' replied Søren, picking up a piece of the chocolate-covered marzipan he had brought with him. 'The lust for power, greed, cruelty...they are all a type of sickness. I can understand how ancient peoples, who were always at the mercy of wild animals and the elements, could see them as their enemies and long to make themselves safe. It's an instinct we still have, and which can take control when people's better qualities have not had the chance to grow.'

Since Karla was listening intently, Søren realised the subject was truly one that troubled her. 'I believe most people have a sense of awe and wonder at natural phenomena,' he said, 'as well as a wish to belong to their surroundings and to experience some sense of harmony. On the other hand, humanity has always needed to have a balance between security and challenge. Without this balance, we don't seem to function at all well. In fact we have so many complex, competing drives, it is amazing to me that we function as well as we do! However, the problem is that for such a long time, the more aggressive races amongst us thought they could endlessly change and plunder the Earth without any repercussions at all...or they thought they could avoid the repercussions if they were clever and powerful enough. They were wrong, of course.'

'Yes, they were, Søren, and even now, there are still a few who haven't learnt. Perhaps Wyvern Meridian, for example. Chiu Liow recently told me how Shela reacted to Kenjiro Kakura when she and Freddi met him in Myanmar. Just as well, by the way, *this* little detail wasn't entered into the Judge before Possum's trial.'

'Why? What was her reaction?'

'She became completely hysterical. Freddi was so affected by her rage, she nearly fell, and when Kakura's bodyguard was ordered to help by taking her leash, Shela attacked him, drawing blood. Luckily, the injury wasn't serious, but at the same time, Kakura caught Freddi by the arm, which we think the cat objected to, because she was then about to attack *him* as well. Freddi managed to calm her down in time, but it was Shela's reaction that really made her suspect Wyvern Meridian was behind the damage done to Myanmar Forest Industries.'

Søren raised one elegant eyebrow. 'That *does* put a different slant on things! Freddi could not have been under any immediate threat. Therefore, based on what we have learnt about cat behaviour, Shela must have been terrified of Kakura. Why was I not told earlier?'

'I suppose everyone had so much else on their minds, it was simply forgotten.'

'Not by Shela, I'm sure. It will be interesting to hear what she has to say if they ever meet again. Still, that's now in the past, and unless it becomes relevant, I see no point in asking Freddi to add the incident to the Breeding Centre's database. Do you?'

'No, at least not yet, although Welcome has managed to ferret out even more financial information about Kakura and his company. Apparently his bondmate has substantial commercial interests, too. They are, as it turns out, the most individually wealthy people on the planet. They're worth something in the order of five billion credits! I can't even conceive of that much wealth.' Karla shook her head.

'What does Peacekeeper Jones think about all this?'

'He thinks we're still in danger, which isn't too wonderful.'

'No, but realistic,' replied Søren, toying with another chocolate before popping it into his mouth. 'Given Wyvern Meridian is as large and as ambitious as we now know them to be, and assuming Shela's instincts are correct, they won't stop until they have everything they want from us, as well as from the companies they may have sabotaged or corrupted. Presumably Kakura isn't at all interested in serious competition from anyone, even the Federation. I do wonder, though, how long it will be before their Australian application is evaluated. Has Chiu Liow heard anything?'

'Well, yes, he has. The evaluation process will be accelerated now that the company's to be investigated by the Assembly. They'll want a fresh copy of our model to compare with the previous one, just to make sure we haven't changed anything important in the meantime. Also, with their work progressing so well, Meng Jarrah is ready to check the latest version using the simulations they've updated at Lamington... Did you know she's back?'

'No, I didn't. I *have* been out of the loop lately. Oh well, I promise not to sulk. There's no reason at all to have told me. Did she speak with Tamara?'

'Yes, just yesterday. Tamara decided to pay us a visit and catch up on gossip, as well as work. She and Mik will arrange for their research to be sent to the Assembly via Coordinator Zago, who'll make a personal presentation. In the meantime, they're planning to take a trip to Lamington.' Karla grinned. 'I suspect they'll treat it as a holiday. I can't say I blame them. They could do with a break. You and I have been very lucky, really.'

'They do have each other. That makes a difference, don't you think?' Søren returned the smile, delighted his two friends had found a lasting bond, not only in their common work interests, but also in their personal lives; he adored the air of romance he now associated with them. 'Which reminds me,' he continued, 'how are Meng Jarrah and Freddi managing?'

'I didn't know you knew about them! How *did* you know?'

'Whatever do you mean?' replied Søren, startled yet again.

'Oh, sorry, I thought you meant, how are they managing their relationship now that Meng Jarrah's back in Australia!' Karla laughed at his confusion.

'Well, I *am* delighted, though I live in hope that no one is able to ferret out Chiu Liow's secrets this easily. You'd make a dreadful spy, my dear.' Søren patted her hand, semi-serious in his comment. 'I was merely wondering if there was any more news from Myanmar, and assumed they would still be communicating with each other, given the investigation there is still ongoing.'

Karla blushed. 'Yes, well...you're right, but thankfully I don't need to be a spy, and I don't talk about our situation with anyone outside our group, so I *think* I can be trusted not to sink the Federation. At least, I hope so! But thank you, it's a good reminder that Chiu Liow *is* putting a lot of faith in us. He could lose his position if anyone found out what he's doing.'

'True, and I think it would be best if we kept our distance from Rohan Maerz...if we *can*. I still don't quite trust him...or his cat! If anyone could find out that Chiu Liow is ignoring the restrictions the Judge set, it would be him. It's fortunate he has been suspended.'

'Do you honestly think he'll stay out of it? I don't,' said Karla, with a grimace. 'How could someone who's spent something like forty years as an investigator of the highest calibre simply leave it all alone? I'm quite certain he'll find ways of staying in touch.'

'You are most likely right, and if he does, I am perfectly sure we will not be aware of it.'

The resident flock of sulphur-crested white cockatoos flew back and forth over the research station at Lamington, screeching deafeningly as they went. They sometimes rested decoratively in a tall tree, ripping some of its bark with their huge beaks as they searched for food, then took off again, soaring high above the treetops. Martha was caring for her test plots and hardly heard their noise, so deep was her concentration. In any case, she was used to their cacophony and not bothered by it. The old echidna living in the nearby patch of forest also ignored them. In fact, it ignored everyone and trundled around hunting for food as if there was no one else in the world at all. She had found a good nest of juicy ants and was contentedly snuffling them up as they scurried along their trail. Her strange, backwards-facing legs scuffled the ground while she ate, making intricate patterns in the dry soil. Meng Jarrah looked up from her work to watch, entranced by the sight of this creature going about its business, oblivious to all the troubles the human world created. With a wry smile, she eventually checked her comlink: Tamara and Mik were due to arrive within the next couple of hours, leaving her just enough time to finish what she was doing.

The time since her return from Myanmar had been satisfyingly productive, and working with Gwenllian and Owain, highly enjoyable. Martha had double-checked all the simulations produced by their combined results, as well as the integrity of the micro-organisms, brought back in secure containers. To bring them with her, Meng Jarrah had needed formal permission from Research Coordinator Zago, as well as the approval of the Australian authorities, who received early notification of her plans while still in Myanmar. This necessity made them uneasy because it unavoidably entailed the use of the lattice. Still, Meng Jarrah concluded, with a quarantine of the entire Lamington test area having been declared, their work could hardly be kept a total secret.

At that moment, screaming from within the forest brought Meng Jarrah to her feet. Martha gasped, and for several seconds, they gazed at each other, stunned. Overcoming their confusion, they ran towards the sound, which continued as a ghastly drawn-out wailing, rising and falling in pitch, scarcely human, yet unlike any animal either of them had ever heard. Before they could reach its source, the sharp crack of a high-powered projectile rifle came from the same direction, and the screaming stopped, as suddenly as it began.

Both women stopped as well, panting for breath, not sure which way to continue: towards the screaming, or away from the rifle fire? Before they could make up their minds, Gwenllian almost collided with them, her eyes wild, barely recognising her two friends. Sharp thorns and twigs had torn her clothes as she ran.

Gwenllian grasped Meng Jarrah by the arm, and as she did, the impact of what Meng Jarrah saw in her mind was so great, she almost fell, but Martha caught her, then cried out, overcome by the same image. They saw two men lying on the ground near the edge of the clearing where Owain had almost finished preparing some of their first test beds. One had been shot through the head. A rifle lay nearby, where it had dropped when he died. There was little left to show who he might have been. The other lay on his side, arms and legs flung out, his head stretched far back, his face contorted into an expression of extreme pain and fear. Owain sat some metres away on a moss-covered log, head in his hands, shoulders shaking. He had been violently sick. Another rifle lay at his feet.

Gwenllian and Martha both released their hold on Meng Jarrah at almost the same instant, pausing only long enough for her to regain control before running on towards Owain and the two men. Meng Jarrah followed. When they found him, Owain was sobbing uncontrollably. Gwenllian knelt down and took his face in her hands, drawing his head to her shoulder and holding him until the sobbing eased. Meanwhile, Martha took a cloth from her pocket to cover what was left of the face of the man who had been shot. It was an odd thing to do, but she couldn't bear to see such a grotesque travesty exposed for a moment longer. Meng Jarrah checked the other man in the vain hope he might still be alive: he wasn't. After a quick look around, she sat down on the log next to Owain and waited. After what seemed a long time, he was able to speak.

'I heard a twig snap, but didn't take any notice, then a bird shrieked and I looked up. There were two of them, taking aim...at me! I flung myself to the ground and all of a sudden one of them started screaming. I've never heard anything like it in my life. It was horrible! Then, instead of aiming at me, he turned around and shot the other one in the head, before collapsing on the ground. I ran over and picked up his rifle, in case he wasn't dead. And then I threw up.'

He started trembling again, his chest heaving in great gasps as he tried to control himself. Gwenllian still held him, her arm around his shoulders. Owain took her hand in his and was able to continue. 'It was you, wasn't it?' he said, turning to his sister, who nodded, her face pale and ghastly, despite having run so far through the forest.

'What do you mean, Owain?!' exclaimed Martha. 'What has Gwenllian done?'

Gwenllian grimaced. 'I seem to have developed some sort of telepathy. Meng Jarrah knows. I've tried to pretend it never happened, but today I saved Owain's life, even though I was more than five hundred metres away when they were about to kill him.'

Martha struggled to comprehend. It just didn't make sense! 'What do you mean, "Meng Jarrah knows"? Knows what, exactly?'

'We didn't tell you because it was up to Gwenllian whether she wanted others to know or not,' replied Meng Jarrah. 'She and Owain found out about these powers shortly before I went back to Myanmar, and showed me. Gwenllian needed to know if the effect was something that someone other than Owain could experience. You felt it, Martha, when you both touched me at the same time. Søren knows too, which is why he came here for a while. We wanted to do some testing and he seemed the ideal choice because he understands so much about cats and what they can do with *their* minds.'

Gwenllian reached out to touch Martha, but changed her mind. Instead, she simply said, 'I'm really sorry you had to find out in such a horrible way. I didn't realise what I could do. Since the first time, even when I've touched Owain, it didn't happen again. I think I was willing it not to. What should we do now?' She was struggling to prevent herself from crying.

Martha took one very deep breath and with both hands brushed her hair away from her face, quickly accepting the situation in her usual calm, stoic way. 'We need to be practical. If you tell us exactly what you did, Gwenllian, we can support you when the peacekeepers get here. We can't put off calling them for much longer, I'm afraid.'

Owain looked as if he needed to throw up again, but managed to control himself. 'Go on, Gwenllian. They have to be told,' he said.

She held her brother a little tighter and said, 'I was working, then virtually saw what was happening...as if I was there. I reacted without thinking and reached into one of the men's minds, twisting it, as if my hand was inside his head. Then I forced him to shoot the other one. There was no choice! I couldn't control them both at the same time! I didn't kill the first one on purpose, but he died anyway. As soon as he was dead, I just started running...and that's all there is to tell.' Gwenllian looked from one woman to the other then burst into tears, weeping hysterically. Brother and sister clung to each other while Martha and Meng Jarrah watched helplessly.

Martha eventually moved away to make the necessary call. Meng Jarrah did the same. This attempted murder was clearly related to all the other incidents, and as far as she was concerned, Chiu Liow Jones needed to know – now, and not later. She didn't want to be in the position of trying to explain everything to the local peacekeepers either.

Chiu Liow listened to her brief account, ran a hand over his face, then through his rumpled hair. 'When the Brisbane peacekeepers arrive,' he said, in a low voice, 'just give them a brief account of who you all are and what has happened here and now. Don't go into any theories about how it might link into everything else that's happened, but you can tell them the FSIU and the Assembly are involved. Once you've done that, ask them to call me. It will be a difficult story for the BPF to swallow, even though they were liaising with me earlier when Lamington was first broken into. And, Meng Jarrah, keep Gwenllian and Owain calm, if you can. We don't want them reacting as badly as they did when she was under suspicion the last time.'

While they waited for the Brisbane Peacekeeping Force to arrive, they all noticed how silent it had become. Even the birds and animals seemed to have been affected by what had happened. Nevertheless, the sun shone into this small gap in the forest just as it had done before, and if it weren't for the bodies, blood, and spattered brain and bone on the ground, the scene would have been one of beauty and harmony. Meng Jarrah shuddered in disbelief, but forced herself to face the reality of it all. She breathed deeply and slowly, and saw Martha doing the same. Gwenllian had stopped crying, but her breath came in short gasps, like an exhausted child. Owain was hunched over, his head down, still holding his sister's hand. None of them spoke. There was nothing more to say.

Meng Jarrah's troubled reverie was interrupted by the arrival of two BPF airjets. She had completely lost track of time and could not have said how long they had taken. There was enough space in the clearing for them to land. Three burly men and one unusually tall woman descended, hands on their sidearms, ready for anything. Taking in the scene, they approached cautiously.

'Which one of you called?' asked the woman.

'I did. My name is Martha. I'm the coordinator of the Federation research station here at Lamington. This is Meng Jarrah, who is a government research coordinator, but usually works in either Papua or Myanmar. She's here helping us.' Martha introduced Gwenllian and Owain, who had approached, but were struggling to control their anxiety. 'Gwenllian is on leave from the Central Computer Site in Melbourne. She's an information technologist and also does private research that's now part of our Federation effort here. Owain is her brother and colleague, on leave from the Department of Agriculture, where he works as a research coordinator. We don't know who the two dead men are, but we think they might be connected to a series of crimes the Federation Special Investigation Unit have been dealing with since late last year. The matter's currently under the jurisdiction of the Federation Assembly. You may have heard of one of the incidents, which happened here not very long ago.'

The peacekeepers were frowning as they listened. Before they asked any more questions, Meng Jarrah stepped forward to let them know that the Melbourne Peacekeeping Force had been contacted. 'I've spoken with Chiu Liow Jones of the MPF. He was involved in the Australian investigation before the Assembly took over, so could you please call him? He should be able to explain everything.'

The peacekeepers didn't appear at all concerned by her news and actually seemed relieved. A double homicide, or even a single one, was an uncommon event, so although they were more than capable of dealing with the situation, it would help matters enormously to obtain assistance from another peacekeeping unit at the outset.

Meng Jarrah listened while one of them spoke quietly with Chiu Liow, although it was difficult to catch everything being said since the peacekeepers had moved several metres away. They occasionally glanced at Gwenllian, then at Owain, and then at each other. As Chiu Liow said, the story was a hard one to swallow. She was deeply thankful he already knew about Gwenllian's extraordinary new powers and that one of his own peacekeepers was a witness to their existence. Without this knowledge and proof, Owain would have had difficulty giving any plausible alternative to his having killed the men himself.

Martha stood nearby, arms folded, also listening, but in dismay. They had been so optimistic their troubles were behind them, but now this! She checked her comlink. Tamara and Mik were due to arrive any minute and if no one was there to greet them, they would worry. Martha realised their cats would be with them as well. Having little experience with cats, yet knowing theirs would pick up on what had happened as soon as they were within a relatively short distance, she touched Meng Jarrah on the arm and silently mouthed, 'Mik and Tamara.'

Meng Jarrah nodded, then abruptly shook her head, mouth pursed in a grimace of annoyance. She was obliged to ask for permission to leave, but doubted if the peacekeepers would be happy to give it. Well, needs must, so she walked over and waited until one of them noticed her.

'Two of our colleagues from Melbourne will be arriving very soon,' she said, 'and they'll wonder what's happening if one of us isn't at the landing site to greet them. Their names are Tamara Solanum and Mik Theophanous. If you ask Peacekeeper Jones, he'll confirm they've played a major part in this case.'

The peacekeeper spoke briefly with the others and they huddled together, discussing the situation with Chiu Liow. At last they gave Meng Jarrah permission to return to the research station. She went over to Gwenllian and Owain and knelt down in front of them. They were sitting on the log as they were feeling too shaken to stand for long.

'I have to go back, otherwise Tamara and Mik will be frantic. It's best if they don't come here before they've spoken with one of us.' Meng Jarrah took Gwenllian's hand in hers, pressed it gently and said, 'Gwen, just remember, you saved Owain's life...perhaps even ours. You did what you had to do, and thank the Sun that you could. Chiu Liow knows all about the experiments Søren and his blessed peacekeeper conducted when they were here, *and* he knows all about how the cats communicate, so I'm sure he'll work something out with these people. Just be patient and try not to worry. Martha will stay here with you.'

As they stared at her, unable to say anything, Meng Jarrah stood up to run back through the forest, ashamed at how glad she was to leave the scene, where the ants and blowflies had already begun to crawl all over the corpses.

After she left, one of the peacekeepers came over to speak with Gwenllian and Owain. He had thermal blankets with him and draped them carefully around their shoulders, then insisted they drink the hot, reviving liquid he had brought for them. A second peacekeeper remained on guard, while the other two donned protective clothing and began their forensic study of the bodies and the clearing.

Mik and Tamara left Melbourne in a holiday mood, anticipating with glee the warm, fine weather they expected to find in Queensland. The skies were grey and overcast all morning and it began to rain heavily while they waited at the Parkville transport exchange. Fortunately, they didn't have long to wait and were under cover anyway, but it just *looked* so miserable. When they reached the airport and their airjet finally lifted off to fly high above Tullamarine, they gazed out the window at a break in the clouds below, admiring the vista before settling down to enjoy the flight. The cats had their own seat and peered out as well, although with a slightly frantic note to their constant purring. They were becoming accustomed to short trips in lower-flying, smaller airjets, but this was their first in a large, high-speed craft and they had never flown above the clouds before.

When he made the bookings, Mik had insisted that the cats accompany them. 'They're not animals,' he replied tersely when the bookings clerk attempted to convince him they should remain in cages in the cargo hold. 'They're cats!'

'Uh, cats *are* animals, aren't they? They're not human, therefore they're animals,' spluttered the clerk in frustration.

'True, they're not human, but they aren't animals either, unless you want to call us all animals, which of course we are, but cats are special. They can talk to us, you know, and as far as we're concerned, they're people, just like us. I promise they'll behave themselves,' pleaded Mik, trying to pacify the clerk now. 'Please,' he said, 'we can't put them in the cargo hold. They just wouldn't cope. They'd create havoc.'

'They'd be in cages. That's why we put animals in cages in the cargo hold...so they *can't* create havoc,' reasoned the clerk, sure he'd won his point now.

'No, these cats would cause havoc if they *were* in cages. If they're with us, they'll behave. All the other passengers would be just as upset as the cats if they're put in the cargo hold. They'd make sure of it.'

The clerk's eyes boggled. 'What do you mean, "they'd make sure"? How?'

'Well, they're telepathic, which I thought you'd know.'

Mik realised the clerk would most likely think he was crazy, but the man dealt with all types of strange people on a daily basis and wasn't about to be seen as not knowing something he should have. So, just in case this was all true, apologising, he put Mik on hold, and with some effort, overcame his initial frustration at this unusual customer request.

'Well,' the clerk said, when he returned to the screen, 'it appears you're not being unreasonable after all. You're right, in fact. Cats *are* special and *can* be treated as people.' Mik grinned when he added, 'Someone should have told me. I gather it's a new regulation. Sorry if I've caused you any upset. We'll make that four seats, shall we?'

'No, no, they can share one. They like cuddling up,' said Mik calmly, 'but if you could make it the window seat, that'd be great. They love watching the scenery go by.'

During the flight, Possum and Fliedermus pressed their noses to the windows, fascinated by the occasional clouds below. Some of the children left their seats to take a closer look at these novel creatures, but at first didn't dare touch them, even though Fliedermus did her best to entice them to pat her. The children giggled and ran back to their parents, but kept coming back time and again. Possum, on the other hand, wasn't fond of children and so ignored their antics when they tried to get her attention by making little clucking and cooing sounds. Tamara was happy to chat about the cats, although she discouraged them from stroking Fliedermus. Given the cat's sense of humour, she wasn't sure what the children might experience and didn't want to risk their newfound status as passengers on an intercity flight.

When they arrived, the airjet circled over Brisbane several times before landing. With the airport so busy today, they had been put into a holding pattern, which gave the cats time to see the city below. Concluding that flying at altitude was highly amusing, they managed to project their excitement to the other passengers, who smiled and waved at them.

As they left the aircraft to find the Brisbane transport exchange, the cats pranced and tugged at their leashes, savouring the new smells and the different climate, yet were unable to comprehend how things could change so much after what seemed to them such a short trip. Mik and Tamara carried very little luggage, so could walk arm-in-arm and still manage to control the cats' high spirits.

Tamara kissed Mik enthusiastically on the cheek and said, 'We should come here more often, you know. I'm sure Martha wouldn't mind.'

Fliedermus agreed, but Possum was still a little wary of her strange new surroundings, even though, overall, she was enjoying herself.

Returning Tamara's kiss, Mik affectionately ruffled her hair. 'Once we've finished the comparisons, we should take a holiday,' he agreed, musing over the idea and mentally running through possibilities. 'I don't think anyone would object; we haven't had one in over three years. We could even take a tent and go on a walking trip for a few days, though we'd have to leave the cats behind. I don't suppose we could carry their food as well as ours.'

Fliedermus stopped in her tracks, turned around and glared at him, while Possum walked on a few steps, until the leash reached its limit. She sat down, disgusted, tail swishing from side to side, her eyes narrowed.

'Ah,' said Mik, twitching his eyebrows, 'I gather that's out of the question. Alright, you two, we won't go anywhere without you, we promise. Can we get going again, please?'

Tamara laughed. A real holiday – even a week or two in her home town of Gembrook – would be wonderful.

Having reached the exchange, further discussion of the proposed holiday was put off until they were in the air again, this time on a smaller domestic craft servicing the Lamington region. The flight didn't take long, so there was little time to go into further plans before they were circling the small airfield near the research station. As they descended and were within metres of landing, Possum screamed.

Meng Jarrah could hear her heart pounding as she ran. She was extremely fit, but the shock was affecting her. Ignoring it, she ran on, then stopped at the sight of Mik and Tamara's airjet. They were scrambling out as fast as they could, dropping their backpacks onto the ground in haste and running towards her, led by the two cats, now off their leashes.

Fliedermus reached her first. The cat stopped for a moment, placed her paws on Meng Jarrah's midriff, gazed into her eyes, then ran off again at full speed, towards Owain and Gwenllian. Possum didn't follow. She had decided *her* role was to guard the wights. Able to see into Meng Jarrah's mind, Possum now knew exactly what had happened. Immediately, Mik and Tamara saw it all too and cried out in horror. Mik, frightened for his cat if she was confronted by a group of suspicious peacekeepers, gave Tamara a quick, reassuring hug, then ran after Fliedermus.

'When Fliedermus last saw Gwenllian, she was still hostile and suspicious, but now her only thought is to rescue her!' exclaimed Tamara.

'We'd better go after them... There's no point staying here. Do you want to let the pilot know we're alright?' Meng Jarrah briefly grasped her by the shoulder.

'Yes, I'd better,' replied Tamara, her eyes wide. 'He almost crashed when Possum screamed. The autopilot took over, but we were terrified for a while there!'

'What? Did Possum know this was happening even before you landed?' Meng Jarrah's voice rose, incredulous.

'They both did, but Possum reacted first. We didn't know *exactly* what was going on, just that you were all in danger and that someone had died.'

Tamara turned away and ran back to where the pilot was waiting, pacing back and forth in agitation. Once he was sure they didn't need any help from him, he left to return to Brisbane, and the two women and Possum walked swiftly back to the clearing. They arrived to find one of the peacekeepers studying Fliedermus, who was sitting at his feet, quite relaxed, ears erect and a smug expression on her face. Mik stood a few metres away, shoulders hunched and hands clenched, looking totally bemused. Martha stood next to him, watching Fliedermus, while Owain and Gwenllian were still where Meng Jarrah left them. They appeared less anxious than before and were speaking with one of the other peacekeepers. The two bodies were nowhere to be seen. Presumably they were now in one of the BPF airjets. The remaining two peacekeepers were still examining the scene and gradually erecting an exclusion field.

The peacekeeper standing with Fliedermus looked up as Meng Jarrah and Tamara approached. 'This cat of yours is remarkable, isn't she,' he said.

Tamara waited apprehensively to hear whatever it was Fliedermus had done, although she needn't have worried. The peacekeeper's mouth twitched in something resembling a smile.

'She turned up at the edge of the forest and sat watching us. We thought she was just one of the research station's pets and didn't take much notice. Before long, your friend here,' and he pointed at Mik, 'turned up as well. Straight away, the cat bounded over to the other two, jumped onto the log next to them and rubbed her head against Gwenllian's. When Gwenllian put her arms around the cat, we *still* thought she was a pet, but then she came over here and showed me what happened, which was as real as if I was seeing it all for myself. I've heard of this type of thing before, but haven't experienced it until now.' He turned to Mik and added, 'How reliable do you think these images are?'

Mik rubbed a hand over his face before replying. Possum crouched by his feet, staring intently at the peacekeeper. 'Oh, completely, as far as I know. I've had these cats for a long time and as well as being our personal security guards during the past nine months, they've played a role in some of the investigations we're involved with. We don't go anywhere without them. This grey one, Possum, saved Tamara's life earlier this year.'

The peacekeeper raised an eyebrow, hesitated, then glanced at Tamara, but said nothing.

Suddenly realising the peacekeeper might not know who she was, Tamara stepped forward and held out her hand, saying, 'I'm Federation Researcher Tamara Solanum from Willsmere.'

'Thank you, I thought so,' he replied, shaking her hand. 'Now, I'd like to go over things one more time, if you don't mind. Meng Jarrah, you and Martha arrived at the same time as Gwenllian, didn't you?'

'Yes, we did. We met Gwenllian on her way here, found out what had happened, and ran on as fast as we could. Once we got here, Owain gave us his version and Gwenllian explained it all from her point of view.'

'Both men were dead when you arrived?'

'Oh yes, very dead indeed.' Meng Jarrah folded her arms and stared at the ground, then took a deep breath and met his eyes.

'And what was Owain doing?'

'He was crying, looking horribly sick, and had vomited. He told us the two men appeared at the other end of the clearing where he'd been working and were taking aim at him. Without any warning, one of them turned and shot the other one, then collapsed. Owain said that he ran over to see if the man was dead, then picked up the rifle in case he wasn't, but soon saw that he was.'

The peacekeeper nodded. This was exactly what the cat had shown him. 'What was Gwenllian's role in all this?' he asked, this time looking at Martha.

Martha realised the simple truth was the only option they had. 'I have only just been told today that Gwenllian has telepathic powers, but it appears Meng Jarrah and others have known about it since she developed them a couple of months ago. When we ran into her on the way here, she touched us, and we saw what had happened, in the same way that Fliedermus showed you. When we got here, Owain asked her if she had killed the two men. Gwenllian said that she had, though obviously didn't think there was any choice in the matter as otherwise Owain would have been shot. She was utterly distraught.' Martha put a hand to her mouth and gasped. The others assumed it was a reaction to the memory, but in fact, she had felt Possum's mind lightly touching her own.

The peacekeeper nodded again, satisfied Martha was telling the truth. Still, the brother and sister might both be required to stand trial, although he could see little point in arresting them. Based on Chiu Liow's information, this was far too complex a case for the BPF to handle alone, beyond the initial interviews and forensic examinations.

'So, this little cat saved your life, Researcher Solanum?' he went on, looking down at Possum, who steadily met his gaze. 'How did she do that?'

'In pretty much the same way that Gwenllian saved Owain,' answered Tamara, with an unusually fierce expression on her face. The peacekeeper plainly wanted to know more, so she told him how an assassin had tried to kill her, but that Possum killed him instead, using her telepathic powers. 'Possum was tried by the Judge and found to have committed justifiable manslaughter,' she concluded.

'Possum was tried?!'

'Oh yes, she was even given formal bail by the MPF before they let her go, but had to remain under house arrest until the trial. Possum was treated just like a human being.' Tamara smiled fleetingly at the memory.

'I'd like to think the case could set a precedent for the Judge to take into account if and when Gwenllian and Owain are charged,' said Mik, looking hard at the peacekeeper.

The peacekeeper frowned slightly, but said nothing further. He would read the cat's trial transcript for himself when he had time. It would no doubt make novel reading! Instead, he turned to Meng Jarrah and asked her to explain how she knew Gwenllian's telepathic powers were real, and how much control the young woman appeared to have over them.

Meng Jarrah related how she had been present when Gwenllian first discovered her strange abilities, then told him about the visit by Søren Thorup and his security guard, and the various experiments they conducted. 'I gather Søren put together a record of everything we did, including the role his peacekeeper, as we call him, played. He said it was important to keep a record because as far as he knew, no other human has ever been able to positively demonstrate having these abilities. He also saw it as important that a peacekeeper be involved in the experiments, to lend them credibility. I'm sure the record could be made available if you wanted it.'

'Yes, the record would be useful. Thank you. Has she used her powers at all since those experiments?'

'No, she seems to have been trying to forget they exist. I'm sure discovering them must be overwhelming.' Meng Jarrah looked over to where Gwenllian sat, still pale, but a little happier. She had an arm around Fliedermus and was slowly stroking her head, while the cat had her tail wrapped firmly around Owain's wrist.

The peacekeeper thanked Meng Jarrah then spoke to Martha, who had moved closer to Possum, wondering whether she imagined the cat's contact. 'We'll need to keep the exclusion field in place until the Federation Assembly decides it can come down,' he said. 'I gather from Chiu Liow Jones you already have a quarantine of your own on a fairly large area, but that it's only a notification, not a field? Pity, otherwise it wouldn't have been this easy for the two men to get in.'

'Yes, that's true,' agreed Martha, in a low voice, grateful for Meng Jarrah's hand on her shoulder.

CHAPTER TWENTY-FOUR

Rohan Maerz knew his task would be difficult, but there was little choice. At least the night was perfect for a long walk – that is, for someone able to walk without undue effort. Lately, he had become even more exhausted than usual after physical exertion, so needed to plan this trip with great care. Besides, he didn't want there to be any incriminating transport records for the Central Computer Site to detect. Aurora would stay home, despite her protests. The electronic device that enabled entry into Willsmere did not include entry requirements for a cat – and the security scanners were now programmed to require cats to identify themselves. Worst of all, during his circuitous trip she might cause a passer-by, or fellow passenger, to remember him, and this was a chance he did not wish to take; he was memorable enough as it was. His clothing was therefore simple and sombre, and he grimaced at his reflection in the mirror. The clothes simply did not look or feel right at all! When Aurora rubbed herself against his legs in sympathy, Rohan stroked her head one last time before leaving.

Unable to walk the entire way, he had plotted a transport route that would take him to a popular leisure centre, where he could rest for a while before departing on foot. Once his work at Willsmere was finished, he would return to the centre for the remainder of the evening.

The trip there took almost thirty minutes. He entered quietly and surveyed the crowd – they were all occupied with amusements of one type or another, laughing and chatting. In one particular section, couples were gliding across a small dance floor to the rhythmic strains of a twentieth-century jazz band. Rohan found himself enjoying the sight and watched for a while before moving over to one of the small bars serving alcohol and other refreshments. Finding a comfortable chair, he perused the menu and ordered a light sparkling ale, as well as a bowl of salted pistachios. When the waiter smiled at him, Rohan returned the smile. It was pleasant to relax and to be anonymous. While waiting for his order to arrive, he surreptitiously attached a tiny case containing a duplicate identity chip to the underside of the tabletop and then inactivated the chip embedded in his forearm.

Once the drink and the nuts were finished, he strolled over to where a group of younger people were playing a complex card game. The game allowed a person's place to be taken by someone else if they scored the lowest number of points in any given round. The rules were posted on a sign above the table and were, to Rohan's mind, relatively simple. He soon conceived of a system that could be used to win most of the rounds, given reasonable odds. However, having no wish to become the centre of attention just yet, Rohan resisted the temptation to sit down when the next person was obliged to leave. Instead, he applauded with the rest of the audience when a particularly good hand was played, then left to continue his journey.

He walked the remaining four kilometres, stopping now and again for a short rest. A breeze had sprung up, which was fortunate because he was feeling hot with the unaccustomed effort. After almost an hour, the sound of water lapping the banks of the Yarra River told him Willsmere was close by. Rohan stopped for one last rest before painfully moving on towards the main gate, where he activated his electronic device. The gates silently opened. He proceeded as swiftly as he could to the front door and then, to ensure no one was inside, accessed the entry log for the second time since first leaving the apartment.

The whole building had a strange, deserted air and Rohan felt like the intruder he was. He withdrew a fine hairnet and facemask from his pocket and put them on, ensuring no stray lock escaped, then left his shoes outside and exchanged them for a pair of clean cloth slippers. A pair of gloves completed the ensemble. Inside, the security lighting was dim, yet sufficient. After taking a moment to double-check his bearings, Rohan walked directly to Mik and Tamara's laboratory. The door was locked, but proved easy enough to open. It was a gamble whether they would leave a back-up copy of their work here, and if so, that it could be found within a reasonable period of time.

The laboratory contained two computers. Their work could be kept on either. He once again activated his electronic device and both machines turned on. Rohan sat down, first at one and then the other, meticulously checking for the files containing the latest version of the model taken to Lamington. Neither machine had them. Well, that was to be expected, given they were avoiding the lattice for anything other than trivial matters. No doubt they had the sense to use back-up drives instead, he thought approvingly. It also meant someone, probably Melrose, had taken the unusual step of supplying them with local versions of their software. While thoroughly searching the laboratory, Rohan idly wondered if the systems technologist had done the same for others.

He soon found what he was looking for: a single, neatly labelled drive. Humming to himself, he disconnected Tamara's computer from the lattice, activated the back-up drive, and examined its contents. To his immense satisfaction, all the files were exactly the same as the ones currently being evaluated by the Federation Assembly. Rohan knew precisely which one to change.

The next step was to amend the computer's system time and date to a setting prior to the original timestamp of the file in question, then make the necessary changes, making sure not to alter its size. Finally, a small program he had brought with him was used to save the changes at just the right moment so that without close scrutiny, the file would appear unaltered. His immediate aim was to replace the file Mik and Tamara brought back from Lamington with this new version. To this end, Rohan inserted a hidden program onto the back-up drive that would automatically activate as soon as they used it. The program would copy the altered file to their original, instead of copying the original to the back-up.

Being one of the oldest and most fundamental to their research, the file he had chosen to modify was the least likely to be updated. He certainly did not want to overwrite any of their more recent work, as overwriting material they still accessed frequently would raise immediate suspicion. On the other hand, even when someone did eventually notice something unusual, the gamble could still pay off if their suspicions led them to examine all the files closely enough to find exactly what he wanted them to find. Either way, Rohan was fairly certain the end result would be what he needed.

Naturally, there was the risk a new back-up would not be made immediately, yet Rohan believed the odds were in his favour. There was every chance Mik and Tamara would make changes to their model while they evaluated their research, based on input from Meng Jarrah, Gwenllian and Owain.

After correcting the system date and time and then erasing each computer's event logs, Rohan reconnected Tamara's computer to the lattice and shut them both down, knowing that few people ever looked at event logs. Satisfied, he returned the back-up drive to its original place, checked that nothing had been accidentally disturbed, then left, carefully locking the laboratory behind him. His luck held: no latecomers entered Willsmere as he was leaving. Once outside, he removed the hairnet, facemask, gloves and slippers, put his shoes on, and left the grounds, using his electronic device to ensure no record of his departure would be made. He walked slowly back to the leisure centre, disposed of all the protective clothing in the nearest recycling chute, retrieved the duplicate identity chip, inactivated it, and immediately reactivated his own.

Although tired from the physical exertion of the evening, the former FSIU coordinator managed to make himself memorable by winning eleven consecutive games of cards before leaving to the applause of the gathered crowd.

*

The Brisbane peacekeepers soon came to the conclusion that it was unsafe for anyone to remain at Lamington until a full quarantine field was erected over the entire test area, a far from trivial exercise requiring Federation resources. As a result, Meng Jarrah, Gwenllian and Owain packed their personal belongings and essential equipment and arranged to return to Melbourne with Mik, Tamara and the two cats. Meng Jarrah accepted Tamara's offer of a room with Mik and herself, while Gwenllian and Owain were to stay in the same communal house as Karla, where they could share Red Matilda's 'guardianship' as well as enjoy Karla's company. Mik offered Fliedermus to them, but they felt that under the circumstances, this wasn't necessary.

When Karla and Søren first heard from Tamara of the complete change in Fliedermus and Possum's attitude towards Gwenllian, Søren, for once, had absolutely nothing to say. He simply stared at Tamara's letter and mulled over the idea for some time, before finally suggesting that perhaps they now saw her as a fellow cat? Karla burst out laughing, but admitted it was entirely possible and might even explain their earlier behaviour: it seemed likely the cats had detected Gwenllian's latent abilities, yet were confused and angered by what they saw as a refusal to communicate in the manner they expected. Now that she could, at least to some extent, their attitude had changed.

On the day everyone finally arrived, Søren, his peacekeeper, Red Matilda and Karla were waiting for them at the Parkville transport exchange. As soon as she detected Gwenllian's approach, Red Matilda began pacing back and forth in excitement, head held high, sniffing the air, the tip of her tail twitching. When she saw Mik, Tamara, and the other cats, she greeted them somewhat perfunctorily, then bounded forward, nearly pushing Gwenllian over in the process. Gwenllian knelt down to put her arms around the huge cat and promptly burst into tears. Her face was thoroughly licked and before long she stopped crying. Instead, a remarkable expression crept over the young woman's face as the two gazed into each other's eyes. Occasionally Gwenllian glanced at the others, who were all watching, intrigued, but soon refocused on communicating with the cat. Eventually, she stood up, turned to her brother, took him by the shoulders, and spoke very quickly, her face a picture of joy:

'Red Matilda says I'm like a very young grimalkin...which is what they call themselves...and if I go to the Breeding Centre to meet the nursing mothers, they can teach me to use my mind in the same way they do! Even though I'm a wight...which is what they call us...it won't be a problem – she's certain all the cats there will recognise me as one of their own kind. Owain, we'll be safe now! She says no one will be able to get close enough to harm us – I'll soon be able do everything *they* can, and one day, might even be more powerful!'

After a relatively short period of deliberation, the Federation Assembly confirmed Chiu Liow to be the most appropriate person to continue the existing investigation on their behalf, although he was now obliged to report everything to a panel of senior FSIU personnel and forensics experts, appointed by the Assembly, with the assistance of the new interim FSIU Coordinator. Since they could not make progress without access to rapid global communications, they were using the overlay lattice and, for security reasons, avoiding the public network. Accordingly, Chiu Liow told them about the silver brooch and earring; the items found which suggested a possible link between Wyvern Meridian and the crimes in Papua and Myanmar. The panel also had the latest results from the inquiry into the duplicate applications for access to Tumucumaque, made by Epsilon and its competitor.

The peacekeeper now surveyed the group of people he had gathered together for the purpose of reviewing the situation and bringing everyone up to date. Research Coordinator Zago had travelled from Brazil to be there, while Welcome, Søren, Karla, Mik, Tamara, Freddi, Meng Jarrah, Owain, Gwenllian, Martha, Eduardo Arreza, Sirinya, Erminio and Lance Melrose Naylor were also present, as were Red Matilda, Possum, Fliedermus and Shela. Yuen Fong Lau had been invited to attend, but despite his interest in the case, could not be present.

All Mik's cats were clustered around Gwenllian, almost protectively. Possum was literally sleeping on her feet, while Red Matilda was partially sitting on her lap, huge paws flexing and kneading her thighs. Fliedermus occupied a chair close by and sat fully upright, with paws and tail neatly tucked in, and with all the appearance of listening to everything being said.

Those who had previously met Gwenllian were still becoming accustomed to the startling change of eye colour. The bright green lenses were gone, revealing her natural colour of light hazel. Her old air of slightly aggressive tension had also disappeared; she appeared composed and at ease. In turn, Owain was also looking a great deal better than when they last saw him.

After introductions and a preamble from Chiu Liow, Zago handed each person a small storage module, then explained what they were for: 'These contain the full details of the Tumucumaque inquiry and can be read later. For the time being, I will give a brief summary of the events leading up to the investigation and then its outcome. You have all been introduced to Erminio,' and she nodded to him, 'and know it is due to his quick action that we, and now the Federation Assembly, have circumstantial evidence that Wyvern Meridian attempted to steal the research Epsilon was conducting into a new pharmaceutical with the potential to be both extremely effective and, for Epsilon, highly profitable.

'For several years I have kept a close eye on applications for entry into rainforests for research purposes, and recently noticed two highly similar applications had been made to the Federation for plant material from Tumucumaque. The first was by Epsilon, and the other, fifteen months later, by Wyvern Meridian. As most of us would know, duplicate applications are not usually granted, which indicated that one of them was in all likelihood false. When I studied the required plants more closely, I concluded the likely research objective was a new antifungal medication.

'In light of the damage done to them by the Claviceps incident, it seemed doubtful that Epsilon had falsified their application. This meant either Wyvern Meridian was the culprit, or someone else was attempting to implicate them. Taking into account the recent series of crimes committed throughout the world against private companies and government research centres dealing in forest products, as well as the nature of these crimes, it was apparent to me that this incident could be yet another one.

'As a result, I met with the Brazilian Attorney General in person. He agreed to look into the matter as a priority and to use the parliamentary lattice for communications. Not long afterwards, Epsilon themselves discovered that all their research results, including back-ups, had been tampered with in such a way as to alter their findings. In short, the composition of the medication had been altered in a small but significant manner, which resulted in its having too many serious side effects to warrant production. Also, even if these side effects could be overcome, it appeared the medication would not be cost-effective to produce.

'An urgent lattice meeting of all Epsilon researchers and directors was arranged, which, while unavoidable, was unfortunate, since use of the network may have given warning to those responsible for the alterations.' Zago paused to clear her throat. 'During the meeting,' she continued, 'it was discovered that no intact records of their original research remained: *everything* had been changed. Can you conceive of how much time and effort, as well as ingenuity, it would have taken to do this?'

Everyone remained silent. Many shook their heads in disgust.

'It is to Epsilon's credit that they immediately contacted the office of the Attorney General. Consequently, a meeting – a very lengthy meeting

– was arranged. Over the next four days, we examined every detail of their work, attempting to retrieve from memory and from hand reader entries, anything that could be salvaged. All aspects of the research could not, of course, be re-created. This can only be achieved by obtaining fresh plant samples and beginning again – which, hopefully, will be possible within the not too distant future.' She smiled briefly at Erminio, who returned the smile, then concentrated on listening to Zago's next words. He was conscious of the responsibility he had towards his company, who had given him the honour of representing them. It was important he report back to the directors as accurately as possible.

'At the same time as we were piecing together all this information,' said Zago, 'the Assembly traced and froze all the Wyvern Meridian information stores that could be located, then searched them for any traces of similar research, or research applications. The problem was that any number of stores could be held anywhere and never be found. At first, nothing at all was discovered, but during the search, each board member was interviewed, including Kenjiro Kakura, the director. It turned out that one of them had died recently, quite suddenly, and not long after Epsilon's lattice meeting.

'The death was recorded as natural, from heart failure, and the body cremated soon afterwards, which meant no autopsy was possible. However, prior to his becoming an employee of the company, and later a board member, this particular person gained extensive qualifications and experience in the development of lattice systems, as well as their associated security methods. The Assembly now had sufficient cause to search his home and to interview his bondmate and son. Nothing was found in his home, but his son lived elsewhere, and when *his* house was searched, they found a copy of the research results, similar to the altered version Erminio discovered. However, the altered file did not have the same timestamp as the one in Epsilon's database. It was a few weeks older, and also had some small differences, such as less convincing costing scenarios.'

Zago straightened her back and smiled grimly at her audience, some of whom nodded in satisfaction, although no one attempted to interrupt. 'Apparently the son, who specialises in biochemistry, is not, and never has been, an employee of Wyvern Meridian. Our educated guess is that he collaborated with his father without the permission of Kenjiro Kakura. His father may have wanted an independent opinion of at least some of the files he was about to substitute and thought his son was well qualified to provide it. When the son was interviewed, he denied all knowledge of his father being associated with an elaborate deception. He seemed to be honestly under the impression he was providing a review of a genuine scientific endeavour that was, unfortunately, flawed. The son may have thought he was giving his father excellent advice and kept the report out of pure interest...fortunately for us. I will let Freddi tell you what happened next.'

They all watched as Freddi walked over to a large display screen, brought up an interview record, then stepped back, ready to watch with the others.

'The Assembly contacted me,' she said, 'requesting that I conduct this interview with Kenjiro Kakura since I'd already had a fair degree of involvement with the case and had interviewed him before. Apparently no other peacekeeper, FSIU investigator, or Assembly member has ever met him in person... Astounding, really... However, the Assembly located Kakura in Paris, France, where he was negotiating the purchase of a highly sophisticated manufacturing complex, used primarily for the production of a relatively narrow range of the more profitable pharmaceuticals currently in high demand.'

Delighted that Freddi was here in Australia for the time being, Meng Jarrah couldn't help being slightly distracted as she admired her calm, competent manner and impressive self-assurance. Nevertheless, she soon turned her attention to the display panel as the interview commenced:

The requisite Witnesses were present at the Reconciliation Centre where Kakura was taken, so gave their names and status once Freddi had introduced herself and Kenjiro Kakura formally confirmed his identity. Meanwhile, Shela crouched in a corner, as far away from Kakura as possible, ears laid well back and tail lashing angrily from side to side. Neither of the Witnesses cast her even a glance, concentrating instead on what was being said.

The room was sparsely but well furnished. Chilled and boiling water dispensers were located discreetly above a small, elegantly functional bench containing a dark blue ceramic sink, a highly polished chrome tap, a coffee servery, and a small thermolyte underneath. A range of teas and sugars, an attractive bowl of fruit, as well as jars of savoury and sweet biscuits, stood neatly on the bench top. Also paying no attention to Shela, Freddi occupied herself taking a number of pretty floral cups, saucers and plates from the cupboard above the bench. Whistling softly, she artistically arranged a selection of biscuits on the larger of the plates, then placed them on the table around which the Witnesses and Kakura were seated. Next, the bowl of fruit was positioned at the centre with a view to its visual effect, after which she brought fresh coffee, a pot of tea, a jug of milk and a bowl of sugar over to her 'guests'. Finally, the cups, saucers, teaspoons and plates were added and Freddi stood back to admire the entire, pleasing arrangement.

Meng Jarrah held a hand over her mouth to hide a quick chuckle of amusement as she watched this play-acting. A few smiles were to be found on other faces around the room, too. Naturally, Chiu Liow and

Welcome had done as much reading as possible about Kakura and had also seen some of the footage taken in public places, although very little existed. However, never having met him, neither they nor anyone else in the room knew what to expect and so were fascinated when they saw that while waiting for Freddi to finish her artistic presentation, he lost none of his poise whatsoever, simply watching her, with the merest hint of a smile on his face.

While Freddi solemnly served the tea, coffee and other refreshments, the silence continued. When she had finished her second cup of green tea and a rather delicious-looking banana, she wiped her hands on a serviette and opened a red folder lying on the table near Kakura.

Selecting three sheaves of paper, Freddi placed them side by side in front of him and said, 'Please read at least the first few pages of each of these reports. Afterwards, I want you to tell me if you have ever seen or heard of either the research they refer to, the organisation named, or the source of the research material.'

He picked up the first sheaf without comment and began reading. After some time, he picked up the second, read it, and then the third. Looking up, Kakura crossed one leg over the other, carefully adjusted the crease in his elegant trouser leg and spoke for only the second time since the interview began.

'I am, of course, familiar with the company named in these reports... Epsilon... They are one of our competitors in the pharmaceutics industry. I have also heard of Tumucumaque. It is famous for its beauty, its diverse ecosystem and its range of plants, many of which are used for a wide variety of purposes. As to the content of the reports, I find them puzzling. One version is almost the same as the other, and both indicate an Epsilon project has failed, while the third predicts quite startling success. I am at a loss as to why you have shown them to me.' As Kakura politely inclined his head, Shela growled from her place in the corner of the room, but no one appeared to notice, least of all Kakura.

Freddi settled back in her chair and studied him before replying: 'We found one of these versions on a computer belonging to the son of a former Wyvern Meridian board member, recently deceased. Another of the versions was discovered by Epsilon in their system. Would you care to guess which one?'

Kakura shrugged his shoulders. 'I have no idea, but I fail to understand how three different versions could exist, and how one of them ended up on the computer you refer to. Perhaps you will enlighten me?'

Freddi smiled, but said nothing.

'Well, perhaps not,' continued Kakura, also smiling. 'Is there anything else you would like to speak with me about?'

'Yes,' said Freddi. 'When was the last time you saw your recently deceased board member before he died?'

'Ah, the classic question. His death was from natural causes, or so I was informed. I saw him at a meeting the night before. He did appear somewhat uneasy, but otherwise, his usual self.'

'Did he eat or drink anything?'

'Yes, we usually partake of a small something before we end our meetings. I passed around a good malt whisky and he joined us in drinking a glass.'

'Why do you think he might have been uneasy, as you put it?'

'I didn't inquire. I don't usually pry into the private concerns of either my employees or associates.' Kakura raised an eyebrow and looked straight at Freddi, who suddenly received a disturbing image from Shela, but managed to control her expression.

'I understand your bondmate, Michiko Yamada, is a gifted designer, specialising in silverware and jewellery,' said Freddi, with a pleasant smile. 'She has a particular interest in using the wyvern, which isn't difficult to understand, given the name of your company. The finished items are created by a mining and manufacturing company in Patagonia that produces silver of exceptional quality. It's also a company noted for keeping meticulous records of who buys their pieces, with each piece bearing the initials of the designer, together with a serial number.'

Kakura nodded, as if agreeing.

'Do you happen to know how many pieces of jewellery have been sold, based on your bondmate's designs *and* which depict some form of wyvern?'

Kakura shook his head and folded his hands loosely in his lap, to all appearances uninterested in the answer to Freddi's rhetorical question.

'The company has records for sales of only four hundred and twenty-three, presumably because they are expensive. They have the names of everyone who has purchased a piece. Out of interest, we checked these names against the Federation database, to find three hundred and twelve were purchased by employees of your company. Another fourteen were purchased by people for whom no Federation record exists. We contacted the remaining ninety-seven fortunate owners of this unique jewellery – all of whom appear to be highly respectable citizens – and found that they each still have it in their possession.' Freddi paused. 'You must compliment Michiko for me... Her work is exquisite. I would like to show you two of my favourite pieces.'

Kakura started for the first time, but immediately recovered and said, 'Please do. I always enjoy seeing her creations. As you say, they are very beautiful.'

Freddi placed the brooch found in Papua and the earring found in Myanmar, both in their protective coverings, on the table. Kakura examined each closely, although without touching them.

'What do you think the odds are that two such unusual and expensive items would turn up at two of the sites where a certain series of crimes we're investigating were committed? And what do you think the odds are if I told you that both of them belonged to purchasers for whom no Federation records exist?'

'Clearly, low,' he replied, and once again Freddi received an image from Shela, who was busily pacing back and forth in her corner, all the while staring at Kakura. It required all Freddi's self-control this time not to react and to continue her questioning.

'Does it concern you that a piece of jewellery designed by your bondmate, and which symbolises your company, was found at these sites, one of which was that of a particularly gruesome murder?'

Kakura stood up. Raising her hackles, Shela snarled and took a few steps towards him, then sat down again, glowering at him, her eyes a pair of golden slits. He took no notice whatsoever.

'Of course what you say concerns me. I am horrified to think my bondmate's work belonged to anyone associated with a crime, particularly a murder. If there is anything we can do to help find the culprits, be very sure that we will.'

He placed both hands on the table and leaned towards Freddi, speaking in even, controlled tones. 'Do you think I don't know how it looks? To anyone who studies the stock market, it's easy to see that although we are, as a whole, trading well, we are also making significant losses in our Southeast Asian subsidiaries. As I am sure you know, we have tried to better our position by purchasing an interest in companies able to help us, with priority being given to land and forest restoration. Also, we are still awaiting an independent Federation evaluation of our Australian leasehold application, which is critical to our future plans and the main reason we wish to further improve our research methods and models. However, I am fully aware we are in direct competition with the Federation for many of the products we sell, or wish to sell, and that our approach to land regeneration is very different to, although substantially compatible with, the Federation approach. I am also aware that this past year has seen a significant number of private companies whose main income is from some form of forest industry either suffer market setbacks or become part of the Wyvern Meridian conglomerate.' Kakura paused, drew breath, and sat down. Meanwhile, Freddi continued to gaze calmly at him, saying nothing, despite Shela's agitation and her own inner turmoil.

'Our company is quite possibly the most successful private enterprise in the world,' continued Kakura, his face now flushed. 'It takes little imagination to see that this may not be palatable to some elements within the Federation, or even to some of our main competitors within the private sphere. We provide an example to the world of just how valuable individual initiative is, and how much the private sector can contribute if given sufficient freedom. There are many who would prefer *all* goods and services to be completely controlled by the Federation. *That* is a recipe for total disaster, and I personally am not prepared to see it happen – which is why *I* choose to compete rather than simply produce luxury goods, as most private concerns do.'

Freddi waited to hear if he had anything further to say, but Kakura remained silent and turned towards the window to focus on regaining the habitual control he had ever so slightly lost.

Freddi stopped the recording and surveyed her audience. 'He couldn't be drawn any further, although I tried for almost another forty minutes. It's remarkable how plausible he is. If Shela hadn't been there, I might well have believed him, but let me ask her to show you what she showed me,' and the peacekeeper concentrated on silently communicating with her companion.

Shela uncurled herself from the spot where she had been lightly dozing and sat up. Everyone in the room simultaneously saw first one scene and then a second. The first showed the extraordinary luxury of the Wyvern Meridian boardroom, the anger on Kenjiro Kakura's face as he forced the members seated around the table to join him in a ceremonial glass of whisky – and the expression of fear on the face of the one particular member who died so very suddenly the next day.

No one uttered a sound, appalled at virtually witnessing this cold-blooded murder. They then saw another scene, where two men with shaved heads, naked torsos, and arms bound tightly behind their backs, were kneeling before Kakura in a darkened room lit only by candlelight. Their heads were bowed, so their faces could not be seen, yet it was clear they were soon to die, for Kakura was dressed in the armour of a Kendo warrior and the sword in his hands was real and terrifyingly sharp.

'Did their bodies turn up anywhere?' asked Tamara in a low voice, breaking the stunned silence.

'No, and there was nothing we could have done to save them,' answered Freddi. 'We've kept Kakura under surveillance for a long time, but we can't follow him everywhere and we can't account for every person he deals with. His movements are rapid and extensive. All over the world, his contacts reach everywhere. It's obvious he has a network of assassins and saboteurs in his employ, and is adept at finding ways and means of corrupting others if he needs to. The problem is, we can't prove any of it. We did confirm, though, that he is a master of kendo.'

'Luckily for us, the Judge already has them in its sights,' remarked Welcome. 'I can but hope this additional evidence will add to its view that they *could* be guilty of having engineered all the various crimes that've been plaguing us.' He looked at the ceiling and sighed mightily, then put into words what they were all thinking: 'I must admit to being glad Shela didn't see those two actually lose their heads. I don't think I could have coped.'

CHAPTER TWENTY-FIVE

When the group adjourned for a short while to recover from the distress of the scenes Shela had shown them, Søren typically busied himself in obtaining the refreshments he insisted they all needed, then served the food and drink in the most comfortable private area available. Discussion of the morning's revelations was then studiously avoided until they were back in the conference room.

'Based on what we've heard today and now seen, I don't think Wyvern Meridian *is* behind all the crimes,' said Chiu Liow. 'Two don't fit in. The incidents involving Morag in Papua have a different feel about them, as does the *Claviceps atropurpurea* affair. Both situations were almost laughable, and in the end, didn't cause any real harm. In contrast, nearly all the other crimes were either murders, attempted murders, or had fairly strong elements of violence about them.'

Welcome scratched the tip of his right ear and pursed his mouth. 'Almost from the beginning,' he said, 'we've thought that Rohan Maerz might be involved. To my way of thinking, having met him several times and discussed his personality many, many times with Morag MacIain, those particular crimes you mention bear his stamp. He has a well-developed sense of the ridiculous, a cutting sense of humour, and as the Judge found at Morag's trial, is capable of having committed them. The question is, why? And then we must ask, what about the others? You see, I have the intuitive feeling Rohan Maerz doesn't approve of outright violence.'

Both Mik and Søren agreed, as did Freddi and Karla, who had already reached the same conclusion. Mik then told the gathering about the dinner party Rohan invited them to attend, as well as the time the former FSIU coordinator paid him a visit. 'I'm quite sure Rohan is a very lonely man,' he concluded. 'Now, the most remarkable thing is that all the cats like him, and during the visit, Fliedermus showed me an image of what appears to be a recurrent dream of his.' Mik silently asked the cat to show everyone what she had seen.

Tears ran down Tamara's cheeks as she felt the intensity of the longing Maerz himself experienced during the dreams. Others put their hands to their eyes, bowing their heads. Welcome, although used to sharing people's innermost secrets, felt the pain of this revelation as much as any.

'This wasn't the only scene she showed us,' said Mik. 'The cats had some incredibly tense moments during the dinner party and refused to explain why until we were home, when I insisted Fliedermus tell me what really happened. If you agree, Chiu Liow, I'll ask her to share the information with everyone?'

'Yes,' replied the peacekeeper, 'but before you do, let me clarify something. I think some of the people here will need to be prepared.'

Some of those who had not already been shown the murder of Mervyn Bradshaw, and therefore did not know what to expect, stared at the cat apprehensively. 'Not everyone here would be aware,' said Chiu Liow, 'that one of the murders – that of Marika, who worked at Melbourne's Central Computer Site as a talented information technologist – was committed by someone she knew well: a man by the name of Mervyn Bradshaw. Mervyn Bradshaw was never brought to trial because he himself was murdered not long afterwards.

'At the time of his death, Rohan Maerz was the one who first determined Bradshaw was in fact Marika's killer, and then almost immediately located him, making a strange comment that left me wondering, yet with nothing to really go on. He said it was likely Bradshaw wouldn't live very long and that the Judge was not the only "arbiter of justice". Sure enough, Bradshaw was dead when our peacekeepers found him. He'd been sent a gift containing cyanide, and died almost as soon as he opened it. The scene Fliedermus is about to show you is of his death, and it was this scene, together with an intense feeling of satisfaction at having caused it, that she found in Maerz's mind the night of the dinner party.'

Gwenllian put a hand to her mouth and shook her head in dismay, while Lance Melrose Naylor's eyes were wide with surprise. He still grieved deeply for Marika and knew who had murdered her – as did a number of the others present – but to actually see the killer die? He raised his head as if to speak, but changed his mind and remained silent. Eduardo Arreza, Sirinya and Erminio were not previously aware of who Marika was, or what her involvement had been in the sabotage of Willsmere, so looked confused.

'Why was Marika murdered?' asked Sirinya.

'We may never be sure, but we think she was the one who engineered the Willsmere security breach, and may even have been involved in the attack on Lamington,' replied Chiu Liow. 'However, we believe that once her task had been completed, whoever bribed or convinced her to do it decided she was now a liability. One of the other information technologists, Thanh Fong Lau, was murdered too, and we still don't know if he was involved as well, or simply removed to use up our time –

or for that matter, as a piece of gratuitous intimidation. Welcome, you have yet another theory, don't you?'

Before replying, Welcome tilted his head to one side and clasped his hands on his somewhat ample stomach, gathering his thoughts for a moment. 'Yes, I do,' he said slowly. 'Based on what we now know about Wyvern Meridian, it's reasonable to assume that they didn't want him around in case he chose to turn sleuth himself. I gather Thanh was ambitious, exceptionally skilled, and well on the way to becoming Victoria's foremost expert in developing and maintaining the type of security systems commonly used to protect buildings. Wouldn't you agree, Melrose?'

'Yes,' replied Melrose, 'I would.'

'Now, it's always bothered me,' continued Welcome, 'that they wiped Karla's computer at the Willsmere laboratory and not any of the others, and even that they took the trouble to wipe hers at all. They stole material from her and Søren's laboratory, yet not from Mik and Tamara's, even though they had ample time. Also, they could easily have harmed you, Mik, far more than they did...even killed you...and could have killed Fliedermus as well, given how easily they appear to have caught her. Therefore, it seems to me they either found what they wanted relatively quickly, or wanted it to look that way. Do you catch my drift?'

Melrose was the first to react. 'Do you mean something might have been done to one of the other computers which they didn't want us to find?'

'Exactly,' said Welcome. 'The question is, what? It's something Thanh may well have begun thinking about. I can easily imagine someone as dedicated to his work as that unfortunate young man would have wanted to do a little investigating of his own, particularly since his integrity was at stake, as well as his professional relationship with Gwenllian and Marika, which he apparently valued.'

The four Willsmere researchers stared at him, all turning over in their minds what had been on their computers at the time, and how they could check if anything had actually been done to hinder their work. Their frantic thoughts were interrupted by Chiu Liow, bringing them back to the death of Mervyn Bradshaw.

'I think we should follow up on that issue without delay,' he said, 'but in the meantime, if there are no other questions, we had better ask Fliedermus to show you what she saw and felt.'

Sirinya gasped in horror as she experienced being virtually present at Bradshaw's death, while Melrose wept, not because of the death, but because of the freshly opened wound. He still found it almost impossible to accept that Marika could have been guilty of any involvement in the events at Willsmere or Lamington; yet even if it were true, her death was hardly justified. To his surprise, he found himself sympathising with Rohan Maerz, although logically, he could not condone what had been done.

Welcome, of course, already knew what had happened, but it was a different matter to experience it directly, and even he was shaken. 'Bradshaw was a wealthy and powerful man,' he said, after taking a kerchief from his pocket to blow his nose, 'although certainly not a scrupulous one. Still, it's remarkable that he'd kill Marika. For quite some time, they appear to have been, if not friends, then at least colleagues, in the world of theatre.'

He put his kerchief away, cleared his throat, and continued by saying, 'On the other hand, Bradshaw may have simply used her for his own ends – it's certainly a possibility. He was a major shareholder in Teak Australia, so in my opinion, it's not unlikely he was Wyvern Meridian's contact point in Australia. Given the complexity and scale of their undertakings, the whole scheme may well have been brewing for quite some time. Bradshaw may even have become Marika's artistic sponsor with the goal of one day co-opting her.

'Now, he didn't return any of her calls during the weeks before she died – I find that illuminating – then calmly killed her with a particularly classy weapon. So, the chances are, he even enjoyed it! Personally, I think Bradshaw was the one who killed Thanh as well. It would make sense, because he would have known about him from his conversations with Marika and probably realised that Thanh was the one most likely to work out what the real purpose was behind the attack on Willsmere. Thanh's murder was also elegant, if you'll pardon me for putting it that way, and in this sense fits in with my picture of Mervyn Bradshaw.' Welcome stroked his chin in thought, waiting for his stunned audience to comment.

'What you say seems to imply Rohan Maerz knew beforehand that Bradshaw was to be the killer and planned to execute him once he'd completed his task,' said Freddi, frowning. 'It also means Maerz was either working *with* Wyvern Meridian, or that he was unable to prevent the murders, but was intent on avenging them. I don't think the speed at which he acted after Marika died would allow for any other possibility. But why couldn't he have warned them?'

Both Chiu Liow and Welcome shook their heads. 'I doubt it would have made any difference if he had. Marika was under full surveillance when she was killed. If he'd warned *us*, it might have been a different matter, but at the time, Maerz may have thought we could protect them and simply didn't want to show his hand. I don't know...' Frowning, Chiu Liow shook his head in frustration.

'If we assume Maerz was telling the truth when he informed you that Bradshaw was the killer,' said Søren, standing up as he spoke, 'it means you could be right, Freddi, when you say he murdered him to avenge Marika's, and possibly even Thanh's, death. It would make sense, then, why the cats like him. What *they* see is someone whose concept of justice is outraged, whose sense of responsibility, even, is so great that he takes it into his own hands to commit murder rather than risk Bradshaw going free. *We* may not see this as morally correct, but perhaps *they* do?'

He went over to Fliedermus and looked into her eyes, gently holding her face in his hands. 'Is that what happened, my little friend?' Fliedermus gazed back at him, but 'said' nothing. 'You don't want to tell me, do you? Perhaps you *cannot*... You may *sense* the truth, but not know for sure, or even how to tell me what you sense.'

Gwenllian took a deep breath and made a decision. 'What if *I* met this Rohan Maerz?' Owain put his hand on hers, but didn't try to prevent her from making the offer. If she was prepared to do this, then *he* would be there with her.

'Have you already learnt so much from the nursing mothers at the Breeding Centre that you are able to take such a risk?' asked Søren dubiously.

'Yes,' answered Gwenllian, 'I think I have. When I'm with them, we form a natural connection. There isn't the strain as there is with people. Our thoughts and memories seem to flow together, even though they don't think quite like us and we don't think like them. We have rather different views on life too, but that's to be expected. I'm gradually gaining control as I learn to accept this ability. For example, I don't send anyone to sleep any longer when I touch them, and if I want to, I can avoid having an aura appear.' She smiled, a little hesitantly.

A number of her listeners had opened their mouths in wonder, staring at her as if she had suddenly become some form of bizarre chameleon. However, for the time being, they thought it best not to interrupt with questions; the cats' abilities had opened their minds to many strange things.

'We need to know if Rohan Maerz is working with Wyvern Meridian or not. It's just so important and I can't think of any other way of finding out, can you?' Gwenllian looked around the circle. Most of them shook their heads.

'Gwen, is there any chance he might know you have these powers?' asked Karla.

'He *might* know, if he's still able to tap into the lattice, but I doubt he'd know exactly how far I can go. He could even be curious to see what would happen if we met. Anyway, if we engineer a meeting, I don't think he'd refuse to shake hands. In most circumstances, I still need the physical contact in order to see what's going on in someone's head. The situation at Lamington was different; Owain was in danger – I haven't trained with the cats long enough to know what's happening at a distance, unless it's something fairly extreme.' Gwenllian hesitated and looked down for a moment, then in a tense voice said, 'If we do this and I see what his motives were, can it be used in evidence at a trial?'

'I think so,' answered Søren. 'I've sent a comprehensive description of our experiments at Lamington to the Brisbane Peacekeeping Force, as well as the account Meng Jarrah gave me of her experience when you first discovered your powers. The BPF also have firsthand evidence of what you can do, my dear.' He inclined his head in acknowledgement when Gwenllian winced. 'I think all this should give you *some* standing. Also, the research done in conjunction with the Breeding Centre can easily be verified, and if necessary, you could demonstrate your abilities to a Witness. Oh, and for those of you who do not yet know, our Gwenllian of the brown eyes,' and he smiled mischievously at her, 'thinks like a cat. At least, she seems to have developed their extraordinary ability to see into people's minds...and even to affect them. So, we must all hope she remains on our side!'

Gwenllian relaxed slightly and gave a small laugh. She fully understood just how uncanny her situation was, as well as the potential for harm the powers gave her. The young woman also knew that, like the cats, she was incapable of using them to hurt others. 'Yes, it's true,' she said quietly, looking directly at those who were not already acquainted with her situation. 'I have no idea how or why this happened, but it was sudden, and not very long ago.'

Zago studied her curiously, pleased to find life still had surprises like this in store. Erminio, Sirinya, Eduardo and Melrose also regarded her curiously, but compared with the surprises and upsets they had already received, both today and during the past year, this revelation, at least, was nowhere near as alarming.

Chiu Liow made a quick decision. 'I believe we should accept your offer. I can't see any other way of sorting this out, and we must. We could discuss arrangements after we finish our conference. What do you think?'

Gwenllian agreed, satisfied she could at last make a real contribution to the investigation. It would help her come to terms with the loss of Thanh and Marika, as well as being responsible for the deaths of two people.

Mulling over what he had said a little earlier, Welcome arrived at another startling conclusion. 'Do you know,' he said eagerly, 'I think Rohan may have fiddled with the Papuan lattice in order to have Morag placed under house arrest. It's the only sensible explanation I can come up with – if indeed he *is* an avenger, and not an accomplice.' He beamed at everyone, waiting for their reaction.

Chiu Liow raised an eyebrow and slowly said, 'I thought that was obvious... I don't see what you mean. He *wanted* her out of the investigation. We realised that was the most likely explanation.'

'Yes,' and Welcome beamed again, 'but what if he did it because he wanted her out of harm's way?'

'You mean that Rohan cares for her a great deal, don't you?' suggested Mik, his expression thoughtful. He was remembering the dream Fliedermus showed him and how well it fitted with Rohan being in love with Morag, who was, he imagined, unobtainable.

'Yes, I think he does.' Welcome's homely face was creased in a sympathetic frown. 'Poor man,' he added, also thinking of the dream. 'Morag brought the case to a point where taking it any further might have put her into extreme danger. Rohan could have thought that having a little fun with the Papuan lattice would be safe enough; at first it would appear to be yet another series in the same set of crimes. At the time, no one had any reason to think it was him, or at any rate, couldn't have proved it.'

'Poor man indeed, if that's the case,' agreed Freddi, 'but he might still be an accomplice. Given Kakura's commanding personality and immense power, I can't see Maerz as the prime mover, but what if he's worked undercover for years, helping Kakura build his empire?'

'It's possible,' said Chiu Liow, brushing a stray lock of hair from his forehead. 'A company like Wyvern Meridian is an anomaly. Helping Kakura may have appealed to Maerz as an intellectual challenge. His own power is immense as well, or *was* until recently. He also has a taste for the grandiose, so I can imagine he and Kakura would have found each other fascinating. It could even have been a refreshing change for them to work together, particularly if there are few people either of them would see as complete equals.'

Shaking his head, Søren disagreed. 'For me, this does not fit well with the cats being fond of him. What if not only Gwenllian meets him, but she takes Freddi and Shela with her? Freddi has official standing in the case, while Shela has met Kakura. We know how badly she reacts to him, so Freddi, if your cat behaves well with Maerz, it may be evidence that he hasn't in fact been working together with this elegant devil.'

'Good idea, Søren. Also, if things don't go to plan, Shela and I can provide some protection for Gwenllian. I don't know how dangerous Maerz can be on a personal level, but it's better not to take any risks.' Freddi noticed that Gwenllian's already pale face became even paler. She appeared not to have considered this possibility when she made her offer.

'Very well,' announced Chiu Liow, 'Freddi and Shela will go with Gwenllian.'

'And so will I,' said Owain. 'You can be sure of that!'

Tamara was following the discussion closely, as were they all, but had also been thinking about her research. She had never fully accepted their Willsmere model could be compatible with the one proposed by Wyvern Meridian for the reforestation of the Australian leasehold, yet had been unable to find faults in either to explain what appeared to be a total contradiction. Now that everyone seemed to be in agreement that Freddi, Shela and Gwenllian attempt to resolve the questions they had about Rohan Maerz, she decided to change the subject back to their computers at Willsmere.

'I'd really like to send more of our simulations to the Federation Assembly for comparison with Wyvern Meridian's,' she said. 'We've made some significant improvements to our model since Meng Jarrah obtained her soil analysis results and brought back the critical microbes for use in our Lamington trials. Also, Gwenllian and Owain have helped Mik and I modify our approach in some small but extremely useful ways, although we still need to make a few more adjustments. We haven't had a lot of time lately because of everything that's happened, but I hope it'll only be a few more weeks before we'll be ready to send our new version to the Assembly. So, Melrose, before we use either Mik's computer or mine again, could we ask you to take a good look at them? We don't want to risk there being something on them that shouldn't be.'

'Yes, and mine too, please!' said Søren.

'Sure,' answered Melrose, glad to be in a position to help. 'What about tomorrow morning, at around 11:00? It could take a while... Are you able to work somewhere else in the meantime?'

'Yes, that won't be a problem. You can take as long as you like,' replied Tamara, with a smile of thanks.

'Will you let me know when you have the results?' asked Chiu Liow, keenly interested in what might possibly be new and critical evidence.

'Of course,' said Tamara. 'We'll call you as soon as Melrose finishes.'

As evening was fast approaching, everyone was beginning to feel hungry, so agreed to adjourn for a meal at the nearest restaurant. Once the meal was over and the others had gone their respective ways, Søren, Freddi, Gwenllian and Owain stayed behind to debate the various options they had for arranging a meeting with Rohan Maerz. By the time they parted, the wind, which had sprung up half an hour since, brought the tang of salt air in from the sea.

Shela sniffed the breeze, her eyes glowing in the starlight. She was pleased her Wight had met Meng Jarrah again, and happy they were to sleep at the house of the three grimalkins. Karla was staying overnight as well to have a chance to talk to Meng Jarrah and to get to know Freddi a little better. This meant Shela could spend more time with all three of her new playmates! She had particularly enjoyed meeting Red Matilda, quickly detecting her mischievous streak and her willingness to mock fight, something which Shela thoroughly enjoyed too, although she rarely had the chance to do so with another grimalkin.

Although she had yet to see the house for herself, Shela decided to send Freddi a clear image of them both lying snugly in bed with Meng Jarrah, in one of the guest rooms Mik and Tamara had prepared for them. Freddi immediately realised the cats had been 'talking' amongst themselves, and, with a surprised smile and a shake of her head, called Meng Jarrah.

'Hello,' said Freddi, when she answered. 'Sorry we're so late. Has everyone gone to bed?'

'That's okay, I was still reading, and yes, they went to bed about twenty minutes ago. How did your planning session go?'

'I think we have something that should work. I'll tell you about it when I see you.'

'Oh, I think it can wait until morning.' Meng Jarrah grinned and added, 'I'd rather we forgot about everyone else for a while... The shower here is easily big enough for two. I was waiting to have mine until you got here.'

Freddi was silent for a moment. 'Are you sure?'

'Yes, I'm sure. Don't be long.'

'I won't. See you in about fifteen minutes.'

That night, they slept together for the first time. Even though Freddi and Meng Jarrah had become so close to each other in Myanmar, at the time, neither felt ready to make the full commitment they knew the other deserved. This time, there was no holding back.

CHAPTER TWENTY-SIX

The air felt cold and crisp against his face as Lance Melrose Naylor, in his sturdy boots, crunched his way along the gravel path leading to Willsmere's entrance. The temperature was an unseasonable five degrees Celsius, and even at this late hour of the morning, a light fog lay on the ground in curling wisps, evidence of the heavy blanket previously covering the entire city during the night and long into the day. He glanced at his comlink and was relieved to see he was only a few minutes late. Melrose had been delayed due to various annoying oversights on the part of Thanh Fong Lau's replacement, who, although highly competent, had a far less systematic approach to his work than Melrose found acceptable. Shrugging his shoulders inside his thick jacket, as if to dismiss the morning's woes, he waited while the massive doors opened then found his way to Mik and Tamara's laboratory. They were both there, hard at work, but looked up as he knocked politely and entered.

'Sorry, I'm late,' said Melrose, taking off his jacket and hanging it neatly on the coat stand, a precious bentwood antiquity from the early days of Willsmere's former architectural glory.

'Would you like a coffee or tea...or something else?' asked Tamara. 'You look half frozen.'

'Thanks, that'd be great. Tea please, without milk or sugar, and while you're doing that, I'll start work on your computer, if I may?' Melrose raised a hand to forestall her reply. 'Yes, I know, you just want me to get on with it. One of the things I'll do is compare its system settings with Mik's. That'll help me work out if anything's wrong with them. By the way, when was the last time you took a copy of your work?'

'Oh, the day before yesterday. I wanted to be sure not to lose anything. We haven't worked on either computer since. We're helping Karla and Søren at the moment with a few updates they wanted, and our hand readers are enough for that. Anyway, I'll get your tea.'

'You don't mind if I just keep working, do you?' asked Mik. He was trying to make up for lost time. 'Just do whatever you think you need to do to that machine of mine. I've got everything on back-up drive and hand reader, so if it blows up, I really don't care.' He grinned and waved his hand at the computer.

Melrose returned the grin, then meticulously examined Tamara's keyboard, desk surface and surrounds for traces of DNA or fingerprints.

'May I have one of your hairs, please?' he asked Mik. 'I need it for comparison purposes. And if you don't mind, just your fingerprints as well. We have them on file, of course, but I like to get fresh samples on site to be certain.'

Mik obediently inclined his head towards Melrose while one long, curly black strand was gently extracted. Next, he placed his fingers one by one on the comlink screen as it was offered to him.

'Thanks for that. Tamara, may I have yours too?'

Tamara handed him the cup she was holding and gave Melrose her prints, together with a hair to complete his collection.

'Do Søren or Karla ever work in here?' he asked them, sampling the tea.

'Not really, but they sometimes come in to socialise, so I guess you'll want theirs too. I'll go and get them.'

Shortly afterwards, two more sets of records were entered into Melrose's comlink. 'Is there anyone else you'd normally expect to be in your laboratory?'

'No. We don't usually have visitors and, oddly enough, we prefer to clean the labs ourselves. It reduces the chance of anything being accidentally interfered with and helps with security too.'

'Certainly makes it a lot simpler, which is good,' replied Melrose, still smiling while he began his scrutiny of Mik's workstation.

'Well,' he announced, after a short time, 'there haven't been any obvious intruders. At least, not in here – not since the original break-in, anyway. Mind you, it doesn't mean there hasn't been anyone at all. Some people are a little too good at avoiding having their DNA remain in places they'd prefer it didn't.'

Mik frowned and met Tamara's eyes. Despite the alarming events of this past year, they were still finding it difficult to think in terms so devious and outside their usual experience. Tamara sipped her tea, but Mik scalded himself on the coffee she had given him. 'Damn!' he exclaimed, setting it aside to cool off a bit and saying, 'I suppose it's possible for someone to hack into our computers and do it so well even you couldn't detect it?'

'Possibly, but it's hard not to leave any trace at all. It may be difficult for me to find out precisely what, if anything, has been done to them, but if they've fiddled with either the files or any of the settings, I'm fairly sure I'd find *something* different. Anyway, I'll turn them on and see what happens. Just ignore me.'

Almost forty minutes went by before Melrose sighed and switched off both computers. Mik and Tamara turned to him expectantly.

'Have either of you worked on the event logs of these machines?' he asked, looking at them closely.

'No,' they replied in unison. 'Why would we?' asked Tamara.

'Well, you wouldn't, unless something went seriously wrong and you wanted to know why. I gather nothing has, or you'd have told me?'

'Yes, of course,' said Mik. 'What've you found?'

'Both event logs were erased during the evening of the day you arrived at Lamington. There's no other explanation, because they contain no earlier records and there's absolutely no reason why both computers would have deleted their own event logs at precisely the same time. No, someone was here that evening and has done something to either one or both of these machines. There's nothing else untoward in either the operating environment or your software that I can detect, so my guess is, they've changed your files. Do you keep additional offsite back-ups of your work?'

'Yes, we do. We send periodic copies to Research Coordinator Zago for safekeeping and for her to review when she needs to,' replied Mik, leaning against a storage cabinet and staring at Melrose, his dark brows drawn together in a frown.

'Did you have your work checked against the back-ups last year, after the break-in?'

'Yes,' answered Tamara. 'A routine check of file sizes and timestamps was done, and nothing looked as if it'd been changed. We weren't thinking in those terms, though. We were more worried about Mik and the damage done to Karla's work.' She was doing her best to remain calm, but was beginning to see a possible motive for what appeared at the time to have been totally senseless destruction. Standing up, Tamara retrieved her back-up drive from the desk drawer and handed it to him. 'I think you'd better look at this, too. The Federation Assembly has the previous version of our model, but not this one. Maybe we'd better get a full comparison done of *all* the files.'

Melrose turned the drive over in his hand. He was beginning to feel sure of what they would find.

While his and Karla's computers were being examined by Melrose, Søren called Rohan Maerz. As he hadn't received an invitation to the dinner party held for Karla, Mik and Tamara, they had all agreed that another dinner was the best pretext for Gwenllian to have an opportunity to be introduced to him.

'Well, what do you think, Maerz? Would you be willing to risk trusting your tastebuds to my culinary abilities? You have yet to meet two of our colleagues, Gwenllian and Owain. It would be a wonderful occasion to do so, and,' Søren paused dramatically, winking at Rohan for additional effect, 'you would have the chance to meet one of the most astounding people *I* have ever come across... Chiu Liow's sister, Freddi. She happens to be in Australia paying a family visit and I'm sure she could be persuaded to come along.'

Rohan paused before replying. He knew perfectly well who Chiu Liow's sister was, *and* her profession. Still, there was no point telling Søren this, or that he was aware something peculiar was happening. For all the researchers and research coordinators, as well as Freddi, to be here in Melbourne at the same time was hardly mere coincidence, of this he was sure. They wanted something from him and the dinner was just a ruse. Well, he was more than happy to cooperate. The evening could be both informative and entertaining.

'I'm honoured to be invited, my dear young fellow. When is it to be, and where?'

'Would next Tuesday be convenient?' asked Søren politely.

'Most convenient, thank you,' replied Rohan, just as politely.

'Good, good, that's wonderful. Now, I am so sorry to ask this, but would it be at all possible for us to have the dinner in your apartment? Mine is far too small. It was too much of a bother to set up anything elaborate as I expected to be back in Greenland before long. I would only need to arrive a few hours beforehand with all the shopping. You could always help if you wanted to, but if you would rather not, please don't worry. You could, of course, keep me company while I cook. What do you think?' Søren smiled impishly.

'I'll look forward to it, I assure you. I'd be more than happy for everyone to come to my home. Is there anyone else coming along?'

'Oh yes, Meng Jarrah may accompany Freddi. They are very close friends and she would love to meet you. Does 19:00 sound like a civilised hour?'

'Yes, indeed, and it sounds like we'll have a wonderful time. Until then,' said Rohan, waving a hand in farewell before ending the call.

'He knows something is up,' thought Søren, no longer smiling. 'Ah well, it makes little difference whether he does or doesn't. At least he will be there, as will Gwenllian and Shela. So, we will see what we see.'

He turned to Karla, who had been listening to the conversation, and said, 'Well, that went as we'd expect, though I think he will have been surprised to hear that you, Mik and Tamara won't be there. Do you suppose we *could* invite Meng Jarrah to make up for it? He seemed to be agreeable to the idea.'

'Yes, I think she might enjoy the evening, out of sheer curiosity, but have you realised Aurora may shield his mind?'

'Oh, I am sure you are right, but she won't know what to expect. Still, Gwenllian must be the first to greet him. I will be busy in the kitchen, so

Maerz will be the one to open the door, which he would most likely do in any case. She will have the advantage of surprise when they shake hands. With luck, Aurora will fail to notice straight away that Gwenllian has a mind similar to hers... So, our 'cat' has until next Tuesday to practice her shielding. Now, if I can just catch her to make sure she does...' Søren was soon deep in conversation again.

Karla decided it was time for their midsun meal, so checked in on the others to see whether they wanted to join her. She was startled by the sombre expression on their faces. Melrose had the results of his morning's work and was just about to find her.

'Have you discovered something on the computers that shouldn't be there?' she asked him.

Tamara answered instead, tapping her fingers against the doorframe and scowling. 'We're pretty certain something's been done to our model. We don't know exactly *what* yet, but Melrose will do a full comparison between what we have now, the versions the Federation Assembly has, and earlier back-ups we sent to Zago. The results should be here by this evening.'

They were all silent for several seconds, wondering if their world would ever return to normal again.

'What did you find, Melrose?' asked Karla, frowning.

'I suspect someone's been here during the night, after Mik and Tamara left for Lamington. I found nothing wrong with your or Søren's computer, and no personal traces left behind in either lab, but the event logs on both Mik and Tamara's machines were erased on that date. I'm almost certain we'll find a small but critical change to their model, since there's no other logical reason why someone would've done this. The question will be, what, exactly, has been done to it? Whoever did this knew what they were doing, I'm sure.'

'Then, depending upon what you find, this could explain why our model and Wyvern Meridian's didn't seem to contradict each other,' suggested Karla.

'Well, yes, it might, if there were changes made during the first break-in, though why they'd want to make more now, is something we need to find out,' replied Melrose, standing up to leave. 'Before I go, is there anything else any of you need to ask me? And what about Søren? Do you want to tell him, or do you want me to?'

'Why don't you stay for a meal with us, and we can all tell him,' she suggested, making an effort to smile. 'We can discuss it over a decent hot soup and some lovely fresh bread. Mik, you've brought some peaches from your greenhouse, haven't you?'

'Yes, I have...' he agreed, but without his usual grin.

They all silently followed Karla to the kitchen, where they found Søren already cutting the bread into neat slices. He turned around, ready to tell them about his conversation with Gwenllian, but stopped when he saw their expressions.

'Ah, Melrose, something is not as it should be with our infernal contraptions. What is amiss?'

'I'm glad you still have a sense of humour, Søren. All the work each of you has done needs to be checked against the Federation back-ups. I don't think you or Karla have much to worry about, but it's best to be safe. Unfortunately, it's a different story for Mik and Tamara.' Melrose repeated what he had already told the others.

Tamara put the hot soup onto the table, holding up the ladle to emphasise what she was about to say and ignoring the drip marks it left on the floor. As Søren hastily wiped them away, she said, 'I guess you'll check our security records now, as well as your own?'

'Yes, that'll be the first thing I do, although my guess is, I won't find anything this time. It's possible they were capable of overriding the building's security system with some sort of gadget that temporarily dealt with the scanners and also allowed access to your computers. It makes my hair stand on end just thinking about it!' Melrose took a seat opposite the high, mullioned windows so he could at least enjoy the view of the gardens.

They each served themselves a bowl of soup and began to eat. With the stress of all the recent events, it seemed best to behave as normally as possible and take one small step at a time. The researchers didn't say it, but each of them desperately hoped that the time and effort required to redevelop an accurate and reliable version of their work would not be so great as to set their regeneration project, or any of their other schedules, back even further.

Zago was still in Melbourne so was able to be present while Melrose examined the various versions of Mik and Tamara's work. She had listened quietly as he summarised the situation for her and told her that, as expected, no trace of this latest security breach at Willsmere was to be found anywhere in the Central Computer Site's records, or at Willsmere itself. When Zago then informed the Federation Assembly of the action about to be taken, they insisted that a Witness be present. They did not want Wyvern Meridian to be in a position to mount a challenge if it turned out that some of the files had indeed been modified in order to give the company a better outcome for their leasehold application.

The comparison software now trundled its way through all the back-up copies of the model made over the past eighteen months; the versions held by the Federation Assembly; and the latest version, which Melrose brought with him from Willsmere.

'This will take a while to finish,' said Melrose, 'and I have copies of Karla and Søren's work with me that I need to look at as well.' Feeling concerned for such an elderly person, he added, 'Would you like to wait somewhere more comfortable, Coordinator Zago?'

Amused, although understanding his concern, Zago smiled and said, 'Thank you for being so considerate. I can see you know what you are doing, and we have a Witness here, so even though I am not actually tired, I will take a break. Where do you suggest I have it?'

'I'll show you... Excuse me,' said Melrose to the Witness, 'I won't be long.'

The sun, which had shown itself only briefly during the early afternoon, was now almost gone, yet the transparent dome of the solarium still glowed with a multitude of colours, giving an impression of light and warmth. Immediately noticing the fountain, Zago delighted in its sparkling water and delicate splashing, and even though the beautiful polished timber floor was an expensive luxury, she could appreciate how well it contributed to the overall effect of the solarium. Looking around, one of the small alcoves immediately appealed to her and she turned to Melrose to thank him, adding that she could quite happily take care of herself now. He nodded, glanced at the time on his comlink, and asked whether she would like anything to eat or drink.

'Yes, but I can see where to go to obtain something. I am sure it is more important that you supervise the comparison than look after me.' She leaned on her staff and smiled. With a grin, Melrose went back to his office.

Left to her own devices, Zago contemplated her surroundings more closely and immediately noticed an oddity in the form of an old-fashioned cedar cabinet with well-fitted leadlight doors. Taking a closer look, she saw that it contained books, and opened one of its doors. Selecting what turned out to be a beautifully bound copy of an eighteenth-century Danish treatise on fungi, she was soon absorbed in studying the delicate drawings and detailed descriptions within this very early work, commissioned, extraordinarily enough, by the Danish King himself. The book was a most unusual one to find in such a place as this, she thought. Well, Thanh had been a talented musician and Marika a highly gifted artist. That being the case, why *not* an ancient botanical work in this small library? Perhaps even Gwenllian had chosen it? Ah yes, there was her neat signature, unobtrusively located on the inside of the back cover.

Much to her disgust, Zago had recently begun to feel her age, and decided that just for once, it would be excusable to indulge herself a little. She put the book aside to fetch a cup of hot chocolate and a piece of rich fruitcake from the nearby servery, then settled down to enjoy reading further. It seemed as if hardly any time at all had passed when Melrose returned to fetch her. He was looking pleased with himself and smiling broadly. 'I think we've found what we were expecting,' he announced. 'Come and I'll show you.'

Zago followed him to his workstation and sat down, patiently waiting for him to explain. 'It was remarkably simple after all,' he began. 'The comparison has taken so long because I wanted to eliminate any possibility of coincidence. Going back to your earliest copies, we did some simulations using a series of standard test data supplied with the Willsmere model. Next, we repeated them with the Wyvern Meridian version the Assembly has, using a dataset we developed that was as consistent as possible with the Willsmere series, but which took into account the different emphasis within the Wyvern Meridian approach. We then repeated the simulations with each subsequent Willsmere version, recording the changes to the outcomes as the model became more complex and was improved. We eventually found that the Willsmere and Wyvern Meridian models contradicted each other on all significant environmental outcomes for any period greater than one hundred and twenty years!'

Melrose looked triumphantly at Zago, who nodded thoughtfully but didn't interrupt, waiting instead for the rest of the explanation: 'We repeated the series with the versions supplied by Mik and Tamara to the Federation Assembly and found that, instead, the two models remained in agreement indefinitely. Then, when we used the latest version, which was on the back-up drive Tamara gave me this morning, they began to diverge again, as dramatically as before. It was therefore reasonable to assume that a critical change had been made to one or more of the files at the time of the first Willsmere break-in, and that now, for some reason that's way beyond me, the change has been reversed by whoever managed to break in the second time.'

'Why under the Sun would anyone want to do such a thing?!' Zago stood up and peered into his face, as if she could find the answer written there. 'But leaving that aside for now, did you find where the modification was made?'

'Oh yes, once we knew what to search for, it was straightforward. We found the modification, as expected, in an older file containing some of their most fundamental working premises. It turned out that the back-up drive held a hidden set of instructions that made certain the recently changed file would become the current version when Mik or Tamara copied their work to the drive.'

Chapter Twenty-Six

'How remarkably clever of them,' murmured Zago, with a frown.

'Yes, it's all very clever, that's for sure,' agreed Melrose. 'It had to be, or the original change would have been picked up when the model failed to remain consistent with the aims of their research project. Also, as I've already mentioned, the problem with Wyvern Meridian's approach only shows up in long-term scenarios, which is equally ingenious. Otherwise, if Wyvern Meridian's Australian leasehold was granted, the flaws in their approach would show up too soon and they'd lose their right to use the land.'

'The company was not performing at all well until quite recently,' said Zago, tapping her staff on the floor in a rare sign of agitation. 'I imagine they stole a great deal of good research and bought into other companies to improve their own situation, but almost certainly knew that our aims and theirs were totally opposed. This meant that unless they *appeared* to have the same long-term goals as us, the chances of them obtaining approval for the leasehold would have been remote. I also suspect that along the way, they have attempted to eliminate any realistic competition.'

'Do you know,' replied Melrose, earnestly taking her by the arm, 'it's even worse still. If we hadn't found this change, your own model would have eventually failed and the Federation would have been discredited in a fairly big way. Your soils would have become depleted again and the forests would have gone into early decline. I think that's part of what they were hoping for. Fortunately, though, nothing seems to have been done to either Karla or Søren's work.'

Zago shook her head and put an arm through his. They walked around the room together as they spoke. 'What it comes down to is this,' she said. 'Wyvern Meridian has no concern for soil regeneration or the natural environment at all! They wanted to grow timber for commercial purposes on a short rotation cycle and knew permission to use the land would never be given if they came straight out and said so. Therefore, we need to ask, who has stopped them in their tracks?'

'I can think of only two possibilities,' said Melrose, massaging his neck, which had become stiff from sitting for so long staring at complex scenarios and sets of data. 'Maybe someone within Wyvern Meridian has finally become fed up with Kakura's heavy-handed methods of running the company, or else Rohan Maerz has finally caught up with them and has chosen this way of exposing their schemes. Personally, my bets are on him.'

'Perhaps,' said Zago, 'and I sincerely hope you are right!'

*

Although it was late in the evening, they wanted to give their news to both Chiu Liow and the research team immediately. With a Witness present throughout, and all the relevant material and conclusions now entered into the Judge, it quite likely made little difference whether or not anyone overheard their conversation. However, as a temporary measure, the calls would be encrypted, so Melrose gave Zago a single-use security key to utilise. While he then contacted Chiu Liow, Zago called Tamara, who sleepily rubbed her face and eyes, her curly brown hair more tousled than usual. Yawning, she made an effort to concentrate, and soon woke up properly once it became clear to her what was being said.

'Mik!' she yelled, turning away and transferring the call to the screen on the bedroom wall. 'Come here! They've found it!'

Mik appeared almost immediately, eyes wide and expectant, although otherwise dishevelled. He had just finished showering, but hadn't yet combed his hair. 'What did they do?' he demanded.

'They stuffed up our model so it'd appear to agree with their piece of crap and even made sure ours would fail! That's what those misbegotten mongrels did!'

Tamara was beside herself with anger. All the misery and fear of these past months finally came to the surface in an almost uncontrollable fury. Mik's face was pale and his expression tense as he sat down and put an arm around her shoulders. In the background, Possum started howling.

'Possum, Possum, I'm sorry, my darling!' Tears of rage and frustration were running down Tamara's face as she rushed to comfort the distraught cat. In the meantime, Mik tried to grapple with Fliedermus, who was frantically trying to climb onto his lap and lick his face. 'What did you find?' he managed to say, even though Fliedermus had her face pushed so close to his, he was having trouble speaking.

Zago repeated what Melrose had discovered, and although she deeply sympathised with their distress and was upset too, she had to make an effort to prevent herself from chortling at the picture before her.

'How can we be sure that's all they've done? What if there's still something there that's even worse?' said Mik, who had finally succeeded in reassuring Fliedermus, convincing her to stay still and stop cleaning his face. By this time, Tamara had reappeared, clutching Possum.

Zago stared at them, then turned to Melrose, who had finished speaking with Chiu Liow and was now listening in on the conversation.

'It's possible,' he admitted. 'They could have realised they mightn't get the Australian leasehold now anyway, so reversed the change as a blind to something else they've done that would ruin your work. I'll have to put some more thought into this, but it's too late now to do it properly. I'll run some probability-based analyses first thing tomorrow to compare the internal consistency of your model before and after both changes. The other thing I suggest you do...tomorrow, not tonight,' Melrose could see Tamara getting ready to jump at anything he said, '...would be to ask Gwenllian to double-check your simulations using some of her research into self-diagnosis, early-malfunction warning systems. The enhancement to the latest version of their module isn't finished yet, as far as I know, but was well advanced last time she talked to me about it. I don't suppose they've had much time to work on it lately, though I'm sure she'd be keen to test it, particularly as she can use my results for comparison.'

Wiping away her tears, Tamara gazed hopefully at him. 'How long do you think the analysis will take?'

'Oh, not too long, once I've worked out a few parameters. I should be able to have something for you by tomorrow evening, as long as nothing else comes along here at the Site to take me away. Luckily, it's my day off, though if I'm already here, that won't stop me getting roped into anything urgent.' He pulled a wry face.

'You're a gem, Melrose!' said Mik warmly. 'I hope we can do something for you one day that's as big a help as you've been to us.' He was so sincere in saying this that Melrose felt deeply touched. Much of his effort received little in the way of personal thanks, though he was certainly aware of how valuable his contributions were.

'Well, thanks for saying so,' he mumbled, blushing. 'I'll call you tomorrow when I know what's going on. Hope you can get back to sleep now, Tamara.'

She smiled and nodded, daring to feel optimistic again. 'Thanks, I'll try, and Mik's right. You *are* wonderful! I'll let you know how it goes with Gwenllian...tomorrow...'

CHAPTER TWENTY-SEVEN

Storm clouds had gathered, dark and gloomy, over Port Phillip Bay, where two-metre waves were already pounding the shoreline, the ripples flowing through into the flooded streetscape of the old, central city. Chiu Liow watched from his office window as the few remaining people still outside drew into safety as quickly as they could. He was angry, and his anger seemed to be reflected in the sudden streak of lightning flashing across the sky. Several seconds later, thunder crashed around the building.

While the peacekeeper paced the floor, frowning and muttering to himself, the storm built its force and continued to punctuate his thoughts. Stopping yet again to gaze at the scene outside, he noticed a pleasure craft in trouble on the bay, but was relieved to see that the air rescue service was already on its way. Once he was sure the rescue was going well, Chiu Liow turned away, trying his best to collect himself. Until the events of this past year, it had been rare for him to have difficulty dealing with his emotions. Part of the problem was Morag. He missed her dreadfully and hated the thought of her being cooped up in her house in the Swiss mountains, no matter how beautiful it all was!

Since speaking with Melrose last night, the implications had troubled him all day. He was now almost certain that no one other than Rohan Maerz was capable of having entered Willsmere without any security alarms being triggered and without leaving any trace – other than the erasure of the event logs on the two computers and the presence of the hidden file on the back-up drive. The 'elegance' of the procedure did, he had to admit, resemble the Epsilon situation, but unless Wyvern Meridian had yet another security and computing expert up its sleeve, the culprit simply had to be Maerz. He *was*, after all, in Melbourne. The peacekeeper found himself grinding his teeth at the thought that Maerz had played him for a fool, even though he had suspected this to be the case for a very long time.

Chiu Liow checked the time as yet another bolt of lightning streaked across the grey sky. Surely Melrose would produce those results soon! Just as the rain began, pouring down in vast moving sheets across the bay and beating against the windows in a cacophony of sound, his comlink chimed an incoming call. To his immense relief, it was Melrose. Even better, the systems technologist was smiling.

'I gather you have good news?' exclaimed Chiu Liow eagerly.

'Yes, I do, which is just as well! I'll come over to give you the details, and should be there in about thirty minutes at the latest. I'll bring Research Coordinator Zago with me. She was here until late last night and needed some rest, but came back later this afternoon once we'd started to get some results. Is that alright?'

'No,' said Chiu Liow, 'the storm is far too heavy for safe travel. I suggest we wait another half hour to see if it eases. Either way, though, it would be best if I came over to you.'

An hour later, Chiu Liow entered the Central Computer Site and quickly found his way to where Melrose and Zago were waiting.

'I've been here since 08:00 this morning, setting up our analyses, and Gwenllian came in a little later to join me,' said Melrose. 'Once we were ready to begin, we called Tamara and Mik, who turned up soon afterwards. Just to make sure, we've run their test data three times using controlled scenario changes. We're certain the latest model is good, which puts my bet back onto Maerz as the one who broke in...at least the second time.'

'Yes, I agree,' replied Chiu Liow slowly, relieved by the news, yet still puzzled. 'Given his style, I doubt very much whether he was party to the first break-in...unless he was somehow led to expect there wouldn't be any violence.' He turned to Zago for her opinion.

'Chiu Liow,' she said, initially with a hint of optimism in her voice, 'I believe we may be moving towards a resolution at last. Everything we have produced today will be sent by messenger to the Assembly. They may want the Judge to examine the information as well, but either way, I think our efforts will justify an even more intensive examination of Wyvern Meridian's affairs and will almost certainly result in their Australian leasehold application being rejected. Naturally, they have the right to appeal if it is. Unfortunately, however, we cannot prove beyond doubt that they were the culprits here. In fact, they could even claim someone else is sabotaging their reputation!' With these last words, Zago frowned and banged her staff on the floor, looking away for a moment.

She seems tired, thought Chiu Liow, as he studied her lined and delicately faded features, surprised by her small outburst. Strange, he had never noticed her age before. Perhaps, like other mortals, even Zago had her limits? He closed his eyes for a moment, heaving a sigh. He *still* did not have anyone firmly in his sights. This meant pinning his hopes on the results of Gwenllian and Shela's meeting with Rohan Maerz.

After a little more discussion, they wished each other well and went their separate ways: Chiu Liow to his lonely contemplation of the storm still raging outside, and Zago to an early bed for the first time in many years.

Fortunately for Søren's shopping trip, the weather improved for the day of the dinner party. Preferring to be outside as often as possible, he tended to frequent the outdoor market areas, especially those along the foreshore. After several hours pleasant selection of foodstuffs, interspersed by a coffee break, and later, a quick meal at a pavement café, Søren at long last had what he wanted. He and his guardian laboriously carried all the shopping to Rohan's apartment, whereupon the peacekeeper returned to normal duties, satisfied Søren would be safe for the time being.

Despite the devious reasons for holding the dinner, Søren still wanted it to go well and for them all to enjoy his cooking. Therefore, as long as Gwenllian didn't 'see' anything terrible when she met Maerz, there was no reason to think they wouldn't – even if a certain sardonic aspect tinged the evening's progress. However, Søren wondered if including Owain had been wise since he seemed the least capable of dealing with things if they went badly. Too late, he supposed, and hoped Gwenllian's beloved brother would manage to contain his erratic temper if the worst happened.

When Søren pressed his palm to the apartment's identification panel, the door opened with a flourish and Rohan immediately relieved him of the heaviest bags. After carrying them into the kitchen, he displayed a childlike glee in unpacking and scrutinising the contents, nodding approval every now and then and casting glances around his well-equipped kitchen to make sure he had the necessary items for their preparation. He was clearly guessing, with a high degree of accuracy, what Søren would need. They had, of course, discussed the menu, as otherwise Rohan would have felt unable to properly select the wines, which, together with the other liquid refreshments, were his contribution to the meal.

Food was apparently a *very* wide field of common interest, so despite the intent of the evening, Søren found himself immensely enjoying their pre-party conversation. He now fervently hoped that whatever Gwenllian found when she met Maerz would somehow exonerate him. It was almost strange to remember how recently the man had made his skin crawl!

Rohan fussed around a little longer, then insisted Søren be seated while he made a pot of his finest tea and arranged a selection of honey-glazed fruits on a genuine, classic, blue and white Royal Copenhagen plate, which he had found and bought in his guest's honour. He stood back to thoroughly enjoy the expression of total amazement on Søren's face when he beheld it. The emotion deepened when Rohan brought forth the teacup and saucer to match.

'Who did you rob to pay for this?' gasped Søren.

Rohan laughed – a warm, pleasant sound. 'I robbed my own account, but it was worth it to see your face. As I'm sure you can appreciate, it was also an investment. The set perfectly matches the décor of my home. I'll keep it here for only you to use when you come to visit me.'

A wistful tone, ever so faint, had crept into Rohan's voice. Søren met his eyes and held out his hand, his elfin features beautiful, his expression sincere.

'I will hold you to that promise,' he said softly, 'and make sure I use it often enough to remember what it must have felt like to have been royalty. I am honoured by what you have done and hope that one day I can do as much for you.'

Rohan shook his hand, briefly but firmly. 'Well, well, let's drink our tea then get to work. We've a great deal to do before our guests arrive. I've told Aurora to keep to herself this afternoon. She's so curious about everything, she tends to get under my feet sometimes, and I don't want to trip over her. I'd hate to spoil your dinner by dropping a pot!'

Søren had wondered why the cat hadn't made an appearance, then realised it might help matters when Gwenllian arrived. He was ashamed to have the thought, but forced himself to remember that Maerz was still under suspicion.

The afternoon passed pleasantly and almost too quickly. The two men, so contrasted in appearance, seemed to find a perfect harmony in their tasks and in their conversation. Their backgrounds and life experiences were very different, yet their basic attitudes towards life and themselves were remarkably similar. At one point, when they were laughing almost hysterically at a story Rohan recounted, Aurora, unnoticed, poked her head into the kitchen, then crept out quietly and went back to sleep on Rohan's bed, one paw and the tip of her bushy tail over her face, as if to dim the noise.

By the time the security system notified them of their guests' arrival, the dining table had been set to perfection and everything was ready to be served in grand procession throughout the evening. The setting was magnificent, with silver and crystal sparkling in the light of two grand candelabra, although a simple vase of dark blue daisies with yellow centres made a sunny contrast and introduced a welcome note of informality. The electric fire produced a warm and cosy atmosphere, and on this still evening, with the curtains left open, the view was even more impressive than usual as the full moon rose, large and yellow, over the distant horizon.

When Rohan answered the door, Aurora finally decided to come out, taking up her favourite spot in front of the heater. Gwenllian entered, with Owain several steps behind. She held out her hand to Rohan, who took it in a firm grasp and then found himself unable to let go. He thought she was one of the most beautiful creatures he had ever seen, and as time seemed to stand still, had difficulty breathing. Blushing furiously, he suddenly came back to himself and released her hand.

'For...forgive me,' he stuttered, feeling dizzy. 'I have few visitors, and if you will pardon me for saying so, none as astonishing as you.' Making a considerable effort, he held out his hand to Owain. 'You must be her brother... I can see the resemblance. Please, come in and make yourselves at home while we wait for our other guests.'

Owain took his hand and shook it, composing his features as best he could into a normal expression of polite warmth. He had made sure to be some distance away when Gwenllian took Rohan's hand, as he didn't want to accidentally influence or 'overhear' anything she saw or felt. They needed to be absolutely certain that whatever passed between the two would be clear and true. He avoided even looking at Gwenllian in case her expression was not as it should be.

Hearing Owain's voice replying to Rohan's greeting, Søren came out of the kitchen, wiping his hands on a towel, and before Rohan turned back into the room, he inclined his head inquiringly at Gwenllian. She appeared composed and was taking off her coat, hanging it with care on the rack by the door, but didn't acknowledge his gesture. Aurora, her head held high and tail in the air, fluffed out more than usual, walked slowly over to where the young woman was standing. The cat made a small burbling sound, then sat down at Gwenllian's feet, gazing up into her face and purring loudly. Gwenllian stood still, answering the question in the golden eyes before kneeling down to gently stroke her head. Satisfied, Aurora went back to her heater and settled down, paws neatly tucked under her chest.

Not noticing anything unusual, Rohan made sure Gwenllian and Owain were comfortable. 'Dinner will be served once our other guests arrive, which one hopes won't be too long. Can I offer you anything while we're waiting? I've an excellent amontillado, if that would suit.'

They both accepted, their polite smiles holding just enough warmth to be convincing. Bursting with curiosity, Søren realised the one thing he hadn't allowed for was how to survive the evening without knowing what Gwenllian had 'seen'. 'Drat,' he thought, 'this will be far too difficult,' and returned to the kitchen in disgust.

As Rohan was serving the sherry, the security system chimed, and this time, when he opened the door, there was no hand to be taken and no introduction to be made. Instead, a huge black cat hurled itself into the room and enthusiastically stood up to place her paws on Rohan's massive stomach, licking the hand he put forward to defend himself. He nearly overbalanced from the weight, let alone the surprise. No one had told him Freddi was bringing her cat!

Freddi came to the rescue by grabbing Shela around the middle and hauling her off. 'I gather she likes you,' she said, with a grin, as Rohan grappled with the animal. Meng Jarrah, in the meantime, stood stock still in the doorway, mouth open. A bigger contrast to the reception Shela had given Kenjiro Kakura could not have been imagined! She took a few tentative steps forward, and when everyone appeared to have recovered from the onslaught, held out her hand and introduced herself, noticing Shela had already pounced on Aurora by way of introduction.

Smiling, Rohan accepted her hand. 'I'm delighted to meet you. It's an honour to have you as a guest. Your reputation for excellence and hard work is worldwide... Please, please, come in and make yourselves comfortable. I see Shela and Aurora have met, so we can forget about them for a while and start our dinner. Søren and I have worked hard all afternoon to prepare it. On which note, please excuse me. I think he may need some help.'

Rohan bustled out into the kitchen, leaving Freddi, Meng Jarrah, Gwenllian and Owain staring at each other, not daring to voice their thoughts.

Since they weren't attending the dinner party, Karla, Mik, Tamara, and surprisingly, Chiu Liow, were coping with their intense curiosity about the outcome by having their own gathering. As a result, the three cats were enjoying an evening together in their own home for a change, but tended to get in the way by taking every opportunity to drape themselves over any available part of Mik or Tamara's anatomy.

Everyone studiously tried to avoid the obvious topic of conversation, but failed, coming back time and again to their speculations as to what they would learn when the partygoers returned. It had been agreed that no matter how late, they should join their friends and at long last tell them what they so desperately needed to know.

They were occupying themselves with a game of four-person chess when the security system finally announced the arrival of the others. Tamara had been stifling yawns for the last hour, it now being well past midnight, yet was still the first person up the staircase to greet the revellers – or 'psychic detectives', as she now tended to think of them. The door opened and all six stood there, those capable of it grinning broadly. Tamara's hand went to her mouth in astonishment.

'*You* are blocking the doorway, little Spud,' said Søren. 'It's freezing out here. Do you think we might be allowed to come in?'

Tamara giggled, and stood aside while they all trooped past and then down into the warmth, where Mik, Chiu Liow and Karla were standing, impatient to be told their news.

'Well?' demanded Karla, arms spread wide and trying not to smile at the silly expressions on their faces.

'Sorry,' said Freddi contritely, 'we're all rather drunk, I'm afraid. It was such a *very* good party.'

She and Meng Jarrah stood with their arms around each other, while Shela, who was definitely not drunk, was standing nose to nose with Red Matilda, finding out what had happened while she was away. Søren, in the meantime, had curled up on the sofa with Possum, who was contentedly cleaning his face.

Chiu Liow sighed loudly. 'Freddi, please, just tell us. Is Rohan Maerz on our side or not?'

His sister met his eyes as soberly as she could manage. 'Oh, we're pretty sure he's on our side. Shela nearly floored him when we first walked in. Love at first sight, it seems. He apparently has a way with cats...and it's not because he *is* one, like Gwennie here.'

Gwenllian laughed softly and stood on tiptoe to put her arms around Freddi's neck, giving her a kiss on the offered cheek before telling them what she had seen.

'I managed to get three strong images before Aurora put a type of cloak over his mind. It seems he has an intense fatherly love for Morag MacIain, which I don't think is a surprise to anyone, although the *type* of love might be. Also, he's deeply attached to Aurora, and this affection is now one of the mainsprings of his life, which is no surprise either. What I *did* see, though, is that he despises, hates and abhors Kenjiro Kakura and his entire operation. It's as if his mind is totally focused on the destruction of Wyvern Meridian.'

Søren broke in at this point. 'Gwenllian wasn't in a position to tell *us* for most of the evening and of course we were all dying of curiosity. Shela obviously thought he was wonderful, which helped a great deal, but *she* was keeping it from us as well. Fortunately, by the time we were ready for dessert, Gwenllian had managed to catch each of us alone to pass on the images, which is why we are all so beautifully happy...and I must say, the dinner was a masterpiece. There were no leftovers to bring you, though. Sorry.'

Fliedermus, who had joined Possum on the sofa, put out a paw to scratch his hand, ever so slightly. When Søren playfully swatted her, she took hold of his wrist with her tail, gripping it tightly. He sighed theatrically and gave in to being reprimanded for not having thought of bringing *her* a midnight snack!

It was all very well for those who had gone to the dinner party. They were already used to the idea of one of their main suspects being innocent of nearly everything they had suspected him of, but it was still news to those who stayed behind. Chiu Liow broke their stunned silence.

'Assuming we accept what you and Shela saw in him, Gwenllian, which presumably we should, I can see only one reasonable explanation for his actions. He's been working underground for what must be many years, gaining Kakura's trust by occasionally giving him information and assistance, and all the time trying to find some means of bringing him down.'

Chiu Liow took a seat, as did the others, waiting for him to continue: 'His feelings for Morag would explain why he stage-managed the Papuan situation in the way that I'm now certain he did. It would have had the double advantage of putting her into safe custody while at the same time giving Kakura the impression her position as an investigator was being compromised...badly. It's even possible Kakura intended to have her assassinated. Otherwise, I can't see any reason why Maerz would have done it.

'It also explains why the Claviceps affair was effective. It temporarily put Epsilon into a difficult financial position and appeared to harm their reputation, while not doing anyone any serious damage. This may have helped convince Kakura that Maerz was on his side. I think it was extremely well done, and even more so when we take into account Wyvern's intention of stealing Epsilon's most recent, and possibly most lucrative, research. Once they eventually discovered the theft, with their reputation in tatters, it would be much harder for Epsilon to claim their product had been stolen.'

Karla finished this line of thought for him: 'Which also means Rohan was probably the one who reinserted Epsilon's application for access to Tumucumaque, don't you think?'

'Yes, it had to be,' replied Chiu Liow, smiling now. 'Kakura is a genius at covering his tracks. Maerz needed to find some means of giving us proof Wyvern Meridian was at the root of all our forest industry troubles. I now believe he was the one who gave them the idea of the duplicate application in the first place, as well as the idea of stealing Epsilon's research. He would have known far better than Kakura what the Federation processes were for making assessments, and therefore knew the duplicate entry would be picked up fairly quickly. I'm sure that's why one of Wyvern Meridian's board members died. Epsilon's application should have been erased and Kakura blamed him for what appeared to be a failure to have done so. I must say, when he blames someone, they pay a high price!'

'I suspect that's the reason all the cats like Rohan so much,' said Gwenllian, stroking Possum, who had deserted Søren and jumped onto her lap. 'They think he behaves righteously. If he loathes Kakura and his methods, that might be why he gave in to temptation and killed Mervyn

Bradshaw. Rohan knew we'd never be able to bring him to justice and couldn't tolerate yet another callous assassin walking the streets. I'm sure he would have mourned Thanh and Marika's deaths just as much as we did, and even if Marika did have some small part to play, he would hardly have thought she deserved to die! At least, that's what Shela just told me, didn't you, my sweet?'

As they all turned to look at her, Shela's eyes glinted and she shared everything in her mind. Her images were as much emotional as visual. They showed Rohan Maerz as a man who, although alone and an outsider all his life, and despite his growing sense of frustration and disillusionment, longed with all his being for a just and kinder world. He had risen to his position of power in order to do everything possible to bring this about and to protect the gains so painfully won in more recent times.

Karla, her head bowed, slowly wiped away the tears trickling down her cheeks. Chiu Liow, who was sitting next to her, put an arm around her shoulders, his expression one of deep sadness. In contrast, Meng Jarrah's face showed only her fierce resolve to do her utmost to continue their work, despite anything Wyvern Meridian might still try to do to prevent them. Freddi had taken her hand and was nodding thoughtfully, as if satisfied she finally understood much of what had seemed so elusive. Meanwhile, Owain made an effort to control his anger as he realised it was almost certainly Kakura who had organised the attempt on his life! Shela stood up and pressed herself against his legs, purring gently as he stroked her head, doing her best to soothe his mind.

Tamara and Mik sat with their arms around each other, profoundly grateful to have reached a point where someone who should have been trustworthy, had proved to be so. They now knew it must have been Rohan who crept quietly into their laboratory to undo the damage that had so nearly ruined their work – ruined one of the key elements in the Federation's strategy to reclaim the world's devastated lands.

The silence continued for some time while they each dwelt on the images Shela had shown them. Søren, who had been sitting with his head in his hands, as if in pain, finally looked up and said, 'There's still one problem. Maerz cannot admit to the Assembly, or to anyone else, exactly what he has done to protect us, as well as our work. You do realise this, don't you? There's no absolute proof that Kakura was the mastermind behind all these crimes. He can simply claim Maerz was an ally who is now disgruntled and could easily fabricate some reason for the betrayal. Or alternatively, he can claim complete innocence... It's all simply a plot on the part of the Federation to discredit the one and only highly successful and influential global private enterprise!'

Fliedermus wailed and the other cats joined her. The brief happiness of the evening was over.

CHAPTER TWENTY-EIGHT

Almost two months of relative peace had passed and yet for Rohan Maerz one last task remained. The Federation Assembly had uncompromisingly rejected Wyvern Meridian's application for the Australian leasehold, although their inquiries into the company's operations found no further evidence of malpractice or criminal activity. He was not surprised and so carefully unwrapped a small package, hand-delivered not long since. Inside was the cicada Aurora had given him, now an ornate masterpiece preserved in a fine coating of Patagonian silver, with the telltale initials 'MY' discreetly engraved underneath its abdomen. Rohan smiled, delighted with this present that he hoped very soon to give to Kenjiro Kakura in person.

After placing it in a new gift box, he set it aside in a safe place and sat down at his computer. He considered his options, adjusted the lattice settings, and sent an encrypted message to the Director of Wyvern Meridian. It was a prearranged signal, appearing a moment later as a red wyvern in the bottom left-hand corner of Kakura's comlink.

For several years, Kakura had possessed an alternative Federation identity number, although he viewed these numbers as gross transgressions of privacy and self-determination. One of the odd quirks of his personality was that he derived a certain childlike satisfaction from travelling in disguise, and therefore took as much time as he needed to enjoy himself while changing his appearance into a reasonable facsimile of his assumed persona. While not strictly necessary, given Rohan's Melbourne apartment was not under visual surveillance, it was a sensible precaution and added zest to the occasion. The two men had not met in person very often, so he found himself anticipating the occasion with great pleasure. The former FSIU coordinator was one of the few people on the planet whom Kenjiro Kakura viewed as an equal – someone with whom he could fully relax and share his innermost thoughts and ideas.

The journey to Melbourne went without incident and he arrived at 11:00 the next morning. Rohan met him at the door, eyebrows raised at his visitor's appearance. Aurora was nowhere to be seen, having been asked to keep herself strictly hidden from view and not to react to Kakura's presence by making the least sound.

Rohan himself was dressed at his most flamboyant, with a long, dark blue tunic that almost swept the floor, deep red shoes, and a fine, purple shawl flung over one shoulder. His medium length silver hair fell in thick waves to his shoulders, complementing the short, well-cut, grey beard. Kakura surveyed the effect and found it pleasant enough, if not to his own taste.

'Do come in,' said Rohan, smiling. 'It's a pleasure to see you again after such a long time. Please, make yourself comfortable. I'll bring you something to eat and drink. I'm sure you must be hungry after your trip. No? Well, perhaps just tea? Good, good. Here, let me take your coat.'

'Thank you,' replied Kakura, handing Rohan his coat and returning the smile. 'I am happy to be here, although I gather you believe we have reached a critical point in our operations?'

'Don't you?' Rohan sat down, and after standing at the windows for a few moments to admire the view, Kakura took a seat opposite.

'Perhaps,' said Kakura, with a slight grimace. 'Without the Australian land, and without the Epsilon research, we are not in as good a position as I had hoped and I admit to being less than happy at being closely examined by the Federation. Of course, they found nothing. They never will. I plan to consolidate the company's business activities, make a few personnel adjustments to improve efficiency, then do nothing further out of the ordinary for some time. Eventually we'll be forgotten, as far as any surveillance is concerned, and can easily begin again.'

'That's what I thought you would say.' Rohan considered him for several seconds. 'It appears that I am dying,' he announced, without showing any emotion, then waved a hand as Kakura gasped in astonishment and began to rise from his seat. 'No, no, please, it's unavoidable. I have, I am told, approximately eighteen months left. It's part of this genetic condition that makes me so dreadfully fat. There has always been the possibility I would not be long-lived. Nevertheless, I have made the best use of my life that anyone could wish for. It is enough.'

Deeply moved, Kakura held out a hand to Rohan, who took it in both his own. For the first time, Kakura noticed that Rohan's hands were strong and finely shaped, with long mobile fingers – one of his few beautiful features.

'I've asked you to come here today because I wish to spend what remains of my life leading a peaceful existence in this remarkable city of Melbourne,' said Rohan, looking directly into Kakura's eyes. 'I'm happy here, but hope you'll forgive me if I no longer assist you in your endeavours?'

Kakura nodded, then pressed Rohan's hand before releasing it, his expression hard to read.

'Thank you,' said Rohan. 'I have a parting gift for you. Michiko assisted me, and I hope you will keep it in memory of your friend? I found it in a forest on the banks of the Yarra River on a day that was very special to me.'

Rohan rose, went over to the ornate cabinet where he kept his dinnerware, took out the silver cicada in its delicate box, now beautifully gift-wrapped, then handed it to Kakura and sat down. Kakura looked carefully at the present before peeling away the layers of decorative paper and lifting the lid. He had never seen one of these strange creatures before, although on hot summer days and evenings had often heard their singing in the trees. Taking it out, Kakura balanced the cicada in the palm of his hand and sighed.

'I have few friends, Rohan Maerz, and it grieves me deeply to lose one. I will treasure this gift for the rest of my life, I promise you.'

'That is enough for me.' Rohan smiled and stood up, then in a brisk tone said, 'Now, let me show you more of the wonderful view from the balcony, then let's think about happier things! But first, I'll make some tea for us both. Afterwards, you must share some midsun food with me. I've made several mushroom pies and have the ingredients for a superb salad to go with them. I know you appreciate a good wine, so there's an excellent local pinot noir we can open. I'm sure, just for once, you can indulge yourself and help me finish the bottle. For dessert, I managed to find a deliciously moist chocolate cake this morning, before you arrived. We can have it with cream and a fine cherry brandy. How does that sound?'

As Kakura smiled at his friend, Rohan's grey eyes crinkled in amusement at the knowledge that he usually restricted himself to a spartan meal in the middle of the day.

They spent the next few hours talking about small daily things, rather than the grand ideas and ambitious plans of previous times. Kakura understood this was the last time he would see Rohan, and in all likelihood, the last time he would even have any contact with him. It was regretful Wyvern Meridian would no longer have such a powerful ally. However, he was confident they would not only survive, but continue to prosper and to vie with the Federation for power.

Once Kakura had gone, Rohan flung open the door to his bedroom and swept Aurora into his arms, holding her close. The cat licked his nose and trilled softly, then followed him out to his study to sleep peacefully at his feet while he began his report to the Federation Assembly. It would take all evening and most of the next two days to put together. He had almost nine years of work to organise and present, as well as all the technical details of his involvement in the *Claviceps atropurpurea* deception; the method he had used to retrieve and then reinsert Epsilon's original Tumucumaque research application into the Federation database; his sabotage of the Papuan lattice that succeeded in placing Morag MacIain under house arrest; the design of the device he recently used to overcome the security systems at Willsmere; the full account of Bradshaw's business and criminal dealings with Wyvern Meridian; plus a copy of the agreement between Bradshaw and Kakura for the murders of Marika and Thanh, which he had located only after learning of Thanh's death, and only three days before Marika was killed.

'I assumed,' he wrote, 'that Marika, being under house arrest and full surveillance, would be safe. That I was wrong on this occasion is something I will always regret.'

An outline slowly grew of how Rohan, in his role of Federation Special Investigation Unit Coordinator, gradually became aware that Wyvern Meridian was growing far beyond the scope of any normal private enterprise, and that their realm of involvement was equally unusual. Intrigued, he began to make discreet inquiries and found, to his alarm, that the company centred itself around a cult of personality, based on its director, Kenjiro Kakura, whose style of leadership was authoritarian in the extreme. In all his long years of working for the FSIU, this was the first time Rohan had ever come across such a company.

He watched their business dealings more closely and discovered certain contracts seemed to have been made with just a little too much cooperation from government bodies. Furthermore, when the company seemed to be trading more poorly in a given area of the market than an ambitious director might desire, their performance sometimes improved dramatically when key competitors were either absorbed into the conglomerate or became weakened to the point of collapse. As the years went by, the occasional employee was even found to have died rather suddenly from unexpected health problems. As Rohan tracked these deaths over time, he saw a pattern emerge and made the decision to find out more by insinuating himself into, firstly, the acquaintanceship of Kakura, and as time went by, the pretence of sincere friendship and respect. In doing so, he became aware that Kakura was fundamentally evil.

Real evil is rare, he thought, as he remembered his initial impressions. The Director of Wyvern Meridian was a strikingly handsome and imposing man, with refined manners and acute intelligence, living a lifestyle that, to all outward appearances, was beyond reproach and highly admirable. His courage, resilience, and love for his family were beyond doubt, yet Rohan, when he met Michiko at long last, was saddened to see how subservient she was to her bondmate. Kakura treated her with kindness and consideration, but with condescension, not as an equal. Rohan was also dismayed to find they had three children. His investigations into this anomaly uncovered an intricate web of bribery, intimidation and flagrant law breaking: after all, once born, what could be done but allow the parents to keep their child?

Nevertheless, he and Kakura shared a great deal in common: their taste for the ostentatious, their deep enjoyment of devising grand and well-laid plans and then overseeing their execution with an unsurpassed eye for detail. They both had an uncanny ability to foresee what the actions of others would be and to plan ahead accordingly. Yet, if necessary, they could also change direction with speed and agility, wasting no time on regrets and might-have-beens. It was easy for him to simulate an effortless and trusting friendship with Kakura, even finding true enjoyment in his company once he had achieved his aims of the moment and could relax for a short while. But at no point did Rohan relax his guard.

As their apparent trust in each other deepened, he discovered Kakura sometimes performed his own executions and each time experienced a profound sense of satisfaction, justifying them in his own mind as a righteous elimination of traitors. Rohan was never able to obtain proof, as Kakura's own words never told him directly that this was so – all the evidence was subtle and indirect, yet in his own mind, he was sure.

Rohan became trusted to the point where he was sometimes consulted as to the best method of breaking down the resistance of some government official, or the board of directors of a company ripe for takeover. At first, he was noncommittal. After all, he had his position to consider, but as time went by, Rohan gave advice when it seemed Kakura would succeed in his aims despite anything he said or did. In this way, the FSIU Coordinator appeared to be assisting without actually doing so.

Eventually Kakura became more demanding, just as his ambitions became even greater, forcing Rohan to give him tangible help in order to maintain his trust. At this point, he gave Kakura the idea of creating an alternative identity. Kakura immediately developed all the necessary accoutrements that might be required, should he ever need to use it. His sense of freedom was now complete.

Kenjiro Kakura believed the Federation model of world governance undermined individual creativity and self-determination. His ambition was to return to a past where large corporations, such as his, essentially managed world affairs. Unfortunately, no sympathy was to be found between the operations of his company and the natural environment. He felt no sense of moral obligation to any other species, seeing the natural world only as a resource to be utilised. In contrast, man-made beauty enthralled him, and he surrounded himself with the finest art, architecture and furnishings obtainable.

The mistaken belief held by Kakura, so common in the past, was that the environmental disasters that plunged Earth into chaos could simply have been prevented by more apt use of technology. Even the lessons of history were forgotten by the Director of Wyvern Meridian, which was strange, given how enamoured he was of ancient Japanese ways and how he had taken the time to study his ancestors in great detail, paying particular attention to their role in world affairs. Apparently his memory was selective.

Rohan waited for the right opportunity to present itself, when either a mistake on Kakura's part could be exploited or a situation could be created whereby a mistake was inevitable. However, as his ambitions grew and his successes accumulated, Kakura became even more dismissive of the rights of others. Violence and murder became a hallmark of his operations. Arrogance had become so great a part of the man's personality that he honestly thought his actions were not only justified, but were wholly right. The FSIU Coordinator could wait no longer.

Some hours after Kenjiro Kakura reached his home, he began to experience violent stomach pains. Michiko insisted a medical practitioner be called, but Kakura wouldn't hear of it. He vomited several times and felt as if he was developing some form of gastroenteritis, but thought it would soon pass. If it didn't, he said, *then* she could call a practitioner. To his relief, he began to feel better during the morning and followed his usual routine for the next two days: attending to business, his training regimen and his domestic duties. Then, without any warning, he collapsed in agony on the way to the airport and was immediately taken to the nearest medcentre by his driver. There was nothing that could be done. Kenjiro Kakura died soon after being admitted. The subsequent autopsy revealed massive liver and kidney failure, caused by the ingestion of *Amanita phalloides*, or Death Cap fungus.

Three days later, when the security system chimed, Rohan turned around to see Welcome and Chiu Liow standing outside his door. He sighed quietly and let them in. The two said very little until they were seated, and then only the usual civilities. Rohan waited expectantly. Before long, Chiu Liow stood up again, clearly agitated. 'Kakura is dead,' he announced baldly, staring straight at Rohan, as if demanding an explanation.

'Good. He was an evil man. How did he die?'

'Of mushroom poisoning. The Argentinean authorities are investigating, but as yet can't trace its source. The fungus was a species with a delayed effect, so although it's clear he ate something he shouldn't have two to three days before he died, it was too late to determine the details. There are no travel records of his having left the country, or even that he left his own city within the space of time he was poisoned. They'll keep searching for evidence of how it was done, but for now, there'll be no public announcement. It goes almost without saying that there's a long list of suspects, including his bondmate. Michiko Yamada states she tried to persuade him to see a practitioner when he first became ill, but Kakura refused and wasn't taken to a medcentre until he collapsed two days later. It seems he was quite well between the first bout of illness and the next. By then, it was too late to do anything for him.'

While Chiu Liow spoke, Welcome watched Rohan. He could see no real surprise in his face and wondered why. Rohan, as if he had read his thoughts, glanced at him and slowly nodded. After a few moments, he stood up and went into his study, returning with a storage module, which he silently handed to Chiu Liow.

'What's that?' asked Welcome, peering suspiciously at him.

Rohan sat down again, considering what to say, then looked at each of them in turn. 'I have expected for some time that Kakura might die of unnatural causes,' he told them, quirking an eyebrow. Welcome harrumphed, but said nothing, prepared to wait for further explanation.

'Chiu Liow,' continued Rohan, 'you have in your hand a complete record of my undercover work for the past eight and a half years. It includes as much direct evidence as I've been able to obtain of the criminal activities of Kenjiro Kakura and his organisation, Wyvern Meridian. It is, unfortunately, rather sparse, but I hope you will now have enough information to piece together much more, particularly in light of the recent events that have tended to put some of their deeds under scrutiny by the Assembly.'

Chiu Liow tried to say something but found he couldn't. The magnitude of Maerz's involvement was beyond anything he had imagined. Even Welcome was at first astounded, then quickly saw how everything fell neatly into place and sighed in satisfaction.

'Rohan, do you have proof you were working undercover instead of in collusion with Kakura?' he asked.

'Not directly, no. I didn't feel I could tell anyone at all, but I think that when you view the contents of this drive, you'll see it's more likely I was working undercover than colluding.'

'Who killed Mervyn Bradshaw?' asked Chiu Liow bluntly. 'Do you know?'

Rohan looked at him almost reproachfully, before folding his hands and resting them on his vast stomach. 'Oh yes, I *know*, but I won't tell you... At least, not yet. There are limits, you see. I suggest you come back once you've viewed this.' He tapped the storage module, now lying on the table. 'Afterwards, you can ask any other questions you like. Perhaps you will even allow me to ask you some.'

Welcome and Chiu Liow spent the next few hours doing exactly as Rohan suggested. His account was so comprehensive and well constructed there was little reason to question him, other than as a formality. He would never, they felt, admit to the murder of Mervyn Bradshaw, and without substantiating evidence, it was unlikely Fliedermus' images could be used to convict him. Privately, Welcome was not entirely sorry.

'Do you think Rohan murdered Kakura?' he asked, as they sat over their third cup of strong coffee.

'I'm almost certain we'll never know,' replied Chiu Liow, rubbing a hand over his face in an attempt to erase the irritating feeling of having been completely outmanoeuvred by Maerz. 'As far as we can tell, Kakura didn't leave his home city during the period when he must have eaten the poisonous mushrooms, and Maerz didn't leave Australia.'

'As far as we can tell,' said Welcome.

Together with the few substantial threads collected in recent times, the evidence provided by Rohan, although sparse, was sufficient to warrant direct Federation intervention into the operations of Wyvern Meridian. Before Federation-supervised shareholder elections were held, the company's board members met for the last time. Those gathered saw the empty chair at the head of the table and experienced a mixture of both relief and apprehension. No one felt safe without Kakura to direct them. His personality had dominated for so long, they had become unused to thinking independently. All of them were due to appear before the Judge to give evidence and to explain their role in the illegal activities that were gradually proving to be far more extensive than the Assembly had suspected. Each person was finally to come face-to-face with their own guilt in allowing themselves to become part of Kakura's vision of a world returned to the past and all its evils.

The next time the Board met, it was unlikely anyone here tonight would be present. The empty chair would be occupied by a Federation-appointed interim director, whose role would be to monitor and to facilitate, but not to vote. At a time yet to be determined, the workings of the company would become public knowledge, and then the shareholders would decide whether they wished to retain their investments, or whether the time had come for Wyvern Meridian to return to obscurity.

Morag MacIain and Chiu Liow faced each other and smiled. The Assembly had wasted no time in submitting Rohan's report to the Judge, which, at a special review held in Luzern, promptly declared Morag innocent of any wrongdoing. Turning to Rohan, who was standing a little to one side, Morag held out her hand, and when he clasped it firmly, kissed him on the cheek. He touched his face, his eyes widening.

'You took on more than you should. I suppose you know that?' she said, gently pressing his hand and then releasing it.

'I couldn't see any other way of bringing Kakura and his wretched company to justice, I'm afraid. I thought of telling you, many times, but decided the risk was too great. I couldn't bear the thought of putting you into more danger than you already were. It may have been wrong of me, I know,' he added, forestalling the interruption from Morag. 'Instead, I've given you a terribly miserable time this past year. I hope you can forgive me?'

'Well, yes, given you thought he was planning to have me killed and didn't feel there was any other way of preventing it. What will you do, now that the Judge has retired you?'

'I'll go back to Melbourne, to my apartment, and use the time to relax and enjoy myself. I've no regrets and have Aurora to keep me company.'

'Won't you miss all the plotting and scheming?' asked Chiu Liow, honestly curious.

'Not in the least,' replied Rohan, with a small laugh. 'Anyway, if I want to test my wits, I can always call Welcome and exchange views on criminology. I may still write another book. I have some fresh material to use! Now, may I invite you both to have tea? It would do you good to take a long walk in the fresh air, Morag, and it would also be good to visit my favourite café one last time.'

Red Matilda was ready to go home. Karla looked into her eyes, holding the cat's face close to her own as they rubbed noses. When Red purred loudly and licked her Wight on the forehead, Karla laughed, caressed her head and returned the kiss.

'I'll miss you, Reddles,' she said wistfully, 'but I know it's time for you to go back to Mik and your other friends. Give me one last cuddle, and then we'd better be off.'

Red obliged, then bounded over to where Karla kept the leash and waited impatiently while it was attached to her collar. She would miss Karla too, but was missing her home more. There was no need to guard her friend any longer. It was time to leave.

They walked the short distance to the nearest callstation in companionable silence, simply enjoying the late afternoon sunshine and fresh air. As usual, Red Matilda spent the journey enthusiastically watching the scenery pass by, ears twitching and the tip of her tail moving slowly from side to side. Every now and then, when she noticed something of interest, Red sent a quick comment and accompanying image to her companion, who either laughed discreetly or silently replied with her own opinion, keeping her expression as neutral as possible; Karla felt the public wasn't yet ready for someone to be seen having an apparently one-sided conversation with a cat!

The homecoming was timed to coincide with a farewell party for Søren. He too had arrived at the conclusion it was time to go home. The Greenlander missed his own cat dreadfully, and the work he had come to Willsmere to accomplish was nearing completion. The remainder could be done long-distance, particularly now they could use the public lattice again. At first it seemed to Karla she was almost being deserted, but she shrugged off the feeling. After all, they would now be seeing a great deal more of Meng Jarrah and Freddi.

The two women had purchased a lovely old home in Brisbane to set up house together. Meng Jarrah saw no reason to stay in Oslo, since her work could just as easily be done based in Brisbane as anywhere else. She particularly wanted to be part of Martha's team at Lamington, continuing to assist in the growth trials and the forest regeneration project, now that they could do so in peace. Freddi's application for a position as a peacekeeper with the Brisbane Force was quickly accepted, particularly since Morag MacIain, the new Federation Special Investigation Unit Coordinator, had acted as one of her referees. As a result, Chiu Liow looked forward to the prospect of seeing his sister more often, as well as to the possibility of working together on other cases.

Gwenllian and Owain remained at Lamington, where, with their assistance, steady progress was being made. Karla was amazed at how well Gwenllian was adjusting to becoming the first known human telepath. All her earlier tension and restlessness seemed to have disappeared. To Lance Melrose Naylor's keen disappointment, however, she had resigned her position at the Central Computer Site in order to concentrate on her research into soil rehabilitation and to regularly return to the Werribee Breeding Centre for more lessons from the nursing mothers. Gwenllian's growing insight into the minds of the felines allowed a variety of projects at the Breeding Centre to blossom. She quickly became a favourite with the human staff and, as her powers developed, was fast becoming a trusted consultant. The events of this past year had shown that the potential for cats to be employed as personal guardians was great enough for the centre to devote additional resources to its further exploration. Gwenllian's specialised knowledge of security systems was useful in this respect for she was able to recommend how the cats' abilities could best be used, in combination with more standard electronic surveillance methods.

Freddi, Meng Jarrah, Gwenllian, Owain, Melrose and Martha were all delighted to be asked to attend Søren's farewell party, which promised to be quite a gathering. The guest of honour had decided to share the position with Rohan Maerz. Since the review in Luzern, his role in bringing Wyvern Meridian's operations to an end had become common knowledge amongst the circle of friends – under the circumstances, and given the bond they now shared with them all, Chiu Liow and Welcome hadn't felt it necessary to hide what they knew.

Even Morag was to be at the party. She had arranged to spend part of her working life in Luzern and the remainder in Melbourne. Rohan was extravagantly pleased when she gave him the news, and needless to say, so was Chiu Liow Jones. Naturally, he and Welcome would be there this evening as well.

Research Coordinator Zago, Sirinya and Eduardo were still in other parts of the world and unable to be present, but sent their best wishes to everyone, particularly to the guests of honour. Zago included a personal message to Rohan to circumspectly let him know she was vastly relieved to learn that his role this past year had been as an undercover agent, and not as a traitor to the Federation. Her own faith in the Federation was restored with this knowledge, although she agreed with the Judge that he should retire: Rohan Maerz was altogether too powerful a person to remain in the role of FSIU Coordinator. If he had shared his undercover work with even one other investigator, the Judge would surely have allowed him to retain his position, but working solely on his own set a highly dangerous precedent that was to be strictly forbidden in future, no matter what the stakes. Checks and balances were essential. Even in these more enlightened days, such power was still potentially a deeply corrupting influence.

The investigation into Kakura's death and his criminal activities was not yet complete. They all had the niggling suspicion that Kakura met his end at Rohan's hands, but given they couldn't be certain, buried their doubts, together with their lingering horror at his murder of Mervyn Bradshaw. They even began to develop a slightly uneasy friendship with him. In reality, there appeared to be little choice. He seemed so kindly and in need of friendship, he was virtually impossible to resist, presenting himself on their doorsteps at unpredictable times, always bearing a small gift of some type and always with Aurora by his side.

When Karla and Red Matilda arrived at Mik and Tamara's house, the door soon opened and there stood Søren, smiling with pleasure at seeing them both. Karla impulsively bent down and kissed him, something she had never done before and which Søren remembered for a long time afterwards. Red sat watching them for a few moments before deciding they were perfectly capable of keeping each other entertained. She bounded into the greenhouse then down the staircase, where she was met by Fliedermus and Possum in a leaping frenzy of furry happiness. Laughing at their antics, Karla and Søren followed more sedately. Tamara, who had been waiting for them to arrive, kissed Karla's cheek, while Mik came out from the kitchen to say hello, then crouched down to hug Red Matilda, obviously pleased to have her home again. Smiling as he watched them, Rohan was standing next to Morag, dwarfing her with his size, while Aurora and Possum were now settled by their feet, cleaning each other's faces – it seemed the two cats had grown especially fond of each other.

'Well, Karla, now that you have arrived, we can eat,' announced Søren, with a dramatic flourish, indicating they were all to proceed to the dining room – forthwith!

His friends obeyed and were greeted by the sight of a dining table laden with the finest dishes Søren, Mik, Rohan and Tamara could put together in one day of hard work. The brightest flowers from the greenhouse decorated the table in a glorious display, while Rohan had provided his best crystal wine glasses to complement the setting, as Mik was a little short of suitable ones for so many guests. A wide variety of Australian wines sat waiting on the sideboard, together with dishes of fresh fruit, their warm, ripe colours matching those of the flowers. A special section of the sideboard was even devoted to Rohan's favourite chocolates, a treat he had delighted in providing.

'Sit down, sit down, please!' Søren insisted. 'I expect you to have good appetites and not to let any of this wonderful food go to waste.'

Later during the evening, when everyone was relaxing after their feast, Rohan called Karla aside.

'I'd very much like to speak with you in private, if you don't mind. Will you accompany me outside to walk in Mik's garden for a while?'

Although surprised, Karla agreed, so they carried their glasses of wine out into the fine, mild evening, where they took a slow turn around the garden beds. Rohan stopped to admire a miniature lime tree, then turned to Karla and said, 'I suspect you've had Chiu Liow's confidence for many months and I'd like you to have mine as well.'

Certain Chiu Liow had kept their discussions secret from his former colleague, Karla's eyes widened in surprise. However, she nodded and Rohan continued: 'Aurora has told me you'll greatly miss both Søren and Red Matilda, so I've come to a decision about something that's worried me a great deal lately. You see, I'm dying, and I need someone to take care of Aurora once I'm gone. Will you do this for me?'

Shocked, Karla put her hand on his shoulder. 'How long do you have?' she asked softly.

'Oh, perhaps twelve months, possibly a few months longer. I've known for some time, but, fortunately, have been able to continue my work. However, I'm becoming fatigued of late and am not at all sorry the Judge decided to put me into retirement. I think it was to be expected.'

'What is it you're dying from, if you don't mind me asking?' said Karla, making an effort to control her voice. 'It's rare for anyone to die these days when they're only your age.'

'It's genetic,' he replied. 'Something to do with the same condition that causes me to be so dreadfully overweight. No doubt my heart and other organs are wearing out with the strain. Nothing can be done.'

'I am so very sorry, Rohan. I'd hoped we could keep you for a long time yet... And yes, I promise Aurora will be happy with me. I promise...'

Karla took his arm in hers and they walked slowly over to a garden seat, placed with an eye both to the view and to comfort. Once they were seated, Rohan patted her hand and said, 'There's something else I want to tell you. You can pass it on to Chiu Liow after I'm gone, but not before. Will you promise?'

Feeling awkward, Karla nevertheless agreed.

'I *did* kill Kenjiro Kakura,' he confessed, in a quiet, resigned voice. 'There was no other way to stop him.'

Karla jumped up, her hand outstretched towards him, staring in horror.

'Yes, I know most people would think it a very terrible thing to do,' said Rohan, reaching out to gently touch her, 'but I need you to understand why it became necessary. Please, will you sit down and listen?'

Karla sat, keeping as far away from him as the garden seat allowed. She felt dizzy at the thought that this man had killed not once, but twice!

'I found out many years ago that Kakura was living in the past, and wanted the past to return,' Rohan explained, when he was sure she was listening. 'I thought at first that the peace and prosperity the Federation had gained for all the world's people, together with the efforts we were making to return the Earth to health, would ensure evil such as his could never again flourish. I monitored his activities and those of his company,

Wyvern Meridian, watching for anything that might alter the balance and threaten everything we have worked so hard to achieve. Sadly, he became more and more powerful, and with that, more and more ruthless. He has murdered countless people, but always used such devious methods that I could never prove it.

'I managed to trick him into becoming my friend, pretending to admire what he was doing, and after a time, gained his confidence to such an extent that he began to tell me his plans. He had the ability to corrupt people in government, at computer sites, in the research centres, everywhere! He could make people disappear by removing their entire set of Federation identification records... Kakura had almost as much access to the lattice as I did!

'Although it was difficult, I gathered evidence where I could. At the same time, I began to develop a plan that would give the Federation Assembly reason to investigate him and his company, but he was too clever, even for me. Yes, Karla, the Federation would have placed controls on his activities and would have monitored him closely, but he was a young man and patient. One day, all the monitoring and all the controls would have been taken away and he'd have begun again. His type always does.'

'But why did you kill him? *Surely* all the evidence you collected would have been enough to have him placed under permanent surveillance!' Karla put her hand on his arm and looked into his eyes, trying to understand.

'Real evil sometimes has a beautiful face, Karla. It attracts people and is subtle. For some reason, every now and again, a person comes along who sees only what they themselves want and have no interest at all in what anyone else wants, yet make it appear that they do. They deceive others into thinking that what they need is what is being offered. They also bring out the evil in others. They bring out the selfishness in us all – the wish to dominate and control, the need to be seen as the centre of all things – and they cause it to flourish. They bring out our primitive tribal instincts that make us fear anyone who is different from ourselves. They justify their actions to themselves and to those who follow them. There have been too many forms of justification over the millennia and they have always led to destruction. I was not prepared to have it happen again, so I chose to kill him before he could do more harm. I do not regret what I did.'

A long silence followed Rohan's words. Karla sighed and could find nothing to say, so instead, took his hand and held it in her own.

*

Warning of the long, hot summer to come, the cicadas were singing so loudly they drowned out most other sounds. A kookaburra laughed, and was soon joined by others of its family, adding to the general cacophony. As if in competition, a lone magpie warbled tunefully, while a small flock of brilliant red and blue rosellas flew overhead, quickly disappearing from sight. Running along the riverbank, side by side, Aurora's keen enjoyment of the late springtime warmth added to Karla's contentment. A blue-tongued lizard dashed out into her path and she quickly changed direction to avoid it.

www.ingramcontent.com/pod-product-compliance
Lightning Source LLC
Chambersburg PA
CBHW060416030726
47495CB00003B/603